Vermilion Ink

by David Su Li-Qun and Diana Gore

ISBN: 1451590008
ISBN- 13:9781451590005
LCCN: 2010905171

*This book is dedicated to our families
who have supported, inspired and
motivated us each and every day.*

Main Characters

Giuseppe Castiglione (1688 – 1766) known in China as **Lang Shi Ning**

Ai Xin Jue Luo Xuan Ye, the emperor **Kang Xi.** A wise and tolerant emperor, he held power from 1662-1722. He was curious about foreign knowledge and brought in many skilled Jesuit teachers to instruct him in mathematics, mechanics, geography, astronomy, art and music. Unfortunately, his tolerance led to enormous corruption in the court. For many years before his death, his many sons began clambering to be chosen to succeed him. In the end, he chose Yin Zhen out of admiration for the characteristics he saw in Yin Zhen's son.

Ai Xin Jue Luo Yin Zhen, the emperor **Yong Zheng.** He held power from 1723-1735. In his short reign, he brutally suppressed opposition and foreign religion. He rewrote historic records to establish his legitimate claim on the throne. His policies created a wealth of enemies. Despite enormous precautions, it is believed that he was poisoned in 1735. His actions succeeded in limiting corruption among the ruling classes and laid the basis for the economic revival of his son's long reign.

Ai Xin Jue Luo Hong Li, the emperor **Qian Long.** He held power from 1736-1795. His was an extremely long, fruitful reign. He was an intelligent, perspicacious ruler who presided over a period of enormous economic growth and international trade.

Anthonio Vassali known in China as **An Dong Ni.** Italian missionary and mathematician. Castiglione's closest friend. Preceded him in China by five years. He was executed by Yin Zhen. Antonio is modelled on historical persons.

Brother Jerome Villier known in China as **Lin Zhi Xing:** A French painter and Jesuit missionary. He is modelled on historical persons.

Father Michel Benoit known in China as **Jiang You Ren** (1715-1774) He was a French Jesuit and astronomer. He came to China in 1744 and put his hand to many things for the Emperor including maps of the earth and the stars. Most importantly he developed the hydraulics for the fountains in the western garden of the Yuan Ming Yuan.

Paolo Lambrezia known in China as **Luo Huai Zhong,** a physician and friend of Castiglione. Fictional character.

Su Ge Lu: A Manchu aristocrat and relative of the Qing emperors. He was a Catholic convert and friend of Castiglione. The entire Su family is modelled on historical persons.

Su Er Qing: The eldest son of Su Ge Lu and Castiglione's first Chinese teacher.

Wu Yu: a famous Chinese painter and a Catholic convert. He became Castiglione's first teacher of Chinese painting. He is modelled on various historical persons.

Chen Yuan: a merchant from Fujian province and an agricultural specialist. He laboured long and hard to introduce a viable sweet potato into China to ease starvation. Modelled on historical persons.

Chen You Min: daughter of Chen Yuan. Fictional character.

Xiang Rong Fei: (Fragrant Beautiful Concubine) A beautiful Uighur captive given to emperor Qian Long as a gift. He was entranced with her unusual beauty and kept her a concubine. Castiglione painted a tender oil portrait of her late in his life. Conflicting historic records exist on her life and death.

Jiang Shan Ren: Also known as 'Little Brother' (Xiao Di) and Cocco. An orphan adopted by Wu Yu and later by Castiglione. He became a painter, the husband of Chen You Min and. Fictional character.

Wang Rong: A eunuch in the Imperial Court who became a close friend of Castiglione and his protector. He rose as high as was possible in the ranks of eunuchs. Fictional character.

Jin Kun: A famous artist and court painter. Lifelong friend and colleague of Castiglione. Modelled on historical characters.

Duan Shi Lian: A eunuch in the Imperial Court but highly dangerous and vindictive. Fictional character.

Ruth: The fourth wife of Su Ge Lu. Fictional character.

Mandarin Pronunciation Guide

Consonants:

Zh: a hard 'j' sound, made by placing the tip of the tongue on the roof of the mouth directly behind your teeth;

Ch: same as above but with the tongue only lightly touching the roof of the mouth while pushing more air through

Sh: same as above but the tongue no longer touches the roof of the mouth

R: Made by curling the tongue and lightly closing the teeth

NOTE: Zhi, Chi, Shi are very common sounds and are made as if they had 'er' on the end

Ji: a soft 'g' sound made by touching the wide middle portion of the tongue on the palate

Qi: a soft 'ch' sound made by touching the wide middle portion of the tongue on the palate but pushing more air through

Xi: a soft 'sh' sound made by pressing the edges of the tongue onto the top teeth and pushing air through.

Ze: A sound similar to 'dz.' It's made by placing forward portion—not the tip—of the tongue touches the roof of the mouth

Ce: As above but with more air pushed through

Se: As above but with even more air pushed through

G: always a hard 'g' as in garage

B, D, F, H, K, L, M, N, P, T, W are similar to English

Vowels:
A: short as in father

E: short as in yet

I: like saying the letter 'e' as in 'week'

O: short as in naughty

U: like oo

Ü: does not appear in this book but is pronounced 'oo' but wit the lips firmly puckered.

Diphthongs and Triphthongs: These are very common in Mandarin

Ai: aye

Ao: ow

Ei: like a long 'a' as in weigh

Ia: like ee-ya

Ie: like ee-ye

Iu: ee-oo

Ou: long 'o' sound like in whoa

Ua: oo-a (short a)

Ue: oo-e (short e)

Ui:oo-ei

Iao: ee-ow

Uai: oo-ai

Part I

Gazing in All Directions

The wind blows wherever it pleases. You hear its sound, but you cannot tell where it comes from or where it is going. So it is with everyone born of the Spirit.

John, 3:8

1

Springtime, Beijing, year of our Lord 1766. I look down at my wrinkled, twisted fingers and study them. These fingers that have served me well for many decades can now only grasp a brush with the elegance of a sow and the strength of a tadpole. When I become bored or anxious and try to soothe myself with calligraphy practice, the strain is as great as ploughing a muddy field by hand. I am further impeded by failing eyes, disobedient limbs, and other embarrassing aspects of an aged body. I can accept the deterioration of my body as the tariff of a long-lived life, but I detest the lack of co-operation of my hands. We were a partnership, my hands and I. They granted me opportunities that I would never have dreamt of in my early years, when I lived by stealing food and begging for charity on the streets of Milan.

Now I wake each morning and wonder if today will be the day that my earthly existence ends. I am content and more than ready to join the friends who wait for me, beyond the great wall. I talk to them frequently—Antonio, Chen Yuan, Paolo, Su Er Qing, Father Ignatius. Oh, yes, many people come to see this old Jesuit. As I have passed over the line that turns one's eyes towards those one has lost and weakens the bonds to those who remain, their visits remind me that I am alive and have lived.

Mine has been a life devoted to art. Art and friendship are truly all that have mattered; though sometimes even friendships were battered by the storms and calamities wrought by my passion for art. My debt and gratitude to the Society of Jesus is great. It trained me and brought me to China. In my heart, I know that had I not been a celibate Jesuit, I would have been denied the opportunities in China that enhanced and challenged my talent.

Chapter I

Though I have lived as a Jesuit for almost sixty years, my passion for art is my master, not my faith. When I approach Saint Peter and ask to enter heaven, I will not be able to lay my achievements as a Catholic missionary before him, and I would not even dare to try to convince him I have been devout. As I have spent more years tolerating my faith rather than trusting it, I expect to have a difficult time talking my way past the gatekeeper to the hallowed halls of eternal life. I will try, as I always have, to find the truest path to the gate. It will not be a straight one, but it will be the path that speaks to my heart. For that was the path I always took to achieve my aims. I, Giuseppe Castiglione, never trod in another man's footsteps. By relying on instinct and blind determination, I found my own unique destiny, despite stumbling many times along the way.

A young servant taps me repeatedly on the shoulder and bends down to my ear. 'The emperor is here, the emperor is here!' he whispers. I can see he is trembling from scalp to toes.

A second later the Qian Long emperor sweeps into the room, brilliantly clothed, smiling broadly, and ever in a hurry. I try to get up, to kow-tow at his feet, but he gently places a hand on my shoulder.

'How is my favourite painter?' he asks. 'Zhen is forever concerned for your well-being. Do you need anything? Are these servants to your satisfaction? And this house? Are you comfortable here?'

Despite living in China for so many years, I still tremble at the sound of the word 'Zhen', a word meaning 'I' but uttered by only one man—the emperor. I have heard it from the mouths of two others who held that title: his grandfather and his father.

I assure him that everything is to my satisfaction, that my surroundings are far more than I deserve as his humble servant and as a Jesuit.

'Jesuits,' he sniffs. 'They abandoned you when Zhen gave you your noble title, yet you remain loyal to them. Zhen has known you longer than any Jesuit serving in my country. Though you have the appearance of a foreigner, you have the skill and knowledge of the rarest of Chinese painters. You are the emperor's personal painter, my living national treasure.' He chuckles into his hand until his eyes fall upon an oil portrait that hangs on the wall in this room. It is one of four I made of the greatest love of his life, Fragrant Concubine. For a moment his smile is gone and his sadness re-opens wounds in my own heart. We never talk about her, but she binds us together, a silken thread of love and loss.

He clicks his fingers and a servant runs forward with a scroll.

'Zhen has made a painting of a horse. Judge it and speak honestly.'

The servant holds the scroll open and I gaze carefully at it though my sight is poor. I motion for the emperor to come closer so that I may speak quietly. He leans toward me.

'Ten-Thousand-Years-Living Father, it is terrible. I have been a worthless teacher and deserve to be punished.'

The emperor laughs heartily and puts his hand on my shoulder. He lets it linger for a few seconds before leaving the room. It is a strong hand, the hand of a confident man.

'Your life is special,' the emperor said during his previous visit. 'Very few foreigners have understood our culture so well. You knew my grandfather, my father, and Zhen since Zhen was a small boy. You must tell your life's story. Zhen would like to see the history of my country through your eyes. Zhen will order Wang Rong to make the necessary arrangements. The task must begin immediately.'

An emperor's wishes cannot be disobeyed even by a silly old fool like me. The emperor chose my scribe carefully for he must realise that I can deny Wang Rong nothing. This gentle, wise eunuch has been not only one of my greatest friends but a man loved by two other Jesuits who were my brothers in spirit if not in blood, dear departed Antonio and Paolo.

I look down again at the first line of the poem I have finished and wet the brush to start the second line. But I am weary and close my eyes for just a minute. Wang Rong will be here soon.

I must have gone to sleep, for when I open my eyes, Wang Rong, the emperor's most senior eunuch, sits with his robes elegantly arrayed over a chair, waiting somewhat impatiently with a brush in his hand, ink mixed and ready. He should have retired by now, but the emperor is loath to lose such a genuine, intelligent servant. Though he is only my junior by a few years, his body is still erect and his eyes unfailing. They look at me now, bright and full of warmth.

'May we begin, Emperor's Painter Lang?' he asks gently. 'Are you ready?'

I stir myself. 'As ready as I ever will be, I suspect. I don't know where to begin. Does the emperor need to know everything?' I smile ruefully at distant memories.

'Perhaps you should tell us how it was that you came to China?'

It is an easy place to begin, avoiding the painful memories of my early years as a homeless orphan. Although the heart of my story lies in China, the country where my life took on its true meaning, I am Italian by birth and that was where gentle hands rescued me and guided me towards my destiny.

'Ah, Giuseppe. What shall we predict for your future? You were born with the face of an imp. Charming though it may be, and we have grown fond of it, it is a signpost to the wilderness in your soul. Even when you reach manhood, I fear your.face will retain the cast of a mischievous child. There will be those who will instinctively want to correct you or protect you. They will see the potential, as we have done, and believe, as we do, that with a little tweaking here and there, you too could see the measure of your worth. But there will be others who will interpret the gleam differently and will not be so kind.'

The old priest glanced at me briefly while he wiped the lenses of his spectacles with a measured circular motion and sighed. 'I have already spent five years turning a wild urchin into a responsible youth. I have not yet succeeded in transforming him into a *sensible* youth. You are now seventeen and we are at a crossroads.'

I never called the old priest by his full title; I merely called him Father. I loved pronouncing the word. It filled my imagination with possibilities of what could have been, had my own drunken father not disappeared and died. My mother died so early that I had no memory of her. I became a street urchin, always hungry and living on instinct, anger, and wits. Perhaps he felt the hunger of my dreams, but he never let on.

I met the old priest when I hid in his church after fleeing from a soldier—whose purse I blithely thought I had deftly snatched—and his friends. Knowing I could not escape, the soldiers laughed raucously and bantered about what they were going to do to me. Their search of the dark side chapels was stopped by the arrival of a group of priests. I watched the confrontation from my hiding place. The eldest priest, to my amazement, cleverly convinced the soldiers that it was in their best interests to leave the church and wait outside after which he would promptly restore the purse and ensure that God would decide how justice should best be served.

Though I had no intention of giving up my treasure, the priests were far more clever than I and quickly extracted me from my hiding place and the purse from me. I was taken to the priest's library where he offered me a plate of the most delicious cheese and bread I had ever eaten. He watched with kind eyes while I fell upon the food, asking a few questions which I answered as arrogantly as I had learned from others like me living wild on the streets of Milan. Unperturbed, he asked if I wished to have a room and meals within the monastery in return for simple chores. I was only twelve, but I had already discerned that whatever the meek are promised in the next life, the clever eat better in the present. Opportunities ignored do not come again, so it did not take me long to accept his proposal.

This father was the kindest, wisest man I knew. After he had succeeded in modifying my manners towards people and food, he taught me to read. It was a relief to discover that I was not a thief or liar by nature, only by necessity. Those habits floated away leaving no trace and I discovered that I was hard-working, loyal, and cheerful even if I was also criticised as opinionated, stubborn, and quick-tempered. A smile from Father or a word of praise inflated my insides better than the richest stew. Not only did I know his every gesture, but I could often guess what he was going to say.

Yet today I could not and the tone of his words came as a surprise. Was he about to ask me to leave this sanctuary? I knew I could take care of myself, but could I bear parting from him and these walls and all the security they represented? He replaced the spectacles, carefully aligning them with two thick hands along the line of his eyebrows. As soon as he released them, they slipped down his nose and he pushed them up, knitting his brows in the vain hope of keeping them in place, a movement he repeated a hundred times a day.

'Giuseppe Castiglione, you are a fine artist,' Father went on. 'Father Andrea Pozzo was very impressed with your sketches and paintings and the work you've done for Master Cornara.' He chuckled. 'Perhaps we can put your impetuous behaviour down to your artistic temperament. Whatever the reason, your tendency to opt for trouble instead of restraint is why we are having this discussion today. It is time to decide what to make of your life and to take a step towards becoming the man you wish to be.'

I had drawn for as long I could remember. Even when I lived on the street, I would pick up sharp stones with dirty, stubby fingers and rub the sharp edges along dusty steps. When Father saw that I could draw he nurtured my skills and found me a teacher, Master Carlo Cornara. Though I learned a great deal from the master, the rules and hierarchies of working in a large studio did not sit well with my independent nature and we parted company without regret on either side.

In recent years I had been supporting myself by cutting silhouettes of wealthy merchants and their families, perched on a stool in the piazza around the Duomo. I liked to daydream about how many homes in Milan were decorated with my artwork. As much as those thoughts pleased me, I also enjoyed the weight of money in my pocket. Until this moment, it seemed a happy enough existence for a lad of seventeen.

'My son, I will speak plainly with you as I always have. You are old enough to leave the shelter of this monastery and clever enough to prosper outside, but you have a nature that is instinctive, fearless, and reckless. If you decide to follow wherever your nose will lead, you will find success and joy in the short term, but mark my words, a prison will be your home in the long term. To avoid such a fate, you need discipline and structure. Life within the walls of a religious brotherhood can give you both these things. Yes, many aspects of such a life will frustrate you, and I cringe at the thought of how often you will be in conflict with your superiors, but within its structures your talents will flourish and your dangerous tendencies will be tamed. Of all the religious brotherhoods, I believe that the Society of Jesus is the correct one for you. It is more tolerant of individual natures than the others and is full of talented men from all aspects of science and art.'

I swallowed hard. Though I had lived in a monastery for five years, I had not taken my prayers seriously. I loved the stories of the Bible and the lives of brave men and women whom we revered as saints and I gazed in awe at the art they had inspired. The only world that had shown kindness to me was this church and its priests.

'Within the society,' Father continued, 'you will be free to pursue your talent as an artist without worrying about finding patrons, shelter, or food. Your commitment will be to God and the talent He has graced you with.'

Perhaps it was the idealism of youth that created a picture in my mind of happiness and security within the society. Perhaps it was something else, a voice calling to me, telling me that something wonderful was waiting for me. All that was required was for me to make a commitment to something for the first time in my life.

'Yes,' I said, 'I agree with what you propose.'

True to the predictions of my old priest, I was an annoyance to my superiors in Genoa as a noviciate. They knew by the way I intoned my prayers and raced through my studies that my heart and mind were elsewhere. I refused to accept their criticism of my nature as sinful. What they described as vanity, disobedience, and sloth, I saw in a different light as essential to what made me Giuseppe Castiglione. I would not bow my head, accept every order, and perform tasks that 'were for the good of my soul'. Though they quickly realised that endless acts of penance could not humble me, they still banished me far too often to solitary contemplation. Fortunately there were a handful of teachers that I respected and admired. They were not the men who taught me religion but those who patiently answered my questions about the world, about all the things I hungered to know.

At the end of my two years as a noviciate in 1711, my obstinacy was punished in the cruellest way. I was judged unworthy to become one of the Solemnly Professed. 'Brother' was the highest title I could obtain. My education was stopped and all the things I yearned to study were denied. Kinder fathers, who had argued on my behalf, convinced me to remain in the society despite the humiliation, telling me that my prospects would be better in a foreign mission where I would have the chance to learn without the strictures of a college.

I swore my vows of poverty, obedience, and chastity with anger. The father who heard my vows smiled and whispered in my ear, 'The ways of the Lord are mysterious. Do not mistake this setback as an omen of the life before you. I am convinced that He has great plans for you.'

Whatever my faults, my skill as a painter was respected and I was given many commissions in Jesuit churches. When I was invited back to the college after a few years to embellish its walls, my resentment got the better of me and I put the faces of my superiors in murals as sinners, moneylenders, and tormentors of saints and our Lord. In the midst of the furore that ensued, I announced my fervent desire to serve the society abroad—in China. It was viewed by everyone, for different reasons, as an ideal solution. After all, a foreign assignment was a permanent one. I would never set foot in Italy again. What I did not know at the time was that the mission in China had recently requested Jesuit artists although no one in Italy understood why.

Within a very short time, I was dispatched to the University of Cöimbra in Portugal for two years to learn how to become a missionary. Unfortunately, my studies were interrupted when the Queen of Portugal insisted that I paint several portraits of her family. This too came to an end when I told Her Majesty that her children were brats and that I would rather paint the devil in hell than continue with the commission. It did not take long for a ship to be found to take me to Macao.

I left Portugal on a ship called *Notre Dame de l'Esperance,* Our Lady of Hope. The sea crossing, even with stopping at the Cape of Good Hope and Goa, should only have taken six months. Because of ferocious storms, which caused severe damage to our sails, it took us eleven. Many succumbed to sickness with fatal consequences while others were swept overboard and drowned.

Though I was not a father, the passengers and crew turned to me for guidance and solace, more and more often as the nightmares of the journey increased. When I saw that the prayers that had caused me such trouble brought peace to frightened faces, I crossed over a line between boyhood and manhood and began to understand the weight of the cloak I wore and the vows I had sworn.

As we neared the end of the journey, I made a pact with God. I accepted that, by entering the society, I was part of a greater good and promised that I would do my part to serve Him provided that I was not required to lose my own identity in the process and central to my being was my art and my fervent need to paint.

Macao was the first stop for any missionary, a vital base of education for anyone heading into the interior of China. It often took six months to receive the necessary permits to enter the kingdom and learn enough Chinese to be of use to whatever mission one was assigned to, but my stay was cut short; my temper, once more, the cause.

Macao was another example of my nature prevailing over good sense and one that I most regretted, since I thought I had left that immature part of me behind. Though I tried to remain placid, a situation arose with several belligerent Benedictines that I finally settled with my fists. My superiors hastened my departure and asked my language teacher, a young Manchu Christian convert named Su Er Qing, to accompany me. Perhaps they believed he had found some way to tame me, since, uniquely up to that point, he had given only the highest praise of my behaviour and devotion to study. Er Qing was delighted with this unusual request; only the two of us and no official escort, stopping for a few days in the middle of our journey so that he could visit his parents in Kaifeng.

'Welcome to Beijing,' said Er Qing.

I looked at him and smiled. He was small and thin, with the appearance of a youth, not of a man only few years younger than I. His jaw was long and protruded forward ever so slightly and was wider at the jawbone than at the cheekbones so that he always seemed to be smiling. His features and manner, forever soft and unhurried, never failed to soothe me as if they exuded some sort of magic potion. Behind a young face lay an older, wiser soul.

'Today, Er Qing, is the fifteenth of November, Year of Our Lord 1715. Fifty-five days ago we left Guangdong and are finally within sight of the capital of China.'

'Would you like to stand here for a moment?' he asked, and I nodded.

The city was only a short distance away protected by enormous walls. The surrounding land was dry and windswept. At first glance, it was hard to imagine why a capital had been established in such a forbidding place, yet it sat there solidly, timelessly, drawing people within like a powerful magnet.

'During my years in the society in Genoa, an older Jesuit, a famous painter named Andrea Pozzo, told me stories of China, igniting a fire in my imagination that never subsided. Now, many years later, I am standing at the gates of its capital. Dare I enter this great city? Many great Jesuits have lived and died here. Who am I to tread in their footsteps?'

'You are too hard on yourself, Brother Giuseppe. I am sure that you too will be remembered as a Jesuit friend to the great Qing dynasty. The time I have spent with you has shown me that not only are you a great artist but you are intelligent, eager to learn about any subject, and kind-hearted. You do not wish to change us, as so many missionaries do. You seek to find a way in which we can learn from each other. The Chinese will love you for these qualities and you will love us. I am sure of that. My prayer is that you will remember this moment with fondness your entire life.'

I turned away from the walls, from the hordes of people and animals coming from all directions, to look at the young Manchu man at my side.

'Er Qing, your words are very kind. I will always treasure the memories of our journey together.'

He permitted himself a brief smile. 'Not kind, merely true.'

There was much more I wanted to say, but my mind was weighed down by many strange emotions. Er Qing, born into a noble Manchu family, had converted to Christianity as a boy. His fluency in Latin had made him the perfect guide between my old life and my new one. These facts alone did not begin to describe the sort of character he was. During our two months of travel from Guangdong to Beijing, I had enjoyed every minute of his companionship, never once wishing to be alone. Though I had shared very few of my deepest thoughts and feelings, it was not because of unwillingness, only hesitation. How could I explain to him what a novice I was in the arts of friendship and family? In his quiet way, he had won my trust, respect, and affection. It was only as the hour of our parting approached that I felt how deeply I would miss him.

Er Qing was suddenly abruptly elbowed aside as a horde of curious faces surrounded me, unashamedly pointing, peering, and reaching out to touch my hair. Where most Italians have shiny black hair, mine was a golden reddish colour; my head ringed by unruly curls like a figure in a Botticelli fresco. My eyes did not blaze dark and mysterious but were green and capped with long, insipid eyelashes. My skin was not olive but pale and spoiled with freckles that increased in quantity and intensity in full sunlight. Even if I were typically Italian in my looks, I would have been an object of curiosity to Chinese such as these for whom the sight of an Italian was a rarity.

I squirmed and tried to ward off the cascade of hands, but they were persistent and unmoved by my displeasure. Somewhat unsettled, I shouted to

Er Qing while pushing and elbowing my way towards our carriage. 'Get me out of here!'

Er Qing flicked the reins and we disappeared into the flow of beast and man heading for the open mouth within the vast walls that was the gate to the city.

'You have attracted many large crowds before, but never so many people in such a short amount of time,' he mused with a chortle. I knew he was thinking about the day when we crossed the Yellow River on foot because the riverbed was dry and hundreds of people had followed us, silently staring, making me feel like Moses at the parting of the Red Sea leading the Israelites out of Egypt.

'Brother Giuseppe,' he went on, more seriously. 'Since you are now beginning a new life, it is time for me to bestow your new name on you. You are well aware that every foreigner who wishes to live in China is required to have a Chinese name. It has always been that way, perhaps because our language does not adapt well to foreign sounds. After all, we have no alphabet. It is my privilege to give you your new name.'

'Will I never use my Italian name again?'

'Only with your own kind. Among ordinary people and all officials of the Qing dynasty, only your Chinese name will matter.'

'If it's so important, why couldn't you have done this earlier? A new name needs time to sit on a person. I've had the name Giuseppe for twenty-seven years!'

'Since the granting of a Chinese name is a profound duty, I decided to wait for this moment. It has not been easy keeping my choice to myself. Do you not agree that this is a most auspicious time? I had many ideas for a new name, but during our brief rest in Kaifeng I conferred with my honourable father. He reminded me that a painter is a link between the present and future and that you, in particular, add another facet, that of joining another culture to our own. The choice was his. Lang is your new surname. It is one of the honourable "one Hundred Surnames. Its meaning is not so very important, but I will tell you that a *xin lang* is a bridegroom. Shi Ning is your given name. It means Generations of Peace and Tranquillity. I will show you how it is written.'

A shiver shot up my spine to think that I was no longer Giuseppe Castiglione, a poor orphan from Milan, but Lang Shi Ning.

'Peaceful and tranquil are not words anyone ever used to describe me. I fear your father sees my weaknesses too clearly and hopes that I will grow into this wonderful name like a child approaching maturity. Please thank him for me. I am honoured to have been given this name and pray that I will be worthy of it.'

The Eastern Church had been easy to find, in a city of low-lying buildings. The steeple and cross were visible from a distance. Er Qing pulled the horse to a halt.

'Will you come in and stay for a meal? I'm sure there will be a spare bed as well.'

'No. Though it saddens me, the time has come for us to part.'

We silently unloaded my cases from the back of the carriage.

Er Qing lowered his head and clasped his hands in front of his forehead. 'We will meet again, Missionary Lang Shi Ning. I feel certain the Lord has brought us together for a reason,' he said. Then he reached inside his robe and pulled out two letters.

'These are from my father. The first is an introduction to an elderly man named Wu Yu, a great artist, who is a devoted Christian. My honourable father believes that you will find no better teacher in all China. The second letter you may not open. My father wishes to remind you that it is not easy to be a Christian in China. As you know, even during the reign of our present emperor, Christians have been persecuted. Only if you find yourself in perilous circumstances may you open this letter.'

My jaw dropped.

'Say nothing. My father is a wise man. He has far-seeing eyes. He believes you will succeed in China and that you have a nature that is in harmony with ours, but that your path will nonetheless be a dangerous and difficult one.'

'I'm not sure that I want to know that.'

Er Qing laughed and left.

I watched him until he disappeared around the corner of the narrow, cluttered lane, followed by scolding hens and other noisy animals.

Even when Er Qing passed from sight, I waited many minutes before I pushed the door open and entered the church grounds, heavy with regret that I had not said more to express my gratitude and affection. Then the realisation of my situation finally sank in. I was one of the first artists selected to join the Jesuits already here, a dreamer among scientists and engineers, in a strange land, a stranger even among my own kind.

3

I wake with a start. My arms are outstretched as if I am pushing something open. They drop, weary and weak. A soft cough brings my mind back into the room. Wang Rong sits by my side in his usual spot. He's smiling, but his brows are furrowed. How long will this memoir take? I wonder. I must get my thoughts in better order if we are ever to successfully record fifty years of experiences.

'I fear I have become very boring company, a drooling, drowsy old man.'

'Even the great Lang Shi Ning must bow down to nature and accept the restrictions of a silver head. If I may be honest, I will admit that you have given me sufficient excitement in this life to accompany me into the next one. How my heart has beaten for the dangerous situations you faced. Ai ya. Those memories cause me shame, for most indicate my failure to foresee the dangers and protect you from the evil traps set by Eunuch Duan.'

'Not true. Souls with malice will always find ways to cause suffering. A ring of goodness cannot repel them.'

So many heartfelt words tumble around my brain, but nothing coherent emerges. I want to tell Wang Rong what a true friend he has been all these years. I will never forget how much he risked to warn Antonio of the dangers he faced. I open my mouth and shut it again, knowing how uncomfortable he becomes at my overt displays of emotion.

Wang Rong clears his throat pointedly. 'Pardon my haste, but we have much work before us. The emperor will be displeased with me if I am asked to reveal how little we have written.'

'It is really so important?'

Wang Rong hesitates. 'The Son of Heaven has affection for you that is composed of many thick layers. He tells me that he was but a boy of four when you first came to court. What other foreigner has served three emperors so honourably? The emperor is saddened by the years that bear upon your shoulders. He has changed a great deal since the death of Fragrant Concubine. He seems to desire only pleasure and diversions. When he is with you or coming to see you, I witness the emperor of old. Perhaps that is why he demands this memoir. Neither the palaces you designed nor the paintings that remain are sufficient to satisfy the emptiness he suffers. When your god calls you to his side, he still wishes to hear your voice, perhaps to remind him of earlier times.'

These sincere words bring tears to my eyes. 'Let us continue then.'

'I think it best if we place you under the guiding hands of calm, more reliable Jesuits,' the rector announced bluntly, shortly after he led me into his study. As I had expected, he glanced from time to time at pages of reports on my character and transgressions. 'They will be responsible for your proper integration into the community of Christian orders as a whole. Please remember, at all times, that you are a representative of the Society of Jesus and of our Lord, Jesus Christ. Whatever talent you possess is by the grace of God and you must always serve Him. Let us pray together. I suggest the prayer of humility of Saint Ignatius.'

I knelt down and uttered words I had said countless times.

'Take, O Lord, and receive all my liberty, my memory, my understanding, and my entire will. Whatever I have or hold, You have given to me; I restore it all to You and surrender it wholly to be governed by Your will. Give me only Your love and Your grace, and I am rich enough and ask for nothing more.'

I left him and wandered into the church hoping to find a way to ease the uncomfortable feelings that pricked at my stomach and chest. It was relatively small, like a church one would find in a fair-sized Italian village, devoid of all decoration save the wooden crucifix. I followed the sound of voices and wandered around the outer buildings. This was an industrious mission, full of geographers, scientists, botanists, astronomers, and physicians. Perhaps out of these walls the first maps of China had emerged, a mammoth undertaking of Fathers Jean-Baptise Regis, Pierre Jartoux, and Matteo Ripa who had recently sent forty-four copper plates to France and Germany for printing. Or was this where the observatory was designed or the first Chinese calendar agreed upon with the emperor's ministers? Everywhere I looked, I saw books and scientific instruments and priests with heads bowed together in earnest discussions.

Later, as I hesitantly entered the refectory, the rector motioned for me to sit near him.

'Tonight, with God's blessing, we welcome *Brother* Giuseppe Castiglione. He brings the skill of an *artist* and we all look forward to the contribution he will make to our humble mission.'

Though there were soft mumblings of welcome, my impression was of a sea of faces staring at me as if I were an oddity. Some of the fathers whispered to each other until we began to eat. I hardly swallowed a mouthful throughout dinner as I furtively glanced around the long room and perceived only dour, disapproving stares.

After dinner, the rector introduced me to three Jesuits. 'This is Father Paolo Lambrezia, a physician.'

I looked at a man of about thirty just shy of average height with dark, soft eyes but with the aura of a much taller man. He had full lips and a broad smile that was warm and welcoming.

'Brother Jerome Villier, a teacher and fellow painter.' Jerome made a small bow as he greeted me. My immediate impression was of a man with a nervous disposition or some internal agitation. He was tall and thin, as if his body had been put in an olive press. Jerome's brown hair was so thin that the pink sheen of his scalp glowed in the candlelight. His lips were also almost non-existent and set in a straight line. He issued smiles while he spoke in short, sporadic bursts. His fragile temperament was palpable and I wondered how old he was.

'And this is Father David Webster, one of our astronomers.' He was at least a head taller than I and large boned. He shook my hand heartily with two hands. 'The four of you will share a house.'

My spirits rose at the sight of these three friendly faces.

'Welcome, Giuseppe,' Paolo said warmly. 'Let us help you carry your things to the house. You and I will be sharing a room, by the way,' he added as we walked to the courtyard to retrieve my belongings. 'Did you have a good journey? The three of us came together and we've been here over a month. After that miserable journey in a two-wheeled carriage and being forced to live together, we're sick of each other. We're looking forward to having someone new to poke fun at.'

'So what made you decide to come to China?' Jerome asked.

'It was the furthest spot away from the college I could think of,' I said.

'Quite right!' They all laughed and launched into stories about the hard times they had had with the fathers during their studies.

'Officious bunch, aren't they?' David concluded. 'I never felt so worthless as I did during my noviciate and the years that followed.'

'I thought I was the only one who they treated so badly,' I said incredulously.

This caused a roar of laughter.

'They treat everyone badly. I think their motive is to strip every shred of self-confidence from your soul so that they can remake you into some sort of ideal priest. The best thing to do is to get as far away as fast as possible.' David looked at me with wide, bright eyes.

'Here we are!' Jerome pushed open the door of a small three-roomed house within the church grounds.

'It's a typical Beijing house,' David explained, 'low and rectangular. There are two bedrooms and a central room where we sit, read, and work. All of the meals are taken in the refectory so we don't have a stove. Many of the missionaries live further away, in Chinese communities, but the houses are no different.'

I felt relaxed among them and was grateful for their company. Paolo helped me unpack. 'David is a bit older than the rest of us. He's thirty-five and has already served in Jesuit missions in Africa and India. I have never seen him other than calm and thoughtful. He's a brilliant astronomer. Don't let his manners deceive you, though. Behind those innocent eyes lies an observant, sharp wit. Nothing escapes his gaze.

'Jerome is excitable and has moments of great sadness. He's the only child of a widowed mother and feels very guilty for having left her. I am the middle one of seven children. My eldest sister is already a grandmother several times over. I'll miss seeing our family expand, but I have no regrets. There is so much for a physician to accomplish here. There's a lot to learn as well. Chinese medicine is so different from ours.'

To my eyes, Paolo's manner and gestures exuded strength and compassion, from the fullness of his head of dark curls to his broad, olive-skinned cheeks, the subtle curve of his chin and the slight droop to his shoulders. Every movement was slow yet firm.

'How old is Jerome?'

'Twenty-seven. The same age as you are.' He smiled to himself. 'He does have the manner of an old man, though. I can see why you would be confused.'

Jerome knocked and interrupted. 'I'd like to see the art supplies you've brought. I probably have enough canvas to last two lifetimes, but I don't think I have enough pigments.'

'I'll leave you two to discuss these things alone,' Paolo said and walked out of the room.

'We're the only artists in this mission,' Jerome said as I organised my few possessions. 'They've given us quite a responsibility, don't you think?'

'What do you mean?'

'As I understand it, we're meant to win over the emperor's heart with our paintings. There've been Jesuits here for a century and certainly since the founding of this dynasty in 1644. The emperor has been extremely fond of many of them and impressed with their knowledge and all they've done for China, etc., etc., but it hasn't won the prize everyone wants.' He paused to see if I was understanding him. 'This emperor has no interest in our religion. He's had no epiphany and he has, in the past, sealed our churches.'

'Surely there are many converts? And more all the time?'

'No and no again. Thanks to Rome and the behaviour of certain emissaries of the pope this emperor is growing more and more antipathetic to Christianity.

'And we are meant to change that?'

'Umm-hum.'

'And if we don't succeed?'

'I have no idea.'

The next day, Paolo offered to take me to the Bureau for Managing the Emperor's Affairs, the Nei Wu Fu, to formally register me as a missionary of the capital. A bored Chinese official barked a question at me without raising his head. When I did not reply he lifted his long face and repeated the question.

'Have you come to swear the Christian missionary pledge, based on the principles of Li Ma Dou?'

Li Ma Dou was the Chinese name given to the great Father Matteo Ricci who had lived in China during the previous dynasty. He had died almost eighty years before I was born. He came alone to China to spread the word of our Lord, ignorant of the language, an explorer of an unknown land. Countless stories survive of his sixteen years here, of his intelligence and commitment. He had impressed the literati with his knowledge and his ability to learn Chinese and memorise great swathes of poetry, but he had also roused the fear of mobs who tried to kill him.

I looked back blankly at the sullen, droopy face of the official with sacs under his eyes of the same shape as his oval head. I felt unsure of what to say.

Paolo whispered in my ear. 'Well? Why are you hesitating?'

'I fear I'm not worthy enough to swear it. I'm not the most obedient or devout of Jesuits.'

'This is not the moment to doubt your convictions or weigh the goodness of your soul,' Paolo said in my ear.

The official watched us with one eyebrow raised.

'But Father Ricci was a giant of a man. What a fool I was to think I could be like him.'

'Giuseppe, you reveal your sincerity and honesty by having these doubts. It shows that you are a true disciple to the path he laid down for us.'

'Thank you, Paolo.' I quickly nodded to the official and repeated the words he uttered: '*According to the precepts laid down by the Jesuit Father Li Ma Dou during the Ming dynasty, I, Lang Shi Ning, agree to respect all Chinese traditions and religious practices.*'

The official quickly wrote on a piece of paper and threw it towards me. 'By the order of our ten-thousand-years-living emperor, this piao grants you the privilege to live in the capital of the great Qing dynasty and to carry out duties as a missionary of the Christian Church. Guard it well, Missionary Lang.' He grunted and turned away to tend to other bits of paper.

'Did I embarrass you?' I asked Paolo. 'There's no Jesuit I admire more than Father Ricci, even including our founder.'

As we started to walk back to the Eastern Church, Paolo put his arm around me. 'It's rare to meet someone who speaks from the heart as you do. All you've done is shown me that your conscience is powerful and functions as your moral guide whatever the consequences. You mustn't worry about what others view as right and wrong when your thoughts are clear and your motives pure. I believe there are always great men around and they make their presence felt when the times demand such vision and courage.

'Ignatius Loyola founded the Society of Jesus when the Catholic Church was under severe attack during the Reformation. His reputation and the principles of the new order were so respected that there are those who say he saved Catholicism. But these are different times and call for another sort of Jesuit. One thing is certain, though, great men also have great sorrows.

'Have you heard the story of Father Ricci and the Plantin Bibles?' Paolo continued. I shook my head. 'Near the end of his life, he had gone south for several months to meet other Jesuits and was given passage to Beijing on the boat of a prosperous eunuch. He travelled with a young Chinese disciple, a boy he had nurtured and educated for several years. While they were sailing downstream on the Northern River, a terrible storm arose.'

Paolo stopped walking. His brows rose so steeply that lines criss-crossed his forehead. 'The boat was heavily laden and wallowing violently. He advised the eunuch to lower the sails, but the eunuch ignored him. It wasn't long before the boat keeled over and sank. There were many deaths; Father Ricci's adored disciple was one of them. Seeing Father Ricci's grief, the eunuch offered to buy another boy from a nearby village to replace the one who had died. He thought he was comforting Father Ricci by assuring him that it would not cost much to replace the youth.' Paolo shook his head. 'I think about this story very often.'

'What meaning do you take from it?'

'I believe that the very acts of living and loving are dangerous, fraught with danger and pain. Father Ricci continued to learn about China and preach about Christianity when his heart must have been broken, not once but many times. The meaning I take from this story is that one must have a clear goal in mind in order to be able to withstand the trials and tribulations that block the path to it.'

I awoke early on my second morning in our small house with an urgent desire to get as close to the emperor's palace as possible. We were meant to do nothing before early prayers when everyone's attendance was required, but I could not resist the impulse to see the city. I set off silently, waking no one, aware that there was no way I could explore and return in time for prayers.

I knew that Beijing was composed of three parts, like boxes within boxes: the huge, outer Capital City; the smaller, refined Imperial City where I lived; and the Forbidden City, the place that captured my attention, the jewel in the centre.

I walked, wide-eyed, through the streets, taking in the sights and sounds of the city as it began to wake, the city that was now to be my home. Gutters on the roadside oozed filth and foul odours. Animals wandered freely on the lanes. No buildings were higher than a single story, though many were hidden from view by walls and gates. Very poor people with dirty children drew brackish water from wells dotted along the way and returned to their makeshift homes. Servants came out of gateways to collect heavy water barrels from carts pulled by donkeys. A man with several pieces of iron tied together suspended from a thin bar above his cart stopped, pulled out a stick, and ran it along the iron. The iron resonated like a dull chime. People rapidly appeared with cooking knives or scissors for him to sharpen.

Street hawkers pushed their carts, muscles bulging, veins throbbing, and chanted songs praising their wares. I passed several small markets with piles of fresh vegetables. Once or twice I caught a glimpse of an ornate palanquin, heavily shrouded and surrounded by guards on horseback. The men who carried the chairs wore little, and what they had was worn and ripped. They perspired heavily but their faces were expressionless. I saw only resignation in their demeanour, as if their spirits had deserted them.

I was anxious to note every detail, to burn them into my memory, and an enticing lane or an interesting face sent me down one alley after another. Before long, I realised I was hopelessly lost and asked for directions to the Forbidden City. An elderly man with tiny eyes motioned for me to follow him. He glided, barely touching the ground, with quick, small paces in shoes made of rags and secured around his calves, glancing repeatedly over his shoulder to see if I were still behind him.

As I followed him, I saw that many of the homes in the Imperial City were refined, even richly decorated, visible through open gates. Some were quite old and fragile, their wooden structures limp and wispy.

Suddenly we emerged from the maze of cluttered streets and reached a large open space. Massive walls and a moat told me where I was. I caught a glimpse of the brilliant yellow roofs at the eastern and western corners of the Forbidden City, their cornices and beams peeking over the tops of the high walls. The old man pointed and left me, bowing his head repeatedly, smiling and shaking his hand while I stumbled over words of gratitude.

I stood near the Xi Hua Men, Gate of Western Glory. I knew from my studies that the bridge over the moat led to the Wu Men, the Noon Gate, and beyond that was Tian An Men, the Gate of Heavenly Peace. Wu Men opened several times to allow carriages, palanquins, and horsemen in and out, but I could see little beyond the outer protective walls; the walls were too thick and the passageway too long for my curiosity to be even remotely sated. I turned away, disappointed, and hoped that I could find the Eastern Church again easily and quickly.

When at last I found the church, I noticed several carriages waiting outside the walls. As I entered the monastery, red with embarrassment and self-recrimination, I was met by a wall of stone faces. I could see Paolo, Jerome, and David at the back of the hall, huddled together.

'We have all been waiting for you, Brother Giuseppe,' the rector said with suppressed irritation. 'Prayers, breakfast, and morning chores are completed. We have been summoned to meet the emperor but could not leave until you returned. In future, Brother Giuseppe, until you have become familiar with the city, do not venture out without either permission or another more *reliable* father at your side.' He gave a look that should have left a burn mark on my forehead.

While I kept my head low, a stream of Jesuits passed me heading for the carriages. Paolo, Jerome, and David came last and stood around me.

'You left without a word to any of us. It's not fair to put us in such a difficult position,' Paolo said. 'We cannot lie for you, nor should we be your keepers.'

The three of them walked off and I followed behind. Paolo's words cut deeply. He spoke without anger, but his tone was one of hurt that I had betrayed the friendship he had offered.

It took over two hours to reach the emperor's summer palace called Chang Chun. The carriage we travelled in was spacious and more comfortable than most. I sat with Paolo, Jerome, and David, who had generously accepted my apologies for my thoughtlessness. 'The incident is forgotten,' Paolo had said.

None of us knew much about Chang Chun other than the facts that it was a large estate with many palaces, lakes, and gardens and that the emperor spent many months of the year there.

'Goodness,' I commented as we arrived, 'I haven't seen so many European faces since I left Macao. And they all appear to be missionaries.'

'Yes, and notice how all the brotherhoods stand apart from each other,' Paolo observed.

He was right. There were distinct clusters of robed men standing outside the large wooden gate united by the sombre cloaks and hats that identified them: Franciscans, Dominicans, Augustinians, and Benedictines. As we dismounted and joined the rest of our order, other groups glanced at us briefly without a single nod of welcome or recognition before resuming their conversations.

'They would not be here were it not for a Jesuit.' I did not disguise the irritation I felt. 'Yet they are united in their dislike of us.'

Paolo nodded. 'Father Ricci in his last minutes on earth said: *I have opened the door*. But though many have come through that door, China is no closer to becoming a Christian country.'

A small gate opened next to the enormous entry gates and a servant appeared, richly dressed.

Chapter 4

'The emperor invites you into the Chang Chun palace. Enter.' The voice was shrill and high-pitched. As he spoke, the large wooden gates creaked open.

'Is that man a eunuch?' I asked Paolo.

'Undoubtedly.'

I could not take my eyes off him as we walked through the gates, my mind full of questions that I both did and didn't want the answers to.

The servants within were clothed in bright silks with beautiful embroidery that contrasted with our browns, blacks, greens, and greys. Our hard shoes made a noise as we filed past, but they glided along in cloth slippers.

The procession was silent and the air chill. A few birds chirped. The palace estate was a maze of paths and gateways leading in all directions. I caught glimpses of pavilions, small cottages, mansions, walled gardens, ponds, and orchards. What I saw was beautiful and serene.

We walked on a stone path, inlaid with patterns of flowers, which split into a Y. One branch led to the door of a small palace; the other, which we took, entered a small, square courtyard. The flower motif continued to the edge of the courtyard, which was framed by a thick wooden railing. A large number of men wearing similar hats crowned with red feathers and purple robes sat cross-legged in rows on fur-covered cushions leaving a central path clear.

Seven shallow marble steps led to an empty rectangular hall supported by large columns. The floor was a chessboard of black and white marble. The ceiling had a central spine with ribs flowing left and right, each one disappearing into carved, brightly decorated beams.

A servant called out: '*The emperor is arriving.*'

'When the emperor arrives you are forbidden to look at him. Lower your heads immediately,' the rector reminded us. 'If he speaks to you, refer to him as Bixia.'

'What is *Bixia*?' I asked.

'We use it as if it were "Your Majesty", but it literally means 'beneath the stairs that lead to the throne room' as far as I can ascertain. Most Chinese refer to him as Son of Heaven or Ten-Thousand-Years-Living Emperor, which we find impossible to say. Jesuits have used Bixia for many years now.'

Another voice called out. '*The emperor is arriving.*'

I recalled Er Qing's history lessons during our long journey north. 'I am Manchu,' he had explained. 'We are descendants of a people once called the Jurchen. In early Chinese records, from AD 300, we were called the Eastern Barbarians. At the beginning of the twelfth century, my ancestors established a dynasty called the Jin that covered much of northern China and the lands beyond. But a stronger military force was afoot, the Mongols. By the end of the twelfth century, the infamous Genghis Khan controlled territory in Europe and Asia from the Caspian Sea to the China Sea, including Siberia and Tibet. His grandson, the Kublai Khan, destroyed the Southern Sung and established the Yuan dynasty, which controlled China for almost one hundred years until the Ming dynasty was established.

'The Mongols had fallen into many factions and were weakened. They continue to mistrust and fight among themselves. But we Jurchen or Manchus learned much and our armies grew stronger. In 1644, the great-grandfather, Nurhachi, and grandfather, Abahai, of our ten-thousand-years-living emperor, with their powerful armies and allies, conquered China and put a Manchu on the throne of China. He was the Shun Zhi emperor and his son, the Kang Xi emperor, is sixty-one years old and has ruled China for fifty-three years.

'His father was only ten when he was crowned as the first emperor of the Qing dynasty, seventy-one years ago. If you hear the term "Han", it refers to pure Chinese who are neither members of a minority nor Manchu. When you meet the emperor, remember his heritage.'

Now we all stood, eyes towards the ground. As the officials rose, I could hear small sucking noises from their cushions. The most senior member of the missionary group, the Portuguese bishop, tiptoed forward and knelt down humbly on both knees, his head low. I watched him by turning my head slightly, peeking from the corner of my eye. A hand gently touched his head. A rustle of silk grew louder as someone walked purposefully forward.

'The head of the Board of Rites,' someone whispered.

A heavy brocade robe rustled passed us and stopped before the assembled officials.

He called out: 'Yi kou tou.'

We threw ourselves down to our knees. As Er Qing had taught me, I hit my forehead three times on the ground, rising and doing it again, three times in all, nine knocks of the head. The ritual made me feel somewhat dizzy and very foolish. As I kow-towed, I heard the sound of countless bodies dropping to their knees. Some were soft and graceful, others old and heavy, murmuring, grunting, and huffing with the exertion. Glancing around quickly, I saw an array of purple robes and red feathers spread across the stone. When we finished we stood again with our heads bowed.

'Ai ya,' I heard. I looked up and blinked at the sight of the Kang Xi emperor, the man formally named Ai Xin Jue Luo Xuan Ye. He was wagging an outstretched finger.

While we had been prostrating, chairs, cushions, and screens had arrived on the raised platform at the top of the stairs. Lacquered screens, half the height of a man, were placed carefully around the emperor.

Er Qing had told me about his selection as emperor, a story of good luck arising from misfortune. His father fell ill with smallpox at the age of twenty-seven. Suspecting that death was near, he chose Xuan Ye, the third-born prince, to succeed him, primarily because he was the only son who had contracted smallpox and survived. Only eight years old, Xuan Ye was proclaimed the new emperor, even though he was not full-blooded Manchu, his mother being Han, pure Chinese. His father had obviously seen sufficient good qualities in the boy to believe this did not matter.

At sixteen, Xuan Ye revealed his strength and commitment to his destiny by dismissing the regents appointed to rule while he was under age, arresting any who threatened him and assuming power fully with no one strong enough to oppose him. Among the Jesuits, his reputation was that of an intelligent and devoted monarch.

Trying but failing not to stare, my eyes scoured every detail of the Kang Xi emperor's appearance. A small hat of fox fur rested like a skullcap on his head, decorated by one milk white pearl sitting in the centre. His robe was embroidered in gold with stylised forms of dragons, each paw baring five claws. On top of the robe, he wore a mink jacket, lined in what looked like black newborn lamb fleece. He sat cross-legged on a huge chair with carved dragons protruding from every corner, cushioned by a thick fur that extended beyond the seat and hung stiffly over the sides.

His eyes swept over the assembled Europeans and Chinese while he leant his head to one side and spoke to an official. His face was wide with lines that accentuated an expression of concern and responsibility. His eyes hung down at the corners and were set deep into his head, the lids so parsimonious that he appeared to have large brown orbs for eyes. A pencil-thin line skimmed along his top eyelid, dropped to the outer corner and continued to his cheekbones.

A eunuch poked the bishop and pointed to a wooden stool covered with a large square cushion. The bishop stumbled as he walked, recovered, bowed again, and sat down. Another Jesuit, thin, almost translucent, appeared like a spectre from somewhere behind the emperor. This was Father Francisco, a Portuguese-born Jesuit and long the official interpreter. He was a thin man with sparse, dry grey hair. He had enormous droopy eyes and a heavy, lined brow with thick eyebrows. His reputation was without equal among Jesuits, not just for his skill at language but for his wisdom and humility.

Two gifts that had been delivered by the Portuguese Office for Missionary Activity waited on a nearby table: a telescope and a Meissen porcelain clock.

'Bixia, our great and powerful king sent you these two tokens of the great esteem he feels for you. He has sent his kindest regards through our new missioners,' said the bishop with a bowed head.

The emperor turned towards the gifts. Curiosity and pleasure shone in his eyes. 'Aha. This is very good.' He gesticulated at us. 'Among you, who knows how to use this?' He was pointing to the telescope, speaking slowly and clearly with a sharp northern accent.

David stepped forward. 'Bixia, we are—'

'You are the astrologer named Zai Dawei?'

'Yes, Bixia. This is an excellent telescope, one of the newest designs. Unfortunately, it will not be possible for me to demonstrate its qualities in daylight. It will not be effective.'

Behind me, several of the purple robed officials began tittering.

'Then nothing can be done. You must return to this palace this evening.'

With the snorts and noises in the background the emperor's face had changed, assuming an air of innocence. He raised his voice and pointed towards an old sour-looking man who was still tittering and elbowing his neighbour.

'Bai Kui Rong, you are my greatest scholar of the heavens. Come tonight and look afresh at the stars with me.'

The whispering instantly died away. 'Zha. I obey.' The man's face became serious and sullen.

'Now at least Zhen knows how to amuse oneself with this clock.' The emperor's eyes swept across the missioners. He unfolded his legs and stood up from the chair. He strode down the shallow stairs and came closer to us. Standing, he was taller than the average Chinaman and full of figure, a well-fed man with a classic oval-shaped contour. When he turned, the back of his head was flatter than I expected, as if the skull had been moulded upward. His face was like an old mountain, its features softened and polished, subtle and mysterious.

I still held fast to my first impression of Chinese faces: none equalled those of my countrymen and women. They were too bland, too muted, devoid of bold features sharpened by great contrasts in colour or shading. To me Italian faces, overflowing with life, revealed character openly, challengingly, with their proud noses and enormous eyes. Though I had grown accustomed to the lack of diversity in hair and eye colour and found many other distinguishing features—hair texture, noses, eyes, and foreheads—that made each face unique, I was troubled by the fact that Chinese faces were by and large merely masks, hiding and diffusing character.

The emperor's brow tightened in concentration. He spoke slowly, surveying everyone present. He gestured with his hands, light and graceful cadences, hands with long fingernails.

An attendant brought the Meissen clock to him. The emperor found the key and pushed it into the lock. He wound the mechanism and waited. After a pause, a soft melody hummed and he chuckled and clapped his hands. He pointed to the clock, smiling to his servants and ministers. Sounds of admiration buzzed amongst the gathered men. The emperor's face changed again. He shook his hand for silence. We listened until the lullaby slowed and stopped and the still air filled with a steady tick-tock. He picked up the clock in both hands and walked in a large circle. He handed it to his attendant and returned to his chair.

'Very good. Truly very good. The Spanish king sent me a different clock last year. This one…is even more refined.' The emperor's eyes turned toward Jerome, Paolo, and me. 'Lang Shi Ning?'

I nodded and he smiled at me.

'Lin Zhi Xing?'

Jerome nodded and received the same gracious smile.

'Zhen has been told that you are painters. This makes us very pleased. In a few days, Zhen will invite you to paint for us. And then this last one must be the doctor, Luo Huai Zhong.' The emperor paused. 'You have been given a very good name. Zhen is pleased. Zhen has a very good French doctor at the moment. But our concubines are frequently unwell. Are you able to tend to women as well as men?'

'Women and children, Bixia,' Paolo said, keeping his head lowered.

Clucking, mumbling, and hissing arose behind us. The emperor looked up with his eyebrows knitted together.

'Are there some of you who disapprove of my question?'

The chattering stopped.

'Zhen has heard that my French doctor has been dispensing quinine and other medicine to many of you. If you do not approve of Western doctors or their medicine, why do you request his help for your ailments?'

He waited for a response, but none came. After a pause, he said, 'Perhaps you are hungry after your journey? Zhen has asked my cooks to prepare a meal for you.'

As abruptly as he arrived, he departed, and eunuchs came to escort us to another pavilion.

We entered another large hall where scores of low tables had been laid with bowls, plates, and cups. We sat on the floor around the tables, each missionary sitting with others of his order. The interior was luminescent with intricate designs painted on the ceiling, beams, and walls in vibrant greens, blues, and gold. Though we were numerous, there was ample space for entertainers as well. Seated musicians played unusual stringed instruments. Gigantic Mongols, with legs like tree trunks and chests like warships, wrestled wearing nothing but loincloths. Delicate, waif-like female dancers twirled on tiny feet making patterns with long scarves. Scores of servants moved among us carrying trays of food, each dish more colourful than the last and festooned with delicately carved fruit and vegetables.

A plate was shoved under my nose and a brusque eunuch indicated that I was to lift the cloth covering it. Beneath it was a green cylinder of stone, the width of two of my fingers, resting on more silk. I picked up the stone off the plate and held it, not knowing what to think.

'The emperor gives each new missionary a present,' someone said as I turned the stone over, wondering what it was. It had a delicate, soft, cool feel to it.

The eunuch returned with a book on Chinese medicine for Paolo.

'This is exquisite. I only hope I can read it someday,' he commented as he turned the delicate, beautifully illustrated pages.

David received a long, shiny lacquer box. He nodded with muted pleasure. 'Very nice. Perfect for holding scientific instruments.'

Jerome came over and unfolded a small cloth to show us a pearl. 'The eunuch who gave this to me said it once belonged to the Dalai Lama. He was very impressed that I was given this. Apparently it can change bad luck into good, though he became offended when I asked him how it did so.'

'Look what I've been given,' I said to him, having looked at the pearl. 'Some sort of green stone. What's the significance of this?'

'It's jade, a gemstone that's valued in China as much as gold is in Europe, if not more.' I turned to face the speaker who wore the black robe and hat of a Jesuit. 'May I see it? Yes, this one is probably from the far west. It's beautiful. Feel it; it's hard, yet translucent and cool. And there are subtle veins of brown running vertically from top to bottom.'

He looked at me and gave a soft laugh. 'It's clear you're not impressed. Believe me when I tell you that jade is used in China to symbolise the finest human virtues, as it is something that can be carved yet is pure, fragile yet surprisingly resilient. You have been given something very special.'

The man had a captivating voice, deep and rich with a hint of playfulness.

'Let me introduce myself. I'm Antonio Vassali from Verona. Pleased to meet you, Giuseppe Castiglione. That is who you are, isn't it?'

I nodded and stared. Father Vassali was highly respected. Jesuits in both Macao and Beijing whispered that he was one of the most talented missionaries in China, a priest destined for the highest levels of the society, as well as a brilliant mathematician and linguist. It was rare, many said, to combine such a privileged background and keen mind as his with a nature that was generous, fair, and kind.

From the way his name was spoken, I had expected someone older and more reserved. The man before me was young and very handsome, blessed with features that any artist seeking to portray male beauty would desire—large hazel eyes decorated with multi-coloured flecks like veins in rich marble and thick black hair. His face was triangular, wide at the cheeks tapering to an elegant, firm curve. His lips were full and well defined and curled up at the ends so that he always had the hint of a smile.

'What do you think of this palace, the Palace of Eternal Spring, Chang Chun?' He looked around and I suddenly felt that in him I saw everything I yearned for: intelligence, confidence, authority, and charm. 'The emperor loves to be here where he can escape the heaviness of the Forbidden City and concentrate his mind on the problems of state. He tries to live here during the summer and autumn.'

Again I nodded but found myself tongue-tied. He either didn't notice or did not mind that I was ineloquent.

'I've heard a great deal about you. Let me reassure you that I believe there is room for individuals in this religious brotherhood. And the fact that you are here proves it. Others believed in your abilities even if your character is one that challenges authority. You would not be here, in this mission, in a country as sophisticated as this one if you did not have something unique to offer.

'I know as well as anyone that we cannot always please those who think they know best. If I had followed my family's wishes, I would still be living a life of indulgence. They had pinned their hopes on me, the only son among five with an ounce of sense, to continue the family business and make them even more wealthy, but it was not for me. I sought knowledge and adventure, not revenues and profits. This is the most exciting mission on earth and we are here at an extraordinary time. During these five years in China, I have begun a great journey of the mind and spirit. It is a country that demands the best you have to offer.'

I looked down at the jade in my hand. I could feel his eyes on me. but I was still at a loss, not sure what to say.

He saw my confusion, and when I looked up, I saw kindness in his eyes. 'I'm not trying to embarrass you, Brother Giuseppe,' he continued, 'but I have been curious since I heard of your escapades.' He put a hand on my shoulder. 'I'd like to hear from you what happened in Macao. Knowing our superiors as I do, devout souls that they are, I doubt anyone truly listened to your version of events. They would have been terrified by the accusations and more concerned with preserving our reputation, weak and unsalvageable though it is.'

I paused, wondering as I looked at his face how much I could trust him, but instinct, not logic, made my choice. Could anyone feign eyes like that?

The history of my behaviour in Macao was something everyone knew about but no one dared to mention. I had longed to have the opportunity to discuss the incident calmly with a sympathetic ear, but no one had asked, no one had offered to listen, until now.

'I'm pleased to meet you, Antonio,' I managed to say at last, 'and I'd like to tell you what happened in Macao. Until I arrived in Macao, I had no idea how disliked we Jesuits are. I spent a lot of time walking and exploring on my own during which I found out that the term Jesuit was tossed about as an insult among the European traders to describe a lying, two-faced hypocrite. As if that were not bad enough, it seemed every other religious order detested us as well. Wherever I went, I was insulted. The worst were Benedictines and Franciscans. They kept asking me how it felt to be part of an order that had poisoned the papal emissary, Cardinal de Tournon.'

Once I started, I poured out months of pent-up frustration and anger. Macao had been a hideous place; a place of jealousies, cruelty, greed, and mistrust, not just among missionaries and traders, but between Europeans and Chinese, among all nationalities and races.

'I tried to ignore them, to find some common ground, but they were intransigent. Then one day, in a market, while I was sketching a portrait of a young Chinese boy and his parents, a group of Benedictines surrounded me. They ridiculed me, saying I was a member of a corrupt order, shouting about our supposed illicit financial arrangements and denigrating us as evangelists for Christ.'

As I described the incident to Antonio it appeared as fresh in my mind as if I were living it again. Four of them surrounded me as I sat. The Chinese boy looked scared, but his parents hid their feelings and their eyes. Several other stall holders gathered and watched with blank faces.

'He has red hair. You know what they say about people with red hair,' one of the Benedictines commented.

'What?' another one asked.

'They're liars and thieves. I heard this one had to beg to be allowed to remain a Jesuit. He's lucky to be a brother after all the things he did.'

'What sort of things? Tell us!'

The Benedictine never got the chance to finish. I swung around and punched him square in the face. His nose broke and blood poured down his face. The curious Chinese moved away quickly but watched intently. I kicked the second Benedictine in the stomach before hitting his ear hard. The two remaining tried to jump on me, but I moved aside and grabbed the backs of their cowls and banged their heads together. One of them lost a tooth.

'My early years of surviving on the streets of Milan had given me good skills and strong fists and feet. Instinctively, these took over. My rule from those harsh times was never to leave an enemy with an ounce of strength left. I found a heavy piece of wood and started closing in on them. I don't know what else I would have done, since for the moment I had forgotten all of my religious training, but I did not get the chance. They took one look at my face and ran off with their hands on their wounds. I was surprised at how good it felt to respond in such an un-Christian way. Several Chinese were laughing while others looked at me as if I were insane.' I told Antonio all this.

'It did not take long for them to tell their tale to the entire religious community. Everyone chose to side with them.' I concluded. 'You know the rest; how I was blamed for putting our mission at risk, how I was forced to leave well before my training had finished. At least I was not sent back to Europe.'

Antonio shook his head and sighed sharply. 'What you did, you did as a man, and no amount of prayer can change an independent nature. We can all serve the Lord in our own fashion, as long as we are honest and sincere. Our society should be able to tolerate those who would use fists and weapons as well as more peaceful means to protect the principles of Christ. Your street brawl will prove of little consequence to our position in Rome or anywhere else. Many of us fear that the future of our society is bleak. We made many enemies at the Council of Trent because our opinions were too liberal for the prevailing mood. In China we stand alone in opposing the Vatican's position on Chinese converts to Christianity.'

I listened, fascinated, as Antonio described things I had heard of but had failed to grasp their importance. He put them in a clear light and opened my eyes to the complexities of Chinese and Vatican policies.

'Cardinal de Tournon brought an edict from Pope Clement in 1706 stating that all Chinese converts to Christianity must no longer practise any of the rites of their former religion, a totally preposterous policy to anyone who understands Chinese culture. The emperor was so furious at the impudence of the pope that he imprisoned the cardinal. It was unfortunate for him, but more so for us, that he died.' Antonio continued, 'Five years has not dulled the rumours of our supposed misdeeds.' Then he winked at me. 'Enough of this grim talk. Today we are celebrating your arrival in Beijing.'

I realised I was trembling inside. I felt I had met someone, a contemporary, who I could trust, admire, and emulate. He radiated confidence and charisma and I felt elated.

With a quick nod of the head, Antonio began to eat. When he had finished he put down the bowl and gave me a gentle slap on the back. 'I believe we shall be good friends,' he said, before going on to tell me more about himself. 'Growing up in the lap of luxury in Verona, I could never have imagined a place like Tibet. How grateful I am to have been sent there. Because of my language skills, I was chosen to write the first reports of that mysterious country and learn its language. It is a kingdom within the highest mountains you could ever imagine. The Alps are mere rolling hills in comparison. I think it is the most beautiful country on earth. The life is harsh: it's difficult to breathe at first and little grows there, so their diet is tedious and tasteless, but the people are handsome, happy, and gentle. Perhaps it is their religion, Buddhism, that makes them so. I was welcomed into the king's household, learned Tibetan and Mongol and studied at the Buddhist institute. When I was there, the rest of the world faded away. I could have stayed forever.'

He was interrupted by the arrival of a large group of men and boys. All talking ceased and the servants fell to their knees.

'These are the princes, the sons and grandsons of the emperor,' Antonio whispered. There were at least twenty of them, ranging in age from three to forty.

'How many children does he have?' I asked.

'Over forty, I believe.'

Once the bowing and formal greetings were over and the cacophony of eating and talking resumed, several older youths rushed towards Antonio, talking at once, giggling and vying for his attention. My Chinese was too basic to follow what was said, but their affection for him was unmistakable. Then an older prince strode over and ordered the gaggle of boys to leave An Dong Ni alone. He sat down and spoke so softly and intently near Antonio's ear that I hardly heard a word.

I glanced up and noticed another prince staring at the two men. His expression was hard, almost angry. He noticed me watching him and turned his cold eyes to me and I shrank. His gaze spoke of superiority and ruthlessness.

5

Wang Rong has left for the day. I watched him stride briskly away, showing none of the frailties of a man of more than seventy years. In the fading light, memories are my company and fill the room. The line between the past and the present is blurred. I see myself again as a young man and find I feel no envy or regret. What a life I have led, mistakes and all.

Antonio's friend Yin Ti was the fourteenth-born son of Xuan Ye. The brooding prince Yin Zhen was the fourth-born, by far the most intelligent and disciplined of them all but a mystery even to those who knew him well. By one of those ironies designed only by God, both princes were born of the same mother. Two completely different characters, Cain and Abel, the sun and the moon; one open and bright, the other dark and dangerous. But although Yi Ti was an innocent victim of the events that ensued, my heart is cold when I think of him. His foolish dreams had terrible consequences for my treasured friend. Though they knock from time to time on the door of my guarded memories, neither Yin Ti nor Yin Zhen are among the crowd of spirits that keep me company. I open the door only to those I loved.

The Kang Xi emperor was an old man when I met him. After fifty years at the helm, he was tired. He encouraged me as an artist without ever praising my work. I never realised how subtly he nurtured roots that anchored my feet to the soil of China. Why he did it, I'll never know. Though his grandson has been my greatest champion, I miss the Kang Xi emperor more than ever. He was one of only a handful of men whose praise I sought. His praise of my adaptation to Chinese art softened the hidden, sad recesses of my heart.

Within days of my arrival at the Eastern Church, I was put to work in an orphanage. I was the only missionary assigned work that had nothing to do with his special talent. In the mornings, after prayers, David went to the observatory, Paolo to the hospital, Jerome to a school, and I began scrubbing floors and privies. Exhausted at the end of each day, I left my sketchbooks untouched. Even my daydreams were blank, my mental canvas un-stretched. My spirits sank low and my concerned housemates could do little to rouse me.

'The work I am assigning you is what I consider best for your soul. It should teach you humility and respect,' the rector had announced. 'I do pray that you learn the lessons well.'

'It's ridiculous,' I protested. 'I was sent here as an artist, not a nursemaid.'

The rector glared at me. 'Then prove you are worthy of the men who sent you here.'

I started to open my mouth, but closed it again. The Lord works in mysterious ways, I reminded myself. Let Him take charge of my life for a change.

All the brothers and fathers of the Society of Jesus lived close to each other in homes surrounding the Eastern Church. Antonio lived alone in a small three-roomed house, sparsely furnished but full of books. I went to see him a few times, and he welcomed me warmly. He regaled me with stories about Tibet, Mongols, and Manchus and other exotic tribes from the wild north and I began to tell him the story of my life, the first time I had ever done so. How different our experiences had been. His family had been patrons to great artists over the centuries. He walked along corridors and prayed in a family chapel decorated with paintings by Titian, Tintoretto, and other masters of Venice. He went to concerts, operas, and carnivals, and was educated by the finest minds in whatever field took his fancy. Yet he assured me over and over again that no matter how different one's beginnings, friendship was indiscriminate, and talent, the evidence of God's grace, could land anywhere and would always shine through.

Leaving him to return home, though my housemates were good companions, was difficult, like abandoning sunshine for fog. Some naïve part of me foolishly sought to imitate him and thus become a being who walked on clouds. Thinking spirituality was the first step, I spent hours studying the *Spiritual Exercises* of our founder, Saint Ignatius Loyola, hoping I could emerge from such meditations a new man, but the old skin failed to shed; I was no butterfly, only a pale moth.

After three weeks, the rector asked to see Jerome and me. 'As you are well aware,' he began, 'you two are the first Jesuit artists to arrive in Beijing. The decision to bring you here was taken at the highest levels. For fifty years, eminent Jesuits have served at court. We have built an observatory, produced the first maps of China, standardised the calendar, and taught science and mathematics to the emperor, princes, and high-ranking officials. However, despite the honours bestowed on several Jesuits in the past and the respect they earned in the emperor's eyes, we have not succeeded in our true mission. Our superiors pray that art will achieve what science has not.'

From his haughty tone, I could tell how little faith he placed in our use. 'An order has been received this morning from the emperor,' he continued. 'You have both been asked to create paintings of your choosing. He has expressed his curiosity about Western art,' he added as an afterthought with a dismissive wave of his hand. 'I do not need to remind you how important an event this is. We will all be watching and praying for your success.'

A flurry of excitement swirled around our communal buildings. Jesuits who had studiously ignored me sought me out to offer advice and encouragement. Everyone had an opinion and no hesitation in expounding it. In the end, Jerome and I discussed the possibilities with our housemates.

'Paint what you love. Anything else will not be true to who you are,' Paolo said.

'I disagree.' David's expression was tight. 'My advice is to paint only what the emperor loves.'

I was inclined to agree with Paolo. 'Why do you say that?' I asked David.

David turned to me, sighing. 'My recent encounter with the emperor did not go as I would have expected.' He paused, clearly embarrassed. 'I arrived in a buoyant mood, confident that he would be impressed with this telescope. The emperor, after all, was not only familiar with telescopes having been introduced to them by several astronomers over the years, but was surely familiar with the concept of empirical studies. I was the lucky Jesuit astronomer poised to demonstrate the most powerful telescope he had seen in his life. He asked me to set up the telescope for him to see the moon.

'He smiled broadly saying, "I shall be the first to see..." before turning to peer through the telescope. He never finished his sentence. He pulled back and looked again, repeating this several times, until he turned towards me with his eyes blazing and said, "This is very wrong, very wrong." He gestured to his relatives and ministers to look, and one by one, they stared at the moon and shook their heads as they finished, casting angry glances in my direction. I was ordered to leave, which I did promptly.

'Can you guess what made them all so angry?' David asked me, swallowing hard, his Adam's apple bouncing up and down.

I shook my head. 'I have no idea.'

David rested his forehead on his hand. 'It's almost impossible to comprehend. You see, according to their beliefs, the moon is home to gods, immortals. They expected to gaze through the telescope and see the dwellings and faces of their deities! This isn't science I'm being asked to teach but magic.'

Paolo stood by with a bemused look on his face. 'Perhaps the emperor is not ready for our Western concepts of science yet. There's still a lot for you to do here, David. Let Giuseppe have a go now. For good or bad, he acts instinctually. And he's a survivor. He'll surprise us all.'

Jerome and I agreed that no medium had more majesty than oils nor was more representative of our heritage. Jerome preferred nature and set off westwards with a carriage full of supplies determined to paint a seasonal landscape. From the moment I discovered I could draw, I had concentrated on the human face and body.

I wasted several days feeling lost for ideas, overwhelmed by the significance of the commission. Which person and what composition would stir the passion of this man? Male or female, saint or sinner, victor or philosopher, old or young? I mulled over the little I knew of him. He was a Manchu, a ruler, a husband, a father of over forty surviving children. How many children had died over the years? How often had he grieved for their loss? Perhaps I should draw a child, the symbol of purity, the hope for our future, and the proof of our past.

One girl at our orphanage stood out from the others. When I first saw her, she was in a frail state, underfed and weak. After a short time, nourished by plentiful, healthy food, she blossomed. I found her an intriguing character. Before, hunger had robbed her of playfulness and joy, but once her belly was full, she was transformed into a whirlwind of giggles, playfulness, enthusiasm, and curiosity. She had one speed—fast—and a natural ability to organise and lead her peers, even older children. The children's favourite games were always ones she had created.

It took some doing and plenty of bribes, but I managed to sit her still long enough to sketch her. The painting took three solid weeks to complete. My aim had been to capture childhood and innocence, but when I looked at it, I perceived wistfulness, and feared I had put my own memories of childhood into her eyes.

Jerome returned with two paintings, a village scene and a gentle panorama of a mountain valley in winter. The entire mission gathered to inspect our finished canvases and showered them with praise. Antonio said very little though I hungered for his words of encouragement.

David took me aside. 'Even if your paintings are not accepted, do not lose heart. This emperor is a man who wrestles with many ideas and I do not admire him less for how he treated me. The rituals of ancient customs, not just Chinese but Manchu as well, weighs heavily against the lure of new ideas. I can see how difficult it is for him to allow foreigners, with their strange ways, to infiltrate his kingdom. Your art is far less offensive than my astronomy. I sincerely believe it gives you a greater chance of success—ultimately.'

Several days after delivering our paintings, we were summoned to the Chang Chun palace. When we arrived in mid-afternoon, the palace grounds were still. We passed servants dotted here and there, sitting on small stools, leaning back against walls, quietly resting or sleeping wrapped up in thick coats. A few others hurried by on padded feet carrying trays.

Jerome and I whispered to each other, struggling to contain our excitement and anticipation.

'If we have succeeded in impressing the emperor, I will feel less guilty about leaving my mother alone in Paris,' he told me with tears welling in his eyes.

'Your mother is proud of you, no matter what you achieve. I have never heard of a parent objecting to a son serving God.'

'You're probably right, but I would like something good to come out of this painful separation.'

'You are to wait here,' a eunuch said as he opened a door.

I could smell the aroma of polished wood even before I glanced inside.

'What a splendid room,' Jerome gasped.

Occupying the centre of the room was an enormous desk, made of rich mahogany with a purple hue. A colourful lacquer border covered its base, depicting four dragons trapped in an endless chase. Porcelain vases, some as tall as my waist, were scattered throughout the room. A low lacquer screen with a frieze in ivory of clowns and jesters stood behind the desk. The remaining space was filled with bookshelves, or so I believed, as the books were either bound with silk and cloth or were rolled, made up of hundreds of vertical strips of bamboo. In a corner, barely visible behind a vase, was David's telescope. I nudged Jerome and gestured towards it with my head.

'Is that a good sign or a bad one?' he whispered.

'I hope we don't have to wait very long, or I –'

The door creaked open and we instantly dropped to the ground, performing our nine bows. The emperor swept past us and sat down in his chair.

'Rise.'

Father Francisco, the Jesuit interpreter, and two eunuchs stood behind him, holding our paintings.

'Bring out the paintings.'

The eunuchs leaned our pictures against the lacquer screen. I felt my stomach sink as I saw the glare from the sunlight rob the paintings of all depth and colour.

The emperor turned to me with a blank expression, giving no hint of either a smile or annoyance. I felt a knot in my insides.

'Lang Shi Ning. This picture is a clear likeness of a young child. But Zhen is not pleased to see only the outside form of an object.' Father Francisco translated literally. I tried to catch his eye, to get some clue from him, but he stared at the painting.

'In China we prefer to express the interior of things as well as the exterior. A great painter conveys both the likeness and the spirit to the viewer. Observe the cheeks of this child. Zhen accepts she is a beautiful child. But it is not for nothing that our poets compare female cheeks to peaches or lotus flowers. How can you use such strange colours here? Blues and greens? You have made her face patchy and rough. The brush strokes are heavy and obvious. These shadows around her nose and eyes are most distasteful. Even in comparison to other paintings from Europe that I have seen, it is poor. This is really not a pleasing picture to look at.'

'Bixia,' I spoke quickly in Italian, 'your humble servant requests that you change the placement of the picture. Placement and light are all important to the overall effect.'

Father Francisco turned pointedly in my direction, signalling me to cease.

'What is he saying?' the emperor demanded of Father Francisco. I did not fully understand Father Francisco's reply, but it seemed to have something to do with the fact that I was new to the country and accepted that I had much to learn about Chinese painting styles.

The emperor smiled broadly and continued. 'Lang Shi Ning, what was your purpose in giving Zhen such a painting? Are you trying to show Zhen that you like this child? Well, what do you like about her? Your art must inspire us to understand your feelings. I am completely unmoved when I gaze upon it.'

'Father Francisco, speak for me. I don't know what to say.'

Father Francisco lowered his head and said something quickly to the emperor. The emperor nodded with a satisfied smile and proceeded to tear apart every feature of Jerome's two canvases in much the same tone.

'Landscapes should be in your head,' the emperor told him. 'That is what Zhen wants to see. What is in there.' He pointed to Jerome's dark, balding head. 'That is where the mountains, lakes, and forests are.'

He started to laugh. 'If you two want to paint well, you must find skilled teachers. Zhen will make sure you are introduced to the royal painters. Zhen thinks it would serve you well to see great Chinese art. Come with me.'

A fat eunuch lurched forward, bowed before the emperor, and spoke quietly and quickly. He glanced several times in our direction.

To our surprise, the emperor slapped him. The eunuch bowed lower and apologised profusely as he crawled away.

I could feel the eyes of the eunuch boring into my back as we left the room. I glanced at Father Francesco, hoping he could explain what we had done wrong and offer some words to soothe us, but the emperor was deep in conversation with him.

'Pride was our undoing,' Jerome whispered in a humble tone.

'How can you be an artist and not have pride? Ignorance is more to blame, and naïveté. What can we hope to achieve?'

'We have no choice but to persevere. I will not let you give up, Giuseppe. And you must serve as my bright-line as well.'

As we traversed a zigzag bridge, I saw the wind ripple the water and watched the gentle movement tickle the large lotus flower leaves resting on the surface. *How simple,* I thought, *to be a flower and not an artist in an incomprehensible country*. Leaving the bridge, we came to a building composed of a middle section with a wing on either side built at right angles.

As we entered, the emperor said, 'My eunuch does not believe foreigners have the right to see national treasures. In fact, very few Chinese have been privileged to see them. In this building are some of Zhen's favourite paintings. Zhen comes to look at them to find solitude and wisdom.'

As Father Francesco translated the emperor's words, he added some of his own. 'This is a great honour, young Jesuits. Remember this generous gesture forever.'

We both bowed our heads and expressed our gratitude as best we were able.

'Good. Let us begin.' The emperor described each painting vividly, clearly excited to be near them. He talked about the painters and the periods in which they lived. When we came to an ancient silk scroll from the Warring dynasties period painted two hundred years before the birth of our Lord, he lingered silently and was so moved that I thought I saw tears glistening in his eyes. It was a simple figure study, no more than a few strokes of a brush.

I could not feel a fraction of the emotion that the emperor displayed. Panic grew in my chest, tightening and choking the breath out of me. The art that had nourished and inspired me had no power here and, possibly, no place either. Was I to turn my back on all that I knew and treasured and adopt the style of these flat, lifeless paintings, devoid of colour and passion?

Father Francesco accompanied us to our carriage. His face was unmistakably kind but he had deep lines down his cheeks that ended in pouches beside his chin. I could not begin to imagine the things he knew and held close to his chest. He was rarely around other Jesuits. It was rumoured that the emperor poured out his deepest feelings to this man.

'Please, my sons, do not dwell too long on this event or punish yourselves. The emperor is respectful of art and artists. It is a quiet passion, but no less important for its lack of expression.' He spoke slowly and deliberately. 'He has not approached this meeting lightly. He has taken time with you and shared his treasures. His manner today may have appeared harsh, but he was not angry. True, he is not interested in Western art, but he has laid a challenge before you. How you respond will determine your future. You are both young, not constrained by age or prejudice. Go and free your minds and talents. He looked at us intently, waiting for us to reply.

'Thank you, Father,' Jerome said.

'Your words are kind, Father, but do you really believe that there is any role for us here?'

'That is not for me to judge, but I have faith in two things: the power of the love of our Lord and the ability of art to enable men to see universal truths, whether it be painting, literature, poetry, or music. Art, like religion, knows no boundaries and nourishes the soul.' He bowed slightly and walked slowly backwards. 'God has placed you here for a reason. Do not give up on him or on yourselves.'

'Excuse me, Father,' I said, and he stopped. 'Who was the eunuch, the one the emperor slapped?'

'Ah. That was Duan Shi Lian. He is one of the most senior eunuchs but has few friends who sing his praises. I too have to remind myself that he is one of God's children and should be loved as such. He is clever and efficient. I assume that is why the emperor allows him to rise in rank. I will convey your apologies for his embarrassment today, but I fear that he is not a forgiving creature. I pray that any future encounters you have with him will be more pleasant so that you can forge a favourable relationship.' Father Francesco shook his head sadly. 'Good day, young men. I wish you luck and wisdom in your journey of discovery.'

I knew that Father Francesco's words were important, but my hurt pride won the day. The paintings were waiting for us in the carriage. During the journey back to the capital I destroyed mine entirely and threw the shredded remains into the river. Jerome looked at me strangely as I did so. 'It was a good painting,' was all he said.

During the days that followed, I was surprised by the sympathy offered by my fellow Jesuits. I had expected ridicule and criticism, but was instead showered by words of comfort from all save the rector, who said nothing.

'It was to be expected,' they said. 'Our first encounters were equally embarrassing.'

'You have much to learn about China,' Antonio told me one afternoon, 'but rest assured, when you do you will be very strong. A child who learned to survive on the streets of a city like Milan will never let adversity triumph. Remember that, brother. It's a source of your strength. That and the fact that God is always with you.'

The word 'brother' moved me. It had a different tone from other times. Did he have a tiny corner reserved in his heart for me?

'Come and take a walk with me and I will tell you about my most embarrassing encounters with the emperor.'

He didn't need to ask me twice. We left the church grounds and strolled around the bustling neighbourhood. As he told me stories about teaching the emperor and his sons mathematics, I tried to imagine his earlier life, but could not. I had never seen inside a home such as his or witnessed more than brief glimpses of family life.

'Would it not be nice if we had the chance to choose if not all but some of our family?' I heard him comment.

'Since I don't remember any family life, I can't say whether chance is a good thing or not.'

'I wish I could pass on my memories to you so that you could see and then decide. We were raised by servants, some competent, some not so. Our parents hardly noticed us until we were of marriageable age. Children were a necessary accident of marriage, something to endure. Sometimes my absent-minded mother would forget which of her sons I was, so rarely did she see me. Once one of my sisters was absent for two weeks before anyone thought to ask where she was.'

I looked askance at him.

'It's true. She had taken herself off to stay with a friend's family. The servants assumed my parents knew and my parents assumed the servants would tell them if anything was amiss with one of their offspring.'

'I can't believe that.'

'It's true.'

'You are trying to tell me that whether one is rich or poor makes no difference and that a child can feel just as neglected in such a family as the child who has none.'

'Is that so hard to comprehend?'

'You do have treasured memories. Don't you?'

'A few, but not many. I was unusual from the time I could talk. My parents often teased me that I must have been a changeling. I don't miss any of my five brothers and three sisters. Good riddance to a bickering, selfish, vain flock of ne'er-do-wells.'

I was silent for a time allowing what he had told me to sink in. 'Antonio, you called me your brother earlier. Does that mean that you see me in that light?'

He chuckled. 'You feel such a loss in never having had a family while I feel regret that my years in that household were utterly wasted.' He paused and looked at me while I held my breath. 'I would be honoured to assume the position of older brother to you.' He smiled when he saw my face light up. 'I can think of no one else whom I would wish to call a younger brother.'

I sighed, 'Thank you.'

'Don't be,' he laughed and slapped my shoulder. 'I'm a pretty lousy brother. Maybe you can help me change that.'

In the evening as we sat reading in our home, I turned to Paolo. 'Paolo, do you remember that we once discussed how wonderful it would be to meet one great man in our lifetime? Do you not think that Antonio is such a man? He is brilliant, eloquent, inspired, a true leader. I've never met his equal.'

Paolo looked at me for a while before he spoke. 'I must be honest and say that I don't see him as you do.'

'But why?'

'I agree he is a talented man and an asset to our mission, but I sense a great conflict in him, a battle so deep and personal that it clouds his actions. We cannot expect to guide others to truth if we lie to ourselves. His inner turmoil, I believe, will cause him to act rashly, perhaps even recklessly.' Paolo placed a soft hand on my shoulder. 'I accept that there is much you can learn from him. He's like an older brother to you. But Giuseppe, never forget that David, Jerome, and I are also devoted to you. If you decide to trust us, we too can be like family to you.'

'I received an order from the emperor yesterday. It concerns you and Brother Jerome.' The rector put on his glasses. They had no wires to hook behind his ears, so they slid down his long nose and were only stopped by an abrupt rise at its end. He read from the decree he held in front of him. 'I will translate. The painters Lin Zhi Xing and Lang Shi Ning are hereby granted the titles of "Painters Awaiting Royal Commands." It is the desire of the Kang Xi emperor that both of you avail yourselves of the palace art institute and any teachers you choose to train yourselves in the principles of Chinese art. When you are trained, if your work is of a satisfactory standard, you may take your places with other royal painters.' He looked up at me over the top of his glasses. 'What the emperor demands, the emperor shall have.'

I rushed to Antonio's house to tell him the news but was startled to find him surrounded by a supply of food, medicine, and clothing.

'What are you doing? What's happening?'

'I'm going back to Tibet. I have received word that the situation is very precarious and I am needed there.'

'What do you mean?'

'The kingdom is in grave danger from a Mongol tribe, the Dzungars, a fierce, bloodthirsty lot who have massed at the border of Tibet. I know they will stop at nothing short of total control of the country. None of the missionaries or diplomats has succeeded in negotiating a truce. Perhaps I'm already too late, but if not, I must try everything to avert war.'

'How do you think you can help? What they need is an army not a priest. You've only just learned the language and their customs. Surely you will be putting yourself in grave danger?'

'I have no choice. I gave my word to the king that I would always be a friend to his country.' Antonio spoke with his back to me while he rummaged through the medicines, foods, and other goods. 'If I am to die, then it is God's will.'

'But you do have a choice.' I watched Antonio intently when he turned his face around, but his eyes were dull. They did not see me.

'Please ask me no more questions. If you are truly my brother, you must trust that I go with my whole heart. Do not try to dissuade me.'

'Antonio, as your brother, I fear for your life. As far as I can see this is a hopeless mission. There is so much for you to do in China.'

He shook his head.

'Then at least let me go with you.'

He turned around with anger in his face. 'Under no circumstances are you to even consider coming with me.'

'Why? You seem different suddenly. Are we not brothers?'

'Even brothers have to accept that duty overrides everything. At this moment, the safety of Tibet is my duty. Yours lies in another direction entirely. You cannot follow in my footsteps.'

When I reached home, Paolo took one look at my face and put a hand on my shoulder. 'I can see that you've heard Antonio is leaving.'

'Yes. In his mind, he is already there.'

'He goes for a good cause. Don't be so foolish as to think that he doesn't care for you.'

'Why do you always think you know everything?' I snapped. I stormed out of the house.

I accompanied Antonio as far as I was permitted, to a small town west of Beijing that marked the beginning of a thousand-mile journey. He was travelling completely alone until the northern Muslim capital of Xining, where three other missionaries would be waiting for him.

'It will be months before you reach Lhasa.'

'I'll go as quickly as I can.'

'Is the route very dangerous?'

'I'm afraid so.'

'I'll pray for your safety.' My voice was weak and I could hardly bear to look at him as I spoke.

Antonio smiled. 'Thank you, Giuseppe. And I will pray that you become the emperor's favourite artist.'

'My prayers have a greater chance of success than yours.'

'Giuseppe, just look at that dark face of yours. Listen to me. If I don't return, that's God's will. You are not alone anymore. You have three very fine housemates who will stick by your side whether you want them there or not. Say nothing more. We each have a task to perform for our Lord. Let's do them to the best of our ability.' He hugged me quickly, but I was bereft. 'Goodbye, Giuseppe, and God be with you.'

As he walked away, I saw the light he had brought into my life flicker and die, leaving me with that old, unwanted companion of my childhood: loneliness.

8

'Giuseppe,' Paolo confronted me several days after Antonio's departure. 'I would shove medicine down your throat if I believed it would cure you of this pointless lethargy, but the cause of the problem lies elsewhere. You do not have the right to fall apart because your friend is gone. What a waste of your abilities to be morose, aimless, and petulant. Your future is wide open so why do you persist with this idleness? And I won't take any more of your sarcastic insolence. Or I will give you a purgative to end all purgatives.'

His words hit true to the mark and jarred me out of my stupor. I searched among my belongings and pulled out the letter that Er Qing had given me as we parted. It was addressed to Eminent Painter Wu Yu.

'How will I find this man?' I asked Jerome, who had already found a teacher through the Royal Institute.

'I've met several painters already. One of them I find very sympathetic. His name is Jin Kun. Perhaps he knows Wu Yu. Come with me and we'll find him.'

A short distance from the walls of the Forbidden City, a group of painters sat together in a teahouse along a canal. One of the young men stood out, and he turned out to be Jerome's new friend. He had an aura of maturity and confidence. A young, handsome man with a calm, assured demeanour, he smiled broadly as we were introduced.

'Of course,' he said when we asked him if he knew Wu Yu. 'Everyone knows the great master. When he became a Christian and gave up painting, we could not believe it. No one was his equal. But it is highly unlikely he would agree to teach you. Many Chinese painters have made the same request, but he has always refused.'

'Perhaps it is God's will, and if I don't ask, I will never know the answer.'

'You talk in the same fashion as he does. Come, I will take you. It's not too far from here.'

Jin Kun explained that Wu Yu served as a deacon in the Mading church. I knew of the church, which had been established by a collection of small European Catholic orders.

An old man praying inside the church heard us enter and turned around. We went up to him, and he peered intently at us. His eyes were clouded by a milky substance, making them look like bowls of gruel. In the centre of the pupil a greenish hue shimmered unnaturally, luminescent like the scales of an exotic fish. His skin was smooth and healthy although dotted with large brown spots of age.

'Master Wu, it is Jin Kun. I have brought a young foreign missionary who wishes to meet you.'

'Ah, young Jin. I continue to hear wonderful things about your paintings.' Wu Yu came very close to look at my face. His thin beard touched my chest. 'What is your name?'

'Lang Shi Ning. I'm a Jesuit brother from Italy.'

'Brother Lang, you have the strangest hair I have ever seen. May I feel it?'

'Yes, of course.'

He reached up with his right hand and softly rubbed his fingers on a clump of curls. 'Most interesting. Who would have thought that hair could be the colour of a sunrise. You are a most lucky man to carry the sun with you at all times.'

'I've never thought of it in those terms. In fact, I have often wished for dark hair.'

'God has given you eyes the colour of the sea and hair the colour of ripe wheat for a reason. Do not wish for what you cannot change. Why have you come to see me, young man?'

'I've brought these greetings from Lord Su Ge Lu. His son was my Chinese teacher in Macao. I stayed with him for a few days in Kaifeng.'

I placed the envelope in the palm of his hand. He tore at the envelope with his long fingers and pulled out the thin rice paper. He held the letter up until it brushed his nose.

When he finished reading, he turned his strange eyes to me. A smile stretched across his face, a glorious smile that squeezed his eyes shut and sent long lines scurrying from the corners of his eyes to his chin.

'Welcome, Missionary Lang,' he said, stroking his thin white beard. 'Su Ge Lu is one of my oldest friends from my stay many years ago in Shanghai.

He suggests that I become your painting teacher. He believes that your future in China is a bright one.'

'My beginning has not been very auspicious.' I explained my encounter with the emperor to him.

'Yet the emperor has made you a "Painter Awaiting Royal Commands." Does that not tell you that he, too, sees a future for you in China?' I shrugged. After a pause, Wu Yu said. 'I cannot refuse any request my old friend makes of me.'

Jin Kun gasped. 'This is a great omen. You are most fortunate, Brother Lang, to have found the finest teacher in all China.'

'If that were ever true, it is no longer so. I will merely serve as this young man's guide to our culture. The rest will be up to him.' Wu Yu clicked his fingers and a scruffy-looking young boy appeared.

'Come. I invite you now to my home. Xiao Di.' He turned to the boy.

Holding the supportive hand of Xiao Di, Little Brother, Wu Yu walked home, his black robe sweeping from side to side, like a child's swing, and we followed him. Those we passed on the streets and alleys greeted him warmly, touching him gently if he failed to see them and he smiled benignly at them.

Wu Yu lived in a single room that contained little more than the essentials: a bed, a desk, and a few chairs. During our journey from Macao to Beijing, Er Qing and I had often found shelter in the simple homes of farmers, quietly leaving a small amount of silver when we departed in the morning. Some of the dwellings could hardly be called homes. At such times, Er Qing mumbled a phrase to describe our surroundings: *Dong bu yu han, Xia bu bi shu*: In the winter it gives no heat, in summer it provides no shade. Wu Yu's room was such a place. Little Brother made some tea and we sat together sipping from small cups.

'Brother Lang, how old are you?' Wu Yu asked.

'I am twenty-seven years old.'

He laughed and said something to Little Brother in dialect before turning back to me. 'Eighty-five, I am eighty-five now. Brother Lang, in China we say that only when you share a language can you be friends. The emperor wishes you to study Chinese painting. My opinion is that you must study the Chinese language first if you are ever to grasp the richness of our traditions.'

Wu Yu caressed the shiny hair of the young boy. 'Little Brother, a big brother has come here for you. You are to call him Da Ge, Big Brother.'

He turned to me. 'His child eyes see the things I can no longer perceive.'

Little Brother and I eyed each other, nodding stiff greetings.

'Young Jin, you must help as well. Today we have formed new companionships.'

Chapter 8

Each day after morning prayers, I made my way to Wu Yu's studio, which was in a small dwelling within the Mading church grounds. He taught me to use a thick Chinese brush to draw characters. When I improved, he gave me poems to copy, explaining their meaning as I struggled to master brush, ink, style, and form. I became a willing slave of calligraphy, bound by its elegant dots, lines, curves, and sharp corners. My rewards were the characters themselves, emerging stroke by stroke, a marriage of images, ancient ideas, and harmony.

As soon as I mastered a skill—a new thickness of brush, a more difficult calligraphy style, a change in paper or ink, or more complicated characters—Wu Yu moved the obstacles or raised the barrier. At first, I failed miserably, but with time and unflagging persistence, I gained confidence and earned praise from Wu Yu.

In every sentence Wu Yu uttered, he hid a kernel of knowledge and wisdom. Much of what he was trying to teach me about life probably floated past my addled head, but much took root, waiting for more fertile times. My heart ached to see him struggling with dim sight.

I asked Paolo if there was anything he could do to help Wu Yu, but he shook his head.

'It's a disease where we understand the process but lack the skills or medicines to change its inevitable course.'

Little Brother studied alongside me, his legs dangling from the chair and his tongue peeking from the side of his mouth as he concentrated. I could feel his eyes watching me intently from time to time. We began to tease and play fight with each other. I was very gentle with him, a frail, bony ten-year-old. He had been a street urchin, homeless, until Wu Yu rescued him. The parallels between Little Brother's life and my own were not lost on me.

Daily, Wu Yu stretched my mind to its limits by obliging me to speak only 'Beijing hua.' When I moaned about the difficulties of learning the language, Wu Yu laughed in his gentle fashion, a laugh that tinkled like crystal while his shoulders trembled.

'We have all made the same complaints, even those born to it. It is not an easy language. For instance, Chinese characters are not immutable. Their meanings and pronunciations can change in different contexts. To truly learn Chinese, one must study phrases, not just individual characters. You are well aware now that two characters join to form another word, and then three or four or five characters join to form a completely unrelated phrase. For example, the characters for red, *hong*, and for dust, *chen*, put together don't mean red dust, but the world of mankind.

'Does Little Brother ever complain the way I do?'

'Rarely, but Little Brother is young, and youth walks through the obstacles placed in its path.'

'Where is he today? It's too quiet without him.'

'He is doing some errands for me.' Wu Yu came closer and peered into my face with a mischievous air. 'Do you not prefer the silence? Do you miss him?' He leaned back and grinned.

I smiled. 'I must admit, it's very dull without him.'

'He does have spirit. You two have become close. It pleases me that he senses you are a man he can trust implicitly. Even I can see that he follows you around like a puppy. And I don't mind telling you that he never stops talking about you in your absence.'

'I am equally charmed by him. He's remarkable, intelligent, funny, and bursting with life. Without his taunts, I would have learned half as much.'

'Brother Lang, if anything should happen to me...'

'Teacher Wu, please don't talk like that.'

'No, don't look away. I am an old man. My days are finite. I must think about his future. When I found Little Brother, he was living like an animal in the lanes and alleys. My eyes were better then but even half blind I could not have missed what a jewel he was. I shudder to think that his life could have ended before it began. If I should die before his maturity, do you care deeply enough for him to ensure that he is educated and set on a proper path?'

I was silent, musing about coincidences in life. Was I ready to take charge of a young life as someone had once done for me?

'Am I asking too much of you?' Wu Yu put a hand on my arm. I touched his hand with mine and was surprised at how translucent his was.

'Teacher Wu, nothing would give me greater pleasure than to be his guardian. I have some knowledge of the life he came from and would not wish it upon anyone. I only pray that we both have the fortune of your presence for many years to come.'

'I am grateful that my great friend Lord Su chose to introduce us. I have long worried about what would happen to Little Brother after my death. I've never asked about your visit with him. He is a remarkable man with great insight into people. Tell me about the Su family in Kaifeng.'

I told Wu Yu the things he wanted to hear: what a wonderful family they were and how much I enjoyed our short stay in their house. When we left, the entire household accompanied us to the Ten Mile Pavilion outside the city to say goodbye.

Wu Yu nodded contentedly and smiled. 'Lord Su joined me in Shanghai once after a flood had ruined the city. For three weeks we hardly slept or ate while we tended to the sick and homeless. He is a true Christian and the most honourable man I have ever met.'

What I did not tell Wu Yu was how preciously I savoured the memories of every minute of my stay in Kaifeng, how often I revisited the smiling, tender faces—and one face in particular.

When I met the Su family, I was new to China and barely able to communicate with them. The entire family came out to greet us: Er Qing's father and mother and his eight younger brothers and sisters, along with every servant. We ate a delicious meal, and Er Qing translated everything into Latin for me. The impression I had was of a loving, lively family.

The first night, I could not sleep and decided to wander around the gardens. I could see in the central room of the house Er Qing and his father kneeling in splendid brocade robes before a small, shiny, carved wooden cross. Their hands were pressed tightly together in prayer and their heads were bowed. I tiptoed softly past the window across the garden.

'The tea has just been made. Come and try some,' Er Qing called out through the window.

He and his father lifted the lids on the cups and blew along the surface of the steaming water, moving thick tea leaves away from their lips. When the tea touched my tongue, I gasped in pain as it scalded me. Er Qing and Su Ge Lu laughed, their eyes twinkling over the rims of their cups.

'You will learn to drink tea the Chinese way and spare your tongue such agony,' Lord Su told me.

They showed me a grey stone portrait of Confucius and explained that though they did not pray to the great sage they respected him as an important ancestor of the Han people.

'While we may humbly bow to his formidable gifts and foresight, we know that his philosophy is not capable of saving the souls of ordinary men. That gift lies in the wisdom and love of Jesus Christ.' They were, however, very sceptical about the ability of Christianity to find a home in China.

Lord Su told me a great deal about Kaifeng, whose name means Enlightened. He was proud of a city that had served as capital to seven dynasties and tolerated many foreigners. It once had the largest concentration of the children of Jacob, Jews. They arrived in small numbers, he said, during the Tang dynasty, but their numbers grew in the Song and Yuan dynasties. 'Their places of worship grew as the population prospered. Certain surnames became known as Jewish, Ai, Zhao, Zhang, and Li. They were an intelligent race and quickly blended into Chinese society. As they intermarried, foreign features melted away. Wishing to excel, they entered the imperial exams and succeeded well. The community shrank rapidly when the young civil servants were dispersed to serve as officials throughout the empire. Several families still existed, but there were fewer and fewer and they knew very little of their old traditions.

'There is a monument in town near the old building where they worship. It says: *"The religions of Confucianism and Judaism differ in only minor details. They share many of the same beliefs which can only serve to strengthen the ties between Chinese and Jews."* It goes on to list several beliefs such as filial piety, respect for ancestors, a desire for harmony in the family.'

Our discussion was interrupted by Er Qing's mother, who shuffled into the room, followed by his brothers and sisters, to ask whether they might go to sleep or if Lord Su had any requests of them. He gave them permission to go to bed. His youngest child was only five years old.

The last to enter was a beautiful young woman I had noticed during the meal, curious about who she was. She rested her hands on the shoulders of the two youngest children and bowed to Lord Su. He placed a hand on her cheek and smiled. I realised that she was not Er Qing's sister but a wife of his father.

After she left, Lord Su explained who she was. 'Originally, I had not only a wife but three concubines or unofficial wives. Er Qing is my eldest son from my official wife. The next two sons were born from my second wife. The fourth-born son was then born to my official wife. The two eldest daughters are the fruit of my third wife. My last wife gave me another son and a daughter, the youngest children. Four years ago, after I became a Catholic, I came to recognise my sin. To correct my transgressions, I sent my three unofficial wives back to their maternal homes to find new husbands and start new families. Of course, I saw that they were well looked after. Two of them have remarried. While the new husbands are not wealth, they are kind. My young fourth concubine came back, refusing to leave me or her children. I do not have the heart to force her from her former home, although she is no longer my wife. She is a woman of unique spirit, pure and loving, a great asset to our tiny church. Her ancestors were children of Abraham.'

Later, when the house was dark and still, I took another walk around the garden. The lanterns had been extinguished, but a crescent moon gave off a weak, watery light. A soft, warm wind caressed my face and enhanced the scent of flowers.

From the garden, I saw the fourth wife of Su Ge Lu enter the main room of the house, holding a candle in her hand. She flitted quickly towards the cross and knelt down in prayer. I hid in the shadows and drank in her beauty, her profile, the way her hair draped over one shoulder, the tremble in her hands, her long fingers. She held her head down, her hands tight on her breastbone; her face was solemn and sad. She raised her head after a moment and spoke to the carving, her lips moving emphatically. She finally rose slowly and made the sign of the cross elegantly, her long fingers turning in the air. *What a glorious creature you are*, I whispered.

From time to time, Wu Yu, Little Brother, and I travelled to an orphanage belonging to a small church situated at the top of a mountain northwest of the city. Though we took a carriage to the base of the mountain, we had to wend our way to the top on foot. The climb was strenuous enough for me but almost impossible for Wu Yu, yet he refused any help.

During one climb, several months after my education with Wu Yu had begun, Little Brother tested my knowledge of poetry. He quoted one line from a poem we had studied together and waited, looking at me with wide eyes and raised eyebrows to see if I could remember the next. *'By the red gate, wine and meat lay decaying.'* I searched my memory for the next line. *'And in the road lay the frozen remains of people,'* I answered. At the peak, he uttered the line Wu Yu loved best, *'With determination one can reach the top.'* Looking at Wu Yu while he sat on a rock struggling to regain his breath, I continued the poem: *'Gazing in all directions, the mountains are so small.'*

'You know, Da Ge,' Little Brother said with a glint in his eye, 'the Chinese sages say a student should learn a poem first from the top to the bottom and then from the bottom to the top.'

I groaned. 'Do I have any choice in whether I wish to try this or not?

'Not much,' he teased.

Shortly afterwards, on a whim, I recited a poem by Li Bai to several elderly men and women who frequently prayed in the Mading church. Their expressions changed immediately. 'Excellent! More!' they said. Their bright faces and delighted laughter encouraged me, and several poems tumbled out, not just by Li Bai but by Du Pu and Bai Ju Yi. I was amazed at my own transformation. I could not only communicate but I could entertain with words.

'I observe a marked improvement in your manner,' the rector said when he saw me one day at the Eastern Church. 'You seem to have found direction and fulfilment. It is a relief to us all.'

Paolo, Jerome, and David did not hesitate to make their feelings known either.

'Deacon Wu has guided you like a wise father and you have flourished,' Paolo told me. 'It shows you how close to the surface all these qualities were.'

'I am relived to no longer be living with a tinderbox,' David added.

'From what Jin Kun tells me, you are learning poetry and calligraphy but nothing about painting,' Jerome commented. 'Is that true?'

I nodded.

'What are you waiting for? Perhaps he is not the right teacher.'

'I trust him. I'm sure he knows what he's doing.'

Each morning Little Brother and I handed Wu Yu one bamboo brush holder after another, simple cylinders with beautifully carved designs of landscapes or animals. He polished each one, rubbing it on his cheek.

'Only the oil from human skin can change the colour and sheen of bamboo.' He waved the holder I knew to be his favourite in front of my eyes. 'Look. Compare the colour here,' he said as he touched the exterior of the carving, 'to this.' His finger pointed to a tree carved in a deeper layer, closer to the core of the cylinder. The brush holder was a deep red, shiny and soft on the exterior, but faded, layer by layer, to a pale yellow. 'Look underneath. That was the original colour forty years ago.' The underside of the holder was a dry, insipid yellow. I was sceptical, not believing that skin could alter the colour of wood, yet I purchased a small bamboo cylinder and rubbed my chin on its surface each evening, shy and clumsy at first.

Watching Wu Yu tend the tools of his art reawakened an early passion for collecting when as a homeless youth I had seen beauty in what others threw away as useless; broken bits of ceramics or rusted metalwork had adorned my surroundings, no matter how bleak. Following Wu Yu's lead, I began to collect brush holders.

One morning, as Wu Yu polished his brush holders, I broached the issue Jerome had mentioned. 'Teacher Wu, I have learned so much from you about the richness of Chinese culture, but you have not even begun to teach me to paint. I have been in the emperor's presence twice since you became my teacher. I tried to lose myself among other missionaries, but he searched for me among the crowd and called out my name to my immense embarrassment. He asked how my painting had progressed. The first time he was delighted to hear that you had become my teacher. The second time, he told me how he looked forward to seeing my new work. Teacher Wu, the emperor seems to have high expectations of me. I dare not tell him that I haven't painted a single stroke in these many months.'

'Calm yourself, my impetuous son. All things must come at the right time, like the birth of a child. You must not try to imagine the future. It is in God's hands alone. Patience, trust, and love will guide you to the correct path.'

Wu Yu took me to the home of a close friend of his. 'Come and look at this painting.' His sight had deteriorated even more. His breath bounced off the silk as he looked closely at it. 'This is a copy of a painting of court officials and ladies,' he continued. 'The original is over one thousand three hundred years old. Observe the brush technique. It is called *gao gu you si*: fine lines. This painting is a model for others.' His hands fluttered along the surface of the painting.

'For portrait painting, a variety of brush strokes are used to create outlines, and outlines are the key to meaning. Look closely. This painting has detail yet remains cloudy; it is complete and suggestive. This official's silk gown is obviously well cut for his frame, yet he wears it loosely. He is a broad man, conveying a sense of strength, a man of authority but not arrogant. From his relaxed stance, I believe he is a sage. And the lady at his side radiates an allure, a worthy companion to such a man. To convey so much with a minimum of strokes requires an excellent brush technique. See how these thin lines convey the lightness and flow of silk. The thick round stroke suggests shoes beneath the gown.'

Wu Yu grew more breathless as he spoke. I was aware of some of his words: 'thin without being overbearing, luxurious, the model for outlining technique; a talent blessed by God,' but my mind was drifting and I remained unmoved. I was thinking: how could these flat, two-dimensional ink paintings equal the frescoes and oil paintings of my country? Our paintings told stories; the characters could walk off the canvas ready to breathe air, with colour in their cheeks and veins throbbing in their hands.

We moved to the next painting.

Wu Yu spoke. 'This painting is called *Li Bai Walking and Reciting*. It is by Liang Kai, a famous Song dynasty painter.'

I looked and recoiled. The being on the painting bore no resemblance to the Li Bai of my imagination, the man who, one thousand years earlier, had written a poem that had become one my favourites.

You can watch the water of the Yellow River, flowing from heaven to the sea, never to return.
You can sit in front of a mirror staring at your white hair, young and shining in the morning, turning to snow in the evening.
A human life must be spent in happiness, do not shrivel before the moon.
I sing a song for you, please listen to me.

It was simple, a full-length profile of a well-fed, middle-aged man with a topknot and a pointed goat-like beard, his hands clasped behind his back with his head slightly tilted heavenwards and a mere hint of a smile. While I scowled, Wu Yu kept clicking, shaking his head and muttering, 'Excellent, a masterpiece.'

Wu Yu turned and, reading the expression on my face, emitted a short, sharp laugh. 'You have the nature of an ox. How can I, a mere ageing shepherd, change your direction once you have stubbornly chosen the wrong route? Ai ya.' He shrugged his shoulders.

'I am so sorry, Teacher Wu. My heart is pledged to artists of my country. I don't know how to appreciate others.'

'Love has many forms and infinite capacity for expansion. You are not being disloyal by embracing other models of beauty and representation. In the West, you seek truth. Your paintings either explore the artist's external interaction with his subject or a dispassionate observation of events. In the East, we find meaning in emptiness, in what is left out. We try to capture internal experiences.

'Observe again this painting of Li Bai. The artist sought to show us the poet's soul. It was painted very quickly after much thought. For me, it speaks of Li Bai's immortality, that he will live on through his poetry. He stands alone, well above ordinary men. The figure is a simple shape with hardly any ink on the clothes, but the cloak floats, as if the gods are breathing on him. The collar is made up of one single wet stroke. Another stroke leads from the collar down the back. The parallel dry stroke here denotes the sleeve. The moustache is made up of three strokes, soft but determined in nature. The front of the gown is also a single dry brush stroke. Only at the hem does Liang Kai use an ink wash.'

I nodded, hearing his words, and he continued. 'There is another big difference between Chinese paintings and those I have seen from Europe: we ignore light in our wildlife paintings. It is neither day nor night; the sun is neither shining nor casting shadows.'

'But light is so evocative of mood and texture,' I objected. 'A flower can't be removed from its surroundings and put in a sterile environment. A rose is different in every situation, by sunlight, candlelight, through a window, alongside a leafy hedge, direct light, reflected light. Light can remove edges, shadows heighten them.'

'But if one is interested in the deepest meaning of an object, it exists outside time. Here, look at this painting of a peony.' Wu Yu had moved to another painting in his friend's collection. 'It's very realistic and detailed, down to the veins in the petals, but the artist had a philosophical reason for making this painting. The flower is symbolic of something greater than itself. The stamp in the lower right corner says *Shu xian tian yi*: nice, loyal, and peaceful. He was making a morality painting about a woman's virtues. The flower is pretty but arrogant, eternal but fleeting. It is another example of how our paintings combine subject matter, painting style, and poetry.'

'Perhaps if I saw you paint, it would help me to understand better.'

Wu Yu laid his hand on my shoulder. 'You will understand my words someday. Our culture has a way of seeping slowly into one's soul. When the well spring is full you will see the world with new eyes.'

Three days later, on a windy spring Sunday morning, I sat at the back of the Mading church and listened to Wu Yu explain a chapter from the Bible. As he spoke, his beard swung to and fro and his long robe swished in the opposite direction to his beard. I watched the audience, who were mostly black-faced, ill-clad peasants. Several women held newborn infants. An elderly beggar, known to us all, shyly tiptoed along the aisle wearing worn clothing, recently scrubbed clean. At eighty-six, Wu Yu still held his illiterate, impoverished followers spellbound.

Later, I sat down with my charcoal and paper to capture what I had witnessed. The figures flew on to the pages: the whole collection of *lao bai xing*, as the common people were called, the One Hundred Surnames. I paused and looked at Little Brother. He was absorbed with two crickets he had found. He squatted on the ground with a stiff horsehair and prodded the two creatures, which were in a deep bowl hoping to start a battle between them. I turned the page and began to sketch him.

Wu Yu shuffled into the room and squinted at my drawings. He stroked his thin beard while he scrutinised them. 'Good likeness,' he uttered and showed Little Brother my sketch of him.

He giggled. 'May I keep it, Da Ge?'

Wu Yu picked up my ink stone and brush and shuffled off towards his studio. He called over his shoulder to us, speaking while he walked. 'Come. This drawing of Little Brother, can you see the difference in your style, in how you depicted his image? Your technical skill is higher now than before. I am pleased to see his spirit shining through. I am ready to paint for you, Brother Lang.'

Little Brother and I ran into each other in a flurry to get rice paper and ink. Wu Yu placed Little Brother in front of him. With fluttering fingers, he felt every inch of his grinning, ticklish helper, including the soft features of Little Brother's face.

'Now play with your crickets. Next to me. Here.'

Little Brother squatted down on his haunches. Wu Yu felt for his head and then ran his hands along the boy's shoulders and his entire body, causing Little Brother to squirm and giggle. Then Wu Yu gave the boy's bottom a playful smack.

'Grind some ink.'

Wu Yu perched on his stool, unmoving, hardly blinking. His head slanted to one side as he stared towards a corner. Little Brother filled the ink stone and placed it next to his master. Wu Yu remained still, deep in what appeared to be a trance. After a time, concerned that my staring might affect his concentration, I opened my sketchbook and resumed drawing. I became aware at some point that Wu Yu had lifted his brush and was holding it in the air.

When I heard the rapid whooshing sound of the brush on the stiff rice paper, I stood up and moved closer. Wu Yu's hand darted over the paper at great speed. The head, drawn with very black ink, took seconds. The back appeared with one stroke, and a curve reproduced Little Brother's fat buttocks. Simple lines became feet and arms. Wu Yu washed the brush, squeezed its hairs, and flicked off any residual water. He briefly dipped the moist brush into the ink. A few dashes on the paper and a nose, a round fat chin, a robe, cuffs, and trouser legs, and even the wooden balls on his model's slippers appeared.

Wu Yu shook the brush for a few moments until it was almost dry. Without any fresh ink, he painted the bowl holding the two crickets. They were proud and aggressive, their heads touching, their hind legs stiff with anticipation. He twisted the hairs of the brush to a point. Wu Yu raised his head and, without lowering his gaze, painted Little Brother's eyes and eyebrows, using his little finger to determine the spacing. His hand darted right and left, and Little Brother's small, fat hands emerged from the ends of the arms. Wu Yu wet and dried the brush again and used a wash to produce a shadow underneath Little Brother's bottom.

I stared at the painting in awe. Using only black ink, he had created a living, breathing being that spoke of colour in its absence, depth and volume without shadow, complexity through simplicity. Without quite understanding why, I was almost moved to tears. While Wu Yu carefully cleaned the brush, I wondered if the hand of God had caressed this man.

After a fitful night's sleep, I arrived at Wu Yu's studio. 'Wu Yu, I hardly slept last night. For the first time I understood what heights Chinese painting can achieve, but I don't know where or how to begin. Please advise me.'

Wu Yu waved his hand. 'Later, later. We have other things to do. Today, I must preach at the mountain chapel. I need you both to help me.'

Little Brother looked at me and shrugged his shoulders. 'He's been very agitated all morning, short-tempered and impatient,' he whispered while Wu Yu had his back turned.

Wu Yu was exceptionally weak during the long climb. Rather than scorn our help as he usually did, he took turns leaning on my arm or Little Brother's shoulder. When he could hardly catch his breath, I put my hand around his waist and half carried him. He was light, made more of bone than flesh.

At the top, we paused for a long time and looked at the city below. Wu Yu sat on a tree stump, hands resting on his knees. The wind played with his wispy beard and blew his long hair backwards. His eyes glistened and he smiled wistfully. What would a Greek sculptor have made of such a noble man?

He put his hands together in prayer and lowered his head. *'And, behold, there was a great earthquake for the angel of the Lord descended from heaven, and came and rolled back the stone from the door, and sat upon it. His countenance was like lightning and his raiment white as snow...'*

He suddenly fell forward and hit the ground with a thud. Little Brother and I rushed to pick him up. I sat on the ground and cradled him in my arms, resting his head on my lap, but his body was completely limp. Little Brother felt for a pulse, put his ear to Wu Yu's chest, and placed his lips beneath his nose. He looked up at me with shocked, disbelieving eyes. He clutched Wu Yu's hands and began to sob.

I continued the passage from Matthew with a quavering voice. *'And for fear of him the keepers did shake and became as dead men. And the angel answered and said unto the women. Fear not ye, for I know that ye seek Jesus, which was crucified. He is not here, for he is risen.'*

We knelt beside his body and prayed. I don't know how it happened, but people arrived from several directions, up the paths, out of the chapel. I recognised some but felt too numb to respond to their grief and sympathy. Wordlessly we wove bamboo reeds and grasses into a soft bed and found long poles. Others prepared Wu Yu's body, tidying his clothes, hair, and beard, and wrapped him in a soft blanket. We tied his shrouded body to the stretcher and began the slow descent. I moved as if in a dream, scraps of poems running through my head. Little Brother walked with tears streaming down his face.

'Gazing in all directions, the mountains are so small.'

I marvelled at the gift Wu Yu had given me when death was so near. Though I had no idea of the path I would take to become a Chinese artist, Wu Yu had opened a door, enabling me to leave the past behind and set off in a new direction.

9

Wang Rong sits opposite, looking over the pages he has just written. 'Ah. I did not know that the great master Wu Yu had been your teacher.'

'Without Wu Yu and Jin Kun I don't know that I would have ever departed from being a Western artist. Perhaps I was able to change because I was only of moderate talent. Brother Jerome, who was far more gifted, never embraced Chinese art with his heart. I was talking to Jin Kun recently about the discussions we used to have about the differences between Western and Eastern art.'

Wang Rong stares peculiarly at me. 'Have you forgotten, Royal Painter Lang, that he died two years ago? You wrote a memorial for his funeral.'

'Yes, yes, of course. It must have been a dream. I have so many vivid ones.' I choose not tell Wang Rong that when everyone leaves me, my room fills up with faces of departed friends.

Wang Rong speaks again. 'Our ten-thousand-years-living father will be most interested to read that you found a woman attractive. You describe Lord Su's fourth wife so eloquently. One would not expect it from a holy man.' He chuckles quietly and I cannot help but join him. We look at each other, he, the holder of the Receive Love Book, and me, the painter of the emperor's women, both custodians of his carnal secrets.

'The Su family of Kaifeng is no more.'

'I know. There was nothing that anyone could do to help them. I know how much you suffered at their treatment.'

For a brief, glorious moment, I am still standing at the Ten Mile Pavilion outside Kaifeng with Er Qing's tearful family. As we drive away, Er Qing teaches me a poem of which only one small part remains with me, a line that defines the true test of friendship as whether one can bear separation when a long journey beckons. It includes the evocative words fen shou, a parting of the hands. I inhale deeply at the thought of how often I parted hands with my dearest friends as they set off on the longest journey of all, the one from which there is no return. That is the heaviest price of living too long.

'What is to become of me?' Little Brother asked as we made preparations for Wu Yu's funeral. 'Wu Yu said I should ask you if anything happened to him.'

'If it would please you, I would like you to live with my fellow missionaries and myself. They are very learned men and can teach you many things.'

His eyes lit up 'I would like that very much. Big Brother?'

'Yes?'

'I believe you've been sent here by your god to do good things and I am the lucky one, the first one to benefit from your big heart.'

'If anyone was sent by God, it was Teacher Wu. He had a way of coaxing the best out of everyone without a person even realising it. My regret is that my time with him was too short.'

'Wu Yu once told me that a soul never dies if it touches someone's heart, that love is permanent and can spread like seeds of precious plants. True love is selfless and enlightening. The saddest people are those who cannot give or accept love. I know he loved me and I feel him, in here.' Little Brother touched his chest.

I nodded. 'I feel him there as well.'

Jerome, Paolo, David, and I received permission to move to a new house to care for Little Brother, but David decided to find a house closer to the observatory and live with other astronomers. Jerome and Paolo were happy to leave the choice up to me and I leapt at the opportunity to find a dwelling. Within a week, we moved into two sides of an enclosed quadrangle, each part consisting of three rooms. The other two sides were also occupied by missionaries. We shared a courtyard in the centre, planted with vegetables and herbs. We each had a bedroom, and Jerome and I had space for separate studios. Our bedrooms were heated by a wood oven in the kitchen, the warmth passing through hollow cavities that ran below our beds. We slept as the Chinese did using a thin cotton cover on top of bricks that formed beds and a pillow made of crushed rice and corn gleanings that crunched loudly at the slightest movement.

'Our founder would be pleased with our deprivations,' Jerome muttered as he rubbed his back and shoulders on the first morning. 'I hope we soon get used to these beds and what passes for mattresses.'

Little Brother and I carefully arranged Wu Yu's few possessions, mostly brushes, ink stones, brush holders, and carvings made from the large roots of bamboo plants. It was wonderful to wake up and see them hanging on the wall or resting on furniture. Little Brother and I had a ritual every morning, taking turns at rubbing our cheeks on his brush holders, smiling the entire time. For many weeks, I could still smell Wu Yu on his possessions.

'It makes me feel safe living here with you and seeing Wu Yu's favourite things,' Little Brother said.

I put my arm around his shoulders. 'Don't think you'll have it easy,' I teased him. 'We will be hard taskmasters and not put up with any wild and foolhardy behaviour. There is very little you could do that I didn't try at least once.'

One spring morning, Antonio appeared at the courtyard next to the Eastern Church. I almost didn't recognise him. Four years had passed. Gone was the youthful, handsome face and the twinkling eyes. He had not only aged dramatically but he was pale and withdrawn. I instinctively threw my arms around his shoulders and hugged him tightly hoping, as I pulled away, to see a flash of the image of him I had kept alive in my mind, but his expression did not change.

'Did you succeed? Is the kingdom safe?'

He waved his hand, not even attempting a smile. 'I failed. The king is dead and Tibet has been overrun. I am tired and need to eat.'

'Of course.' I rushed to prepare food for him, my mind full of concerns and questions that I did not expect to find answers to.

Neither rest nor companionship brought any change to his demeanour. For several days I tried everything I could think of to bring a smile to his face or brighten his mood, but he was a dark, locked cabinet. Though part of me dreamt that time would heal whatever wounds he carried and the Antonio I knew would return, in my heart I suspected he was gone forever.

'Has he spoken to you about what happened in Tibet?' Paolo asked.

'No. Something terrible must have occurred. He's so changed. It's as if his soul is depleted.'

'I'm sorry to say I am not surprised. I always feared he would seek challenges that were beyond his capability, and when human lives are at stake, the costs of failure are great. Perhaps time will heal his sense of guilt. He has many of the qualities needed to lead the society through the challenges it faces, but his strengths are currently weakened by whatever it is that weighs on his heart. Encourage him to unburden whatever it is.'

'I'll do anything, anything to help him.'

'Of course you will, but you too have changed.'

'What does that mean?'

'When you first met Antonio, you put him on a pedestal. You wanted to emulate him. Once you began to have faith in your own strengths, you no longer needed such a hero. Deacon Wu, more than anyone, set you on the right path, and being a diligent guardian for a lad like Little Brother has affirmed the wise and caring qualities that were always within you.'

'Paolo, such praise embarrasses me.'

'Then get used to it. It's always easier to be one of the flock than to be guided by a strong internal voice, but you were not born to follow and I, for one, look forward to watching where you will go.'

Antonio was restless, impatient to leave Beijing. In a short while, he organised a charity mission to Shandong province where famine conditions were acute. Over twenty Jesuits set off with him, including Paolo and me, with large quantities of food and medicines.

The countryside was parched and barren, scorched earth devoid of life. We distributed food supplies, such as rice, flour, dried beans, and meats, to scores of families in small, dusty villages. When we had the opportunity, we spoke of Christ's teachings, of brotherly love, heaven, and one almighty God, and saw looks of wonder crossing their faces. Their hearts seemed open for evangelical messages, coming as they were on the back of unselfish charity, but our time was limited.

We examined many ill men and children; few women were willing to accept our help. Dysentery, disease, and infected wounds were common within a population weakened by starvation. Paolo believed strongly in what he called hygiene, in the importance of regular bathing and clean water, but no such thing was possible in an area so bereft of water.

One person Paolo tended in one of the villages was a well-dressed youth with peculiar growths and wounds on his face and a thick discharge coming from his nose and mouth. A very agitated servant stood at his side.

'His mother had the same. The master sent her away somewhere. I noticed the first mark several years ago, but his father shouted at me and told me to ignore it. Then more marks and it gets worse. Can you help him? I promised his mother, I would care properly for him. I leave him with you. Tell no one I brought him. I must hurry back now.'

'It's leprosy,' Paolo announced after the servant scurried away. 'I had expected to see more, but this is the first case we have encountered.'

I flinched. 'Isn't it dangerous to touch him?'

'Cleanliness is the greatest weapon against disease.'

Paolo turned towards the crowd of peasants who had come to watch. 'You must separate yourselves from the affected or you will also suffer the illness. There is no cure.'

We had just finished building a small hut a distance away from the village and dug a ditch, filling it with a small amount of water, when an armed militia arrived, forcing all the peasants to scamper away. The militia leader demanded to speak to the leaders of our mission.

His brusque manner changed when he was away from prying eyes. 'You Christians are good people. We simple folk know that. But the big landlords are powerful. Ai ya.' He spit viciously. 'We cannot disobey them. They can punish our families and take away our livelihood if we disobey. Forgive me for what I am ordered to do. In that hut, you have the son of the wealthiest man in Shandong. He accuses you of witchcraft. I am ordered to bring his son back and expel you from this province. You must go immediately or you face great danger. You could die if you remain.'

Wu Yu, like Lord Su, had often lamented the fragile position of Christianity in China. 'The wealthy resent the message of equality, monogamy, and brotherly love,' he had said to me. 'Despite bitter complaints from landlords and nobles, the emperor has largely remained tolerant. He respects your fellow Jesuits at court and appreciates activities that benefit his people. But do not be fooled. Christianity stands on a precipice; one wrong move and it will be gone without a trace.'

Now I was seeing the truth of his words.

Our mission over, we returned to Beijing, where we heard of similar incidents in other provinces. In Hebei, Anhui, Sichuan, Shanxi, Zhejiang, and Jiangxi, missionaries were attacked by soldiers of the local gentry. In Fujian, all missionaries were expelled. But there was an even graver development awaiting us in the capital. It was December 1720, just over five years since my arrival in Beijing.

Our superiors had little interest in our reports of growing opposition from landlords and gentry in the countryside. They were too busy wringing their hands over a disastrous encounter between a papal delegation and the emperor. The senior Jesuits who witnessed the meetings would not discuss them. The papal emissary, Monsignor Jean-Amboise Mezzabarba, was far too eminent a man to be criticised, even in private.

David, in his quiet, tenacious way, unearthed an Englishman who had been present in court during Monsignor Mezzabarba's interview with the emperor. He was the negotiator for a Russian trade group seeking new commercial ties with the Qing dynasty.

Paolo, Jerome, David, and I sat in a teahouse and listened intently to his version of events. 'I wonder if all papal emissaries are as obnoxious and arrogant as this one. He stood before the emperor, unrolled a fancy piece of paper, lifted his chin as if he ruled the land, and began to read a long edict titled *A Papal Constitution of Prohibitions*. Some tall, thin priest, a Jesuit, I guess, dressed like you, translated the Latin for the emperor. From what I could tell, and my Latin isn't what it used to be, the document seemed to declare that the Chinese who converted to Christianity were subjects of the pope! Even I thought that took some nerve.'

He paused to drink his tea, smiling wryly as he recalled the scene. 'The poor Jesuit who had to translate was most upset. He didn't half glare at the monsignor, but his anger was nothing compared to that of the emperor who turned red in the face and began to bellow, stomp, and, I assume, curse in the Chinese fashion. He wouldn't let the papal emissary utter another word. My Russians and I were only at court for three days, but the emperor wouldn't talk to us. He just wanted to insult the papal emissary. In the end, the monsignor stammered and stuttered and offered eight concessions. He seemed, and again I'm no expert, to negate what he had come to say in the first place. He kept repeating that a Chinese convert could have his idols and make supplications to his ancestors as long as it had no sacred significance. Total nonsense. And now the emperor won't even see us.'

I rushed to Antonio to tell him what we had found out. He shook his head. 'This will change our fortunes greatly. You wouldn't know, but after Cardinal Tournon's unfortunate meeting with the emperor, he decided to establish a dialogue with Pope Clement XI. In 1710, the emperor began sending letters to Rome to clarify Chinese religious practices. The pope never answered. The emperor sent over one hundred and fifty *Hong Piao,* Red Manifestos, to Rome, each one written personally in bright vermilion ink, placing them in the hands of missionaries and merchants. The pope ignored them all.

'Six years ago, the emperor sent a young Italian Jesuit, Father Provano, to speak to the pope on his behalf. Pope Clement kept Father Provano in Rome for three years. When he allowed him to return to China. he was expressly forbidden to reveal anything of Vatican discussions or opinions. The young man died on board ship before arriving in Macao. A merciful release, some might say. The emperor's patience has been remarkable. What can Rome be thinking to treat him so insolently? Do they not realise the consequences?'

The next day, scores of missionaries were summoned to the Forbidden City. It was a large contingent that entered a spacious pavilion with the name *Cultural Palace* painted over the door. Eunuchs and guards stared as we made our nine kow-tows and remained prostrate on the ground waiting our orders. My heart was racing, for I feared the worst. Why should the emperor allow any Christians in his kingdom when our pope had insulted him so deeply?

'Stand up,' the emperor ordered. His face was dark and his anger unmistakable.

'In the past, we were tolerant of your religion and your actions in our country for one reason: you were of good heart. You have done many good things for my subjects and shared your Western science. You have always insisted you performed your great deeds without any wish for benefit, for reward. But the price you ask is higher than any remuneration we can offer. You exhort my people to turn their backs on their ancestors. Is this not the same as if we came to your countries and urged you to forget your ancestor, this Jesus Christ? We say this once more: to ask my people to follow you and to forget their ancestors is forbidden.

'Zhen has made the following decision. No Christian missionaries have permission to travel within China. You are forbidden to convert any of my subjects. If you disobey these commands, you do so at the risk of imprisonment or death. Notices of my orders will be placed throughout the kingdom. Chinese will be ordered to inform the court of any disobedience. Notices will also be posted to discourage Chinese converts from continuing in their worship of your religion. Christianity has no place in China if it serves to undermine the values that have guided this country for two thousand years.'

He nodded to an official who shouted at us. '*You heard our ten-thousand-years-living emperor. Now go and obey his orders!*'

As we began to back out, bowing and knocking into one another, to my surprise several other officials were shouting, 'The Jesuit Lang Shi Ning, come forward.'

For an instant, I hid among the dispersing crowd but a eunuch grabbed my sleeve and pulled me to the side. I was suddenly alone and trembling. When the hall was quiet, he led me forward.

The emperor, conferring with officials, turned his head and beckoned me closer. I knelt on the ground.

'Zhen has been told that the south of your country has a climate very similar to ours. What sort of crops do they grow there?'

I swallowed hard, completely perplexed at the question. 'In Italy we grow maize, olives, rice, sugar beet, and wheat. Different types of wheat, winter and summer.' As I spoke the Chinese words slowly and clearly, Father Francesco nodded his approval. A wave of nostalgia for my homeland swept over me.

'What other crops do your people in this southern region grow? There must be others.' He leant forward. 'Think hard.'

'Yes, Bixia.' I searched my memory. There was something in the distant past. What was it?

'Zhen's country is burdened with a huge population to feed,' the emperor continued when I failed to answer. 'It is not blessed with enough arable land or a gentle climate. Large mountain ranges divide my kingdom east and west. The west is high, while the east is low. The great mountain ranges Tian Shan and Kun Lun not only reduce land available for farming, but torment my people with violent weather. Zhen's northern border is desert. Cold winds whistle southwards, often making land barren. They cover thousands of li with a fine dry, loess powder.

'Cold temperatures restrict our choice of crops and the number of harvests. In summer, the north-south winds cease altogether and the wet east-west winds take over, causing many crops to rot. The entire southern portion of the country suffers great rains and floods. Although the south has the most fertile land and can give us three harvests per year, floods often destroy crops. If Zhen fails to feed the people, they may become restless. Then we will suffer a double calamity as a nation: war and famine.

'The north has suffered ten years of drought. My peasants work hard but the earth yields little. Year after year, this bitter labour continues and they weaken. Zhen is told that the south of your country has similar problems. Do your people suffer as mine do? I am told that famine is rare. What knowledge can they share with us?'

Leaning on his throne with one arm, he spoke with passion. His hands flowed, the sleeves and fabric of his robes swishing and crackling. His eyes implored me to answer his question.

I began to pray: *Lord, the emperor is asking me, a lowly brother, an orphan, a misfit, to help his people. I am named Joseph, the same name as that of a great hero of the Israelites, a man who saved Egypt from famine. For some reason I was given his name and now I am being confronted with a similar task. If this is part of Your plan for me, help me now and bring an answer to my lips.*

From the depths of my memory, something came into focus, a special plump delicacy I ate as a young boy. As the image came closer, I could see its bulbous shape, feel its rough skin, and taste its sweetness.

I looked up at the emperor with bright eyes. 'Bixia, we do have a food for the poor. In Latin we call it *Ipomoea batatas*; it is a potato with red interior that is sweet.' I started to speak slowly, thinking as I formed the words. 'I remember seeing these sweet potatoes when we journeyed through Guangdong. Yes, yes. I am sure farmers were eating them.'

'Father Francisco,' the emperor turned his head. 'Do you know the plant he speaks of?'

Father Francisco rushed forward, his hands clasped before him. He addressed the emperor with a bowed head. 'Your Highness, I believe the Chinese name is fan shu.'

'Any plant containing the character *fan* comes from outside China. Yet farmers are growing it in the south. I did not know.' The emperor looked down at his hands, deep in thought. 'If this fan shu *can* tolerate dry conditions, as Missionary Lang suggests, and produce high yields, Zhen is a fortunate Son of Heaven and my people will benefit. Brother Lang, what does a fan shu look like? Draw us some fan shu so that Zhen can see them.' He stood up and snapped his fingers.

Several eunuchs rushed away, bowing rapidly as they backed out of the emperor's presence. In a short while paper, ink, and brushes were shoved into my arms.

'Bixia,' I ventured while trying to hold all of the items firmly. 'With some colours, I could better show you how they look.'

The emperor shouted harshly at his eunuchs. 'Bring Zhen powdered ink in many colours. Hurry.'

I moved over to a small table, carefully ground several colours, and began painting. I was certain that he wanted me to use my Western skills to render these potatoes for him. A picture remained before my eyes that I transferred onto the fresh paper: three oval sweet potatoes on a green cloth viewed from above as if they rested on a low table. The first one was separate from the other two, having rolled away. Of the remaining two, a large one rested directly behind a small one, but the small one still held on to its root. A streak of light illuminated from the left leaving a long shadow. It took me half an hour to finish painting the still life. While I did so, the emperor strolled around the room reading and reciting poetry. From the corner of my eye, I saw that his hands periodically rested inside his long sleeves. Father Francisco hardly moved. The only other sounds in the room were those of breathing and the scrape of my brush on the paper.

'Interesting,' he said when I presented it to him, kneeling with the picture held high above my head. 'It looks like a type of radish Zhen eats. But the radish is not one that fills the stomach, nor could one survive for long on such a food. Are you certain this plant will be of use to us? Brother Lang, tell Zhen about the taste.'

'The taste is sweet. The texture is soft. It is a good food, Bixia.'

'Ai. The question is can it make a home in the north of China? Is the soil and climate of the dry north suitable for this fan shu?'

'I do not know, Your Majesty.'

'*BAI KUI RON!*' the emperor bellowed in a high-pitched voice.

An older official tiptoed forward from a group waiting quietly in a far corner. 'Your Majesty, your humble slave is here.'

'Take Brother Lang's painting and prepare copies for an imperial challenge. Have banners posted throughout the city and the outlying towns. Zhen wants knowledgeable men to come forward to help us. Rush messengers to Guangdong and Fujian. Bring me back plants, seeds, and farmers.'

'Bixia.' Father Francisco stepped forward. 'This plant produces no seeds. It is propagated through shoots and root cuttings.'

'Bai Kui Rong, you heard the father. Bring us what we need as quickly as possible.'

Father Francisco accompanied me a short distance. 'Well done, my son. Your suggestion is an excellent one. It had not occurred to me or to other Jesuits that I consulted. It was the emperor's idea to ask you. Now I pray that the plant will take root and prosper quickly.'

We stared at each other. I would have liked to have spoken more to him but I sensed he was a solitary man. Whether he was always that way or whether it was circumstances that had made him so silent was impossible to say.

He put his hand on my shoulder. 'I have heard about your unyielding nature. It frightens people of lesser talent. Would you like to know why the emperor chose to question you about botany when there are others far more qualified?'

'I can't imagine why he would turn to someone as uneducated as me.'

'He chose you not because of logic or merit but on faith, on emotion. Two of the princes have spoken of your qualities, though they hardly know you. Yin Zhen, the fourth-born son, told the emperor that you have eyes of a clever man and the heart of a child, and that religion is not your master. The second prince is one of the emperor's favourite grandsons, Hong Li. He is very young but precocious and outspoken. He looked at the oil painting the emperor disliked and praised it. He told his grandfather that he had had a premonition that you would be a great friend of both China and its emperor.'

10

Copies of my study of sweet potatoes adorned notice boards throughout Beijing.

'Brother Giuseppe, you have succeeded in introducing European art to the masses of China. Our superiors can inform the secretary general how your illustrious painting of the simple sweet potato, *Ipomoea batatas,* is the most famous still life in China,' Antonio teased.

'Don't they say that great things arise from humble beginnings?'

'That's one way of looking at it,' he retorted, putting his arm around my shoulders. 'We shall wait and see.'

Ten days later, several imperial guards arrived at the Eastern Church, disrupted the service, and bellowed for Missionary Lang Shi Ning. With a bright red face, I broke from prayer and walked up to them. I could hear several disapproving clucks and comments from the pews.

The leader of the guards informed me that I had been called to an audience with the emperor at the summer palace, Chang Chun. Antonio rushed out after me and whispered quickly in my ear.

'It's nothing to worry about. One of the princes told me that your poster has produced a result. Someone tore one of them from a wall and carried it to the Forbidden City. This is how the Chinese acknowledge that they are thereby accepting the challenge laid down by the emperor.'

The rector had also joined us and heard Antonio's explanation. I looked at the rector for some sort of encouragement or approval. 'Who am I to keep Brother Lang from his appointment with destiny?'

I could feel every freckle alive out on my face. I don't think he had ever said anything to me without an underlying current of sarcasm and derision.

At the palace, eunuchs insisted that I refresh myself with a small meal before they took me to the emperor. I ate alone, forcing small dumplings and other delicacies into my mouth, sitting uncomfortably in a hall ironically named the Still Heart Pavilion. Finally, an official politely requested that I follow him. In a remote part of the estate, we left the formal gardens and came to a tiny farm enclosed by wooden fences. There was a barnyard, chicken coop, stable, cow pasture, vegetable garden, and a small three-roomed hut containing farming implements—hoes, sickle, winnow plus yokes and bridles. There were also two date trees with fresh, green fruit hanging. A gardener, head down, dressed in coarse, faded clothes, patiently tilled the soil. When the official bowed and departed, a eunuch touched my elbow and grunted while tilting his head, indicating I should follow.

'Lang Shi Ning! Come. Come.' The gardener was smiling at me. I had failed to recognise the emperor. If I had been more knowledgeable, I would have recognised that only the emperor could wear a four-cornered hat, but I was still quite ignorant of the customs of the imperial household. I instantly dropped down to the mud, my face pressed into who knows what, and made my nine kow-tows.

'Please stand up. Brother Lang, look at your robes. Eunuch, give him a cloth to wipe his face and hands.

Once I was clean, he spread out his arms. 'This is my little village. Zhen calls it Dao Gu Tun. Zhen grows crops here and maintains a collection of animals. Zhen ploughs with either horses or cows. Fertilising, irrigation, Zhen does it all. Sadly, last year was not a good harvest, apart from millet.' He leaned back, surveying his domain.

Then he squatted on his haunches and clasped a clump of earth. 'Come. Is your Italian soil like this?'

I too bent down and dug up a ball of earth. It was useless to feign knowledge when I was so ignorant of Italy's soil.

'Bixia, may you live ten thousand years. Your humble servant is very poor in his knowledge of farming. I cannot answer your question.'

The emperor nodded. 'Honesty is a rare virtue in my experience. Well, in a short while we will see what Merchant Chen Yuan has to tell us.' He looked behind me, and I turned to see the elderly, cynical Minister Bai Kui Rong and another man rushing towards us with rapid small steps. The visitor was a thickset man, carrying a sack around his shoulders.

'Your Minister Bai Kui Rong kneels and bows before you.'

'The worthless Chen Yuan kneels and bows. May the emperor live ten thousand years. Ten ten thousand years.' The visitor's cheeks glowed.

'Rise.' The emperor gestured with his eyebrows at Chen Yuan's sack. 'Where are the fan shu? Hand them over quickly.'

Chen Yuan crawled on his hands and knees towards the emperor and opened the bag. I stretched my neck and could see at least ten sweet potatoes, their red flesh shining through thin yellow skin. The emperor took one after another before lifting the largest one from the sack. It was the size of a melon. He examined the thick heavy root dangling from the potato and looked it over carefully. His face was flushed with excitement and his eyes sparkled.

'Merchant Chen, rise,' Bai Kui Rong whispered, raising his eyebrows. Reluctantly, Chen Yuan rose to his feet.

The emperor turned from us and walked towards a well. He began to turn the handle to lift a bucket from the water. Bai Kui Rong and I leapt forward to help him.

'Not necessary. You both know less than Zhen about farming matters.'

He lifted the bucket and washed the sweet potato slowly and tenderly. The he dried it and a eunuch handed him a knife. He deftly cut the potato in two. He carved out a hunk of flesh and put it in his mouth.

'Ha. Delicious,' he said when he finished chewing. 'Fragrant and sweet, even raw.' He cut another hunk and gestured to me. 'Is this what they taste like in your country?'

I dropped to my knees and put a hand above my head as I had been taught. The emperor dropped the morsel into the palm of my right hand. I put it into my mouth and chewed. The taste evoked images of Italy flowing. I felt the emperor's eyes upon me, waiting for my reaction as I slowly rose.

'This Chinese sweet potato has more flavour than those of my country. It's very good, but we must boil it to taste the full flavour.'

The emperor clapped. 'Yes, but later. First, Merchant Chen, explain to me why you have accepted Zhen's challenge.'

'I will tell you, Ten-Thousand-Years-Living Emperor. Your slave has stayed in the capital for many days in order to complete some buying and selling, but mainly to find a plot of land outside the city. My plan was to cultivate these fan shu. I come from the south, from Fujian, but I have been a merchant for almost twenty years, travelling between the north and south.

'Though my area is blessed with good soil and rain, I have witnessed the effects of droughts in the north too often. With each calamity, the lao bai xing, the ordinary men and women, find it harder to obtain food. They dig up grass and strip trees bare.' Chen Yuan's voice quavered. 'I began to search for a crop that would withstand the harsh climate and poor soil while satisfying hunger. These fan shu were first planted in Macao and only arrived on the mainland a few years ago. Last year my nephew found some shoots for me to plant. After one year, even on poor soil, I was successful. My yield was over two thousand catties. I was determined to come north and plant some shoots.

'My results here were a disaster. I took advice from old farmers but everyone had a different suggestion. That is why your humble slave is here searching for a new plot, to try again until I succeed. I will not give up. When I saw the imperial announcement, I thought, my blessed gods, heaven truly has eyes. A fortuitous message flowing directly from the immortals through the emperor. I came immediately. With your concern for your people, we cannot help but succeed.'

'You have spoken well, Chen Yuan, and made Zhen very pleased. The Qing Empire is lucky to have men like you. Since heaven is smiling on both of us, we cannot delay. In a few days, Zhen will be travelling to Cheng De. You will accompany us. There, Zhen has over one hundred mu of good, sandy soil. Together we will plant these shoots.'

Large tears tumbled down Chen Yuan's cheeks. 'Our ten-thousand-years emperor is truly a father of the people. Your slave, Chen Yuan, makes this promise: until I accomplish these great deeds for you I will not return to my ancestral home.' Chen Yuan threw himself to his knees and prostrated himself.

'If your skills are as big as your heart, we will succeed.' The emperor touched Chen Yuan's shoulder, indicating he should rise.

Listening to Chen Yuan speak, a visionary seeking to help those less fortunate, I felt I was witnessing brotherly love in action. His compassion for his country and countrymen demonstrated as pure an example of Christian love as any I had witnessed.

11

'You have been given a wonderful honour,' the rector began. His lips were pursed as if a sour taste had shrivelled his mouth. He held his spectacles in one hand and a thin piece of rice paper in another. 'The emperor obviously wishes to express his gratitude for your valuable contribution to his country's agriculture. There are many among the fathers here who wonder how you have risen so high in the emperor's esteem, but I say it only proves how correct we were to bring artistic *brothers* to China.'

'Do these fathers believe I have sinned in order to rise in the emperor's estimation? Am I suspected of improper behaviour?'

The rector stared at me coldly before replying. 'It never hurts to examine your heart and seek out your sins. We have an entire lifetime in which to improve ourselves and make ourselves worthy to enter the kingdom of heaven.'

'Thank you for your advice, Rector.' I glanced at the paper he held in his hand.

'Ah, yes. He put his spectacles on the end of his upturned nose while he read. 'You have been ordered to establish a school to teach Western art techniques.' He looked up at me. 'You are to be its director.'

When the decree was publicly announced to the mission, I tried to avoid everyone but my closest companions. From the moment my education stopped in Genoa and I was forbidden to become one of the Solemnly Professed, I believed my lower status would cripple me. A brother was never expected to be granted a position that made him stand out from his superiors. As director of a school that would require the assistance of Jesuit fathers, I would be giving instructions to those who should be ordering me. It would have been inconceivable in Europe.

Paolo leant his forehead against mine and put both hands on my shoulders. 'You must never be intimidated by what others in our society may think or say. You received this honour because of who *you* are. If I can see your talent and sincerity, why can't they? Their prejudice blinds them. In fact their reaction disgusts me.'

Although the emperor had already selected several young painters as my first students, I took the opportunity to make a bold request. 'May I include a student of my choice, Bixia, a young man with great promise?'

'As you wish.'

I hurried home to tell Little Brother the good news. He hopped from foot to foot and danced around before stopping to hug me. At fifteen, not only was he considerate, enthusiastic, and resourceful, but he absorbed knowledge from my fellow Jesuits like ink on blotting paper. How had Wu Yu known that such a bright jewel lay hidden beneath the grime of a homeless waif?

'I've never asked if you have a proper name.'

'I have no formal name.'

'Well, we must decide on one.'

'I would like a grand name. One that will command respect.'

Not only did Little Brother prove to be very opinionated, but his own choices were flamboyant. He refused to listen to Paolo, Jerome, or me. Only when I brought Jin Kun into the fray did he calm down. I don't know what Jin Kun said to him, but he suddenly capitulated and accepted the name of Jiang Shan Min, Good Person Jiang.

The four of us, Paolo, Jerome, Little Brother, and I, moved again, this time to a house north of the Forbidden City in an area full of artisans. It was a bustling, friendly neighbourhood. They welcomed us warmly, delighted to have two foreign Jesuit artists, a court physician, and an adopted Chinese boy in their midst.

For my school I was granted a small building, the *Qi Xiang* or Give Fortune Palace, in a corner of the sprawling palace grounds. I appointed Jerome immediately as a teacher and asked for assistance from several Jesuit fathers, who, though not artists, were excellent teachers. My biggest concern was how to convey the grandeur of Western art to the students when we were hampered by a lack of examples. Whereas I had been nourished by paintings and sculptures in churches, schools, guildhalls, and piazzas around me, they were denied such feasts.

I was also concerned that a school teaching Western art techniques alone could not be a successful or long-lasting endeavour. My students had aspirations to emulate great Chinese artists of their choosing. Perhaps I could find a way to blend the two traditions so that they were no longer opposing schools of thought but complementary ones. In that frame of mind, I approached Jin Kun and asked him to become a teacher as well.

'I have never thought of teaching,' he said. 'I am quite a solitary person. Most of my life was spent in the company of one man, a Buddhist monk, who had long periods of silent meditation. Though I eat and drink with other artists, I always feel strange doing so. What you ask will be a challenge for me, but because it is you who is asking, I accept.'

We developed the skills of our students in much the same way as I had been taught. Drawing was the basis for all other media. We exhorted the students to copy from life, plaster models, and assembled groups of objects. I led them into and through a dark, bewildering forest of bizarre terms and techniques: perspective, light, dimensions, composition, oils, silverpoint, etching, gouache.

When we progressed to portraits, several members of the court expressed their willingness to serve as models, including high-ranking officials and a few of the princes. The emperor's favourite grandson, the young prince Hong Li, a bright lad of no more than seven or eight, was among the first to pose.

'I wish to learn to paint and be an inspiring artist,' he announced to me. 'At the moment, however, I am concentrating on my poetry. When I am ready, I will ask Emperor Grandfather if you can be my teacher.'

The students complained about the strange art forms and flourished despite our inadequacies as teachers. Their minds were young and supple and they were pleased to be part of such a novel experiment. They talked and bantered with the Western teachers but treated Jin Kun with deep respect, accepting every word he spoke as Gospel.

'Painter Lang, this school has proved to be an exciting place for teachers and students,' Jin Kun commented after several months. 'I had no idea I would enjoy it so much.'

'It would not be so were it not for you, Painter Jin. You are an excellent teacher and the students are inspired by you.'

'Impossible.' As he began to blush, I realised that I had said enough. Superstitions or cultural taboos forbade my Chinese friends from accepting compliments.

'Painter Jin, I've reached a point in the teaching where I need to make a request of the emperor and I am worried. You see, in Italy, we are accustomed to drawing the human body from life.'

'Are you not already doing so?'

'I mean bodies, unclothed bodies.'

Jin Kun's eyes widened. Then he shook his head. 'Painter Lang, this is not a Chinese custom. I do not think the emperor will approve, but if you feel it is important you must try. Make your request carefully and wisely.'

I could not delay any longer. I asked for an appointment and stammered out my request. It went badly.

'What an immoral suggestion!' the emperor replied. 'Zhen has never heard of such a thing. Is this how you behave in Europe? People stand bare while others gather around to examine them? This is not our way. This is lewd and disgraceful.'

I backed away apologising profusely, my face hot with embarrassment.

Several weeks later, the emperor asked to see me. 'Zhen has spoken to Father Guo,' he said, referring to his translator, Father Francisco, 'and he has explained your artistic traditions. He talked to me about Greece and Rome. Our cultures are very different. What is viewed as immoral in one may not be in another. Make your request again, Missionary Lang. A bit clearer this time. Zhen is listening.'

I stammered out my proposal, emphasising how important it was for my students to understand the entire human body. The emperor stood up and walked around, stroking his chin.

Thank you, Father Francisco, I mouthed to the thin form who hovered behind the emperor. He smiled and nodded benignly.

'Granted,' the emperor said after a long silence. 'But only this time. It is not an experiment that will be repeated. You may not use men and you may not use women as participating would damage their morality. The room must be sealed to outsiders. These are my orders, respect them, Missionary Lang.'

I backed away, completely perplexed. If I could draw neither men nor women, who would I draw? Children? How much would that teach my students? When I repeated the emperor's words to Jin Kun, he choked with laughter.

'What is so humorous?'

'If you take away masculine and feminine, what is left?'

'I don't know.'

'Let me put it another way: if you take away that which makes a male, what do you have left?'

'Oh. I see.'

'Yes, the emperor has given you permission to paint eunuchs.' He wiped tears away with a cloth he kept in a small bag that hung from his waist. 'Isn't having any sort of body better than no body at all? You must accept the emperor's generosity. You see eunuchs all over the palace, but do you understand their origin?'

I shook my head.

'You know about Yin and Yang, that heaven is completely Yang, earth is completely Yin, mountains are Yang, water is Yin, man is Yang and woman, naturally, Yin. The *Book of Changes* states that "one Yin and one Yang is the way of life." Lao Zi wrote, "Everything carries Yin and embraces Yang." Since the emperors could not allow Yang slaves to serve their Yin women they created a slave that was neither one nor the other.' Jin Kun pointed to his loins. 'Do you know what we call this area?'

I felt my face redden. Peddlers and peasants had long ago taught me the coarse terms for male organs.

'We call it *Yang Ju* or *Yang Wu.*'

I understood this to mean the Yang Instrument or the Male Object.

'The eunuchs call it shi.'

The shi he referred to, showing me the character by writing in the air above his palm, meant 'thing', 'activity,' or 'business.'

'Oh, I see. Rather descriptive'.

'In the Ming dynasty, a eunuch, Wei Zhong Xian, rose to the position of Head of Rites and Rules. He not only controlled a vast chain of commercial enterprises but he had spies in all the ministries. He referred to himself as *Du Lan Guo Zheng*, the single ruler, and is often blamed for the decay and collapse of the dynasty.

'The Qing dynasty had no intention of making the same mistake. Eunuchs instantly lost most of their power and wealth. Even the extent of their education was restricted to "one thousand words for morality" and not much more. They are managed by the Nei Wu Fu, the Bureau for Managing the Emperor's Affairs. The head of the bureau, always a relative of the emperor, enforces the imperial palace regulations, the household law, not just for eunuchs but for all servants of the court. There are nine levels of officials. Only three eunuchs are permitted to reach the rank of fifth level and two may reach the sixth level.'

'Jin, I've noticed signs in the palaces: "*Eunuchs, do not forget who you are. Eunuchs, you are the cheapest form of slave.*" Are such notices really necessary?'

'In my encounters with eunuchs, I have come to believe that castration does as much to their nature as to their bodies. There are very few eunuchs I personally trust or like. The more time you spend within the imperial household the more you will share my distaste for them.'

Guards were posted outside the disused room in a remote corner of the Forbidden City that was reserved for life-drawing classes. As we were only permitted to draw a small number of eunuchs, I had asked the official in charge of this 'Western experiment' to select eunuchs who demonstrated different body shapes and ages.

The first eunuch was a thin youth with an intelligent, calm face.

'What is your name, young man?' I asked him as he waited behind a screened area.

'I am Wang Rong and I am not so young, Painter Lang. I am already twenty-five.'

'Please forgive me, but you look much younger than that. I want to thank you for agreeing to pose for us. It is a great help to my students. With your assistance they will understand human anatomy much better.'

'Hmm. But there is a part of my anatomy missing.'

I checked his expression and saw only playfulness in his eyes. 'Yes, well that is not important. We are interested in how the body is put together, in muscles.' I stopped as I saw his shoulders begin to shake with laughter.

'I think I have embarrassed you. Perhaps we should begin.'

I nodded and turned away.

'Painter Lang, none of us volunteered to be your models,' he continued. 'Eunuchs do what they are told. All the palace eunuchs are in quite a state of hysteria at this undertaking. Chinese are very modest people, even eunuchs.'

My back was still turned. 'Are you upset to be posing for us?

'Though I am not thrilled, I am not upset. Nothing, Painter Lang, could be worse than the circumstances that made me a eunuch. I await your instructions. I do not want to shock you.'

I turned around. He stood, stripped of his robes, a wisp of a bony, blushing man. His hands covered his loins.

'Um, if you prefer, you may use this cloth to cover yourself.'

We emerged from the enclosure and I positioned him on a high stool in the centre of the room. I began to review the principles of drawing a body, the dimensions and proportions, translating directly from the lessons of my youth.

When the shuffling sound of chalk filled the room, Jin Kun crossed over and whispered with an innocent air, 'If this is a bare-body drawing class, why is he wearing that hiding-embarrassment-cloth?'

'There's no point in drawing something that is not there.'

'Humph. I do not believe that is your true reason.'

Two months later, we painted the last of the eunuchs, a fat one. I groaned when I saw who it was—the second most senior eunuch in the court, Duan Shi Lian.

Jin Kun took me aside. 'It's rumoured that your first encounter with Eunuch Duan was unfortunate. He was slapped in your presence by the emperor when he objected to you being shown paintings in the emperor's private collection. Well, this will not have endeared him to you any further. I have heard that because he objected vigorously to this nude posing, the emperor ordered him to be punished, beaten, I believe. Though he is one of the most disliked eunuchs of the court, his position is unassailable. I don't know where he draws his power from, but be very wary of him.'

'What can I do now?'

'Pray to your god that he dies young.'

Duan Shi Lian was on the far side of forty. He had a bloated appearance and rolls of white flesh. I tried to apologise for any embarrassment his selection may have caused, but he cut me short.

'It is my duty to serve my emperor in any way he desires.'

When I offered him a cloth to cover his loins, he grabbed it, tied it expertly, and strode out from behind the screen. As I followed, he stopped in the centre of the room, pirouetted, and, in one deft movement, removed the loincloth. He walked to the high stool and manoeuvred his bottom on to it with a bit of effort. When he was comfortable, he spread his legs wide apart. My students gasped. They could not suppress their shock and revulsion. His face showed no emotion, but beneath one eye, the flesh twitched.

What we could not help but see was a male without that which distinguishes him as such and what was there was hideous. The remnants of his penis and testicles hung loosely in all directions, pink, like tentacles on an octopus. I wondered how this could be the work of a careful surgeon.

A pall was cast that robbed us of creativity. When I realised how distraught my students had become, I found an excuse to halt the session and thanked Duan Shi Lian profusely for his assistance. After he had waddled away to dress, all eyes turned to me. I tried to summarise what we had learned about the human body and to lift the heavy atmosphere, but I was unable to do so.

Jin Kun stood at my side as the students departed, shock written on all their faces. 'Do not be hard on yourself. It was a bold venture. That does not mean you should not have tried. It is a shame that such a eunuch was the last model. It is said that he mutilated himself. Imagine what that man is capable of doing to others if he can do that to himself.'

12

One spring morning, I was woken in the early hours by an imperial servant furiously shaking my shoulder. 'Missionary Lang, wake up! You have been summoned to paint a portrait of the fu yuan da jiang. Hurry, we must get to the Wu Men Gate in no more than one hour. I will help pack whatever materials you need.'

It took several minutes for what he was telling me to sink in. A few days earlier, the fourteenth-born prince, Yin Ti, had returned to the capital. He was known as the *fu yuan da jiang*, the 'commander controlling distant regions.' Banners announcing his arrival had adorned the Imperial City for at least a week, but, occupied with teaching and translating Italian art texts into Chinese, I had ignored the festivities.

We arrived at the Forbidden City before sunrise. Little Brother ran off to ask Jin Kun and Jerome to make arrangements for my classes. At the Wu Men gate, I was directed to a handsome steed while my easel and art supplies were taken to a carriage. Not only did the horse appear far too strong and lively for my level of horsemanship, but I had no idea why I needed a mount.

'The prince wishes his portrait to be painted at the Tian Tan palace, not here,' a soldier informed me.

I mounted awkwardly and rode at the very back of the small contingent of servants and soldiers. It took us almost an hour to reach Tian Tan, the Temple of Heaven. To my relief, my powerful horse behaved impeccably throughout.

The emperor came to Tian Tan each spring to pray for fruitful harvests and each winter to thank heaven for granting his prayers. The grounds of the palace were extensive and serene. The most important buildings were three circular temples, laid on a north-south axis. The most ornate was the Hall of Prayer for a Good Harvest, with three concentric blue porcelain roofs, a giant golden bauble on top, and a highly decorated, soaring interior. Here artisans had been permitted to use bright blue, green, reds, and gold on the beams and pillars. I gazed in admiration at the fanciful designs lavished on every surface, extending to the top of the dome. If such ability to paint in colour existed, why were Chinese paintings so muted?

As I strolled around the interior, I counted twenty-eight thick round pillars, four representing the seasons and twenty-four representing the twelve months of the year and the twelve hours of the day. Though the building was round, it was situated within a large, square, stone courtyard. A raised stone walkway led to the other round temples, a tangible embodiment of the saying *'Round Heaven and Square Earth'*.

After daybreak, once the sun had removed the chill from the air, Prince Yin Ti arrived on a beautiful chestnut horse with a flowing white tail and mane. To my surprise, Antonio was riding by his side.

'How do you do, Missionary Lang. We met once before, at a banquet soon after your arrival. My good friend Father An tells me that you are a great artist. I should like you to paint a military portrait. I have brought armour and one of the finest horses in the stable.'

I looked at Antonio. He lowered his head and closed his eyes briefly before speaking quickly in Italian. 'This is important, Seppe. My princely friend is a wise man, open to new ideas, someone who can influence the future of our mission.'

With a smile on my face, I spoke softly to Antonio. 'Why did you not warn me of this request? I would have been better prepared if I had been given some time.'

'It is better this way. The less people know of this the better.'

Maintaining my false smile, I retorted, 'If that is the case, then perhaps you should not be here either.'

I turned on my heel and went to prepare my materials, unable to ignore an uncomfortable sense of betrayal. In the past year, I had spent little time with Antonio. I blamed the fact that we were both so busy, but if I were honest with myself, I knew that a key thread that had secured our friendship had been severed. Antonio lived much of the time in a world of his own. My life was absorbed by the likes of Paolo, fellow artists like Jin Kun, my students, and, most important of all, my young ward, Little Brother.

My attention was drawn to several gold items that emerged from beneath a dark cloth in the carriage: the chest plate of a glittering suit of armour.

Servants helped Yin Ti put them on. He leapt astride his chestnut horse. Yin Ti's own long hair flowed from beneath a golden helmet. A long spike with a horsetail plume pointed upwards from its crown and flaps protected his neck and ears. Golden scales covered his chest armour, his ribs, his upper and lower arms and shoulders, and golden sheaths covered his legs; even his boots shone gold. A pattern of good luck clouds was embossed in the centre of his chest. Baby lamb fleece peeked out from his cuffs. The saddle, which was diamond-studded, rested on a finely embroidered cloth and porcelain tassels hung from the girdle, tinkling in the soft breeze. The sun glinted off small diamonds pressed into the bridle.

I glanced briefly at Antonio and nodded my head. 'He looks magnificent,' I said quickly in Italian.

'Like the true leader that he is.'

All the emperor's sons carried the character *Yin* as one of their given names. It is an intriguing character, meaning 'to have many descendants.' On the outside of the character are two vertical lines that look like legs. Alone, they are pronounced as *ren,* the same sound as the word for man. Between the legs are two other symbols, one above the other. The higher character is *yao,* youngest son or daughter; the bottom character is *rou,* flesh or meat. From his loins, a man produces the flesh of his descendants.

Concentrating on my painting, I only heard snippets of a conversation between Antonio and Yin Ti, most of which concerned the economic future of China.

'...as regards the policy of uniting small countries to defeat larger enemies, one must concentrate on the southwest and the northwest. Tibet and Xinjiang must be tamed and controlled. His Majesty, my father emperor, was delighted with my "Ten Points of Ruling",' I heard Yin Ti say. 'He will take a great deal of persuasion, however, to change the policy banning imports. I insist that our country cannot progress without trade. It must be our priority. The rigorous custom controls need not persist. It has been twenty-two years since my father emperor dispersed rebellions. Our country has many goods desired by other nations all banned for export: gunpowder, minerals, iron ore, rice, crops, fabric, carpets.'

I had completed the first layer of detail when we paused for a midday meal. I looked forward to several more weeks of work to complete the painting to my satisfaction. The finished painting needed to be elaborate, worthy of the fine designs on the armour and saddlery.

'Your Highness, could you spare another day or two so that I can ensure the accuracy of the portrait?'

'Not possible. I will be too busy to sit, as I depart in three days. My father emperor bids me to hasten back to my post.'

'When will you return? Will you want the painting sent to you when I finish it?'

He chortled and threw his head back. 'I expect it done before my departure! You have three days, Missionary Lang.'

I swallowed hard, looking to Antonio for assistance, but he was observing the prince.

Antonio spoke. 'Your Highness, have you seen the second-born prince? Is he comfortable?'

'As well as can be expected after his imprisonment and the poisonous medicine he was given.'

I had heard a bit of the history of the unfortunate second-born Yin Reng, the eldest legitimate son. As the only child of a beloved wife who had died young, Yin Reng had been spoiled by his father. He was twice named crown prince only to be denounced and imprisoned. It was rumoured that he had used his position to enrich and empower himself. Even the emperor suspected at one point that Yin Reng planned to assassinate him. It was rumoured that several of his brothers had bribed physicians to change medicines in order to drive him insane or do worse damage.

After our midday meal, I worked feverishly, hardly aware of anything but the portrait. Only one comment penetrated my concentration.

'With no crown prince named, my brothers vie incessantly with each other. Some of their tactics are shameful. I am glad to be far away from those intrigues.'

'Absence will only make the emperor admire you more.'

'I ask no favours; only that I may honourably serve my country.'

During the late afternoon, the prince dismounted and came close to my portrait, nodding to show his approval. 'Does Brother Lang have experience with fortune telling?'

I shook my head.

'No? I want you to paint a ray of light in the middle of my forehead. Would that be agreeable to you?'

'Yes, as you wish, Your Highness.'

'When the painting is finished, I will send a slave to collect it. Apart from the three of us here, my closest guards, and servants, no one else is to know about this painting.' He peered into my face, raising his eyebrows and tilting his head to one side. 'You are not to display it to any other person.'

'As you wish.'

I spent the next three days and nights back in Beijing cloistered in my studio. As requested, I worked in a shaft of light from heaven to Yin Ti's forehead. On the last day, as darkness fell, a servant came to take the portrait away.

Jerome, Paolo, and Little Brother had respected my wishes and did not try to see it. However, Jerome and Paolo uttered several critical comments. 'What is Antonio up to? He should not favour one prince over others. There are no secrets at court. If Yin Ti does not become the next emperor, Antonio will face the wrath of the successor. By asking you to paint this portrait he has made you an accomplice to his own machinations.'

'Then I must trust in his wisdom and foresight.' I retorted more sharply than I intended to.

I finally went to see Antonio, not quite knowing what I wished to say to him. On the wall facing the entrance of his house, a lit candle rested on a small altar beneath a finely carved mahogany crucifix. In the same spot in our home, I had hung three of Wu Yu's largest brushes.

Antonio was contemplative as we sat together sipping tea. 'I can see that you are annoyed with me, Seppe. Prince Yin Ti and I needed to talk privately. There are too many prying eyes and ears in the palace. In the open air at Tian Tan we were able to discuss many issues. The future of our work in China rests on who is the next emperor.'

'Antonio, even I am aware of the intrigues among the princes. Is it wise of you to favour one prince over another? Will they not resent your behaviour if another prince is chosen?'

'He is the finest prince, the one who deserves to be emperor. It will be him. I'm sure of it.'

'How can you be so sure? You seem to be looking at the succession blindly. It is not clear who will be the next emperor.'

'Are you doubting me?'

'I am concerned for you. When I lived on the streets among rival gangs of youths, I never chose sides. In fact, I never stood out from the crowd. I made it a point to be invisible because experience taught me that there is always someone more powerful. The struggle for the succession is no different. It is a battlefield for a great prize and there will be victims, innocent and not so innocent.'

The kettle began to boil. Antonio picked it up off the stove and poured hot water into the teapot. The perfume from the tea leaves seeped into the room.

'By God's grace,' Antonio said in a deep voice with his back to me, 'Yin Ti shall be the next emperor. We will not have long to wait to see His choice.'

13

'It gets hotter every year. There is more dust, the odours more foul, the air more suffocating, and sun more cruel than ever,' I moaned to Paolo as we took a few minutes to sit under a tree in the church courtyard. It was August, my seventh summer in Beijing, and I could hardly breathe. He leaned back and closed his eyes.

'Actually this heat agrees with me. Pity that I will have to leave the capital soon. I have an order from the emperor.' Paolo waved a thin piece of paper, his eyes never opening. 'I've been asked to accompany him to Cheng De palace and to the Mu Lan hunting preserve.'

'Cheng De? In Rehe province?'

Paolo nodded.

'Where everyone says it's cool and beautiful?'

He nodded again and sighed. 'So I've heard.'

'How long will you be gone?'

'Perhaps one month or more.'

'Congratulations. How lucky for you. Please say the appropriate prayers over my dead body when you return.' I turned my back towards him.

'Is this the sin of jealousy I see peeking out from that hole in your head, Brother Giuseppe?' He prodded me with his finger, but I ignored him. 'Now you are being rude as well. I was wondering if you could help me? There is another name on this letter that I can't quite make out.'

I turned around. From the laughter that suddenly appeared in his eyes, I knew what the name would be. I snatched the paper from his hand. When I saw my name, my jaw dropped open and then I pushed him so hard that he fell off the bench. He lay on the ground laughing until I pulled him to his feet.

'What a temper you have, Seppe.'

'I will forgive you if you find a way to bring Little Brother along as well.'

'I have already done so.'

Paolo, Little Brother, and I joined thousands from the court on the journey north as the emperor's family, his military leaders, heads of the six major ministries, closest advisers, servants, and soldiers made the annual trip to the palace known as the Mountain Retreat to Escape Summer Heat. To my delight, Jin Kun, at the reins of a small two-wheeled cart appeared at our side after several hours of slow movement.

'I never thought I would find you among all these people,' he said. 'This is my first journey to Cheng De as well. Young Jiang, come and ride with me.' Little Brother nimbly leapt from our carriage to Jin's and beamed contentedly.

We travelled over two hundred miles towards the northwest. Each morning servants raced ahead to set up tents along the route, some for rest, others for eating, 'tea palaces' and 'residential palaces.'

When we finally arrived at Cheng De, the sight of it took my breath away. The bulk of the estate lay in a large basin surrounded by soft, green mountains. Pavilions had been constructed with great care along lakes, within forests, and on mountaintops. A large pasture held scores of beautiful horses. Many more frolicked in the lake and river on its southern flank.

'I feel content here,' I said to Paolo. 'I don't know why.'

'There isn't always a logical explanation for what we feel. Sometimes the soul is wiser than the head.'

'Does Cheng De please you?' I had been sketching and did not hear anyone approach. I turned around to find the emperor and several officials standing behind me.

I immediately bowed on the ground, scattering my materials in all directions. 'It is one of the most beautiful places your humble servant has ever seen.'

'Good. Zhen chose this spot over twenty years ago. The landscape is like a miniature China. There are mountains in the northwest, ample water in the southeast, and wide open plains in the north. Missionary Lang, please go now and find Chen Yuan. Ask him to show you the fan shu fields and report to me what you see. Take this gift to Chen Yuan as well and assure him of our appreciation for his work.' The emperor waved his hand and a servant ran forward to place a golden hoe in my hand. 'Zhen has personally written on the handle. See here: "*zhuo xin chun yi.*" It means to "farm with your heart".'

I waited with my head low until the emperor walked off, and then collected my things and rushed to find Paolo and Little Brother and ask them to come with me.

'You will like Chen Yuan. He is a remarkable man,' I told them.

Guided by a servant, we hurried to his fields, which lay a short distance from the eastern edge of the wall surrounding the estate. The land was flat for many miles until the next swell of gentle mountains. The servant bowed and left us, pointing towards a straw pavilion. As we drew closer, Little Brother read out five characters that were painted in bright green above the door: '*Sweet fountains make green melons.*'

A voice shouted, '*Lang Shi Ning!* We have been waiting for you.' Chen Yuan appeared from nowhere, rushing towards me with his arms extended and a beaming face. 'And who is this?'

I introduced Paolo and Little Brother. 'This is one of the emperor's physicians and a dear friend of mine, Luo Hai Zhong, and Jiang Shan Min, a rising painter and my adopted brother. But before we say anything more, the emperor asked me to present this to you.' I held out the shimmering hoe before me.

Chen Yuan fell to his knees. He faced the palace and kow-towed three times before he would accept the hoe with his head bent downwards.

'What a wonderful inscription! I will honour this glorious offering from the emperor forever.' After a moment of silent prayer, he stood up and handed the hoe to a servant, who scurried off, peering at it and holding it as far from his body as possible.

Chen Yuan clasped my hand and arm. 'Brother Lang, it is so good to see you, and your timing could not be more auspicious. Tomorrow I will marry. It was chosen as a favourable day for a wedding; now your arrival has proved it is so. Will you join us as well, Physician Luo and young Jiang?'

'How wonderful. Congratulations. Is your fiancée from your village? Someone you've known a long time?' I asked.

'Not at all.' Chen Yuan dragged me along the field, his arm fixed tightly around my own. His round face was flush with excitement and I could feel his hand trembling ever so slightly. 'If you remember, my birthplace is Fujian province where, according to custom, one selects a bride from either one's own or a neighbouring village. My engagement had been agreed upon by my father many, many years ago. But for so long I travelled all four seasons. I began to worry that I was wasting the springtime of my betrothed and asked my father to break the engagement. She married another and produced several children. I gave no further thought to a wife.

'Now that the royal challenge has replaced my former itinerant life, the idea of marriage has relevance. Since I am already past forty years, sooner is better than later. I hired a marriage broker to find me a woman from this area, one who would understand the value of this great undertaking.' Chen Yuan talked with his entire body, his face more lively with each sentence. He walked vigorously but stopped abruptly from time to time to look at me and see my reaction.

'Have you met her? Do you not worry that she may not be the appropriate woman for you?'

'Oh, she is the right one. The marriage broker took me to spy on her in the fields and I was most impressed. She is attractive, strong, and robust with a virtuous demeanour, clearly a practical woman from a simple peasant family. Though the custom here is to wait at least two years before marrying, I would hear nothing of it. Everything was settled within a month. After tomorrow, with the right woman under my roof, I will peacefully, whole-heartedly concentrate on my fan shu.'

'I pray that your respectable bride shares your enthusiasm and dedication and is your equal in energy and persistence.'

'That will be the case. I have no doubt.'

Chen Yuan led us towards several men standing together discussing a field with young plants. 'These are all brilliant agricultural specialists from the south, from Guangdong province. The emperor summoned them north to assist me.' After a short conversation with them, we walked on.

'Dear friends, you will come to my wedding, will you not?'

'Well...'

'I know, Painter Lang and Physician Luo, you are both religious men, Christians. But please, at least drink tea and congratulate me. You, more than anyone, are responsible for my great honour. It is a sign from the gods, a blessing on my marriage that you should arrive the day before my wedding. If there is anything which presents an embarrassment, close your eyes and ignore it. I believe that even your strict god is not so heartless as to deny a man the company of his friends at his wedding.'

I looked at Paolo, who nodded, and Little Brother, whose eyes begged me to agree. 'Yes, we accept. How could we refuse? Does anyone ever say no to you?'

Chen Yuan laughed and slapped my shoulder. 'Not often. Victory comes to the man who has clear sight of his goals. Never be confused by useless aims. Move through life like a spear, that is my way.'

As Paolo, Little Brother, and I walked back towards the palace, Little Brother asked many questions. 'How long have you known him? Why have you never told me about him?'

'I only met him once before today, yet he treats me as if we have known each other forever. Why are you so curious?'

'I don't know. He reminds me of Wu Yu, a man who thought of others before himself. I like him.'

When I asked Jin Kun next day to accompany us to Chen Yuan's wedding he smiled. 'You realise that in a few days we leave for the Mu Lan preserve and many days of hunting. You will appreciate having the pleasant images of the wedding to think about.'

'I've read other Jesuits' accounts of the imperial hunts. I believe I'm prepared.'

'No matter how much you have heard or read, you will still be shocked. I have participated in several and return horrified each time. The Buddhist I grew up with taught me many things, not the least of which was the sanctity of all life.'

'Why have you agreed to come then?'

'One does not refuse a request from the emperor. Could you turn down a king's invitation in your country? Anyway, I am looking forward to our collaboration. Have you not been told?' he asked when he saw the blank look on my face.

I shook my head.

'You and I will prepare a large painting to celebrate the conclusion of the hunt. The emperor is concerned that you have not learned enough about Chinese art. He believes a collaboration with me will help. I'm surprised you were not told in advance. It doesn't matter; I have brought all that we will need. Painter Lang, never forget that emperors are impatient and demanding people. Our service to them takes precedence over everything.'

We found Paolo and Little Brother and walked to Chen Yuan's house. He was perched on a tall horse, with his face powdered and rouged and his hair pulled tightly into a long ponytail, dark and shining. Red silk was wound around his torso forming a cross, then elaborately gathered and tied over his heart into a bold flower design. A long, flowing robe of beautiful, rich blue silk was draped over the horse's haunches. He waved when he saw us.

'Is this not grand?' Chen Yuan shouted excitedly to us.

In front of him stood several men, each holding a red lantern aloft and behind, others carried the bridal sedan chair. Inside a toothless, wrinkled wisp of a woman sat grinning at everyone and mumbling to herself.

'She is sitting in a palanquin normally reserved for family. Probably the marriage broker. She certainly has the fair looks of one of her trade,' Jin Kun noted wryly.

A team of drummers and musicians came to life with a cacophony of banging, thumping, and blowing, which startled birds from trees and set animals braying. Six young barefoot men, dressed in shimmering silk tunics and trousers, rushed to the front of the procession waving red banners.

The wedding party set off for the bride's house and we followed a short distance behind.

At the bride's house, the six barefoot youths paid a small amount of coins and entered. They gently guided the heavily veiled bride towards the door. She was held back by her father, who asked many questions testing her understanding of the duties and obligations of a wife. His feigned reluctance to part with her delighted a large, curious crowd that had gathered. Finally he relented and the bride left her parental home to begin her journey to her new home. The crowd hooted and cheered.

As we strolled back to Chen Yuan's house, more peasants left their fields and joined us. Chen Yuan stood in the middle of the doorway, beaming and bouncing with impatience. He saw us surrounded by jostling onlookers and said something to a servant. We were led through the tightly packed mass into the house.

'When does the wedding ceremony begin?' Paolo asked Jin Kun.

'It is over. They are now husband and wife.' He looked at us curiously. 'Is it very different in your country?'

'Very,' we answered together.

Jin Kun raised his eyebrows. 'Watch closely. Everything that occurs now is symbolic. If the rituals are not strictly adhered to, our gods could be offended. See how a young boy and girl are following the bride and groom. They are carrying pomegranates, dates, and peanuts. The pronunciation of these words—carrying pomegranates, and so on—is the same as words meaning to have a son quickly or to have both a boy and girl. Now the bride is stepping on a cotton sack. Again, the sound for that action is the same as the words for carrying a son in one's womb.'

Chen Yuan approached us, a grin stretched across his face. His face, ears, and neck were bright red. We introduced him to Jin Kun.

'Welcome, welcome. Forgive me for ignoring you for so long. Painter Jin, Missionary Lang, Physician Luo, and young Jiang, your presence has multiplied my happiness.'

Chen Yuan motioned for his bride to join us. I could finally see her face and found it handsome, open, and illuminated by large, glistening eyes. She reminded me of the hardy women from the south of Italy, wonderful mothers and wives, able to cope with any and all difficulties.

She knelt. 'I hope you fine gentlemen are well. I am only from a small farming household. I do not understand ceremony. Please, fine gentlemen, do not laugh at me.' She giggled shyly and only stood up on my insistence.

Before the banquet could be served, Paolo and I begged leave of the newlyweds. Chen Yuan looked crestfallen.

'Please drink one celebratory glass of wine with us.' Chen Yuan and his bride held the bottle together and poured four small glasses. We each proposed a toast to their marriage and to lasting friendship.

'For a Jesuit who arrived alone in Beijing seven years ago, you have established some good friendships with extraordinary Chinese,' Paolo commented later. 'Most Jesuits—I don't know why—cannot form such bonds with people of different races. They prefer to be superior to them, like parents with children. But you see past all the barriers and stand equal with them, to your credit. You are the richer for it.'

'It is because he has a big heart,' Little Brother added, holding on to my arm.

14

The hunting party swelled to over twelve thousand people. There were six thousand soldiers from the eight armies of the Manchus as well as an assortment of fighting men from northern tribes: Qinghai Mongols, Keerke Mongols, six united Inner Mongols armies, forty-nine private armies, and the eight armies of the Chahar who lived near Xinjiang.

'Hunting is as important to Zhen as maintaining a strong army and secure borders,' the emperor proclaimed as we set off for the Mu Lan preserve. 'It is our Manchu heritage.'

I looked ahead and behind. The procession that had left Cheng De in the morning sprawled for miles along a road built for the emperor's use. Soldiers guarded the route on both sides. The surface, made of pressed stone and earth, shone like polished leather. It was wide: two men, head to foot, could easily lie across it, and was separated from the surrounding land by low earthen walls. Markers at regular intervals displayed distances.

It reminded me of sacred roads in Europe, routes for saints' relics and pilgrimages, like the one stretching from northern France to north-western Spain leading to a cathedral at Campus Stellea built to house the tomb of Saint James, one of Jesus' martyred disciples.

'Seppe, there is something I must share with you and you alone,' Paolo said to me as we sat together in a carriage full of medical supplies. He held the reins of the horses, leaning forward. Little Brother continued to travel with Jin Kun, whom he adored. 'The emperor is a very sick man. Over the past two or three months, he's suffered minor heart collapses. The severity of his condition is known only to the prime minister, Long Ke Duo, and me. But, worst of all, he's lost the will to live. I tried to advise him not to participate this year but he refused. "This is my forty-eighth hunt," he informed me. "In fifty years, I have only missed two and those were because of war."

'Why has this happened?'

'He is wounded by the strife among his sons.'

'No one has a claim to perfect happiness, do they?' I finally commented.

'Only by the grace of God may we experience periods of fulfilment that make everything else tolerable, my friend.'

On the high north-eastern plateau, the landscape was flat, a sea of endless yellow earth, thick and mesmerising. Tall poplar trees had been beaten into unnatural positions by fierce winds. The earth was parched and lonely.

That evening, a servant came to escort Paolo to the emperor. He asked me to accompany him. I sat on the floor quietly in a corner of the tent while Paolo examined Xuan Ye behind a curtain. 'Do not look so concerned, Physician Luo,' I heard him say in a low voice. 'Everyone is exhausted today. Even Zhen could not avoid it. Today, Zhen thought about another hunt, exactly forty years ago. One of your Jesuits was with me, Father Verbiest. He was a great man and a loyal friend. Did you know he designed cannons to help us repel barbarian invaders?'

'I have heard the story and how he blessed them with holy water. Your Majesty, your pulse is very fast. And the colour of your skin indicates that you are straining your liver. Would it not be possible to travel a shorter distance tomorrow?'

'Zhen feels very tired. Probably because Zhen is old. But the timetable cannot be changed. Zhen will sleep earlier tonight and tomorrow will be better.' Xuan Ye turned to his relative and prime minister, Long Ke Duo, and issued an order. 'No change. Breakfast begins at five in the morning. There must be no delay.'

Paolo spoke quietly to Long Ke Duo after emerging from the emperor's sleeping area. As we walked back to our tent, Paolo said, 'There is something else I must discuss with you. I have put off speaking about it for too long, but when I see how frail the emperor is, I can no longer delay. It's about Antonio, Seppe. While I agree that he's a very talented man, I am concerned about the risks he takes. Many of the princes are angry about secret meetings between Antonio and Yin Ti. They have knowledge about a portrait you painted outside the Forbidden City and Antonio's role there.'

My heart sank. Though I wanted to discuss the sense of unease about Antonio's meddling in politics, I was stopped by blind loyalty to him. Those few months of companionship in my first year in China had bound us together. Without the confidence I had gained from his affection, where would I be? Who would I be?

'Antonio's motivations are good. He believes he is helping our cause and that Yin Ti is the most worthy prince to succeed his father. If he does become emperor, the cause of Christianity in China will be strengthened.'

'But surely you have more sense than to take sides in such a precarious situation?' Paolo's voice was tense. I shook my head, unable to say anything.

'Sorry, this is not the tone I had intended to take. Let me tell you what I believe. While Antonio may say his motives are solely for the good of our mission I see something else.' Paolo sighed. 'In my years of tending people, I have seen many who have given up on life, usually in the face of grave illness. Antonio, though healthy, displays the fatalistic attitudes I've come to recognise. Something has happened to him, and it makes him court danger. That is my professional assessment. He is beyond my ministrations, but I will do whatever is required to protect you.'

Paolo took my arms and looked me straight in the eyes, demanding an answer.

'Paolo, I love Antonio like a true brother. He makes me angry at times and his distance hurts me deeply, but there is a part of me, though it be foolish, that is prepared to risk anything if it helps him, as I would my own flesh and blood.'

'Make no mistake. The game that Antonio is playing could prove to be a lethal one. These princes are not to be insulted. I will not stand by and watch you waste your enormous talent and possibly your life. You must come and talk to me before you assist in any further trysts on his behalf. Though you may choose to ignore my advice, please, *please* reflect on what I've said.'

I sighed. 'I appreciate your concern and know I should respect your advice. You are wiser than I can ever hope to be.' I paused, suddenly realising how much anxiety I was causing him. Paolo looked at me with large, concerned eyes. My voice dropped to a whisper as I decided to divulge what had been bothering me for months. 'Antonio never informed me in advance about the portrait. I was summoned to the Tian Tan palace to paint Yin Ti and was surprised that Antonio accompanied him. Though I was annoyed at the time and told him so, what's done is done and there is nothing I can do about it.'

The corners of Paolo's mouth dropped. 'How dare he! I believed you were a willing accomplice. Antonio has implicated you by keeping you ignorant. What was he thinking? Seppe, this is not how brothers behave. It's not how friends treat each other.'

The second evening, when we returned to our tent, Jin Kun and Little Brother were waiting for us. 'The emperor treats you both so well,' Jin Kun said. 'You will never be able to repay him in this life.'

'Are we committing an error, in your opinion?' Paolo asked.

'You are receiving better treatment from the Son of Heaven than family and ministers who have devoted entire lifetimes to him. Those who are excluded may feel slighted.'

'Being with an emperor is like riding a tiger,' I mumbled.

'Correct,' Jin Kun said, adding, 'but this tiger also has many male offspring eager to taste blood.'

'Big Brothers, please listen to Painter Jin,' begged Little Brother. 'I do not want anything to happen to you.'

During the night, it began to rain; heavy, fat droplets whipped to a frenzy by strong winds. The storm lost none of its intensity after daybreak. The emperor refused to stop travelling even when pummelled by earth, twigs, and leaves. The road dissolved into mud, snagging the feet of men and hooves of beasts and causing everyone to fall at some point. After the emperor urged his mount towards the side of the road, all the soldiers followed suit, leaving the central path for carriages and sedan chairs.

The fourth-born prince, Yin Zhen, rode behind his father. When servants rushed forward leading a fresh horse, he dismounted to help his father.

'Perhaps the emperor draws strength from the land of his ancestors,' Paolo mused in the evening. 'His condition has improved.'

At dusk on the fourth day of our departure from Cheng De, we paused at the entrance to the Mu Lan hunting preserve. Jin Kun had told me that Mu Lan was the Manchu pronunciation of the words 'deer hunting,' *shao lu* in Mandarin, and that the emperor had created the preserve forty years earlier. It was composed of over sixty separate hunting grounds. Jin Kun described it as a place of lushness and tranquillity sullied by annual hunts.

The emperor's words were recorded by a scribe.

'If an emperor only governs from the safe confines of the capital and does not celebrate his mounted armies, he deserves to lose his throne. Zhen and the united armies come here each year to pay respects to our common ancestors and to listen to the leaders and tribal heads of this region, to humbly receive their wisdom on the direction of our policies. May this hunt be the most successful ever.'

That evening, the emperor invited us to his tent to discuss the Roman Empire. He was intrigued by the stories of its decline and fall. We discussed the tragic saga of wars, excessive taxation, a brutal slavery system, revolts, an entrenched social hierarchy, and ever harsher dictatorships. For some reason I became very vocal about the early history of Christianity, talking about how suppression and martyrdom failed to abate it, and how the message spread among the slaves and grew with each century until Constantine himself converted.

'Missionary Lang, are you advocating your religion here so that the peasants can overthrow their lords?'

'Your servant has been foolish. Please forgive him.'

'You know that your predecessor, Father Verbiest, gave us a bible and talked to me of Jesus and his wise sayings. His relationship with his apostles was similar to that of Confucius with his students. When Zhen probed Father Verbiest to explain the miracles of Jesus, he gave very unsatisfactory answers. Can you do better?'

'Bixia, our Lord performed miracles for people with faith. A good heart is amply rewarded. Even Confucius claimed that the devil cannot take over a body if the soul is healthy. Forgive me, *Bixia*. Your foolish slave has said more stupid things.'

Paolo reassured me later that I had not offended Xuan Ye.

'Are you sure?'

'Sometimes, when I teach the emperor science, I add many unusual ideas, some scientific, others more philosophical, based on personal experience. He takes pleasure in verbal challenges, in sincere debate. He once said to me, "Outside this room, Physician Luo, remember another world intervenes. A world of intrigue and dispute. Do not use the same freedom of speech with my sons. It could be misinterpreted, and you could be severely punished. In my youth, I would not have tolerated your argumentative bent but age has softened my rigidity."

In the morning, Paolo tactfully talked to the emperor about the rigours of a hunt after such a long and taxing journey. Prince Yin Zhen and a small number of close officials were present.

'Hunting is, by its nature, a fearsome, exhilarating sport whether undertaken as a participant or as an observer. Zhen is a Manchu, and hunting runs in my veins. Do not ask a Manchu to sit quietly. If heaven decrees that it is time for Zhen to join his ancestors, what better way and what better place Zhen cannot imagine.'

Yin Zhen followed us out of the tent. 'What can we do to help our father emperor?'

'His Majesty is healthy but not as young as he once was. It would be best if he did not strain too much during the hunt.'

Yin Zhen kept his eyes on me while he spoke to Paolo. 'I will see what I can do.'

As we set off at dawn, Jin Kun walked beside me. 'Where is Little Brother?' I enquired.

'He is with several other boys his age. They are being looked after by several old men, once formidable hunters. It will be good for him. He will learn many things.'

'Painter Jin, have you heard that I painted a portrait of Prince Yin Ti?'

'Yes.'

'What have you heard?'

'Many things.'

I waited but he said nothing more. 'Was it wrong?'

'That will depend on who is asking and who is answering.'

'Can you say something that is not inscrutable?'

He frowned and hesitated. 'You have not been here long enough to understand our ways. People say that dark times are coming. Having seen such periods before, I am worried. I am not a brave man, Painter Lang. I wish only to be left alone to paint and to live at peace. The first emperor of the Qing dynasty tried to make many changes among the Han to enforce Manchu ways, and this emperor, his son, continued to do so. There were times when those who refused to accept new customs were exiled or executed. This emperor was ruthless when he assumed the reins of government from the regents. The next emperor, if he is to survive, must be severe too. He will have many brothers who could plot against him. In such times, it is best to be like a grain of sand, no different from one's neighbour, insignificant and inoffensive. With your foreign looks and strange ways, you stand out. If you displease the new emperor, it will not just be you who suffers.'

A shout stopped our discussion.

'*Form a circle!*'

The Mongolian and Manchurian ministers for hunting rode at the head of the interminable line. The minister for guides divided us into two wings. The completed circle had a circumference of over ten miles. We were required to be silent until given a signal.

Paolo rode a short distance behind the emperor who looked regal on his favourite horse, the Grey Jade Steed, a strong dapple grey with a luxuriant mane and tail, given to him by the Russian tsar. Two young princes rode on either side, his grandsons, Hong Li and Hong Xi.

The signal came and we all began to hoot, scream, bang, and thump. The noise was deafening. In the distance the trees, shrubs, and grasses began to shake. A huge dust cloud rolled in all directions like the smoke from a raging forest fire. While we continued to shout, small pinpricks of brown and grey animals appeared in the distance.

At the same time, the circle moved forward and inward. Even if we stumbled or trudged through water, we dared not stop. The terrain was hilly. Those without horses clambered up steep slopes, holding on to branches and stumbling over roots. We were cut by thorns and trapped by undergrowth. Finally, the minister of guides approached the emperor for his orders.

'The hunt may begin.'

White scarves were waved and the shouting and banging ceased. In the place of our voices, the frightened cries of trapped animals and squawks of birds echoed off the hills. The emperor kicked his horse and sped off. The two grandsons followed.

'Tighten the circle more.'

I was astounded at the number of animals trapped within the human wall. In their mad panic, they raced from one side to another, predators and victims united in a fruitless attempt to escape, raising swirls of dust. I could smell the animals and their fear. The pounding of hooves shook the ground.

The emperor bore down upon a large brown bear. He raised his gun and took aim. A puff of smoke and the whistling of the bullet pierced the air. A second later, the animal howled in pain and wobbled for a second, but instinct urged it to run on, though at a slower pace, grunting and snarling all the while. The emperor followed while loading a new bullet. He aimed again, and blood spurted from a wound in the bear's back. It dropped on the edge of a tiny copse, gave a tremble, and lay still.

'Grandson Li.' Xuan Ye pulled his horse to a stop. 'From here to the dead animal is about one hundred paces. I want you to test your strength with my bow and arrow. You need good arms to use it. This is an adult bow.' He pulled an arrow from his case and handed it to his ten-year-old grandson.

'Respectfully, Grandfather, let me try.' Hong Li took the bow and arrow and pulled back the hard string. With a harsh ping, it sailed toward the fallen bear and struck it in the side.

'Well done,' the emperor shouted. Many other voices joined in.

'Can I go and have a look?' Hong Li asked.

'Go.' The emperor turned to the assembled leaders of various armies. 'This bear is the first kill of the forty-eighth hunt, brought down by both my grandson and myself. The hunt has begun with good luck. The animal will be recorded in the great book as the "Bear Snatched at the Beginning of the Hunt".'

Hong Li ran to the bear's side and pulled the bamboo arrow from the bear, cleaning it on a white cloth. As he held up the arrow to show his grandfather, the bear rolled over and lunged at the boy with a vicious snarl, knocking him to the ground. It raised a gigantic paw and Hong Li scampered backwards on his elbows and backside. The bear swung its paw, catching the hem of his robe and pulling the boy closer. A sound exploded, and most of the bear's scalp disappeared. Hong Li was splattered with blood and gore. The emperor stood with smoke oozing from his gun, his face hard but drained of all colour.

Soldiers ran forward, lifting Hong Li on their shoulders to bring him to his grandfather. Xuan Ye clasped Hong Li to his chest. 'Do not be frightened. Do not be frightened.'

Hong Li pushed himself away from his grandfather to look at him and shook his head. 'Grandfather, it was nothing, really. If only this robe were not so long, I would have avoided the paw.'

'Then so be it, my young treasure.' The emperor looked at him, his eyes glistening. 'Come, cut his robe off just below the waist. Unsuitable clothing almost robbed my grandson of his life.'

While Hong Li's robe was being cut, the emperor seemed lost in thought until the minister of guides whispered something in his ear. His eyes came to life as he nodded.

'Royal princes may hunt now.'

Although Paolo and I had remained a discrete distance away, the emperor turned towards us. 'This precious grandson of mine has a greater fate than most men.' He put his arm around Hong Li and squeezed him fondly. Hong Li hugged him. To my eyes, the affection between the two was deep and sincere. 'The Chinese say: if one faces death and survives, his fortune is great.'

Yin Zhen, Hong Li's father, suddenly appeared. 'Thank you, Father Emperor, for your golden eyesight and strong heart. You have saved my beloved son.' His actions belied his words: he neither hugged nor gazed upon his son. Hong Li did not rush to his father's side. Another prince came to stand with us, the eighth-born, Yin Yi.

'Father Emperor, by saving the life of your grandson you have brought honour for our family for many generations. The Qing dynasty will surely survive for many centuries!'

After two hours, the ground was littered with the blood-stained corpses of mountain goats, rabbits, foxes, deer, and wolves. Fresh and bristling with life at dawn, the land had become a field of death in a matter of hours.

'Good. Now the inferiors can hunt,' the emperor stated. He moved into an enclosure on a hillock led by his grandsons. *'Everyone may hunt.'*

A great cheer sounded. Metal daggers and swords clinked while horses whinnied and beat their hooves on the ground. A few sure-footed animals tricked their pursuers and broke through the circle, only to be caught by other hunters waiting under cover beyond. Two solemn men, ignoring all other game, walked towards the centre of the field.

'Who are they, I wonder?' I said aloud.

'Tiger hunters,' Hong Li answered proudly. 'The bravest men of all.'

The emperor suddenly turned to Long Ke Duo. 'Zhen does not see Yin Zhen or Yin Yi. Find them and serve them with care.' Long Ke Duo called to several guards and rushed off.

As if conjured up by the tiger hunters, tigers suddenly charged into view, magnificent creatures, huge and muscular, fur gleaming, moving with long strides. Behind came the two missing princes, pursuing them on foot. The eighth-born prince, Yin Yi, fired a shot into the air. One of the tigers turned abruptly and charged at him. It leapt, its giant paws outstretched, but the eighth-born prince shifted position nimbly and drew out his long sword. With a shout, the prince held his position and plunged the sword into the tiger's stomach. The animal gave a terrifying howl of pain, rolled over several times, and lay floating in its blood, its legs twitching.

The fourth-born, Yin Zhen, watched the dying animal before he turned and charged after the second animal. This tiger was bigger than the other. It ran to and fro, whipped into a frenzy by the crowds and the rank smell of death in all directions. The tiger hunters moved closer and motioned those of us around them to form a circle. Even the emperor joined the circle, but he forbade his grandsons to leave the enclosure. The tiger's eyes were awash with panic and confusion. He crouched close to the ground, snarling and spitting, his ears flat on his skull.

The hunters pulled their swords out but held them at their sides. The fourth-born son stripped off his fine outer garments until all he wore was a fine short silk robe. He took a small silver dagger from its sheath, and holding a shield in his other hand, Yin Zhen entered the circle and slowly edged towards the animal. His eyes had narrowed into tiny slits. With the knife taut in his right hand and his shield protecting his body, he twisted to the side. He approached until he was no more than ten paces from the tiger. The tiger sniffed the air and lowered his head, then raised it with a roar and a snarl. The tiger's front paws ploughed huge ridges in the soil.

Yin Zhen inched forward with a cold, tense glare. He slowly placed the shield on the ground, never taking his eyes off the tiger. Standing up, he faced the tiger, legs planted apart.

The tiger dropped to the ground and changed the position of his ears. He seemed to mewl. The fourth-born prince walked up to the animal's face and stood above him, legs apart, dagger close to his eyes, until the tiger put his head on the ground and wiped his face with his huge paws, a subdued creature. The emperor turned and looked towards his grandsons with a relieved smile on his lined face.

Suddenly Yin Zhen knelt down and plunged his dagger into the animal's throat. We all gasped as a fountain of red blood shot out. The tiger fell onto his side, clawing the air, choking and flailing until he died. All eyes turned to stare at Yin Zhen while he calmly cleaned his knife and walked away from the limp animal. A pool of blood fanned out in all directions.

'Grandfather,' a young voice broke the silence. 'Your hand is shaking. Is everything well with you?'

'Yes, Grandson. I am well enough.'

The emperor walked stiffly towards Yin Yi. He pulled out his own sword and offered it to him. Yin Yi knelt as he accepted it. 'Thank you, Honourable Father.' With a broad smile, he shouted as he held the sword aloft and turned in a circle. 'May our emperor live ten thousand years.'

The emperor turned to Yin Zhen. 'I am pleased that you are unscathed.' Yin Zhen lowered his head and nodded sharply.

The hunt lasted for twenty days. The quantity of dead animals was indescribable. Howls of fear and pain and the smell of death became part of my waking and sleeping hours. We had turned Eden into hell. I hardly saw Jin Kun, who seemed pale and withdrawn, or Little Brother, who seemed to find the entire occasion a great adventure, or Paolo, who was busy from morning to night working with all the doctors and other practitioners.

Our camp sprawled across a large plain. Scores of animals were barbecued over huge spits every night. The hunters and soldiers ate greedily, drinking and singing rowdily. The sky and hills, illuminated by the flames, looked like angry wraiths glaring down at us.

One night an anxious servant appeared at our tent and begged me to follow him quickly to the emperor. Jin Kun was waiting for me outside the emperor's tent. We entered together.

'The Mongol nobles invite us each year to a grand celebration,' the emperor said to us. 'It is held for three days and nights at Zhang San Gong. On the final night, Zhen will host the feast and plans to present a large scroll to commemorate our years of co-operation and friendship. This is your task. The scroll should convey the wonderful celebrations at Zhang San Gong as proof of the excellent relationship between the Manchus and the Mongols. It must be finished by the evening of the third night. Zhen orders you to leave in the morning for Zhang San Gong. My son Yin Zhen will accompany you. The rest of us remain here for another four days. You have one week to complete this painting.'

We departed before daybreak. Yin Zhen and Jin Kun nodded at each other without uttering a single word. The entire day's journey, with two silent companions, loomed before me.

At mid-morning I broke the silence. 'Your Highness. How did you know that the tiger would not strike you? You put yourself at risk and caused the emperor great worry.' I winced as my question didn't quite come out as I wanted it to.

'My father emperor worried?' He snorted. 'If that is so, I cannot be considered a loyal son, can I, Missionary Lang? In reality, his fears were unnecessary and I was never in danger. Tigers are like men. When they see you are braver and more determined, they admit defeat and seek your protection.'

'Your Highness, please forgive this stupid servant. The tiger relented; it humbled itself and acknowledged you as superior. Why did you kill him?'

'A tiger is always a tiger. Better to strike first and eliminate any possibility of a future attack. I do not believe in allowing danger to exist close to me or my family.'

'Does this philosophy apply to people as well?'

'Naturally. I would not hesitate to kill to protect my country, my emperor, or my family.'

Zhang San Gong was already a city of tents when we arrived and preparation well under way to feed, house, and entertain twelve thousand people.

Jin Kun and I began work immediately. 'This may be your first commemorative painting, but I doubt it will be the last. I advise you to learn well the lessons I teach you here,' Jin Kun said as we began to discuss the layout of the long scroll. 'A painting such as this one is composed of three parts: land and nature, people, and mountains. Each element must be beautiful and harmonious, but man is the feature that binds the parts together.'

The fourth-born prince sat quietly for hours watching us work, never disturbing us. At first, I was uncomfortable with his presence, but soon hardly noticed that he was there.

Soon the structure of the painting was complete even before the majority of the hunting party arrived—mountains in the background, a large, sprawling camp, and trees, rocks, and bushes in the foreground.

Once the camp filled up, we painted without rest, incorporating many aspects of the celebrations: wrestling matches, acrobats, dancers and musicians, soldiers bathing and playing, the emperor presenting medals and titles, troops arriving and departing. We worked rapidly using fine brushes and pens.

Jin Kun admired my use of colours and I marvelled at his skill with landscapes and calligraphy. Little Brother offered to help, but it was obvious that his interest had been captured by the hunters and soldiers. When I told him we did not need him, I watched him skip away with the carelessness and delight of youth.

The scroll was twenty-four Chinese feet long and six and a half feet high. It was an extremely ambitious and, to be honest, tedious work. We painted over five hundred horses, eight hundred soldiers, one hundred officials, scores of artists, servants, saucepans, water buckets, trees, and flowers.

'I never wish to do another painting like this one,' I said.

Jin Kun chuckled. 'That is a wish that will not be granted. Pray instead that you find pleasure in them.'

When the emperor came to collect the painting, I was ready to collapse and Jin Kun's face had a green tinge to it.

'Really excellent. Royal Painter Jin, Missionary Lang, you are both outstanding. Zhen is very pleased with you.'

'Ten-Thousand-Years-Living Emperor, all the credit is due to Painter Lang. My miserable self only assisted. I am honoured to have had the opportunity to work with him on so great an undertaking.'

'My colleague is being too humble. He is a great painter and an inspiration to all. Your slave only worries that this painting is not good enough. If Your Majesty is pleased, then your slave is lucky enough for three lifetimes.'

15

In the middle of December, by which time we were back in Beijing, announcements were posted throughout the capital: '*The dragon's body is not peaceful.*'

One week later, new announcements, signed by Long Ke Duo, prime minister, cousin, and confidante to the emperor, carried the sad news that Ai Xin Jue Luo Xuan Ye, the second emperor of the great Qing dynasty, had departed for heaven, bin-tian.

The Kang Xi emperor's reign was over—sixty years after it had begun. Few people remembered a time when he was not their emperor. Wherever one walked in Beijing, people were crying.

Soon after the notices were pinned up, an exhausted Paolo reappeared at home. I hurried to fill a plate with hot food for him and boil the kettle for tea.

'The emperor's collapse was severe,' he explained while he picked at his food. 'He never opened his eyes or made a sound after his heart attack. Though he still breathed, he was no more than a shell. The worst heart attack occurred on the nineteenth. Two days before he died, Long Ke Duo ordered me to leave the emperor's bedside but forbade me to leave the palace. I wasn't permitted to see him again, either alive or dead.'

I hesitated to ask the question that had been on my mind since the first news of his illness had been released. 'Do you have any idea who will be the next emperor?'

Paolo shook his head. 'The Forbidden City is a bleak, ominous place, full of soldiers loyal to various princes. Everyone speaks in whispers. While there are those who grieve, most are preoccupied with the issue of the succession.'

On the fifth day after the emperor's death, a great commotion in the streets drew us out of the church grounds. Soldiers were pasting notices on walls and everyone was shouting something about a new emperor. We surged forward with hundreds of other curious souls, squeezing to find a place to read the announcements. Those who could not read were pleading with others to know what was written.

Taller than many, I shouted out the news to Jesuits standing behind me. 'The new emperor is the fourth-born prince, Yin Zhen. His reign is to be called Yong Zheng. The reign formally known as Kang Xi is now too sacred to be uttered, so in death the late emperor is to be known as Sheng Zu. Yin Zhen's mother has been renamed Virtuous Concubine and her new title is the empress dowager.'

Paolo dug his fingers into my arm. 'I must pray for your safety,' he said.

'Surely we are too insignificant for him to concern himself with us?'

'You do not understand the nature of this man if you believe that.'

A few days later, more posters informed the capital of the emperor's final hours and how the new emperor was chosen. Paolo stood with me while we read. I could feel his body tremble though he did not dare utter a sound in public. '*Four days before his death, the Emperor sent Yin Zhen to the Tian Tan palace in his stead. He was asked to carry out a special ceremony requesting a good harvest in light of the Emperor's grave illness. In the early hours of the twentieth of December, the Emperor summoned several of his sons, third-born, fifth-born, eighth-born, ninth-born, tenth-born, twelfth-born, and thirteenth-born: Lord Yin Zhi, Governor of Chun Yin You, Baron Yin Yi, Marquis Yin Tang, Governor of Dun Yin E, Marquis Yin Tao. With his sons present, he presented his will to the eminent Long Ke Duo to be read aloud: "The fourth-born son, Yin Zhen, of valuable nature and deep loyalty, has the ability to rule the country. He is the successor of my crown; he is to assume the position of Emperor."*'

Inside the church, Paolo shook his head in disbelief. 'This version of events is impossible. The emperor was in a deep coma.'

The entire city was an unsettled, worried place. Rumours abounded in the Chinese and foreign quarters. Did Yin Zhen make a secret deal with the powerful and inscrutable Long Ke Duo? Did they change his father's will? One senior missionary was adamant that the emperor died before any will was written and that, together, Long Ke Duo and Yin Zhen forged a will of their making.

Yin Zhen was not ignorant of the rumours. He called several foreign dignitaries to the palace.

'I gave no thought to the succession,' he told them, not yet using the term *Zhen* to refer to himself, 'but when my father emperor passed his authority to me, I could not refuse. Until the day he died, I was ignorant of his choice. Had I known while he was alive, I would have refused the honour. There is at least one who believes he can usurp the crown for himself. These ideas and rumours are not in the best interests of the country or its people and must be stopped immediately. For the sake of China, any further discussion of my legitimate claim to the throne will be dealt with severely.'

Yin Zhen was officially enthroned. Though hardly known by ordinary people, Yin Zhen was nonetheless unpopular. The celebrations, simple as they were, were empty and joyless. Many Chinese whispered that the fourteenth-born prince would arrive in Beijing any day as if they believed he would either clarify the situation to their satisfaction or change it.

'Why is Yin Zhen not trusted? Why do so many ordinary people, who have never met either prince, prefer Yin Ti over Yin Zhen?' I asked several Chinese friends, but no one had a satisfactory answer.

Three weeks after the death of Xuan Ye, we were drawn outside again by shouts and the sound of running feet. *It's the fourteenth-born prince. Yin Ti. Yin Ti.* We followed the noise until we could see plumes of soldiers' helmets bobbing as they rode closer. Blocked by a wall of people, we craned our necks and searched for Yin Ti. What a large army, we commented.

Then a wave of shocked stillness swept along the length of the street. The only sounds were horses' hooves and the creaking wheels of a heavy carriage. As we watched, a wooden cage appeared. Inside, dirty and bloody, sat the fourteenth-born prince, his neck, hands, and feet bound in chains. His head hung down, his face covered by his long hair.

The troops hastened him through the city, followed by a horde of people, until they reached the tomb of his father, the late emperor. The soldiers opened the cage and roughly dragged out Yin Ti, a man who could have been their emperor. Gasps and murmurs of pity erupted all around me. A large gap opened in the crowd as soldiers shouted and shoved people aside. Pulled by chains attached to their arms and legs came two more princes.

'Those are the ninth- and tenth-born princes,' Paolo whispered.

The door to the tomb was heaved open by several strong soldiers and the three were pushed inside. The soldiers slammed and bolted the door.

'*Disperse!*' a commander called out and motioned his soldiers to advance upon the crowd. We moved away like terrified sheep, still in shock at what we had witnessed. Like the foolish man who believes the impossible cannot happen, I had been taught a lesson.

Paolo spoke quietly to me as we walked back to our church. 'Yin Zhen will use Antonio's relationship with his brother to destroy both of them. He is very opposed to our Christian aims in his country, but, more than that, for some reason, he has long mistrusted Antonio. I suspect that Antonio was privy to princes' secrets when he taught them mathematics, secrets that Yin Zhen wished to be kept within the family. It did not help Antonio that he made such a point of preferring his brother over him. Damn Antonio for risking your neck as well as his.'

'I must go to him.'

'Giuseppe! Stay away from him.'

'I'll be all right.'

I ran to Antonio's house. The door was ajar and I stumbled on him kneeling before the crucifix, deep in prayer. I knelt next to him, too breathless to speak.

'I know,' Antonio said with his head still lowered, his face drained of colour. 'A eunuch warned me several days ago that Yin Ti had been arrested. Before the emperor's death, it appears that Yin Zhen and Long Ke Duo dispatched messengers to a senior general who was on an inspection tour of the northern border. Long Ke Duo wrote that Xuan Ye was aggrieved to hear that Yin Ti had been plotting against him. On behalf of the emperor he ordered the general to arrest Yin Ti and bring him here as quickly as possible.'

The fourteenth-born prince was tortured and interrogated. Each day information oozed out of the Forbidden City about the crimes he confessed to. In the telling, his crimes and guilt grew larger and more indefensible. Whether people believed the confessions or not, his reputation was shattered.

One morning when we came out of our church after morning prayers, Wang Rong, the gentle eunuch who was our first model in the life-drawing classes, stood at the door waiting. I did not recognise him at first in the disguise of a common servant but knew his voice when he called my name.

'Painter Lang, please listen to me. I do not have long. Your friend, Father An, is in great danger. I have come to warn you so that you can save him. He must flee or he will surely die.'

'What do you mean?'

'The fourteenth-born prince has this morning admitted to collusion with Father An. If he had been named emperor he would have promoted Christianity in China and may even have considered publicly converting to Christianity as an example to his people. He admitted he was a Christian believer and had been baptised with a few drops of your holy water. Father An will be arrested shortly. I came here as quickly as I could and must return before my absence is noted. I am sorry for you all,' he called as he ran off.

Sick with worry, I ran to find Antonio. I did not need to say anything. He was sitting in his house as if he were waiting for something.

'There is nothing I can do now. I am ready to face whatever is coming. This transgression was not a sin. God will understand my desire to try to put a Christian emperor on the throne of China.'

'Come. We must disguise you immediately. You must leave before the soldiers arrive. Hurry.' I pulled his arm but he was rigid. Tears stung my eyes. 'You must save yourself!' My voice screeched. 'You must let me save you. Hurry. Please. I beg you. For me. For your brother.'

He faced me with eyes that did not see. 'This is God's will. It is the price I must pay for…' He could not finish the sentence.

'For what? There is nothing you could have done that can justify your death.'

'Oh, Seppe. You who are unable to lie cannot imagine the lies one can tell. I seek nothing other than a righteous death to cleanse my sins.'

16

Wang Rong fears he has exhausted me and departs. I take off the necklace I wear hidden around my neck and clutch it in my hand. On a long chain, a small Buddha hangs. It is all I have left to remind me of my long-lost friend. My servant looks at me sympathetically. Having helped me bathe and dress for many months now, he is well aware that I wear it as well as a heavy gold cross, the symbols of two very different religions hanging together.

Antonio gave me this necklace on the night before his execution. It had once graced the neck of a woman he had loved, a Tibetan princess. The story of his illicit love had shocked me when he revealed it, but once he told me the story his anguish eased. The guilt he had carried around for so long was far heavier than any man should bear. When I saw how deep his love for her had been and how much he had suffered by her death, I could not help but forgive him his sins and pray that she would be waiting for him in heaven. Afterwards, he was very clear-headed and calm, far more so than I. He made me promise three things.

'Promise me, Seppe, that you will give this necklace to a woman you love. Don't look askance. Not every love of a woman leads to the sin I committed. Promise me that you will protect my diaries and get them safely to Rome.'

I waited for the third promise. His hesitation worried me.

'Promise me that you will live, that you will do whatever is necessary to live, and to serve this emperor with your entire being. I believe in you. If any Christian can reach into his heart, it is you. From the moment I met you I was convinced you had been blessed with compassion and sincerity. It makes people love you.'

I fought that promise. I told him that I would detest this emperor until the end of time, but he was adamant. Numb, I gave in.

I fulfilled two of these promises. I hope that God will not judge me too harshly for breaking the third and keeping the necklace.

The soldiers came for me as well several days later. I was dragged before a scornful Long Ke Duo, told to prepare myself for interrogation, and released. Paolo, Jerome, and David were beside themselves with worry. I know they prayed for hours and tried to think of ways to help me. They seemed to accept that there was nothing they could do for Antonio. I lost nights of sleep wondering if he was being tortured and worrying about how I would react when the same was done to me. The saddest face of all was that of Little Brother, who was approaching adulthood.

'Am I to lose you, too?' he asked with angry eyes. 'You who have been brother and father to me, who have given me guidance and inspiration for all these years. Jin Kun warned me this would happen. Do you realise you have endangered him as well, since everyone knows that he is your friend. You promised Wu Yu to look after me.'

I tried to put my arms around him but he pushed me away and left the house.

In a fitful dream, I heard the voice of Su Er Qing bidding me farewell. He was handing me a letter. *Do not open this letter now. If you are ever in grave danger, you may use it, but use it wisely. . . .*

I leapt from my bed and searched among my things. Within the pages of a book, I found the sealed letter. Inside the first wrapping was another with a few characters handsomely drawn: *'Please give this letter to Prince Yin Yi.'* The eighth-born prince, the tiger slayer, had suffered none of Yin Zhen's suspicions. He had been embraced, named the Jian Qin Wang, the relative closest to the emperor, and promoted to a senior ministerial position. I thanked the Blessed Mother.

'The Prince is unable to see you,' the servant said to me.

'Please show him this letter,' I said. 'I'll wait for his reply.'

He returned after a few moments.

'Prince Yin Yi says that he is well aware of the problem. He can say no more at this time but he begs you to leave immediately.'

On the day of my interrogation, I arrived at the Forbidden City. I was led to the cultural palace where two and a half years earlier I had been asked by the Kang Xi emperor to think of a plant from Italy that might nourish his people in times of famine. Where I had sat and drawn three sweet potatoes, I saw the fourteenth-born prince standing. His head was bare, his face white, his legs shook, and his entire body quivered. The ninth- and tenth-born princes cowered beside him, also hatless. Their faces were wretched. There was no sign of Antonio. No one had seen him for two weeks.

In the middle of the hall, Prime Minister Long Ke Duo sat erect. His face was expressionless. He was flanked by many princes, including the eighth-born. Behind them, partially hidden by screens and a bamboo curtain, sat another man, who, I assumed was Yin Zhen.

I entered and kow-towed to Long Ke Duo.

He wasted no time asking his first question. 'Missionary Lang, do you know you are guilty?'

What to say? How to answer?

'Your slave does not know what he is guilty of. Please, Prime Minister, tell your slave what he has done. If he is guilty, he will certainly admit the truth. If he is not, he will patiently accept your judgement in these matters.'

'If this is how it is to be, we will give proof for you to see.' Long Ke Duo waved his long hand. Servants rushed forward, carrying an object.

'Missionary Lang, stand up. Remove the cover.'

I got off my knees and took the deep blue cloth away. As my portrait of the fourteenth-born prince was revealed, I heard the princes mumbling in surprise, sucking in their breaths.

'This is a painting by my miserable self.'

'Do you know now that you are guilty?'

'Master, I still do not understand. Please tell your slave.' Once more I knelt upon the ground.

'You are a clod with a lying mouth. Smack his face. Loosen his tongue.' A heavy slave ran up to me and raised his thick hand, giving me a vicious clout below my ear. Then another. And another. Blood filled my mouth and poured from my nose. I wiped blood across my sleeve. It trickled down my throat.

'Master, hitting your slave is useless. I have admitted that I painted this picture. But your slave is such a worthless creature that he is too stupid to understand what offence he committed.'

'Missionary Lang, when did you come to our great country?' It was a different voice, that of the new emperor. I bowed low before speaking.

'Your slave has already been here for seven years.'

'And shortly after you arrived, the late Emperor Sheng Zu gave you a title, Painter Awaiting Royal Commands, and, later asked you to establish an art school in the Forbidden City. It is hard to believe that you still do not understand our Qing dynasty regulations.' Yin Zhen spoke very slowly and carefully, putting extra emphasis on 'regulations.'

I said nothing.

'Yin Ti, speak and enlighten Missionary Lang what transgression you made.' The new emperor snarled at his brother.

Yin Ti found it hard to speak. 'I…was not allowed…to wear the armour and helmet of my late Father Emperor Sheng Zu. Even though it was a present from him to me.'

'Father Emperor Sheng Zu gave you armour. He did not give you power over this nation. Yin Ti, you had the dream of becoming emperor. That is why you had the gall to strut in this armour and have it painted by this missionary.' Yin Zhen laughed coldly.

Everything Paolo had feared was coming true. If it should serve Yin Zhen's purpose, I would die as a conspirator. My life hung upon a fine balance.

'Missionary Lang, do you now know why you are guilty?' Long Ke Duo persisted.

I thought before I answered. I was a child of the streets and had learned my lessons well: say no more than is asked for and reveal no more than is necessary.

'Your slave knows.'

'Missionary Lang, when Yin Ti asked you to paint this portrait, did he say anything to you? You are required to tell the truth. Who else was present? What did you talk about?' Long Ke Duo continued.

Yin Ti had been tortured. Antonio probably had been as well. I chose my words carefully.

'This slave is but a painter. If a prince asks me to paint a portrait, I do so. For this picture, there was no special arrangement. On that day, apart from the prince, my colleague Father An Dong Ni was present.'

'According to your school schedule, you were meant to teach that day and the next and the next. It obviously was important enough to you to abandon your students for three days to paint Yin Ti's portrait.'

I felt as if a bucket of ice water had been dumped over my head. Jin Kun had obviously already been questioned. Was he all right? How many more lives could be affected if I answered imprudently?

'Your slave was ordered to paint this portrait. A prince's order must be obeyed.'

'Fine. Let us assume it was as you say. At the Tian Tan grounds, what did you discuss? Tell us everything, missionary, or, I warn you, your skin will rip and your bones will crack under torture.'

My heart pounded. I sailed into mist, relying on instinct. 'I did not participate in their discussion. I was at least ten feet away. I heard nothing. There was a wind that day.'

'So Father An did not share this discussion with you later?'

'Never.' The mist was thicker. I did not know I could lie so easily. The faces of the people at risk welled up in my eyes.

Long Ke Duo issued another order.

My beloved brother Antonio was pulled into the hall like a wild animal. His robes were covered in blood. His hair was matted. Welts, bruises, and lumps obliterated his handsome features. I fought the urge to run to him and clasp him to my breast. It was heartbreaking to see him thus. Through his pain, he looked around for me. His eyes met mine and a flicker of light shone.

'Father An,' Yin Zhen began, 'on the day this painting was made, at the Tian Tan palace, did Brother Lang join in your discussions?'

'Although I had known Brother Lang for several years, the fourteenth-born prince was not at all familiar with him. If we had things to discuss, how could I expect him to do so in front of a stranger?' Antonio's words were slurred. His voice was raspy.

Yin Zhen continued his examination. 'Yin Ti, when did you meet Missionary Lang?'

'At the same time as you,' his brother replied falteringly. 'When Missionary Lang arrived in the capital. Our Father Emperor Sheng Zu invited the new missionaries to the Chang Chun palace for a banquet. Last year, in the eighth month, I returned briefly to inform our father of the situation on the border and ordered him to paint this picture.'

Yin Ti lifted his head. He looked at his brothers one by one. Many of them flinched under his gaze.

'Ai.' Yin Zhen nodded his head up and down. 'So, Yin Ti, I ask you, apart from hatching your secret conspiracies together, if you were a loyal son, when our Father Emperor Sheng Zu had many times ordered the cessation of Christian activities, when our father so loved you, why did you insult him and betray our ancestors, stir up trouble with the people by leaving the correct path and taking up relations with these missionaries?'

Yi Ti stood taller, wincing as he did so. He took a deep breath and spoke carefully, looking from brother to brother. 'I did it for this land, this culture, our history.'

The princes stirred and murmured.

Yin Zhen snorted. 'Eh, that is very good. I am waiting to hear you talk. In front of your brothers, explain your great enterprise clearly. I do not want to be called a murderer behind my back.'

'Good. I wish to have the opportunity to explain. When our ancestor took the throne of China, he was not the first Manchu to rule here.' Yin Ti paused, taking a long breath. 'Four hundred years ago, our ancestor Emperor Hu Bi Lie made the Yuan dynasty strong. But our ancestors who invaded China were ultimately absorbed by Han culture. They did not recognise the importance of changing the three-thousand-year-old Han culture, of influencing it. The result was eleven emperors in ninety-eight years. Our ancestors lost the country for one reason: force alone cannot rule a nation with a strong culture.'

'Ridiculous.' Yin Zhen spit out the words. 'The great Yuan dynasty was lost because Emperor Shun was corrupt. After the Red Scarf Rebellion, Zhu Yuan Zhang founded the Ming dynasty. It was nothing to do with culture.'

'You are wrong!' The fourteenth-born prince raised his voice. 'All the princes share the same ambition. For the honour of our ancestors, we want to stay here in this rich land. We do not want to be defeated by the Han. To do so, we Manchus must have our own beliefs, our own religion with which to rule. With our own religion backed up by our might, we may tame this country. The Han themselves say there are two tools necessary to successfully govern a nation. One is the use of force. The other is the presence of a respected culture. Without the basis of a strong unifying culture, we cannot hope to rule over the Han. A form of Christianity, coupled with Confucian ethics, can do that. I have seen—'

'Nonsense,' Yin Zhen interrupted him. 'Do you really believe that Christianity has a place in this country? It has not saved the countries where it is strong. The history of Christianity, as I have learned it, is full of war and persecution. Is this what you want in China? People turning against each other because of a foreign religion? Never! To suggest it is immoral and traitorous.' The bamboo curtain was wound up. Yin Zhen's face was red with anger and his eyes glowed.

'Father An, this is your work. You wish to undermine the foundations of Chinese and Manchu beliefs and substitute them with your own. Ultimately, you and your kind wish to make China a fiefdom of your pope, to destroy it and plunder it as your nations have done in other lands.'

'No. We are not after territory,' Antonio answered. 'We do not want to rule any people. In the eyes of the Lord we are all His children, we are all one. There are no borders to His kingdom. We are here to save the souls of His children. Once people take the words of our Lord to heart, then the kingdom of brotherly love will be established on earth. He will offer you salvation. There will be no more evil. No more killing. He will walk once more among us.'

Yin Zhen was indignant. 'You speak the words of the devil. You Christians dare to say there is a formless father and a divine son we must pray to. In China, the emperor is the Son of Heaven. There is no other. Your religion speaks of a final day of judgement. This is yours. You are sentenced to death for spreading the devil's religion in order to confuse the masses and for plotting with Yin Ti to kill the father emperor and imprison the princes in order to snatch power.'

Yin Ti tried to speak, but his head was pushed downwards and his arms pinned behind his back.

'Come,' Long Ke Duo shouted to soldiers. 'Take the condemned to the street.'

The court emptied.

Long Ke Duo looked at me. 'You are free to go, Missionary Lang. The emperor gave orders that you were not to be punished. This time.'

I was left completely alone. I knelt down and prayed, bereft, wondering how I could find the courage to go on living.

Help me, Blessed Mother, to find the strength to forgive myself and those around me who do evil.

The fourteenth-, ninth-, and tenth-born princes were tied together with long poles and put in the back of a large two-wheeled carriage. The fourteenth-born prince wore the stained Jesuit robes and hat of Antonio. Antonio was tied in front of them, dressed in the sullied robes of the fourteenth-born prince. My portrait of Yin Ti was tied to the very front of the carriage and the carriage was wheeled through the streets. The commotion in the capital was enormous. Crowds gathered to watch the shocking procession and to stare at my painting. Many missionaries too witnessed the shame.

This was the second time my work was used to stir the public.

The fourteenth-born prince was not executed. He was locked away in his father's tomb with his brothers, the ninth- and tenth-born princes, all kept alive as a warning to any other ambitious prince.

Yin Zhen decided that Antonio should die by fire, a highly unusual form of execution. He gave no reason for his choice, and we were all too numb to think about its significance.

On the night before his execution, the eighth-born prince arranged for me to see him. The jailer removed his yoke and brought him a meal and a large jug of wine. Antonio was cold and frightened. I held him close to my chest. He pulled away and handed me a necklace with a small Buddha hanging on the chain.

'This was hers. She is dead, Seppe. I could not save her. My guilt is great. God has punished her to show me how great my sin was. I have tried to live as a good Jesuit since her death. I only pray that my death will cleanse my sins and that I may sit with God for eternity.'

'Antonio, who are you talking about?'

He covered his face with his hands and cried as if they were tears he had bottled up for a long time. I stroked his back and shoulders until he calmed down. Finally, he began to talk. 'On my first trip to Tibet, I met the king, Lazanghan. He had a niece, Dan Zhu, who was the most beautiful creature I had ever seen. We studied Buddhism together and she taught me the Tibetan language. In time, we became more than friends; we became lovers.'

His face changed when he spoke of her, of her beauty and gentle manner and her knowledge and passion for her culture. I had no doubt that this love was genuine but it was also a terrible sin.

'It was very difficult to leave her,' he continued, 'and return to Beijing, but I promised her that I would return and make a decision whether or not I would remain a Jesuit.'

I was shocked at what Antonio was telling me, but, somehow, not surprised. Paolo had long suspected that Antonio carried a heavy secret. Once more he was proved right.

'When I returned to Tibet, the war had begun. There was nothing for me to do, Seppe. Lazanghan, her uncle the king, was already dead, and Dan Zhu had disappeared. No one knew where she was. I assumed she had been murdered. While I was staying at the Potala palace, it came under siege. Negotiations were useless. In March, the palace fell. I was captured with three other missionaries. We were brought to a camp of a powerful Mongol commander.'

Tears began to fall down his cheeks. I wiped them with a handkerchief. 'Go on, Antonio. You must get this off your chest,' I urged him gently.

'I heard the commander asking another soldier if we were Christians. I answered him in his tongue. He was impressed that I knew his language. The dead lay all around. He began to taunt me. "I hear that you monks don't touch women. Tibetan monks are also forbidden to take wives. But they are like all men. They cannot live on vegetables alone. They need meat sometimes. There's a woman behind that tent. High class. She spits at me and calls me names. I have an idea. You go into that tent and prepare the meat for me. You take her first. You get her used to a man and I will let you go. You will be free to continue your valuable work saving our souls. Is that not a worthy trade?"

'I refused. And said many things to him, begging him to be kind to the woman. Suddenly a voice called out: "Antonio!"' It was Dan Zhu. She was alive! I called back to her and leapt towards the tent. The commander was startled and I almost made it to the tent before soldiers beat me down. As they held me, he walked around me, stroking his chin and thinking. I didn't know what to say. Dan Zhu was frantically calling to me. I shouted to her. I prayed to God to save her, to take me but to spare her, not to punish her for my sins. The commander laughed viciously and issued orders. I was tied to a flagpole and gagged. The commander sneered over his shoulder as he entered the tent with three other soldiers.

'She began screaming horribly, calling to me to save her, while they violated her. I struggled to free myself but to no avail. My hands were cut. The screams ended abruptly. The silence was even worse than her cries. The commander came out of the tent and threw a necklace at my feet. It was the small

Buddha necklace that I am giving to you. "The bitch wasn't so strong after all," he said. I was dragged into the tent and forced to look at her soiled body. Her eyes were open as if locked in disbelief, and tears had stained her face. Her hair was spread out like the wings of an angel.'

How had he kept this secret for so long? Without hesitation, I took it upon myself to absolve Antonio of any sins that he might meet death with a cleansed soul. My only wish was to help him find comfort in his last hours.

'Our Lord Jesus Christ, who hath left power to his Church to absolve all sinners who truly repent and believe in Him, of His great mercy forgive thee thine offences. And by his authority committed to me, I absolve thee from all thy sins. In the Name of the Father, and of the Son, and of the Holy Ghost. Amen.'

'Thank you, Seppe. Thank you.'

The next morning, Christians of all sects were allowed into the Forbidden City. We crossed the moat and passed beneath the outer walls. In front of the inner walls was a huge pile of wood. The emperor had selected the large courtyard before the Noon Gate so that he could watch this death without ever leaving his palace. Hundreds of members of the court stood along the ramparts looking down upon us.

The execution ground filled with priests, friars, and brothers of all beliefs knelt in prayer. Hundreds of soldiers surrounded us to ensure that we did nothing foolish. Antonio was brought from another gate. Guards pulled him from the carriage and led him to the huge pyre. The Portuguese bishop and our rector asked if they could hear his last confession. Soldiers held his arms while the two prelates performed the rituals that should have taken place in the privacy of his cell. As he was tied to the stake, my eyes met Antonio's. As the fires were lit, he mumbled a prayer while looking at me, the *Anima Christi*: *Soul of Christ, sanctify me. Body of Christ, save me.*

We all joined in.

Water from the side of Christ, wash me.

O good Jesus, hear me.

Let me never be separated from you.

Our voices rose into a crescendo. Smoke stung our eyes. I could no longer see Antonio clearly.

From the malicious enemy, defend me.

Bid me come to you,

That with your saints I may praise you

For all eternity. Amen.

I thought about all the saints who endured death by fire. One stood out on this dreadful day: Eulalia of Merida. She was a young girl of twelve who lived in Spain. During the harsh persecutions of the Romans against

Christians in the early fourth century, she protested to Emperor Maximilian. To test her loyalty he asked her to pray to idols. She refused and he sentenced her to death. She faced her death bravely, despite her youth. According to the stories passed down over the centuries, in the midst of her ordeal, a white dove flew out of her mouth and snowflakes fell on her body to ease the pain.

Behind Antonio's head, high up on the ramparts above the Noon Gate, Yin Zhen stood watching the fire consume Antonio. Gasps came from all directions as flames suddenly surged several feet high. The wood crackled louder and the tip of the fire seemed to lick the sky. I could still make out Antonio, standing erect, showing no pain. Perhaps his soul had already departed. He never cried out. Maybe Jesus comes to us in moments like this, to fill us with the joy of forgiveness, to explain the mysteries of divine purpose at the instant of greatest sacrifice.

Suddenly fire consumed his body, his hair, his mouth, eyes, and ears. I was certain I saw flames in the shape of a dove circle his head. Ashes rose and fell around his shell of a body like snow. Mercifully, it was over quickly. His body vanished, and he was only a memory to keep alive inside my head.

Later, we buried a small jar with ashes gathered from the pyre in the Jesuit cemetery that contained the tomb of Father Ricci. Antonio was surrounded by three of the greatest Jesuits who ever served in China. A simple stone marked the dates of his life and death. We carved an epitaph: Jesuit Father, Teacher and Martyr.

While all the Christians present at his funeral prayed that his soul would find eternal rest on the right side of God, I prayed that his tombstone would last forever. I wanted to pray for revenge, but knew how much that would displease God. Instead, I silently intoned the words uttered by the first Saint Ignatius before his martyrdom in AD 107, words that often gave me peace when I thought none was possible.

"I am God's wheat. May I be ground by the teeth of wild beasts until I become the fine wheat bread that is Christ's. My passions are crucified, there is no heat in my flesh. A stream flows murmuring inside me; deep down in me it says: come to the Father."

Part II

How Solitary the City

'For these things I weep; mine eye, mine eye runneth down with water; because the comforter is far from me, even he that should refresh my soul;

Lamentations: 16

1

Many times I tried to thank Wang Rong for his concern for Antonio but he shook his head and hands and said over and over, it was nothing, do not embarrass me.

'I too lost a friend,' he finally blurted out. 'Brother An was a special man. He taught me many things. He treated me as a man despite my position.'

Wang Rong never revealed more. I watch him now as he transcribes my words about Antonio's death. My eyes are poor, but they still see the streams of tears flowing down his cheeks.

A young baby lies asleep in my arms. His parents are somewhere in my house. Everyone refers to him as my great-grandson. His grandfather is an old man now as well, the man I used to call Little Brother. He visits me every day and calls me 'Father.' How I treasure him, a loving soul who has been part of my life since he was ten years old. Without any fanfare, he has been a lodestar. Because of him, I became a brother, father, teacher, and mentor.

I place my hand on the face of the sleeping infant and caress the soft skin. He sighs and trembles as he falls into a deeper sleep.

Within days of Antonio's execution, soldiers hustled the Portuguese bishop and our rector away to the port of Jiao Dong Wan where they waited until a ship bound for Europe set sail. In addition, the three largest foreign churches were closed and any pending requests for new missionaries were denied. The emperor banned any preaching of the gospel and decreed that attempts to convert Chinese subjects were now punishable with imprisonment or death. The majority of missionaries expected to be expelled in the coming months.

Little Brother, without articulating his fears, anticipated the worst. He treated me as if I alone were to blame for the emperor's anger. I endured his silence and his angry glares. I wanted to offer words of comfort, but he spurned my hesitant overtures. One night he failed to come home at all. Like a distraught parent, I wandered around searching for him, distracted by how redolent with poignant memories each lane and teahouse was.

I ran into Jin Kun. 'Have you seen Little Brother?'

'No. Please, I'm in a great hurry.' Jin Kun glanced from side to side, unable to look directly at me.

'If I am forced to leave, please look after Little Brother.' I called out after him.

He turned his head to reply. 'Do not worry about him. I will continue to teach him and help him as long as he needs.'

As I walked away, he ran back to me and blurted out, 'But if you are expelled, he will never get over the loss of your presence.'

One month after Antonio's death, Paolo, Jerome, and I were summoned to the Nei Wu Fu, the Bureau for Managing the Emperor's Affairs, where we were informed that we had been pardoned and our former posts had been restored. Unfortunately, our dear companion David Webster had been expelled. David joined a new mission in Maynilad, the capital of a country known to the Chinese as Lu Song Guo, a collection of islands named the Philippines, after the Spanish king, Philip II.

Little Brother's manner changed immediately. He hugged me. 'I know I behaved foolishly. I'm sorry.'

'I know what you were feeling. It was just as difficult for me. We merely had different ways of showing it.'

'I will go with you wherever you go. Just remember that.'

'Little Brother, someday you will fall in love and make a new family. That is the way of things.'

'And we will live together. All of us.'

There was no point arguing with him. I was relieved to see his humour and good manner return.

He was the only one who broke through the depression I suffered over Antonio's death. He began luring me back to normalcy by using our old games of reciting poems line by line and, in doing so, stirred hidden voices and emotions. '*Gazing in all directions*,' he said at one point and waited. It was a cunning choice. Words of wisdom from Wu Yu, temporarily misplaced, emerged, bringing inspiration and purpose. How could I fail the old painter who had taught me so much about life and art? '*The mountains are so small*,' I replied.

A new era, a new emperor, and a dramatic change in the Christian community combined to give form to nebulous ideas long playing in the recesses of my mind. I was now a transplanted hybrid, born in one place but educated in another. I prayed that Wu Yu, of all people, would have agreed with the path I was about to chart—one of a new art style, never seen before.

I loved charcoal and coloured chalk, using washes to create soft studies imbued with powdery delicacy. Watercolours, chalk, and Chinese ink mixed, matched, and blended opened new avenues for me. I began experimenting with oils and tempura on silk and found that, by treating the silk with a special wash, I could paint with tempura once more. The colours of my native Italy appeared on Chinese silk. It opened up enormous possibilities for solidity, depth, and realism in portraits and landscapes.

The winter was bitter and made almost unendurable by the location of the studio for 'Royal Painters' and lowly 'Royal Painters Awaiting Commands' such as me in the Forbidden City. The Qi Xiang Palace was a vast, draughty space unprotected by nearby buildings. The single stove was powerless to heat it. My feet and hands were incessantly red and painful. It was both an inauspicious place and season for the birth of my new style. Jin Kun, Leng Mei, and Tang Dai, my daily companions, all talented painters, encouraged me to continue developing my ideas. They also took an interest in Little Brother and taught him many of their techniques. Under their tutelage, his skills soared. I rarely saw Paolo, as the emperor kept him close by. Jerome preferred to work alone outside the Forbidden City.

Our new rector, Father Ignatius Kogler, a mathematician and head of the Astronomical Board, was a kind man with an intelligent, perceptive mind. He was small and lively, reminding me of a busy terrier on the scent of something interesting. He had a habit of appearing unexpectedly as soon as an idea came into his head. His enthusiasm was infectious and his good humour a breath of fresh air.

'For the sake of our mission you and Brother Jerome should advance to a higher rank of royal painters,' he told us one evening after dinner and prayers. 'The emperor appreciates sophisticated, delicate pieces of art. He was delighted with a small enamel pot given to him by French priests. He is a man of great contrasts, a tyrannical ruler but a true patriot. Though he appears to be dour and severe, he is dedicated to conserving and supporting his nation's arts and culture. Very few of us have any contact with him any longer. If there is to be any improvement in our status we must rely on the handful of Jesuits who he retains in his personal circle.'

'Your idea is a good one, but I cannot believe the emperor feels anything but antipathy towards me. I came as close to being executed as anyone else.'

'I think you are wrong. The portrait you made of Yin Ti has not been destroyed. I believe he admires the art if not the subject,' Rector Ignatius said thoughtfully. 'He is jealous that you did not paint him.'

'You surprise me, Rector. I believe he keeps me in China only until he devises a way to punish me sufficiently for my association with Antonio and Yin Ti. I await his revenge.'

He sighed. 'Interesting how we see the situation so differently. Let's assume that there is a portion of truth in both these viewpoints. Since we don't know which one of us is right, my suggestion about making something pleasing for him can't hurt, can it?' He looked at me with large, persuasive eyes, and I could not help but smile. He viewed the world optimistically. What a fool I should be not to take a stab in the dark.

I decided to learn enamelling, a skill at which I was a complete novice. I knew only the basic concepts of enamelling: metal on the inside and vitreous glaze on the outside. A Jesuit metallurgist and chemist taught me how to mix flint, sand, red lead, soda, and potash, melting them to produce a clear glass. This was the *fondant,* its hardness dependent on the mix of components. The harder the enamel, I learned, the more difficult to work with but the finer the result.

New terms entered my vocabulary: *cloisonné, champlevé, plique à jour, émail en ronde bosse.* I prepared a base of copper, cut the shape I desired with shears, and formed it with hammer and burnishers before cleaning it with acid and water. With the *fondant,* I added oxides while it was hot and flowing. It was not at all like mixing pigments of paint. I became an apothecary or an alchemist, measuring, experimenting with one bit, adding a dash of this or a bit more of that to produce radically different results. And one could not just paint over mistakes. It took many trials for me to understand how vital it was to maintain a consistent temperature in the crucible while adjusting components, fusing them in some dance of Aristotle's atoms to produce brilliantly coloured enamel.

Having to apply the enamels in their wet condition and wait for each to dry before adding the next colour was a time-consuming endeavour for such small objects, but gradually I improved and went on to try the next level of subtlety, *grisaille* enamels. This required using white enamel over a dark enamel base. The white was enhanced with turpentine, water, and oil. By adjusting the thickness of white applied over the dark background, I learned to create varying degrees of grey. By hatching with a sharp tool, I was able to create relief. I eventually learned to use gold and foil as well since nothing else produced the same impact.

Father Ignatius followed my progress closely, saying very little but grinning and nodding his head as I gained confidence and skill. 'Manchus like tobacco,' he mumbled one afternoon in my studio then moved away, trying to appear nonchalant. 'Wouldn't it be a good idea for someone to make something delicate for their snuff? Something with a Chinese design, of course.'

'Yes,' I agreed, 'someone should.'

The Spring Festival passed and the Lantern Festival. During that time I laboured over two gifts for the emperor, a small oil painting and an enamelled snuff bottle with gold relief. By early May, they were done. The painting, of plum blossoms, was Chinese in its essence though the execution was largely Western. Plum trees are special, producing blossoms while the rest of nature sleeps through the bleakness of winter. On the front of the snuff bottle, which was no bigger than the width of three of my fingers, I made a picture of two mandarin ducks happily swimming in a pond, symbols of devotion and luck.

Rector Ignatius rushed me off to hand the two presents to Duan Shi Lian, the fat eunuch responsible for royal artists. Eunuch Duan assumed the snuff bottle was a trinket to wear around the neck and wondered where the chain was. When I explained its use, he clutched the object, and I feared he would not deliver it. I promised him that I would make a snuff bottle for him if the emperor appreciated this one.

Jerome had produced an oil painting, an exquisite depiction of the Goddess of Mercy, Guan Yin. With his delicate hand, he captured her gentle, watchful countenance yet gave her an angelic and robust air.

Several days after the emperor received our gifts, we were both promoted to royal painters. The post came with a salary, which we passed on to the rector. I had no religious obligations apart from my own prayers and meditation. Kind Rector Ignatius insisted that I keep a portion of it to use as I saw fit.

'I don't know how to thank you,' I said.

'An artist needs inspiration. I've seen the little objects in your house that give you pleasure and it does not worry me one bit,' the rector said. Before leaving my studio, he added, 'Brother Giuseppe, all of the Christian orders have resumed their missionary activities as quietly and discretely as possible. I have decided to exclude you from these obligations so that you may continue painting. If there is to be any repercussion, I want you safe from accusations.'

'Is it wise to risk the emperor's wrath?'

'We are here to spread the word of Jesus Christ. There is no other choice. But you have other strengths to contribute to the mission and I do not wish to jeopardise those.'

He was an extraordinary man, far-sighted and kind. With the regular flow of income, my collection of beloved objects grew rapidly. In addition to brush holders, I added ink stones, ivory carvings, and miniature porcelain figurines. Their delicacy and imaginative designs intrigued me. My most valued ink stones came from Duan Zhou in Anwei province. One end of the oval stone was recessed for grinding and mixing ink, but the other end dissolved into a landscape or scene from a folktale. The heavy stones lay within highly polished wooden boxes, miniature worlds of fantasy and beauty.

'I've received another disturbing letter,' Jerome said. This was in the summer of 1723, six months after the coronation of the new emperor. 'Our society's enemies are swelling in number and they seem intent on destroying us. Jesuits have fallen foul of both the Spanish and Portuguese in South America and we are becoming outcasts in Europe as well. Don't you find it strange that though we are all meant to be doing God's work, there is so much time wasted on attacking each other? The Jansenists are our greatest foes, but no one seems to understand who they are or what they believe in. Pope Benedict XIII listens to their slurs against us. I have begun to fear that it is possible we will be forced to disband.'

'Then if we are forced to return to Europe, it's sure to be a very reassuring homecoming,' I said.

The first year of the Yong Zheng period was memorable. The emperor reduced the bloated administration of the empire, lowered taxes, and implemented a thorough investigation of local government to weed out corruption. He punished those guilty of creating forged documents and false accounts and budgets or of using public funds in any way to support private needs. He released any province or district that suffered natural calamities from its obligation to pay taxes.

On the other hand, his personal insecurities did not diminish. He ordered a loyal follower, Zhang Ting Yu, to write a history of the Qing dynasty slanted for his approval. It led to an inexcusable destruction of historical documents. Any references to Tibet as an independent country disappeared. When Zhang Ting Yu ordered us to hand over Antonio's diaries, we had none to give him. The Jesuits who had left China had long since delivered them to Rome. For a time we feared repercussions, but none came.

The Chinese gods rewarded the good deeds of the new emperor with abundant harvests. Unusual stories circulated of millet plants with two, three, four, or even five heads. The most fertile regions, Guangxi, Guangdong, and Fujian produced three bountiful harvests. The Xian region announced bumper rice and millet production.

To the Chinese, a flower blooming twice, a plant with more than one head, a root feeding more than one stem, a surfeit of seeds, a shell containing more than one nut, or an egg with a double yolk were imbued with divine significance. New ideas for paintings took root in my mind.

An important festival arrived, celebrated on the ninth day of the ninth lunar month of the Chinese calendar. It had many names: Double Nine, Dogwood, or Climbing Chrysanthemum. Its origin was mysterious. According to the fables, a man named Heng Jiang visited an immortal, Fei Chang Fang, to pay his respects. The immortal warned Heng Jiang that a disaster threatened on the ninth day of the ninth month. He was told to sew dogwood stems into a sack and to tie it around his back and climb the mountain with his family, plant the dogwood and drink chrysanthemum wine to celebrate the occasion. Heng Jiang followed these instructions. When he and his family returned home all their animals had died. Each year the Chinese climb mountains to plant dogwood and drink chrysanthemum wine.

Jerome, Little Brother, and I participated in the celebration for the first time. Along with the other royal painters, we left before dawn for the western mountains. After climbing for several hours, we pulled young dogwood shoots from our sacks and planted them. We lit incense and turned towards the mountaintop to kow-tow three times. Pots of wine were uncorked. Our friends sang a greeting to the mountain and sprinkled a few drops on to the ground. We toasted each other and began to drink. Sitting on the ground, either leaning on tree trunks or boulders, everyone took a turn reciting poems or singing a song.

Knowing we were near the spot where Wu Yu had died, Little Brother and I strolled until we found the rock where he had fallen. A chill wind beat my neck and coursed up my sleeves. As I walked, leaves crunched underfoot.

'I believe that man is similar to a leaf on a tree,' I said to Little Brother. 'He emerges as a tender bud and slowly grows, becoming larger and healthier. Spring witnesses his glory and summer his maturity. With autumn, he gives way to age and disease until he falls and decays. Each leaf is unique, the distribution of veins, the colour and shape a secret code. When death comes, experience dies as well. The next generation must begin afresh. The great majority of mankind falls to the forest floor unnoticed. Only a handful, chosen by God, complete their destiny and leave footprints on the tracks of history.'

'I think you are talking about Antonio and Wu Yu,' Little Brother said, 'but it could apply to you as well. You will be long remembered.'

'I don't think so. I have very little to show for my years here.'

'We'll see. I'll remind you of this conversation some day.'

On the journey home, I gathered several plants together for my next painting including double-headed millet stems and a lotus flower. The lotus roots itself in the mud of a shallow pond. Its stem passes through murky water to produce a large bloom that floats on top of the water. And by some quirk of nature, lotus leaves are always clean despite the muddy surroundings. Among scholars, when a friend becomes an official, lotus seeds are sent as gifts to remind him to preserve his virtue no matter how sullied his milieu. The pronunciation of the characters for green lotus and an uncorrupted nature were identical: *qing lian.*

Wang Rong, the eunuch who had tried to warn Antonio, had been promoted in rank and was responsible for the needs of the royal painters. When I discussed the plan of my painting with him, he was enthusiastic.

'Wait here. I will bring you a vase from the national collection.'

He returned with a beautiful, pale green, long-necked celadon vase.

'This vase was fired in the imperial kilns of the Song dynasty. Look at the quality, how shiny its surface is.'

'It is beautiful. I'll base the colours of my painting on this soft hue. Wang Rong, thank you. It's a perfect choice.'

'Oh, yes. I almost forgot. I brought its stand as well.' He pulled out a rich, dark brown support for the vase from a bag he carried around his waist. 'When you are finished, I will personally take it back. If I am fortunate, no one will have missed it.'

'Is this dangerous for you?'

'Not if I say it is for you. The emperor does not hide his appreciation of your work.' Then he asked, 'Royal Painter Lang, may I ask a personal question of you.'

'Of course.'

'Since the death of Father An, you are different. You smile but you are sad. Even in a group of people, you seem alone. It seems to me that, though you have lost a great friend, you have many other good friends. It is possible to commemorate a lost friendship with joy. In that way you share what you have learned from that person with others. You celebrate his life. Forgive me if I have spoken unwisely.'

'No, Wang Rong. You've not spoken out of turn. Yes, I miss Antonio and I am unable to accept the reasons that cut his life so short.'

'Surely he would not want you to be so sad all the time.'

'No, I'm certain he wouldn't, but emotions often have more power than logic.'

'If I am sad, I set aside a few minutes each day to pray about those things I cannot change. The rest of the day is for work and improving the things I can change.

'It's wise advice.'

After preparing the silk, I began by painting a poem in a calligraphic style called the Song style in the right-hand corner of the silk. I could feel Wu Yu's soft, shallow breath on my neck and his voice talking in my ear taking me through every movement of the brush. '*Heng* (horizontal), *dian* (dot), *ti* (left dropping slope), *pie* (right falling slash), *zhe* (corner), *na* (right falling flourish).'

When the painting was done, I placed my name, one character beneath another, and the date, the second year of the Yong Zheng reign, tenth month, tenth day, in the bottom right-hand corner. I entitled the painting *Ju Ru Tu, A Collection of Auspicious Images* and gave it to Wang Rong.

Three days later, Rector Ignatius could hardly wait for morning prayers to end before he leant over and gave me a slap on my back that took my breath away. 'The emperor is overjoyed with your painting. He was impressed at the subtle message of fortune and purity you portrayed and praised the excellent skills you have developed. He said that, as a European, you challenge the rules that have governed Chinese painting for hundreds of years.'

Though such praise should have warmed my heart, it did not. I had never seen any warmth in the emperor's face. The only images I retained were those of a man with cold, calculating, hard eyes, which never gazed upon his father with affection, nor on his own children. I had often heard that he favoured his eldest son, Hong Shi, above all others, yet I had never witnessed his eyes light up when any of his sons entered his presence. In my mind, this emperor was a bitter, vengeful man incapable of mercy or forgiveness, and I wondered when I would feel his wrath.

My next painting was also of flowers, dominated by double-headed peonies. Wang Rong brought me another of the national treasures, a square-sided Ming vase with a lattice-work carved mahogany stand. Peonies, like chrysanthemums and plum blossoms, were national flowers. They symbolised prosperity, dignity, luck, tenderness, and beauty. Again the emperor was overtly pleased and eloquent in his praise.

The officials of the Nei Wu Fu, the Bureau for Managing the Emperor's Affairs, did not hide their disapproval of my new status—a European held up as an example for Chinese artists to emulate. Fortunately, the other royal painters took no offence and the attentions of another prince further ensured that the officials of the Nei Wu Fu kept silent. Often while I was painting, I heard a rustle of satin. Even before turning around, I knew who it was: Hong Li, the young fourth-born son of the emperor. 'Have I disturbed you? Keep working, Royal Painter Lang. It pleases me to watch you. My father emperor is very appreciative of your talent.'

He frequently stood with his chin raised and his hands linked behind his back, a slight smile rising from the corners of his mouth. 'If ever I become emperor only you will paint my portrait.'

My third painting for the emperor was entitled *Song Xian Ying Zhi Tu, The Pine, Hawk and Glossy Ganoderma,* . In it, a watchful white hawk perched on a crag set in the midst of rushing water. Beside the rock stood an aged, knurled pine tree. The richest colour came from deep red *Ganoderma lucidum,* treasured mushrooms that grew among the rocks. I employed a flat light over the scene so that the background faded away. The rushing water in the lower third was highly stylised, while the pine tree was painted in great detail to reveal age and strength.

The hawk gazed out across the landscape with intelligent eyes, turned slightly to the left so that his right wing was in shadow. The pronunciation of the character for hawk was the same as that for hero. The pine tree, reputed to live for almost one thousand years, represented long life. The *Ganoderma lucidum,* said to be the food of the immortals, represented eternal life.

Wang Rong insisted on delivering the painting to the emperor on his birthday.

'Zhen wishes you to make a painting each year for my birthday,' the emperor announced when he sent for me. 'And the subject must be clever, like this one, an animal or bird that reminds an emperor of his duties.'

Later, I went to visit Antonio's grave. I sat for a long time contemplating the changes since his death. My life had been much simpler when I was able to divide things into good and bad, safe and dangerous, and friend and foe. The Chinese say that everything has shortcomings and everything has merits. I was finally beginning to understand the adage.

On a bright, brisk day in the autumn of the Yong Zheng emperor's third year on the throne, there was a loud knock on the door to our house. Before Little Brother could reach it, the door was flung open and a smiling Chen Yuan strode inside. His wife followed, smiling shyly while cradling a bundle tenderly in her arms.

'Chen Yuan! A child. How wonderful. Congratulations.' I leapt up and gently pried apart a nest of blankets until I revealed a peaceful, sleeping, angelic face.

Chen Yuan sniffed. 'Don't bother. It's not a son. Nothing to celebrate. She is lucky that I have not yet drowned her.' He glanced sharply at his wife, who looked crestfallen at her husband's criticism before turning his attention to Little Brother.

'Can this be Jiang Shan Min? When did he become a man?'

'He's twenty already. He's become a respected artist as well,' I said proudly.

Little Brother put his hands together and bowed his head. 'I'm honoured to meet you again, Merchant Chen. Big Brother and I talk about you often. He believes that your experiments will save the lives of millions of Chinese.'

'Bah! I begin to doubt that we will ever succeed. These eight years have been most difficult. Perhaps the gods are angry with us for trying to thwart the whims of nature; they appear to keep putting new obstacles in our path. Each year we find a new problem: one year it is the soil, another year the timing of planting the crops. Weather is our greatest enemy. Too little rain, too much, too cold, too hot. The emperor asked me to come personally to the capital to make a report. Out of one mu, the land only yielded a sparse thirty jin. The harvest is tiny in comparison with what we can achieve with other crops—millet for example.'

'What does the emperor say? He is not one who likes to hear bad news.'

'Yes, I agree, but I gave him several fan shu to taste. Our ten-thousand-years-living emperor was very pleased. He asked me to continue the trials and ordered the Treasury to give me thirty-two catties of silver. What other choice does he have? There is no one else who is trying to help put an end to starvation. Look.' Chen Yuan dropped a large bag on the table. 'I have brought some things from the country to give you.' He reached into his cloth sack and pulled out a huge clump of red dates. 'I am now a northern country bumpkin. Wah, here are a few fan shu. Taste them.' He pulled out three tiny sweet potatoes, the size of duck eggs.

'You will succeed. I'm certain of it.'

'May I see the baby?' Little Brother had moved closer to Chen Yuan's wife and was speaking to her in a quiet voice.

She handed him the infant.

'She's so light,' he said with his eyes wide open and a big grin across his face. 'Look, Big Brother, isn't she beautiful?'

The baby had woken up. She stared at Little Brother with round, curious eyes while her hands darted in all directions. I opened the blankets further and marvelled at the miracle of young life, hardly the length of my forearm. She was fat and glowing with health. I could not take my eyes off her tiny features, miniature fingers, nose, mouth, and wispy eyelashes. Suddenly, with a gurgle and a smile, she clasped my index finger.

'What strength in those hands. She's looking at you, though,' I said to Little Brother. 'I think she wants your finger but captured mine by accident.' He brought his free hand closer to her face. She immediately threw my finger away and grasped his, trying to pull it toward her mouth. Little Brother began to laugh.

'I have fallen in love. Now this is the sort of woman I can understand.'

'I should have drowned her,' Chen Yuan muttered under his breath.

'Why? Because she is female?' I could not disguise the surprise in my voice.

He waved his hand. 'I try to be tolerant. So what if the first child is a girl, I keep saying. My wife's father and her mother are most displeased. They keep insisting that I drown her.'

Little Brother moved closer to me until his arm touched mine and he nudged me. 'You would really consider taking her life?' I asked Chen Yuan. 'Are you insane? You're neither poor nor ignorant. I don't believe you.'

'Eh, Child's Mother.' Chen Yuan barked at his wife. 'Take the baby from Little Brother and feed her. Leave us in peace.'

I stared at him in disbelief. Could this be the same man who spoke so eloquently to Xuan Ye about saving the lives of peasants? A man who could devote his life to helping others but was willing to take the life of something that was his own flesh and blood?

Chen Yuan said nothing until his silent, sad wife had disappeared into another room. His voice was gruff and belligerent. 'Ai, you do not understand our reasoning. The period until the infant is weaned is long. Perhaps one year. A woman cannot fall pregnant during that time so it delays the next birth. I am not young and must have a son. Apart from her mother, no one else will miss her.'

'Big Brother, we must do something.'

Little Brother's imploring eyes spoke volumes. I hardly had time to think before words tumbled out of my mouth.

'I cannot stand by and listen to you talk like this. Give her to me. I'll raise her. Somehow, we Jesuits will raise her. And give her a good life.'

'Really?'

'Yes, really.' What had I just said?

'I will help!' Little Brother raised his voice. He was too respectful to show anger to Chen Yuan but his face was flushed with emotion.

Chen Yuan was silent for a moment. Then a smile spread across his face. 'This is excellent.' He spoke very loudly. 'This child is adopted by you, but, as you are a busy royal painter, we'll raise her for you until she is old enough to be married.'

I swallowed hard wondering how I should break it to the rector that I was now an adoptive father to an infant girl.

'Now that we have settled this matter, I'll take my wife to the Forbidden City. There she will touch the nails of the High Noon Gate. Though it is not the correct time of year, I hope that by rubbing them she will produce a son next time. 'Oh,' he said, flicking his hand, 'I almost forgot. Since you are now her father, you might wish to give this ya tou a name. Do not think too hard about it. Any name will do.'

I could feel my cheeks burning. 'On the contrary, it will be an honour to choose a name that is worthy of such a beautiful child. *Min*. Yes, that is good. The *min* that means to have an intelligent, agile mind.' I watched to see if he approved. He shrugged in a nonchalant manner. '*Xue*. That can be her other name. The *xue* that means to be educated. She will be known as Chen Xue Min.'

Chen Yuan shook his head vigorously. 'No. No. That will not do. A girl must not be educated. Who would marry her? I suggest *You*. It means to be young and naïve. You Min.'

'What do you think?' I asked Little Brother. 'Together the two characters give an image of someone eternally young, innocent yet eager to learn, forever fresh.'

'It's very good,' he nodded.

'Then so be it,' Chen Yuan announced before calling to his wife.

She came into the room with her hand across her mouth trying to conceal a smile. She raised the tiny creature above her face and giggled. 'You Min, precious daughter. You now have two fathers and a big brother, lucky girl.'

Chen Yuan walked over and kissed his daughter gently on the forehead. 'You Min, what a good name.' My mouth dropped open at the change in his manner. He smiled warmly at his wife and nodded his head with a satisfied smirk on his face.

'You cunning fox. You have been tricking me. I was ready to choke you.'

'What are you talking about?' He looked at me with innocent eyes. 'Wife, do you have any idea why he is so upset?'

She giggled and handed You Min to me. 'These foreigners are very unusual people.'

'Why couldn't you have simply asked me to be her uncle or guardian? Why make me so upset?'

'Were you upset? Was that what you felt? Then I am most sorry.' Despite his words, his eyes twinkled with triumph.

Chen Yuan left as abruptly as he arrived. It took me awhile to comprehend what had occurred. Never would I forget the intense rush of protectiveness that had surged through me, albeit with Little Brother's prodding. He had thrust upon me something I could never have had on my own, a brief sensation of fatherhood, of nurturing a newborn. He had obviously thought long and hard about how to thank me for playing a small part in his destiny. What do you give a man sworn to celibacy and poverty?

Little Brother closed the door and turned to me. 'You lost a great friend but now have gained a daughter. Perhaps the cloud that has hung over your heart can lift. It would please us all to see you truly happy again.'

I was surprised at his words and the emotions hidden within them. 'Have I neglected you?'

'No. You have been a brilliant teacher and brother, but I know how much more you can accomplish when you are happy.' I could hear exasperation in his voice. 'If only Paolo were here, but we hardly ever see him, not since the emperor became so dependent on him. He could explain what I am trying to say. We've talked about it. You are producing brilliant paintings, but they are lifeless. You have neglected to put your heart into your art and Wu Yu would be very disappointed.'

'How can I be joyful when others have suffered so much?'

'Big Brother, why must you feel guilty for the actions of others? You cannot change what has happened in the past. You have hidden a large piece of your heart and have forgotten where it is buried. I want you to find it again. We all want you to.'

In the late autumn, leaders of Christian missions were summoned to the Yuan Ming Yuan estate. I was also ordered to be present.

I had never seen Yuan Ming Yuan, but I had heard much about it. The Kang Xi emperor had chosen the site for a second summer palace and began constructing pavilions and gardens in the latter part of his reign. Though it lay closer to Beijing than Chang Chun, he never felt as at home there as he did in Chang Chun. His son was exactly the opposite, ignoring Chang Chun and spending several months instead at Yuan Ming Yuan. Like his father, he often said that a country estate was a haven to bi xuan ting zheng: avoid noise and pay attention to politics. Though frugal in most respects, he made no secret of his desire to enlarge and develop the estate, once the official three-year period of mourning for both Xuan Ye and for his mother was over. The emperor's mother had died shortly after the succession. Only one of her two sons attended her funeral. Yin Ti remained locked in his father's tomb.

The emperor met us all in a building called the Great Morality Mansion.

'Despite my threats and orders, you still dare to convert the masses. From Guangdong province, disobedient priests prowl the coast, seeking to beguile my subjects. In Shandong, churches disallowed for preaching have been converted into orphanages and charity schools, but Zhen is not fooled. Church properties are merely a pretext for other purposes. Outside the capital, under the excuse of caring for orphans, you seek to pervert the souls of my people.'

Rector Ignatius and other leaders tried to speak, but the emperor refused to listen.

'All European Christians have wild, evil natures, seeking to conquer what they do not understand. You want to change our ways, to make us like you when we don't want to be. You obey a pope thousands of miles away who knows nothing of our culture. Zhen's anger at your behaviour will last many generations. Zhen will pass his antipathy towards your leaders to my children and they will tell their children. China will *never* be a country governed by Christians!'

Every priest trembled at his words; the threat behind it rang in our ears. We had found no methods in China to spread the words of Jesus Christ. Time and again we were blocked by any number of obstacles. Perhaps we would all finally be expelled.

The emperor's face suddenly changed. On the surface he appeared to be smiling, but I perceived a sneer, the same scornful face he had worn after he had slain the tiger, a face that spoke of self-satisfaction at doing the unexpected and causing pain at the same time.

'Royal Painter Lang, step forward. You send art that pleases Zhen greatly. Why are there not more like you? My son Hong Li sings your praises.' He looked around the room. 'My government would welcome more men of this calibre,' he announced.

I blushed deeply and lowered my head, wondering what he really meant by his words. Rector Ignatius sighed with relief at my side.

The emperor surprised us again by agreeing to consider two requests that had been submitted several weeks earlier. He re-opened two churches and released two Jesuit missionaries from prison. As I rode back to Beijing, I tried to empty my mind of everything but plans for a new painting.

3

The emperor's anti-Christian sentiments had severe consequences for Chinese Christians, who were ordered to give up their new religion. Amongst them were my treasured friends Su Ge Lu and Su Er Qing. Su Er Qing had been my first Chinese teacher, had given me my Chinese name, and had welcomed me into his household for a few days during our journey many years ago from Macao to Beijing. His father, a wise, perceptive, unforgettable man, had provided my introduction to Wu Yu. They steadfastly refused to renounce their religion, and the cost of their adamantine faith was death.

A few days before their execution was to take place, the emperor granted Su Ge Lu's request to be attended by Christian priests in his final hours and after his death. He also announced that he would select the priest from among the many who served the court, and he chose me.

The Su family were Manchus and relatives of the emperor, but that had not spared them his wrath. Why did this tragedy arise? He had long known that they were Christians but had left them alone. It was only when he decided to destroy another brother of his that they became pawns in a lethal game. And why did he decide to trap another brother? No reason, merely another attempt to prove his legitimate right to the throne.

The story of what ensued came to us in pieces told by many different voices. Those who bore witness felt compelled to unburden their sense of guilt to Christians, particularly those who knew the brave and noble family. No matter what their rank, whether they were officers in the royal troops or labourers who scrubbed the prison floors, they came to us. An emotional thread wound through all the pieces of the story: horror that such honourable people could be treated so cruelly. Many used the words 'Accept our ten-thousand-fold pangs of sympathy for these courageous people.'

Their fate had been decided when the emperor dispatched a trusted commander to Kaifeng with orders to find out if his brother, the eighth-born prince, was a Christian. When he reached Kaifeng, the emperor's emissary announced that Christianity, the religion of the devil, would be stamped out. He peremptorily searched several houses before turning his attention to the one household that was his prize. Many people warned the Su family and begged them to hide their Christian bibles and crosses, but they refused.

Su Ge Lu was the most prominent figure in the province. He had wealth, land, status, and royal blood. Christianity had taught him and his family the importance of good deeds. They opened charity schools, distributed money to the needy, and established almshouses, all rare acts of generosity. The local people honoured them as best they could. The family could hardly walk the streets, as they were constantly beset by townspeople who kow-towed and demonstrated their thanks. They gave the same reply to each: 'Thank God himself. We are hopeless sinners. All the glory belongs to Him.'

When the emperor's commander arrived at the Su family's house, he ordered the soldiers to strip the house bare, which they did with enthusiasm. They ransacked the storehouses and burnt the fields. In the Su family courtyard, a mound of forbidden objects formed an enormous pile: Bibles, crucifixes, rosaries, hymn books. In a startling short space of time, generations of hard work were obliterated and the proud family entered the class of the homeless and destitute.

Su Er Qing and Su Ge Lu were taken to jail, where they were kept without sleep and questioned incessantly, but they held fast to their beliefs. There was only one question to which the emperor wanted the answer: which prince was their confidant? They refused to implicate any prince and reiterated their devotion to all of the emperor's brothers, sons, and nephews and to the great Qing dynasty.

The emperor sent his favourite son, the first-born prince Hong Shi, to Kaifeng. Hong Shi, a sheltered, shy man in his early twenties, was very different from Hong Li, the son of the emperor I knew best, who had an instinctive appreciation of the ways of the world well beyond his young years. Where Hong Li was hungry for knowledge, Hong Shi spent little time thinking. Hong Shi accepted the artificial conditions of palace life as normal and had little experience with ordinary people. Perhaps that was why the emperor loved him so—he was no threat.

Hong Shi arrived in Kaifeng to find silent streets and roads lined with cold eyes. People kow-towed but stared with undisguised resentment. He asked questions and learned things that disturbed him greatly.

In a bold act, Hong Shi wrote to his father and pleaded for clemency for the Su family. Despite their Christian leanings, he argued, they were loyal subjects and performed many good deeds for the city. He described how lowly his noble Manchu cousins had fallen, how they were forced to beg for food.

The emperor's response was immediate. Riders raced back to Kaifeng with his reply and posted his orders throughout the city. '*All guilty members of the Su family will be brought to the capital to be judged and punished. For defying an Imperial ban against practising the foreign religion they are ordered to wear heavy chains and yokes and to travel in cages for all to see.*'

The lao bai xing, the ordinary people, crept up to the prison and whispered words of comfort. They covered the ground of nearby lanes and alleys with white paper flowers. The commander ordered the streets to be swept, but every night the white flowers returned.

When Lord Su, his wife, and sons were placed in the cage to begin the sad journey, the streets were full of silent people. Some went so far as to wear white funeral clothes and break vases.

The commander of the royal troops ordered the arrest of the most blatant mourners. As the soldiers rushed forward, a large group of men, women, and children appeared. Leading the group was the beautiful young former fourth concubine of Su Ge Lu, dressed in white, the woman whose beauty and tranquillity had captivated me during my brief stay in Kaifeng. At her signal, the group knelt before the soldiers who stood looking at each other.

'Who are you? Who dares stop an escort on an imperial mission?' asked Hong Shi.

The fourth concubine put her hand on the bridle of the prince's horse. 'Your Highness, we are one hundred members of the Su family and its household. We come to beg you for mercy. By making our patriarch and his sons travel in these conditions, you may cause their death. It is possible, is it not, if they are healthy, that they may have the opportunity to speak to the emperor and prove their innocence? He may even relent and pardon them. If, by this treatment, they are deprived of the chance to defend themselves, you will have taken our dearest relatives from us.'

'Death is what is coming to them. It doesn't matter if it's now or later,' the commander hollered.

'Do you believe that?' She continued to look at Hong Shi.

'They are worshipers of an evil foreign religion. We have no time for discussion. We must leave now.' The commander looked at Hong Shi.

'Please. One moment. Look at this.' The fourth concubine unrolled a scroll she had been holding in her other hand. 'Your Highness, the numbers who have converted are large. Will you take us all to the capital in chains?'

While the prince read the scroll, the commander dismounted and approached the fourth concubine. 'Do you wish to die, stupid woman?'

She did not answer.

'There are many names here. Which is yours?' Hong Shi asked.

The commander was impatient. 'We can arrest her whether her name is there or not. She is inciting the masses to delay our departure. They all disobey an imperial order.'

She turned and faced the prince. 'I became a believer many years ago but did not receive a Christian name. When Grandfather Su was arrested, I asked his official wife to give me a Christian name. Look here, at the bottom. This is my name. *Ruth*. It has been signed by the official wife.'

'I cannot believe that you show this to me when you know you may die as a result.'

'This is true, Your Highness, but I have no greater wish than to walk the same road as Lord Su and his sons.' She lowered her head as she spoke. 'I am a member of the family. One of the sons you hold in that cage came from my womb. If I am unable to save their lives, I am resolved to die with them.'

Ruth, the fourth concubine, included among her ancestors some of the first Jews to arrive in Kaifeng during the Tang dynasty. Though they had settled in the city seven hundred years ago and all physical traces of her heritage had disappeared, she was an extraordinary woman. I could imagine her as a descendant of the great Hebrew heroines. She exhibited the same fierce determination, conviction, and courage and deserved the name she had been given. On that day, in the people's hearts, she became known as the lie nu, the female martyr.

The assembled group of Su relatives spoke together while they knelt on the paper-strewn road.

'We are willing to die, your Highness, Commander. Take us to the capital with Grandfather Su.'

'Arrest them all,' the commander bellowed.

'Wait.' Hong Shi flailed his whip in the air.

He walked away and pondered the dilemma alone. When he returned, he ordered the arrest of only eight members of the household: Su Ge Lu, Su Er Qing, a second son, a household manager, a cook, two farm supervisors, and Ruth. The rest of Su Ge Lu's family were released from the cage. Perhaps he believed that his father's heart would be won by Ruth's sincerity and eloquent tongue.

He was wrong.

Hundreds of people followed the prison cages for several miles. Slowly they dropped behind and watched until the entourage disappeared from view.

Lord Su was in failing health, suffering from an illness that caused him to bleed from his bowels. It had worsened during the harsh imprisonment and interrogation. To relieve himself, he required assistance. Loss of blood and illness had sapped what little strength he had. Hong Shi granted permission for Ruth to travel with Su Ge Lu in the same cage. He drifted in and out of consciousness. Ruth held him in her arms. When the rocking of the stiff carriage woke him out of his stupor and he moaned in pain, she held his frail body in her lap and soothed him to sleep. During the journey, Hong Shi often rode next to Ruth and Su Ge Lu.

The emperor personally attended the proceedings at the high court. He questioned Su Ge Lu and Su Er Qing repeatedly about their contacts with his brother, Yin Yi, the eighth-born prince, the one who had helped me at the time of Antonio's trial, but was none the wiser. He was not interested in their religion, only in their contacts with Yin Yi.

The emperor employed a new tactic. He lied to the imprisoned prince, Yin Yi, claiming that Su Ge Lu had revealed the extent of his relationship with him and his treacherous dealings with the fourteenth-born prince at the time of succession. With very little prodding, Yin Yi confessed to whatever was suggested to him. He begged his older brother for mercy.

It was frightening to watch the emperor deal with enemies. He found whatever means he could to destroy their souls, to reduce them to begging, snivelling shells. When the fourteenth-born prince had been tried at the time of succession, though weak in some ways, he showed that he was a principled man. At the end of his trial, when his brother had judged him to be guilty, the fourteenth-born prince had asked for death. The emperor refused his request, choosing to imprison him in the tomb of their father, determined to break his spirit. When the weaker Yin Yi begged for life, the emperor sentenced him to death. He locked him in a small room, telling him to prepare himself for death. Each day he waited, growing more and more terrified. He could not eat or sleep. It did not take long for him to die.

The Su family had served a purpose. They had enabled the emperor to rid himself of another potential rival, though no plot had ever been uncovered. As if to validate the allegations he had never proved, he ordered the eight innocent people to be executed, proclaiming them guilty of collusion with Yin Yi without any evidence other than the voices in his own head.

When the emperor announced that I would hear their last confession and witness their deaths, I was stunned.

'The Su family deserves the highest ranking Christian in the land,' I complained to Jerome and Rector Ignatius. 'Why is he doing this to me?

'Sit down, my son.' Rector Ignatius put his hands on my shoulders. 'Do you remember several years ago, we had a discussion about the emperor? I said I believed he admired you and you argued that he wished to punish you.'

'I remember.'

'I have come to the conclusion that we were both right in our assessment. He truly admires your art, but can never forgive you for producing such an exquisite portrait of his greatest rival, his blood brother. He cannot decide which passion has the stronger hand. He seeks to separate you from your fellow Christians as well—to isolate you. There will be much grumbling among other Christian orders that you, a mere brother, have been given the task of attending to their last rites. The emperor knows all too well what he is doing. He wants you to be devoted to him and him alone, to have no other masters.'

'Should I refuse?'

'How can you? Who knows what he will do? He will not kill you, of that I am sure, but he will punish someone for your insolence and the Su family will go to their deaths without succour.'

'Rector, I don't know that I have the strength to witness their deaths.'

'Then you and I must pray for you to find the strength. I have watched you suffer silently these past few years. Jerome, Paolo, and your devoted young ward have been concerned. I don't know why God has put so many trials in your path, but He has His reasons. There is no doubt that to go on with your life's journey you must overcome your fears and anger and find solace in His love. If you find no truth in what I say then I ask you to follow your own conscience. What does it tell you?'

I looked up when he said those last words. He referred to one of the central tenets of Jesuit thought, one that other orders detested us for. We believed that if faced with a moral decision we should follow our own conscience. We even believed that a man is not culpable of error if he acts on a personal opinion, even if the majority of others believe it is a wrong choice and it most probably is the wrong choice. Those few words, *follow your conscience,* reminded me that no matter how hard I tried to hide, I had responsibilities arising from my bonds to many others.

I sighed and a burden lifted from my heart. The condemned were the first Manchus to invite me to their home and offer the hand of friendship. They had guided me to Wu Yu and thus set me upon a solid path. Whatever I could do for them I would do with my whole being.

However, despite the emperor's decision that a priest would share their last hours, when I went to the prison, I was denied entry. When I protested, two guards pushed me back.

'We have other orders,' they shouted. 'Leave now if you ever want to be able to do anything for these Christian scum.' I stood staring numbly at them as they slammed the gates in my face. Then I returned to the church and gathered several priests for a prayer vigil. We returned to the prison and sang hymns and read aloud all night. The guards left us alone.

In the morning, I returned briefly to our church to change into formal robes, clean and bright. Almost every member of our mission seemed to be present. Many whispered words of sympathy and comfort. Rector Ignatius placed a heavy bible in my hands. 'We are praying that you may be permitted to carry out your duty to the condemned, my son. Though you will stand alone, may you take strength from this.'

I looked at the book. It was a volume of a copy of the famous Plantin Bible. The original and the copies dated to the late sixteenth century, made by Christopher Plantin in Antwerp for Philip II of Spain. The precious copies were brought to China in 1604 by Father Ricci. It was one of the most beautiful bibles ever produced.

'Thank you,' I said to him with tears in my eyes.

'I will go with him!' I heard the voice of Little Brother, a confident man of twenty-two. He was standing at the door of the church. 'How can he endure this alone? How can you expect him to?'

'No,' said Rector Ignatius as he walked over to him. 'If you wish to help him, you do so best by remaining here. Brother Giuseppe will feel your strength with him every step of the way. Go now.' He nodded to me while placing his hand on Little Brother's arm, restraining him.

A horse was provided for me at the prison gates. I waited, surrounded by royal guards. Shortly before noon, the huge gates creaked open. An eight-wheeled prison carriage was pushed out into the road. People lunged forward for a better view. They were excited as if the day were festive, as if it were a carnival. Hundreds of men, women, and children came from all directions, running towards the carriage, laughing and shouting. The eight innocents were taken to Cai Shi Kou, a square reserved for execution of the most common of criminals, south of the Forbidden City.

I followed at the back of the procession. In the narrow streets, bodies pressed hard against my legs. Our horses whinnied and stamped, their eyes wide with fear. We moved slowly, a seething mass melded together. The sounds of hooves, wheels, and shouts echoed off the walls, reverberating in my head. Children threw stones at the wooden cages from upper-storey windows. I begged the soldiers to protect the prisoners, but they shrugged their shoulders.

After an interminable time, we arrived at Cai Shi Kou. The doors of the carriage were opened and the eight filthy prisoners pulled out. With their hands tied behind their backs, they landed awkwardly and fell to the ground, one after another. I could not get close enough to help them up. Large wooden blackboards stating their names and crimes hung around their necks. They were dragged onto a tall platform. At the front of the platform was a levelled tree trunk. Two men dressed in red stood to one side. Their scarlet tops were fastened at the sides. Sharp knives sparkled in the daylight, the tips embedded in the tree trunk.

When the raucous crowd fell silent, I was finding it hard to breathe, and the taste of bile burnt my mouth. Mindlessly, I opened the bible. When I glanced down to see where I was, the page before me was Exodus, chapter 20, where Moses receives the Ten Commandments.

As the official for the executioners shouted at me, images of the past came to me: the excitement on our faces as Er Qing and I had set out from Macao, the scenery on our journey, crabs sunning themselves on Dong Ting lake, the open gate of the Su home, healthy proud parents crying with joy at our arrival, our late-night talk in my halting Chinese, and the tranquil, devout Ruth.

Like an ice-cold statue, I willed myself to move closer and touch each person. A glimmer of recognition and hope shone in their eyes; hope, perhaps, that my words might bring solace. I quickly murmured prayers—Hail Mary, Glory be to the Father—lest the executioners stop me before I finished. I struggled terribly with the prayer for a good death, the Bonna Mores, choking on tears.

'God bless you,' I whispered to Su Er Qing who tried to say something. Ruth's lips were devoid of colour and her chin began to tremble. I put a hand on her shoulder. 'God will protect you now. You have served Him well. He is waiting to receive you.'

Somehow, Su Ge Lu remained on his feet, but I hardly recognised him, so gaunt, ashen, and feeble was he. I again made the sign of the cross over each of them and spoke out loud to God in Italian. 'Lord bless these people and keep them by your side.'

Su Er Qing tried to say something, but it was garbled. He was looking at me but could not lift his head. I saw a gaping wound on his neck and gasped. I looked and saw that each had the same wound, a cut that destroyed a major muscle in the neck, forcing the head of the condemned to drop so that no final shout of defiance could be uttered. As if these people would have done so! Oh, the perfidy of this entire charade!

The Plantin Bible shook in my hand and my entire body trembled. I raised my arms to heaven, holding the bible aloft. It was not to pray, but to wail. *Why, Lord? Why are you turning Your back on these people? Why must these good Christians suffer so much for You?*

A roar rose from the crowd. I turned and saw the heads of the condemned dropping off one by one in a sickening sight of mutilation.

Sickness welled up from my stomach. Tears mixed with sweat and saliva dropped from my face. But the hideousness of the execution was not yet over. Their bodies were not surrounded by light. They were not wrapped in wings of angels. They did not ride heavenward on the backs of eagles. Instead, in the most nightmarish act of bestiality, the crowd leapt on to the platform. I was shoved aside. Men, women, and children carried thick pieces of steamed bread. They jostled to dip the bread in the hot blood of the victims. They stuffed the bread into their gaping mouths, blood dripping down their chins and soiling their clothes. Sickness overwhelmed me. I retched, but my stomach was empty.

For many nights, I was tormented by nightmares. Sometimes when I awoke screaming, Paolo was by my side, checking my pulse or applying poultices. Even his devoted presence failed to exorcise the hideous images that sickened and tortured me. There seemed to be no respite. Paolo mixed herbal remedies that eventually calmed me and permitted deep sleep.

I cannot deny that dreams of salvation, from some unknown source in my soul, restored my sanity and faith. In my dreams Antonio, Su Er Qing, Su Ge Lu, and Ruth were laughing, surrounding me and patting my head and shoulders. I was reluctantly boarding a ship while they stood on the shore, waving and wishing me luck. *It's not your time to travel with us. We are not alone here and we are happy, but you have much more to do before we can be together. There are many who need you. You have much yet to achieve.*

One morning I awoke in a strange room that looked very European with wooden screens and panels, wardrobes, oil paintings, and small bronze sculptures. Even the smell in the room reminded me of Italy. Only when my ears picked up sounds in the street—the strum of the iron harp of the passing barbers, the rattle of the junk collector's shakers, the echo of the hollow drum of the oil merchants—did I realise I was still in China.

Rector Ignatius opened the door and carried in a tray with soup and bread. 'You are confused, perhaps. I have spoken to you many times over the past days, but I doubt you understood. You are in my house. I felt it best to keep you here.'

He knew what I was suffering but did not try to tell me to forget it and forgive. Instead, he showed me the importance of love. He reminded me of its power and its ability to heal the deepest of wounds. He repeated the words of Jesus in Saint Matthew, chapter 22. Jesus had been asked which was the greatest of the Ten Commandments and he answered, 'The first commandment: "Thou shalt love the Lord thy God with all thy heart, and with all thy soul, and with all thy might".'

The second most important duty, the rector reminded me, was: 'Thou shalt love thy neighbour as thyself.' He continued, 'I want to read you this poem. It was written in Spain almost one hundred years ago, in 1628.'

No me mueve, Señor, para quererte
el cielo que me tienes prometido;
ni me mueve el infierno tan temido
a no dexar por eso de temerte.
Tu me mueves, Señor; meuveme el verte
clavado in essa cruz y escarnecido;
mueveme el ver tu cuerpo tan herido,
mueveme tus afrentas y tu muerte.

Mueveme en fin tu amor, en tal manera
que aunque no hubiera cielo, yo te amara,
y no hubiera infeirno, te temiera.
No me tienes que dar proque te quiera,
porque aunque lo que espero no esperara
lo mismo que te quiero, te quisiera.

'I'm sorry, Rector, but I don't understand Spanish.'

'Then I will tell what it says. It says that what moves me to love you, Lord, is not heaven or hell. It is you who move me, Lord; it is seeing you nailed to this cross and mocked, seeing your body so wounded, what moves me are the insults done you and your death. What moves me is your love. Even if there were no heaven, I would love you, and though there were no hell, I would fear you. You do not have to give me grounds to love you, for no matter what I had hoped for, I love you.'

These words hit me very deeply and I began to sense that a great change was taking place.

Paolo arrived and scrutinised my face. 'You look different. Your eyes have lost that guarded look you've worn as long as I've known you. What's happened?'

'I had the strangest dream, Paolo, a beautiful one. Though it may have been a message from heaven, I believe it was a wiser part of me that was talking. When I lived in Europe, I cared deeply for only one person, a priest who saved me from the streets. I never told him how much I cared for him; I don't even know that I admitted it to myself. You cannot imagine what it is like to never know security and love as a child. It makes you wary of being vulnerable. Here, in China, people have entered my life and I have felt such love for them as I never expected to feel. But the pain of losing Wu Yu, Antonio, and now the Su family was so great that I wondered why I allowed myself to care. I believe what the dream told me was that I have been loved. I have seen myself through their eyes and been startled by the view. As if to reinforce that message, Rector Ignatius read me the most beautiful poem on the value of divine love. I know now that I cannot protect myself from pain when my soul is urging me to risk everything for what my heart craves. I cannot deny myself friendship, companionship, or a sense of belonging, no matter what the cost.'

Paolo put my hand in his. 'Most of us don't ever need to ask those questions. Growing up with caring parents, a child accepts love as a normal part of life,' Paolo said. 'You have not had that experience, so your emotional journey has been a long and fraught one. The times in which you live have made it more extreme than it should have been. Of course you are loved and have been loved. How could you not be?'

'I would like to go home now.'

After we returned home, I sat for a long time in sight of Wu Yu's paint brushes and brush holders. Paolo entered my studio and cleared his throat in his special way. It always preceded giving a serious diagnosis to a patient. I turned around to look at him.

'I have one more piece of news. Don't look so worried. Your friends are all safe and well. It's about Hong Shi.' He raised his eyebrows and I nodded for him to continue.

'Hong Shi came to me, after the imprisonment of his uncle and the execution of his cousins, with pains in his head and his stomach. I examined him and asked many questions. In the end, I gently explained that his illness, though physical, was the result of emotional stress. I suggested that he live with Buddhist monks for a time—that a simple life of meditation would help him recover. He said that I was correct, but as the eldest son of the emperor he had other obligations. Shortly after leaving me, he confronted his father and demanded to know why he had shown such cruelty to his own brothers and to the Su family. The emperor was enraged by his son's behaviour. On the spot, he stripped Hong Shi of his royal status and ordered him to be evicted from the palace.'

Paolo's head was down and I noticed that his hair was entirely grey. Deep lines crisscrossed his cheeks and brow. His large, compassionate eyes were dragged downwards by heavy sacs. He had aged. I put an arm around his shoulder and guided him to a chair.

'Hong Shi is a rabbit in a den of wolves. He'll be better off now.'

Paolo grimaced. 'At the doors of the palace Hong Shi took up his sword and plunged it into himself. By the time we physicians arrived, there was nothing any of us could do. He was bleeding profusely and we could not stave the flow. We carried him back inside. He died slowly, screaming in agony. The emperor arrived and stood frozen for many minutes, hardly blinking or breathing. Then he went mad, raging around the palace, breaking and tearing things. For three days and three nights he refused sleep, food, or drink. All the ministers and court doctors quaked before him and were useless. Only on the fourth day was I able to encourage him to take some nourishment and rest.'

'You're exhausted, Paolo. Please rest. The emperor doesn't need a physician. He needs a confessor.'

During the sixth year of the Yong Zheng period, the north of China suffered the worst drought in anyone's memory. For the majority who lived in the capital, the drought was little more than a distant rumour. It aroused few emotions. The emperor, who ruled with a heavy hand, only focused his cruelty upon those he perceived as his enemies. However, as a monarch, he truly cared for his subjects. For two years, he waived all taxation for the northern provinces. He continued to reduce the costs of government and hacked away at corruption. But he knew the lessons of history only too well, how often the panic of famine caused revolutions and changes in dynasties. He beseeched heaven in every way he knew for rain.

It was at this time that the emperor commissioned me to paint a series of portraits to honour his ancestors. He explained the task in no uncertain terms: *If the portraits are worthy enough, my illustrious forebears may favour us and bring rain to parched land. Zhen demands them to be realistic. They must breathe life so that Zhen can implore my ancestors directly for their help. The paintings will be hung in the Ru Gu Han Jin, a mansion Zhen has just constructed at the summer palace of Yuan Ming Yuan.*

It was an interesting challenge, to produce realistic portraits of people who had been dead for decades. The emperor imposed a deadline, an auspicious date, the Ghost Festival in April, the most important day in the calendar for visiting family tombs and paying respects to the departed.

I received permission for Jin Kun and Little Brother to work with me. Though I wanted Jerome to join us, he refused my invitation. He was more and more unwilling to adapt to Chinese imagery.

'No, I am not like you. I am a Jesuit first and an artist second. If I cannot paint the images that inspired me to this religious life, I would rather not paint at all. I have tried to paint flowers and animals in the Chinese style and I feel foolish and ashamed in the eyes of the Lord.'

His words stung deeply, but I said nothing. I tried to become a better Jesuit, painting by day and joining my brethren at night to gather money and supplies for the famine victims. Working at night in the streets of Beijing had its own special excitement. We carried paper lanterns to illuminate our way, not just to see where we were going, but to avoid the sewage and excrement that blotted the ground. Hundreds of flickering lights, carried at different heights, rocked from side to side along the lanes and alleys. We arrived at the doors of prosperous houses with students from our orphanages. We swept their paths and took away the refuse while singing Christian hymns. The gentleman of the house, embarrassed by our presence and vehemence, gave quickly to our cause to hasten us on our way. Our supply of food, old clothing, and quilts grew steadily.

As the weeks progressed, profiteering and hoarding forced the cost of supplies to rise. We had exhausted our possibilities of raising more money in the capital. Without asking for permission from the Nei Wu Fu, the Bureau for Managing the Emperor's Affairs, I asked many eminent Chinese artists to donate paintings that we could sell. Jin Kun, though nervous at such an unprecedented venture, assisted me. Jerome was the happiest I had seen him in a long while as he busied himself producing small masterpieces of biblical scenes for sale to foreign residents, Europeans and Russians.

The emperor grew more agitated with each passing month. He led an illustrious group of officials to the Tian Tan palace to pray for rain. He summoned Daoists from every corner of his empire to chant and employ magic spells, but rains refused to comply.

Having exhausted the entire pot of Chinese religious supplications, the emperor cast his eye upon the bottom of the barrel and summoned representatives from every Christian fraternity to the Forbidden City.

I stood in a corner with other royal painters as the emperor sat upon his throne and gazed around the room.

'Zhen is anxious about the state of affairs in our country. What methods do you have to rectify droughts?'

'Bixia, we cannot ascertain the cause of this prolonged drought. We believe it may have internal causes but we still do not know what. We are studying the problem with great diligence,' a Belgian Jesuit astronomer offered.

'Zhen is convinced that you possess ways to make it rain. To resolve this disaster early is most important.' The emperor glanced coldly around the room.

'None of our scientists is aware of methods to bring rainfall...' another priest interjected, but he stopped when he saw the emperor's back stiffen.

'Does the Bible not demonstrate over and over the power of your god and this Jesus Christ? Did your god not cause a flood? Did Jesus not bring people back to life?'

I could hear mutterings, but no one spoke up.

'Well, Zhen gives you twenty-one days to summon your god. He must bring rain by the Spring Planting Festival.'

There were gasps and shocked mutterings among the assembled Christians.

'You will have the full co-operation of the palace during these days. Whatever you need, you may ask. No one will interfere with anything you choose to do. Does this suit you?'

'Your Majesty, our Bible states—' Rector Ignatius tried to speak.

The emperor stood up and raised his hand to stop the rector. He turned and walked away. We all fell to the ground and buried our heads into the floor.

'Pray for rain,' he said before departing. 'If you succeed, Zhen makes this pledge: some of your restrictions will be lifted. If you fail, Zhen will have proof that your god does not exist, and you will stop all activity in my country and return to your homelands. If any choose to stay, they must forsake Christianity. *This* is a test of your loyalty to the Chinese people. Twenty-one days. That is all.'

While we prayed for rain as the emperor asked, we continued our practical efforts to help the famine-struck Chinese. A large group set out to deliver food directly to distant villages. Because of my commission to paint the ancestor portraits, Little Brother and I left several days later than most, after the ceremonies for the Ghost Festival.

Jin Kun arrived as we were packing our cart. 'I am ashamed when I see how much you have done to help my people when I have done so little. May I join you?'

'Great,' Little Brother answered. 'Hurry up.'

'It will not be pleasant,' I added.

'I know and I will try not to let you down.'

We headed northeast with fifteen carriages and a guard of over fifty soldiers under the supervision of officials from Zhili. The soldiers were Manchu banner men.

Our route led us first through several villages that had already received assistance. People, though thin and gaunt, smiled at us. 'More supplies! How fortunate! The others left many days ago! Hurry! Our cousins are waiting for you!'

'Family ties among Manchus are also very strong,' Jin Kun commented. 'Each village is dominated by one clan. That building over there is a temple and a mausoleum which holds chronicles of marriages, burials, and births. These peasants generally prepare for difficult times by setting aside a proportion of the crops in a storehouse,' Jin Kun added. 'But this drought has been too long. The stores have long been depleted.'

Little Brother read from a dusty sign hung above the temple Jin Kun had pointed out. '"*Honour from our monarch is more important than honour from our family. One can live a full life without a father but one cannot survive a day without our monarch.*" I have never seen such a sign before.'

'They are very loyal subjects whether it is times of famine or not.'

After two and a half days, we reached a village called Zhang Tun. The main road was lined with sagging trees that had been stripped of bark. Not a single blade of grass was visible. We bent down to pick up some soil. It had a sickly yellow hue and immediately crumbled and blew away like dust.

In doorways, people lay immobile like inert puppets, with their flesh hanging loose. No birds chirped, no dogs barked. One old man, barely able to stay upright, struggled towards us.

'Ai ya. There are so many of you. Why do you come here? We have nothing to offer as hospitality.'

A soldier spoke, tilting his head towards me. 'This Christian has come with food and clothing.'

The old man began to cry. He covered his face with large, bony hands on which veins protruded like broken twigs. Still holding one hand over his sobbing face, he tried to tug on the rope of a brass bell but did not have the strength. Little Brother gently took it from his hand and yanked it several times. 'Let me help you,' he said.

A young girl of no more than five suddenly hurled herself along the lane. She saw our group and threw herself, screaming, at our legs. A short man followed, too weak to run very fast. He was dogged by a mad-looking woman, with the remnants of her hair standing up in all directions. She was shouting incomprehensible words.

The child reached up her arms and I lifted her to my breast. 'Save me, Uncle,' she kept shouting. Her face was splotchy and tears poured down her cheeks. I hugged her and stroked her, but she could not be comforted.

The man reached up and grabbed the child's waist, but I did not release her. With screams and curses, the woman hit the man. He pushed her to the ground. He reached again to prise the child away from me, but I moved away.

'Uncle, you cannot give the child to him,' the woman shouted, kneeling before me.

'What is happening?' a soldier demanded.

'He wants the life of my Little Flower.' Hatred shone in her eyes. Her lower teeth were bared and protruding.

The man suddenly lunged for Little Flower. The child anticipated it and screamed. I clasped her tighter as the kneeling woman bit the man's leg and he yelped. 'Kill us both,' she screamed, 'and eat me first.'

Little Brother gasped and placed his body in front of mine. I caressed the terrified child's hot scalp.

The man opened his mouth, which was full of rotten, yellow teeth, and howled. 'You cannot do this. Last night her uncle gave us his child to eat. Now it is our turn to give him Little Flower. You cannot stop it.' He raised his leg to kick the woman. Instead, in his weakened state, he lost his balance and fell.

'We did not eat the child. You ate the child. You are the bastard—the cannibal—the beast!' The woman was crying hysterically.

The commander of our soldiers grunted with anger and pulled his sword out of its sheath. The child's father crawled away from him while scrambling to his feet. He scampered off, glancing over his shoulder with frightened eyes. The wailing mother threw herself at our feet.

'Thank you,' she said over and over.

Starving peasants, walking skeletons, slowly crept towards us from all directions.

'Please give us food.'

Soon there were hundreds of people in the square. Many leaned on the arms of others. When they saw the carriages, they fell to their knees.

'An immortal has come to save us. Look at him. Do not make him angry or he will punish us further.'

I tried to explain that I was a Christian missionary, but my words fell on deaf ears. My light hair, red and gold and unruly, my freckles, and green eyes convinced them I was not human.

'How do we protect the little girl?' I asked the commander of our guards after we had distributed food and clothing.

He thought for a second. 'I will tell the old men and women that you have powers. If something happens to the child, you will know and will bring down such punishment as they have never seen before.'

'But that is a lie.'

'Big Brother, be sensible. Isn't a lie that saves a life permissible in your god's eyes?'

'Not one that gives me divine powers.'

It was Little Brother's turn to make a suggestion. 'I will tell them that we have put a hidden mark on this girl and that someone will return next year or the year after or even later to check that she is still alive. If ill has befallen her, the village will be punished. Is that satisfactory to you?'

'Can we not just say that we will return and expect to find her alive?'

'What is to stop them from substituting another young girl? Without fear of retribution from the gods, she is not safe,' Jin Kun intervened.

I acquiesced and watched the faces of the peasants as Little Brother told the absurd tale, probably embellishing it. I saw them look in my direction and quickly avert their eyes. The expression of panic on their faces was unsettling. When the girl's mother threw herself at my feet in gratitude, it took all my strength to stand still and not denounce the lie. If Chen Yuan could not solve the problems of famine, what sort of life did this child face anyway?

Over the next few days, we passed countryside that resembled deepening layers of hell: decomposing corpses, ravaged landscape, a countryside bereft of small animals or birds. The soldiers continuously buried scores of dead. Those who had not died of starvation were too weak to resist the illnesses that raged, but we had no physicians with us.

Only a few days remained until the Spring Planting Festival. We headed towards a village called Ding Zhuang with our last two carts of supplies. We arrived at dusk. As with all other villages, an unnatural silence hung in the air. There was also a thick, grey fog hanging close to the ground. Rubbish and corpses lay mixed together. Muted moans along the road meant that the dying lay among the dead. It was difficult to see anything clearly. The horses pulling the carts began to whinny and snort with fear.

We heard voices and followed the sound until we came upon many people clustered around a well. They were burning incense and praying kneeling on the ground. One man, wearing a square hat, blew ashes into the abyss while chanting some prayer. My eyes were drawn to two thin, frail children, a boy and a girl, sitting in a bucket poised above the well. The onlookers slowly turned their heads when they heard us approach. My heart sank.

A thick-boned man with a long, ugly face strode over. 'You have no place here. Be off.'

'What are you doing with those two children?' I asked.

'It's not your business.'

Soldiers moved forward and reached for their swords.

'Don't you try to stop us!' he shouted angrily. 'The fortune teller there says that the well god is angry. He will only be appeased after he is given a boy and a girl. Then we will have water.'

The fortune teller nodded to the man holding the rope, who abruptly released the bucket into the well. The children held on, screaming as they plummeted. Little Brother and I raced to the well, peering over the edge. We heard their desperate cries echoing over and over in the chasm.

I turned on my heels and charged over to the man. My rage made my head pound. Large pockmarks scarred his cheeks, visible even in this poor light. I slapped him hard and grabbed him by his ragged clothes. My hand left a red mark on his skin. He was too startled even to raise his hand to rub his cheek.

'Take a look at me.' Cleverly, Little Brother rushed up with a lantern and put it next to my face.

The man gasped when he saw me. 'He is an immortal. Red hair, green eyes.'

People gasped all around.

'I saw the suffering here and took pity on this village. I have brought food. If those children are not brought up immediately, I will leave and send even more misfortune so that you will all die.'

His eyes became globes and he began to tremble from head to foot. 'Forgive me, Immortal. Do not harm us. Quickly, bring up the children. Do not harm me. It's the fortune teller who made us do this. Not me.'

The children were quickly hauled up. I could feel the eyes of every peasant on me. No one spoke. The only sounds were the wails of the children. I walked over to them, cradled by their parents, and put my hands on their heads, muttering a prayer in Latin. 'May the Lord bless and protect you..." At the sound of my prayer, their crying ebbed.

As we walked to the carriages to begin unloading the supplies, the commander whispered wryly, 'You changed your tactics quickly, Royal Painter Lang.'

Little Brother and Jin Kun walked behind me as if they were my attendants. 'Oh, great one,' Little Brother said quietly, 'can you please make it rain so that we can go back to being artists instead of delivery men?'

'I'm ashamed at what I just did. How many more principles will I abandon?'

'As many as it takes to achieve a good end,' Little Brother replied.

At daybreak, while we were still burying dead and helping the sick in whatever ways we could, some children screamed in fear when they saw my features. The adults dared not look at me and kept their eyes downcast. I murmured prayers to atone for my lies.

As we sat down to rest, exhausted and disheartened by all we had seen over the past days, Jin Kun commented, 'We've been awake for almost forty-eight hours. Do you realise that today is the Spring Planting Festival? If it does not rain, what will you do? Will you leave China or give up your religion?'

'I have no idea. I've allowed people to believe that I am a god. What more can I do to distance myself from my religion?' I answered cynically.

I looked up at heaven, my bleary eyes tracing the sky towards the horizon. In the east, the colour of the sunrise and the parched soil blended into one long piece of fabric. A tear appeared in the fabric, bright and penetrating. Another streak followed like a spindly tail of a child's kite.

Everyone stopped and stared. A sound rumbled closer, shaking the earth. *Taboom. Taboom.* The sound of thunder.

Little Brother and Jin Kun turned to me with open mouths and wide eyes.

'It's going to rain,' Jin Kun announced. 'I can smell rain in the air.'

'You see, your god is not angry with you,' Little Brother said. 'He is rewarding your humanity.'

Jin Kun put his hand on my shoulder. 'Perhaps, in this instance, you've been spared from making a painful decision.'

5

It rained for five days and nights, making our journey back to Beijing a trial of obstacles. Three weeks after our return, the emperor issued an invitation to a celebratory banquet to all missionaries who had participated in the famine relief work.

'Zhen wishes to thank you personally for your work among the villages most affected by famine,' he announced at the end of the meal. 'Zhen has received word from clan elders that you brought much welcomed food and behaved with respect and concern for the needs of the lao bai xing. My eunuchs will give you each a present.'

Several eunuchs carrying large baskets walked among the tables handing every missionary a small, round melon. We all looked perplexed.

'This is the sweetest of its kind on earth, a ha mi melon,' the emperor announced. 'They are only grown in Xinjiang province, in the northwest. These are prized because they can retain their taste even if stored for six or seven months. *Ha mi* is a wonderful name for this fruit. A good life is one filled with laughter. *Ha. Ha. Ha.* And your days should pass as sweetly as honey or mi. That is why Zhen is giving these to you. In life, if first we know bitterness, then we know sweetness, how much better than the other way around. Do you not agree?'

No one dared utter a word.

'Ha mi melons have another special feature: the drier the soil, the sweeter the melon. It presents Zhen with a dilemma. Zhen loves these sweet melons, but they come at the cost of dry soil and famine conditions, meaning my people suffer. Zhen is torn between my duties as an emperor and the desires of my stomach. Is this not a difficult choice for a man?'

We stared at the emperor. He looked back at us, beaming. A eunuch came up behind Rector Ignatius. He poked him in the ribs and whispered in his ear. 'Laugh. Laugh,' I heard him whisper.

Rector Ignatius did as he was told. His laughter was hollow. Everyone turned to gaze at him as if he were insane. His eyes rolled, imploring us to join in. We feigned delight and mirth, in a bizarre cacophony of forced laughter.

The emperor clapped his hands. 'Good. Good.'

The laughter immediately died down. We hardly breathed, wondering what would happen next.

'Ai. As a point of interest, Zhen is returning your churches to you. You have my permission to open them. But remember that these churches are only for foreigners. None of my subjects may enter for prayer or instruction.'

I was sitting hunched over a delicate snuff bottle, painting a sleek greyhound sitting on its haunches, using all my concentration to paint the miniature image, when a finger gently tapped me on the shoulder. I leapt and turned with a start.

'Wang Rong! I didn't hear anyone come in. You gave me the fright of my life.'

He was smiling at me as he folded his arms within the sleeves of his robe. 'So, sorry, Royal Painter Lang, you were concentrating so intently that you did not hear me arrive. This could not wait. You are to come with me at once. The emperor demands your presence.'

A groan arose of its own accord. 'What is it now?'

Wang Rong pursed his lips and nodded his head slowly. 'I believe you will be pleased. Do not ask me to tell you anything, however. Our ten-thousand-years-living emperor was very specific with his instructions.'

When I arrived at the court, the emperor inhaled deeply before speaking. 'Zhen has an important birthday approaching and has an idea for this year's painting. Zhen wishes you to use the coloured paint you like so much on Korean silk. It is the finest material. Generally, you present Zhen with a nature painting with only one animal, and Zhen is pleased, but this year Zhen wishes you to paint horses, one hundred horses to be exact. Zhen keeps his best horses at Cheng De. It is an ideal place for them. The leaders of the armies under the Eight Banners send their finest animals to me. Only a few are brought here. Go to Cheng De. You may leave as soon as you wish.'

I hurriedly backed away lest he changed his mind. How my spirits soared at the thought of seeing Cheng De again. I had not been there for many years, not since the last hunt that his father, the Kang Xi emperor, attended a few months before his death. And I would be able to see Chen Yuan and his family.

I counted the months on my fingers, not believing my fortune. It was only July and the emperor's birthday was in December—five months of freedom lay ahead.

Little Brother was bent over a small, detailed painting of a large peony when I arrived at our studio. I noticed he was using pinks and reds and I was pleased. He too loved colour.

'I have just received a wonderful commission from the emperor. It means I will leave immediately for Cheng De and can remain there until December. Would you like to accompany me?'

He looked at me as if I were insane. 'Do you think there is any doubt about my answer? We can see your daughter, You Min. She must be five or six by now. And the sons Chen Yuan has written to tell you about.'

In no time, Little Brother had packed for both of us, hired a carriage, and bought food. He nipped at my heels impatiently while I sorted out my affairs. I still had to inform students of my absence and needed to postpone several commissions.

'At last,' Little Brother sighed as he flicked the reins on the horses' backs and we set off.

As we travelled together, I reflected on the many years I had spent with Little Brother and was overwhelmed by a desire to call him by a new name. As a child, for years I had envied my playmates who had homes to return to. They would leave me at mealtimes and rush into their mothers' arms. From a distance I had watched mothers embrace their sons and murmur a loving word: *coccobello*. As we travelled, perhaps tweaked by the euphoria of a holiday, I could not stop myself from uttering it.

'Cocco. From now on, I'm going to call you by this name.' I had said it. I dreaded to think what Paolo would say if he heard me. Coconut, dear one—whichever meaning he chose, he would consider me mad. But even if the appropriate time for the name was long passed, I was determined to bless him with it, for to me it was a name that symbolised a parent's love, for that was the emotion he engendered.

He asked me what it meant and I muttered something. Fortunately, he liked the sound of it and asked me no more questions. He wanted to call me by an Italian name, so I taught him to say 'Seppe'. Then his conversation turned to the painting for the emperor.

'One hundred horses, eh? A number that is twice fifty. Ai, he is a superstitious man. He is asking the gods to grant him a long life and you are the messenger. How does that make you feel, Seppe?'

'My only worry is how to make an interesting study of such a large number of the same animal.'

Cocco chuckled. 'You will find a way.'

It took us four days to reach Cheng De, struggling on narrow paths up and over the mountains and through broken sections of the Great Wall.

When we were in sight of the palace, Cocco shouted as he set off for Chen Yuan's house, 'Race you!' I tried to catch up, but a forty-year-old man runs slower than a twenty-three-year old. I arrived to find him squatting between two young boys who were more interested in ants than in the strange man who had suddenly appeared. Cocco glanced up at me and subtly pointed towards the house.

You Min stood in the doorway with her eyes and mouth wide open. She ran inside the house. '*Baba, Baba,* there are two strange men here. One is the green-eyed foreigner you told me not to be afraid of.'

Chen Yuan emerged wiping his hands on a cloth and a huge smile illuminating his face. He threw the cloth across his shoulder and stretched his arms wide.

'I know everything! You may think we are hidden away in the countryside, ignorant and stupid, but news travels faster here where the air is purer than anywhere else. You must be exhausted. Ah, it is good to see you, Old Friend Lang. Ai ya. And this one,' he said standing in front of Cocco, eyeing him from top to bottom. 'Such a handsome man. That skinny, big-eared youth is long gone. The marriage brokers must be knocking on your door. Well?'

Cocco blushed. 'I'm too busy to find a wife.'

'I once said that. I did not suffer by waiting for the right woman. Perhaps you, Jiang Shan Min, will have the same good fortune to wait until you are almost forty then find the perfect wife to make you happy and proud. Then you will make my good friend here a grandfather.'

He turned at looked at me with such deep affection that I was taken aback; I had spent so little time with this man. How does it happen, I wondered, that bonds of friendship can be forged instantly with some people and maintained over decades as fresh as the day they were made? Jerome, with whom I had lived now for thirteen years and cared for deeply, was not a bosom friend.

'I've burnt a lot of incense praying for you, Missionary Lang, dear friend. This moment has been in my thoughts many times. Now it is reality.' Tears caused his eyes to sparkle. 'Come. Look at my sons. Muddy urchins. This is You Zhang and the other is You Cheng.'

I was pleased that Chen Yuan had kept the same first name for each child, *You*. 'Handsome boys. I like their names.'

'Yes, we made them similar in case you decide to adopt them as well.' He winked as he hooked his arm around my elbow and led me towards his curious sons. They sat together on the ground, staring at me with impish faces.

'He has weird eyes.'

'That is no way to talk about a visitor!'

'Why is his hair so funny?'

'There are spots all over his face. And what a big nose.'

'Children!'

'Is this the man you talk about, Father?' A small hand slipped into mine. 'The one from over the ocean. From *E-da-li*?' You Min was staring up at me.

I laughed heartily and scooped her into my arms.

'They have your gift of saying exactly what they think.'

'It must be a trait of their mother's.'

'Now, child.' Chen Yuan spoke softly to You Min who put her head on my shoulder. 'This is your other father. The one we've told you about. And that man is his other child. You may call him Ge Ge. He's your older brother.'

You Min lifted her head and wriggled to be let down. She walked over to Cocco and put her hand in his while we strolled towards the sweet potato fields. He reached down and picked her up, putting her on his shoulders. She squealed and swung her legs. 'Father, look at me!'

'The drought has made things very difficult. We've fallen behind. The most we've harvested is five thousand jin of fan shu from each mu. By contrast, we harvested a quantity of millet twenty times greater.'

'You will succeed. I'm sure you will. It's a great thing you are doing. You have within your grasp to put an end to starvation…'

'It's still not good enough. Our ten-thousand-years-living emperor constantly inquires of our advances. I feel no pride of achievement. Our yields do not justify the labour and costs we have sunk into the soil these many years. We can't expect peasants to grow fan shu when the crops are unreliable. Our goal is for ten thousand jin per mu. What defeats us is that this plant is not grown from seed. We need roots to propagate. At present, we depend on supplies from the south, from Guangdong and Fujian. They arrive by land or by water. It's not only expensive but prone to problems. The roots and young plants are carefully packed into wooden crates, with earth tucked around them. If they get too hot or too cold, they can be damaged.'

'Can't you preserve your own roots through the winter?'

'This is exactly what our ten-thousand-years-living emperor wants us to do. Last winter, I placed roots in a cave to see if it would work. Just a few days ago, I planted the shoots. Let me show you the results.'

You Min and Cocco went off to play with You Zhang and You Cheng. Chen Yuan and I examined every field. As we talked, I could hear children's delighted laughter. I didn't remember Cocco ever having young friends. From the age of ten, when I first met him, his companions had been only adults. Had I failed him in this regard?

'Pay attention, Old Friend Lang. In case the emperor questions you about this.' Chen Yuan lectured me about his work. The crops and fields were as much a part of him as if grown from his own flesh and blood. He and his team experimented with every variable at their disposal—type of soil, fertiliser, strain of sweet potato, irrigation, timing. Wooden markers along each field listed the significant details. His records were meticulous. For his sake and for the well-being of the peasants I had met, I prayed silently for his success.

'Despite all these years of trials, success is not at hand,' Chen Yuan noted sadly as if he had heard my thoughts. 'I will not give up, but sometimes I wonder if we will succeed in my lifetime.'

'You will triumph. God will not let your devotion go unrewarded.'

'God? Your god? Is he concerned with a man like me?'

'Of course. He watches over all of us.'

'Hmm. If *you* say so, I must believe it.' Chen Yuan looked at me with one eyebrow raised.

Cocco and I stayed in a small house on the estate called Wan Huo Song Feng, Wind of the Pines of Ten Thousand Cliffs. Of all the pavilions and palaces within Cheng De, this one had been Xuan Ye's special retreat, a quiet, simple dwelling where he read, wrote, and thought in solitude. The only child who had accompanied him to this house, according to the older servants, was Hong Li.

'This house is a happy place,' I told Cocco. 'Can you not see them sitting together—the emperor proudly teaching his young grandson portions of the classics?'

'I did not know the previous emperor, but I know how much you respected him. Seppe, do you take it as a sign from your god that he has put you in such a place?'

I laughed. 'I think my Lord has better things to concern Himself with than my petty affairs.'

Our cottage was ringed by scores of pine trees whose needles shook most of the time, brushing against one another to make music—rustling, whistling, howling depending upon the strength of the wind. Beyond the trees, stairs led to the Bridge of the Wind of the Pines of Ten Thousand Cliffs, which joined a long path around the edge of a large lake. From the bridge, we could see the pastures on the far side of the lake filled with grazing horses.

I was ignorant of horses and still only a mediocre horseman. Cocco had even less experience of the creatures than I. Though all the servants were aware of why we had come to Cheng De, they were still shocked when we announced our intention to help with the care of the horses. Laughter hid their embarrassment at seeing a royal painter sweeping out stalls, carrying pails of water, and mixing feed.

'How else can I understand the creatures if I do not spend time with them?' I tried to explain, to no avail.

'A Chinese painter would sit and contemplate for many days. He would not dirty himself or sweat to find inspiration.' The head groom shook his head. 'Stable hands look after horses, not painters. This is most unusual.'

After the first day, I was smitten by the creatures. They were delicate, intelligent, and perceptive with an ability to sense one's mood and react to it. I quickly learned that a calm state of mind was rewarded. I talked to them in Italian while I softly brushed their gleaming coats, watching their muscles ripple and quiver. I grew familiar with individual snorts, sniffs, and whistles and could recognise which animal made the sound. They displayed a full spectrum of temperaments I had only associated with humans: gentle, insecure, needy, loving, playful, unpredictable, even malicious. The affection between us grew and I spent hours wondering about the spirit behind the soft eyes and curious muzzles.

There were a few horses who were occasionally nasty, but only one that was horrid to the core. He was a long-toothed, irritable stallion who used every opportunity to grab a chunk of my skin or tread on my toes. I learned to give him a wide berth, since he took particular pleasure in kicking anyone who came within range of a hind leg. Though I had not yet planned the painting fully, I decided that revenge would be mine in the end. I would paint him separated from all other horses with his best feature forward: his arse.

I ventured into neighbouring villages on horseback and my horsemanship improved daily. In a tiny hamlet called Peach, I met a family who I liked very much. Even though they were desperately poor, they were welcoming and curious to learn about life beyond their hovel. The father (I never knew his name, referring to him as Old Zhang like everyone else) was only twenty-five years old, yet he was already lined and short of teeth. His wife was a typical northern woman, with big feet and a square face with delicate, narrow eyes always illuminated by two round red cheeks. The right-hand side of her mouth tilted upwards when she smiled. She was illiterate and naïve but blessed with a sweet disposition. She was a capable, devoted mother of two boisterous boys both of whom had square heads and enormous ears. I drew all of them as they went about their work and chores.

They lived with less than the bare minimum of comfort: one set of clothes, no blankets, no bedding, and no oil to make a light. Old Zhang gathered what he could from the mountainside. Mrs Zhang wove baskets and straw curtains in her spare time. On the seventh day of every month, she walked to the market with her two sons to sell her work. Depending on how much she sold, she returned with small amounts of salt, oil, soy sauce, and vinegar. Their diet largely consisted of wild vegetables and a thin rice gruel.

I quietly handed Mrs Zhang small amounts of money, food, and useful items—not enough to elicit the envy of their neighbours but enough to improve their circumstances and soften their struggle. I insisted that a smile was sufficient gratitude and refused to allow her to throw herself at my feet as she tried to do.

'You are good people. My God expects me to look after you. I am only His servant.'

Old Zhang was a silent type but not dour. He enjoyed hearing stories that made him laugh. He had a kind nature and treated everyone well. Within the village, he was called the Lucky One—after all, he had married a pretty, strong wife who produced two healthy sons. Her only drawback, they commented, was her feet, which were larger than most men's feet.

Cocco did not wander the way I did. He spent most of his time helping Chen Yuan and his wife. He adored You Min and her brothers. Again, with a stab of guilt, I realised that it was the first family he had ever come to know well. When I tried to apologise for the shortcomings of my guardianship, Cocco would hear none of it. 'If I don't regret anything, why should you be sorry? I was well cared for, loved, and educated far beyond my expectations. You have led me into my adulthood with wisdom and generosity. I will have a family of my own someday and relive childhood through the eyes of my offspring.'

That day, to my delight, he decided to accompany me to Peach village. We carried the makings for a simple meal. It was twilight when we arrived. The atmosphere in the hut was heavy. Mrs Zhang tried to hide her red eyes from me and Old Zhang sat scowling. I looked at Cocco and shrugged, shaking my head. I handed Mrs Zhang my basket of supplies. She was normally excited to see what treats lay beneath the cloth, but not this time. She accepted the basket listlessly and turned away.

'Sit. Drink something,' Old Zhang insisted.

'Perhaps it is not convenient now?'

'Sit. Drink.' Old Zhang did not look at me as he growled his invitation.

'We will stay for a short while.'

'Won't hear of it. Eat dinner, then go.' Old Zhang growled at his wife, 'Make something for us.'

'Ai.' The sound came out like a high-pitched squeak.

'Won't take her long.' Old Zhang waved his hand at us to sit down.

'Seppe,' Cocco spoke softly. I looked at him and sat down.

We sat stiffly and silently. Even the boys hardly moved other than to glance from time to time at their parents with frightened eyes. Mrs Zhang hid herself away in the tiny kitchen. I could hear her forcefully pumping the bellows over the wood fire.

As Mrs Zhang put the food on the table, Old Zhang suddenly turned to Cocco, leaning back against the wall. 'Honourable Jiang, you married?'

'Not yet. I'm still young. And too busy with my work to think about it.'

Old Zhang was silent for a minute. He clucked and cleared some food from his back teeth.

'Old Zhang, are you thinking of making an introduction for him?' I said. 'Who do you have in mind?'

'Nah.' Old Zhang fell back into thought again. He ignored his dinner. He turned his head and flicked his hand to his sons. They rushed off outside.

'Come.' He gestured that he wanted us to follow him to the tiny space that served as their kitchen where his wife was cleaning a pot.

She saw us coming and opened her eyes in horror. She quickly raised her sleeves to cover her face.

'Brother Lang, you're good man. I know from the first time I seen you. Your student, Honourable Jiang, hasn't come before, but is also good since he is a friend of you. I was coming to find you. But, luckily, you come by tonight.'

These were more words than I had ever heard him speak at one time. He stopped again and dropped his head as if he had run out of words.

'Say what you wish to say. Something is troubling you. If we can help in any way, we will use all our strength to be of assistance,' I said, putting a hand on his shoulder.

He opened his mouth but the words got stuck. 'My wife,' he finally uttered.

I turned to her. 'Tell me what the problem is.'

She lowered her sleeve and cast suspicious eyes at her husband.

We all stood there waiting, my head grazing the decaying ceiling. Suddenly Old Zhang strode over to his wife and yanked her rough cotton trousers down to the ground. I saw a flash of white skin before I turned away. Cocco gasped.

'You don't go tonight. Let her serve you. Look. She got white skin. She free from disease. So what if she has big feet. Tomorrow, you give some money.'

I could feel her eyes on the back of my head and shared her shame. I waited but did not hear her bend down and pick up her trousers. I turned around with my hand over my eyes. From beneath my hand, I could see her feet were still covered by the fallen trousers.

My words came out breathlessly. 'Your wife is a fine woman. She does not deserve such disgrace. I am a friend of your family. You have embarrassed me as well as your wife. I have relations with no women. How can you dare ask me something that is so base and immoral?'

Cocco recovered from his shock and grabbed hold of my cloak, dragging me out with him. I kept my hand over my eyes, tripping and lurching until we were in the road.

'That was a memorable introduction! I have never witnessed anything so desperate in my life.'

'I'm speechless. What was he thinking of? I would give him money gladly. Now I can never go back to that house again. Cocco, something terrible is going on there. We must leave them some money. What will he make her do?'

'Wait here. I'll leave money outside the door.' Cocco gently led me to the stump of a tree and helped me sit. I could not stop trembling. What a fool I had been, thinking I could befriend such a poor family without any consequences.

After several days, a young female servant came to see me. She knelt at my feet and would not rise when I asked her to.

'We are all aware of how kind you were to the Zhang family. They are my mother's cousins and she wishes me to thank you and explain what has happened. They are the poorest family in a district where most people have very little to spare. They have debts. The landlord increased their rent for some reason even though he knew they could barely meet the existing rent. Old Zhang told my father that he had no choice but to rent his wife to two brothers in a mountain village. The brothers are too poor to keep a wife. They signed a simple contract promising to keep her only until she produces a son.

'I have never heard of such an arrangement.'

'Royal Painter Lang, it is very common in this area. Most of the land outside Cheng De is very barren. The desert comes closer every year.'

'What can I do to help?'

'There is nothing. If you spoke to the landlord, he might throw them off the land. At least they have a roof over their heads and relatives nearby. This is their fate. You have tried to change it, but the gods are stronger than you.'

I went to see Old Zhang myself, giving him more silver.

'Do whatever you have to, but bring her back. This is unacceptable.' I tried hard to contain my anger, but it crept into my voice. Old Zhang sat mute and immobile. He seemed deaf to my words. His sons, hunched on either side of him, clinging to his arms, had lost all their sparkle and joy. There was no fire burning and no sign that food had been prepared. 'Can't do it,' one boy spoke. 'She is someone else's wife now.'

That evening I sat with Chen Yuan and tried to make sense of what had happened to the Zhang family, hoping to find some way to help them.

'The problems of the poor are endless,' Chen Yuan began. 'Even if you helped this family during the short period that you are in Cheng De, what of the long term? How can we improve the life of their sons and their sons' sons? Did I ever tell you what motivated me to leave my comfortable life in the south for this difficult existence in the north?'

I shook my head.

'Throughout my childhood, my mother lectured me. Our world is made up of two sorts of people, she insisted: those who are merchants and care little for morality and those who are not merchants and care for morality. Child, she said often, you must be a merchant who cares for people. You must be both sorts of men. This is what the world needs. Her words are what made me decide to pursue this dream.'

The word he used for morality was *ren*. I knew it was a Confucian concept with many meanings. No one had yet explained the term sufficiently well for me to understand it. In my mind, it was a word that encompassed all the best of Christ's teachings—the concepts of fellowship, humanity, love, concern and righteousness.

'Great changes are made with little steps,' he went on. 'The Zhang family's tragedy cannot be undone. You cannot change their fate without risking even greater calamities. I believe we must do everything we can to work towards a better future.'

Through the servant girl, I continued to send baskets of food to the Zhang family but I no longer visited Peach village.

I completed the cartoon for my great painting. It was a long scroll, over twenty-three feet long and almost three feet high. It displayed a community of sentient creatures. Every horse had its own nature and story.

Regardless of the sheer number of horses at Cheng De, my deepest affection was reserved for one, a beautiful black mare, fifteen years old and very calm. She greeted me daily with a gentle whinny and searched my clothes for hidden treats. If I playfully turned my back and pretended to ignore her, she tickled my ears with her velvet muzzle. When that brought no reaction, she would push me on the shoulder, once, twice, then harder and harder until I responded.

When my idyllic days at Cheng De were drawing to an end, I took her out for a long ride. I set out for an unusual rock formation, a giant natural pillar that emerged from a cliff top. It had long fascinated me. That day I understood the meaning of a Chinese idiom: *While looking at a mountain, one can ride a horse to death.* Though I carried a full day's food and drink, my destination was far more distant than I could have imagined, and I realised that I should not attempt to return to Cheng De that evening. I noticed smoke and headed towards it.

Three strong men suddenly leapt out of a gully and dragged me from the horse. Ignored my protests, they tied my arms and took me to a cluster of run-down dwellings, where I began shouting that I was a servant of the emperor, a royal painter living at Cheng De. A circle of unkempt, rough peasants gathered around looking at me with disbelief. A toothless, bald curmudgeon came forward and eyed me from top to bottom. He smelled foul and had a vacant look in his eyes. I lowered my voice and spoke slowly and clearly to him, telling him who I was and why I had come to the village, but he did not respond. Gasps and clucks erupted all around me. The old man, still watching me, spoke to several other scruffy men. I did not understand a word of what they said. As the number of hostile faces increased, I switched to bits of other dialects, even a few words of Manchu, but all my attempts were met with the same cold stares.

My sense of danger swelled to new levels when I was tied with rough hemp and tossed, face first, into a filthy barn. *What will they do to me? What an ironic end to my life in China,* I thought. *No religious martyrdom for me—just an obscure death at the hands of ignorant mountain dwellers. No one will find me.*

Children gathered around me. *How can I convince them I am no freak of nature, despite my height, my hair, and eye colour?* Moving to make myself more comfortable, I racked my brains for ideas, but the urchins ran away shrieking. From a distance they began to gather stones. Some of the children ran forward and threw them at me. My bonds made it difficult to avoid the missiles and several hit my body and head. Because of the noise the children were making, several adults arrived. They started to laugh and ridicule me, treating me as if I were an animal captured for their amusement. I could feel blood running down my face. A group of swaggering youths approached and I felt a surge of panic. They undid and removed most of my clothes, despite my shouts and protests. They looked my body over thoroughly, poking and pushing. A couple of the youths held my arms. The leader pointed to my male organ, clearly surprised at its size. He poked it and poked around with a stick until I howled in pain.

I heard the giggling voices of young girls. Savouring the reaction of the females, the youth poked harder. I kicked him and he fell backwards. The other youths began to laugh at him and released their hold on my arms. My victory was brief as the youth, red-faced and annoyed, picked up a hoe and marched over to me with malice in his eyes.

Suddenly the village elder appeared, pushing everyone aside. He spoke harshly to the youths and motioned for them to leave, which they did. He cast a glance at me and snorted before turning his back and walking outside. He shouted at an old man who fetched a stool and sat down outside the barn. From the tone of his voice and the fact that the noise quickly died down, I assumed that he had told everyone to leave.

Relieved that I was not going to die just yet, I gave in to shock and promptly passed out. When I came to, night had fallen and everything was still. The stool outside the barn was empty. I was in pain and very thirsty. *Oh, Lord, do I deserve your mercy? I have been a most unsatisfactory Jesuit. I have doubted and mistrusted you. By my lack of faith I have earned this punishment and am ready to atone for the sins I have committed in your eyes. If I must die, so be it.*

I started to recite prayers of penance, guilty at how little time over the past six years I had spent nurturing my faith. I was a Jesuit only by the thinnest of bonds.

'Brother Lang, I couldn't help you today. You hurt?' a soft female voice whispered in my ear.

Strong hands untied my bonds. Confused, it took me several seconds to recognise the voice of Mrs Zhang.

My arms and legs were numb. She seemed to sense it and rubbed my limbs, ignoring my nudity.

'What are you doing here?' I asked her incredulously.

'I brought your clothes. I'm sorry they're a bit dirty.'

She handed me my undergarments and trousers. She did not wait to be asked, but gently helped me to dress as if I were an infant. It was a few minutes before I could stand and walk around. Though I ached, I had suffered no serious injury.

'What are you doing here?' I asked her again.

'We can't talk now.'

I followed her quietly until we were well away from the village. She had tied my mare to a tree. She whinnied very softly when she saw me as if she understood the danger as well.

'Go quickly. As soon as you go down the hill, you'll be safe.'

I thanked her, touching her shoulder. I even blessed her in Latin, though she had no idea what I was saying. I began to explain how I had given her husband money to bring her back, but she stopped me.

'Brother Lang, I thank you for your kindness. When I finish my work here, I'll find you and make kow-tows.'

'When will you return home?'

'Soon as I deliver a male child.'

'How do they treat you?'

'It works well, but I miss my sons too much. Apart from that, this is fine.' She gave a small giggle like the ones I remembered so fondly. The brothers are both kind to me, not too rough when they use me. If they were nasty, it would be difficult.'

'And if you give them a daughter instead?'

'I beg you, don't talk like that. They spoke to a wise woman. She says that I must get pregnant this month for a boy. Next month and the following four months, I only produce girls.'

'But...?' Words escaped me.

'If there's a bit of money in my home, I'm content.' She laughed and it rang out like chimes. In the moonlight, I could just make out her crooked smile, the right side arching more than the left. 'Brother Lang, talk to my husband. Tell him to take good care of himself as well.' She handed me a cloth bundle. 'Here's some millet. Tell him to give this to our sons to eat. I've eaten less, to save these morsels for them.'

I tucked the bundle into my torn robes. She had already disappeared. I could hardly see, but my intelligent mount picked her way down the hillside. She wasted no time getting us home.

I left the journey up to her. I had too much to think about. *Oh, Lord, thank you for giving me another chance, but tell me what is the lesson I am to take from this? Had I kept the Zhang family together, I could have died tonight. Are You telling me to question everything I take to be morally right or wrong? Lord, if my rescue is the result of another's misfortune, when is it my turn to suffer so that another may live?*

'What happened to you?' the head groom asked, aghast, when he saw me. It was soon after daybreak and I had quickly unsaddled my horse, fed and watered her, hoping to flee before being spotted.

'It's nothing; nothing at all,' I answered and hurried back to our cottage. Cocco helped wash my wounds and applied salves. I told him the entire story.

'It is an unbelievable chain of circumstances,' he muttered. 'She saved your life. What if she had still been with her husband and sons in Peach village? It is too frightening to think about. We must leave here for a few days. The gossip of your injuries will spread very quickly. There will be many questions. The commander will want to know all the details. If you reveal anything, you will bring misfortune on Mrs Zhang's head.'

'I have already thought about that. I am prepared to lie to protect that sorry village. Though they behaved inhumanely, I do not seek revenge.'

'Wait here,' Cocco said and ran off. He returned within an hour. 'It's all arranged. We will go to Chen Yuan's house until you are healed and the incident is forgotten.'

My absence from the palace grounds did not stop the commander of the royal guards coming to Chen Yuan's, but it was several days before Cocco allowed him to see me. When he did, I lied. I was, by nature, a very poor liar and the commander, a canny, battle-scarred man, saw through me instantly.

'I would not insult a royal painter by questioning his honesty. Knowing that you are a missionary, I put this unwillingness to co-operate with me down to the precepts of your foreign religion. I have a duty, however, to protect the distinguished servants of my ten-thousand-years-living emperor and will not be satisfied until I find answers that have more credibility.'

He dispatched soldiers to neighbouring villages and questioned many people, but his enquiries led nowhere. He came to me a few more times, but I held to my story of a fall from my horse.

He grabbed my wrists and said, 'How does a tumble produce marks like these, Royal Painter Lang?'

I shrugged.

'Does this have anything to do with Peach village and the Zhang family?'

'Who?' I looked at him innocently.

He raised his chin and nodded, slowly and thoughtfully. 'Though I am a soldier and you are a missionary, we both have a duty to protect the weak, the vulnerable. How I seek to achieve that and how you do it are in opposition. It puts me in an interesting predicament. Royal Painter Lang, though I am reluctant to do so, I must trust that you know what you are doing. Pray to your Christian god that no one else is harmed by these villains, for that person's suffering would be on your head.'

In the heavy silence that hung in the air after his departure, I was startled by the sound of You Min sobbing. I followed the noise and found her trying to walk around her room. She was wincing in pain and hobbling.

'What's wrong?' I asked her.

Wiping her eyes with the back of her sleeve, she climbed on to a chair and looked at me sadly, not saying anything. She rolled up the bottom of her trouser legs and stripped off her shoes. Her tiny feet were swaddled in tightly bound cloths. I gasped. It had never occurred to me that Chen Yuan would bind his daughter's feet. If he had been planning to do so, he would have done so several years ago, when she was two or three.

'Does it hurt a great deal?' I asked her through stinging eyes.

She nodded.

'Must your feet be bound like this? They were not bound when I first arrived.'

Again she nodded. 'Mamma says small feet are pretty. Then I can walk like a lady. Mamma says no man will want me with nature's feet. Only a beggar will be my husband.'

I bit my tongue to stop me from saying too much.

'Do you want to see my feet, Uncle?' I nodded slowly. 'I show you at night. If Mamma saw me now, she might smack me.' You Min giggled.

That evening she crept into my room and perched delicately on the edge of my bed. She took off her slippers and began to unroll her bindings. Her small fingers were surprisingly deft. I held the end of the cloth. As it unfolded, I rolled the coarse fabric around my hand and elbow while her foot emerged.

The contrast of her flawless face and hands with her distorted, bloodless foot was shocking. This was no misfortune of nature, no accident; this was purposeful mutilation. It was a sin to take a fully formed foot and wilfully cripple it. Her tiny toes had already been fully bent beneath the sole. The arch rose like a bow. The toes were clenched tightly like a fist. When she walked, she rested on her heel and the knuckles of her toes.

I did not want her to see my distress, but I should have known better than to try to hide emotions from a child. She peered into my face, her fingers pointing at me until they touched tears in the corner of my eye.

'Lang Da Da, what's wrong?'

'Ah…' I could not answer. 'How…do you…play games?' I tried to speak normally.

'I can't do lots of things. I can't play tiao fang zi'.' You Min pouted, her lips jutting forward in an expression of injustice.

The game she mentioned was similar to one the children in Italy played, where children mark out a long rectangle and break it into squares, then throw a bean bag and try to hop successfully to where it has landed, claiming it as their territory. Only when all the squares have been claimed can a winner be declared.

'Don't be sad, child. Wait two days and I'll buy you a lamb knuckle to play with. Is that not just as good?'

The four-sided lamb knee joint was used for a game that only required accurate throwing. She clapped her hands with delight and began to wrap up her foot again. She turned on her stomach and slid down slowly from the bed. As she wobbled out of the room, she reminded me of a bird with a broken wing that would never again know the joy of soaring above the earth.

'Cocco,' I asked later, 'did you know that You Min's feet had been bound?'

'Yes. I do not approve, but it is not my place to criticise my elders. My heart is very sad for You Min. Most of the women I've met don't have bound feet. It's not something I have ever thought about before. Do you know why Chen Yuan is doing this?'

'It's a Han custom that refuses to die out. Manchus have never bound the feet of their women. The first emperor of the Qing tried to ban it, but the Han disobeyed and the imperial edicts were never properly enforced,' I answered.

We were silent for a minute. Cocco spoke first. 'If we both are in agreement, should you not speak to Chen Yuan on You Min's behalf?'

'Undoubtedly.'

'I'm most surprised that you concern yourself with such a small issue.' Chen Yuan studied my face. 'Haven't these few months been most eventful for you? You have witnessed wives being rented out to procreate and murderous peasants. Now you encounter the custom of foot binding. It's normal. The child's mother was adamant from the time she turned two. I thought it unnecessary and delayed the decision for four years, but her mother was most insistent. She claims I will harm her marriage prospects. Come with me into the town now. Bring Jiang Shan Min as well. It is fortuitous that today is the start of the annual temple market.'

'What is at this temple market?'

'It is a famous competition to find the prettiest little feet among all the women of the district.'

We walked from the palace walls towards the town. The crowds were enormous, but no one had come to sell or to buy. We joined the strolling gawkers, and what a strange spectacle it was. Women and girls perched on window ledges, in doorways, on stools, or along the tops of low walls displayed their feet. Their clothes were bright and gaudy and their faces heavily painted. Some were barely teenagers, others were older. Not one of them had a foot longer than my index finger.

'Look at the faces of the men,' Chen Yuan noted. 'No one is shocked or disapproving. Am I not right in believing that most find this a feast for the eyes? Look, some of the women have just changed their shoes and returned to their seats. See how the men gather around to stare at them again.

'There is a saying: *Qian, qian zuo xi bu, jing miao shi wu shuang. The beauty of the walk of a woman with bound feet has no equal in this world.* Men seek to be handsome, virile, strong, and brave while women cultivate soft natures. These two aspects of human nature balance each other.'

'Are you absolutely certain that women are happy to have bound feet?'

Chen Yuan thought carefully before answering. 'Yes, I believe they are. From ancient times, we Chinese have held two things precious. The first is the colour white. The second is the idea of "small." We wear white to mourn our dead. Our elderly with their white hair are called many respectful names: Hoary Head, Silver Silk, Snow Crown. White is used to describe morality, humanity, and honour. White is used in countless descriptions of females. We say that "one white beauty hides one hundred ugly wenches." The term *xiao* is often used in a symbolic way. For things we treasure or pity, we add the word *xiao*. *Little* sister is an unmarried woman. *Small* days means to have an easy life.'

'But we have no right to alter what is given by God,' I countered. 'Binding feet is not an enhancement. It is cruel, deforming, and crippling.'

'Have we not altered many things in our world? Do we not breed animals for our own purposes? Look at the work I am doing, defying nature itself. You have told me how women wear strange fashions in your country that sound not only uncomfortable, but unhealthy from our perspective. In our eyes, women appear delicate when they walk on these tiny feet. They sway and wobble like thin limbs of trees blown by the wind. Women with natural feet cannot compare with them.'

Shortly before nightfall, one young maiden's feet were selected as the prettiest of the competition.

'An outline is being made of them then hundreds of copies of the *Golden Lotus Fragrant Picture* will be produced. There will be no shortage of buyers. See, they are putting up banners announcing the winner's name. Do you hear what people are calling out?

'Yes I can understand it. For five coins anyone can touch "the crescent moon curve" of the winner's feet. I still find it very disturbing.'

'I can do nothing about that. But at least you can appreciate how deep the roots of foot binding go in our culture. I can assure you that the winner's value as a wife has soared.'

Cocco spoke at last. 'Honourable Chen, I know many men, learned and talented, who would happily marry a women without bound feet. Please reassure your wife that You Min's future prospects will not be damaged if she has normal feet.'

'I will do so with pleasure, Young Jiang, but I doubt that she will believe it.'

When we returned home, Cocco's irritation spilled over. He took me aside. 'I don't care about what other families do to their daughters. You Min is your daughter. You must stop it.'

'Cocco, she is not really my daughter. It was a gesture of friendship from Chen Yuan, nothing more.'

'I was there when you adopted her. The words were spoken.'

'Yes, but it had a different meaning from a true adoption. You Min is clearly loved and well cared for. Chen Yuan knows how much I disapprove of foot binding, but she is his flesh and blood, not mine. How can I interfere? My actions could affect her entire future. Do I have the right to jeopardise that?'

Cocco snorted his disgust at me and paced the ground for many minutes. Then he said, 'I have an idea. I will speak to You Min personally and tell *her* that we do not approve and why. Her parents are not cruel people, and I agree, they love her dearly. If she decides to continue with foot binding, then it is her fate. Perhaps if she objects, her parents will not force her to continue.'

'Cocco, she is only six years old.'

'She has wisdom beyond her years,' Cocco said as he walked out of the door.

At the beginning of December, Cocco and I sadly bid farewell to Chen Yuan and his family. Though I missed Paolo, Jin Kun, and other friends as well as my students, I found Cheng De to be my Garden of Earthly Paradise. The rest of the world did not intrude. Even my faith strengthened in such ideal surroundings. I felt God's support, reassuring me that, as long as my conscience was clear, I was free to follow my own path. In Beijing, surrounded by passionate Jesuits, I doubted my devotion and diligence. In the pure air of Cheng De, I was free of doubts.

'Wu Yu taught me a saying,' I commented to Cocco at one point. '*At thirty, one must sit up and ask what one is doing. At forty, one must no longer be confused. At fifty, one knows one's destiny.* Yet I return to the capital and the court without either knowing or in control of my destiny.'

'I think that's good. An artist must never be too secure. It means he is always searching his soul for answers and paints from the great spaces that his quest opens up.'

7

I returned to my Jesuit world in Beijing only to discover that my anxiety in leaving Cheng De had been justified. Paolo sadly informed me that rumours abounded among other sects that I, Giuseppe Castiglione, no longer believed in our Lord. It was whispered that I worshipped the emperor as my God. He treated me too well, they said. As much as he and the rector defended me, the rumours continued.

'Other Jesuits must feel the same, but they are too cowardly to come forward and show themselves,' he added. 'They are jealous of your success. This rumour mongering is un-Christian and unjustified.'

The birthday of the emperor was the thirteenth day of December, according to the Christian calendar. The Great Harmony Palace in the Forbidden City had been scrubbed and freshly painted in bright reds, blues, greens, and gold for a ceremony to which we Jesuits and other orders and foreign dignitaries had been invited. The emperor and his consort sat upon thrones on a high platform. Hordes of relatives, officials, leaders of the Armies of the Eight Banners, literati, and provincial dignitaries filled the hall. Musicians played softly in the corner.

The emperor had issued strict orders for his birthday. No subject of the emperor was permitted to bring a valuable present. Many of the nobles and senior ministers grumbled; if the presents could not be valuable, they must be clever. His edict only intensified the anxiety surrounding the event. Only foreign ambassadors were excluded from the prohibition and were free to offer luxurious presents.

My 'present' had been delivered several days earlier. The emperor had been profuse in his praise. He asked his fourth-born son, Hong Li, to create a poem for it. The long scroll was on display in the hall for all to see. The painting consisted of a tapestry of scenes, with all the horses engaged in some activity—playing, eating, drinking, quarrelling. There were very few humans represented, apart from a few who tended the horses. My four-legged friends represented Christian virtues: gentleness, tolerance, domesticity, and obedience. Ninety-nine horses lived in an ideal community, happy, blessed with abundance, and busy. One horrid, hateful stallion lived alone on an island showing only his arse to the viewer, but only I knew why he was there. Many of the Chinese who gazed at the painting made the same comment: *Tian di ren he, ren jing jiao rong*, the harmony of heaven, earth, and man, the confluence of man and nature.

Rector Ignatius insisted that I stand next to him as a sign of his support. He even made a show of smiling at me and touching my arm or shoulder. I was grateful to have such a tenacious, demonstrative man on my side. When it was our turn, Rector Ignatius presented the emperor with a set of silver teacups.

He returned to my side and whispered. 'Thanks to you, we have done the right thing. He was pleased.'

Upon the advice of several senior Jesuits, Rector Ignatius had originally chosen a different gift—a porcelain clock recently arrived from Europe—but when he had asked my opinion, I had pointed out that the word for clock is *zhong*, which has the same sound as the character for 'end.' 'To offer a clock, *song zhong*, has the same pronunciation as the act of seeing a dying relative for the last time. The emperor will be insulted by such a gift.'

A Cantonese official mounted the platform, the first Chinese guest brave enough to offer the emperor a present. I could see a carved jade plate with a red egg in the centre. The egg was not oval, but round, a nearly perfect circle. Such an egg was rare and precious. For the Cantonese, to eat a round, red egg on a birthday was a symbolic act. This egg had many symbolic associations. It referred to the saying *Tian yuan, Di fang*, heaven is round and earth is square. Not only is the universe round like the egg, but at the centre of the universe sits the Chinese emperor, the Son of Heaven.

In ancient thinking, *fang*, square, represented the orderliness of life, so the present was a way of thanking the emperor for protecting the entire country. In the *Book of Changes*, *yuan*, round, symbolised eternity: complete one revolution and begin again; extended to life itself, it symbolised immortality. *Hong*, the colour red, was the colour of fire. *Qian cheng hong huo* meant that the future is bright. *Ji dan* was a chicken egg. *Ji*, chicken, had the same sound as the character for luck.

The emperor was visibly impressed and touched. He asked for his special dragon-phoenix chopsticks. He grasped them and went to lift the egg off the plate. The egg slipped out of the chopsticks. He tried again, his face flushed. He succeeded in raising it from the plate. Higher and higher—then the chopsticks went askew and the egg tumbled back on to the plate. The eunuch holding the plate began to tremble and the egg quivered on the plate.

The emperor stood up. He controlled his frustration and tried two more times to lift the egg. Both attempts failed. His face went from pink to red. As he grasped it one more time, the egg bounced off the plate. It skittered down the gown of the terrified eunuch and danced a merry path down the steps from the platform. The emperor hurried after the egg and bent down. We all knelt with him. Even on the floor, the egg refused to yield.

The emperor stood up and growled. He threw his chopsticks to the floor. He swooped down and picked up the egg with his hand, then pressed it between his palms. He threw the crumbled bits on to the floor and ground his heel round and round. The segments turned to powder.

The only sound in the vast room was the laboured breathing of the emperor. He returned to his throne. Slowly his breathing returned to normal. The poor official from Canton was nowhere to be seen.

'Bring Zhen the prisoners in the Lu Liu Liang case!' the emperor shouted and my heart sank. He so often dispensed cruelty to assuage anger.

We waited, and soon six bound prisoners were brought before the emperor. Two, I was told, were sons of a scholar named Lu Liu Liang and two were students of the sons. The others were a zealot named Ceng Jing and his student.

'Zhen has decided that Ceng Jing and his student are hereby pardoned and may leave, but the sons of Lu Liu Liang and their students will be executed immediately. All of their sons will to be sent to serve as soldiers in distant posts and all the women and girls will be brought to serve in the palace.'

Crying and pleading their innocence, the four men were dragged out of the palace.

A birthday was a day more than any other when pardons were expected from rulers, but this emperor trod a different path. I reflected on the words of the prophet Micah: *What the Lord doth require of thee: Only to do justly, and to love mercy and to walk humbly with thy God.*

In the eyes of scholars and intellectuals who were my trusted friends, the emperor's decision was unjust. *This is outrageous,* they muttered. *They are innocent. With this act, with the murder of sons of such a great man, the gods will be angry. He has surely altered his fate. Huo qi xiao qiang, disaster will begin within his home.*

Knowing little about the case and not wishing to distress these friends more, I sought out Jin Kun for information about the case. He was a reclusive painter. Given his charisma and the joy he displayed in the past in the company of other artists, this change was inexplicable.

'Royal Painter Jin, we miss you. Why do you hide away here?' I asked him.

'I hide because I am afraid of the emperor.'

'Why?'

'It is only a matter of time before I suffer at his hands.'

'*Why?*'

'Because of the man who was my teacher. Do you remember, I told you that, as a boy, I had travelled with a Daoist monk for many years. That man was Zhu Da. He came to Jiangsu and took a liking to me. He asked my parents if I could serve as his "Baby Daoist Companion," the one who carries the pot, cup, and bowl, and they agreed. He changed his name to Ba Da Shan Ren, Man of the Eight Great Mountains. He was a relative of the Ming imperial family and he opposed Manchu rule. Ba Da Shan Ren was a brilliant painter and very productive. His paintings are full of hidden meanings. The emperor, at some time, will turn his attention to those paintings and seek to destroy them and...' Jin Kun stopped talking.

'But they are only paintings which can be interpreted in many ways.'

'The emperor is arbitrary in his application of logic and fairness. I knew Lu Liu Liang and his sons. They did not deserve their punishment.'

'How did they fall foul of the emperor?'

'Lu Liu Liang was a respected Confucian scholar who died several years before our late emperor. Ceng Jing is an idiot, a failed student from Hunan province who never met Lu Liu Liang but read one essay by Lu Liu Liang and discovered his aim in life, to rid China of foreigners. The essay was called *Yi Xia Zhi Fang* or *Contradictions Among Chinese and Foreigners*. Though it said nothing of the kind, Ceng Jing believed it dictated that all Chinese, as a sign of respect to their king, must expel all foreigners. Ceng dispatched his student, Zhang Xi, to find Yue Zhong Qi, a military leader who controlled the armies of Sichuan and Shaanxi. Zhang carried a letter from Ceng Jing in which he urged Yue to join the fight against the "foreign" Qing dynasty, not realising that Yue was Manchu himself and a relative of the emperor. Ceng Jing and his student were arrested, as were Lu's two sons, who had played no part in the conspiracy and knew nothing about it.'

Jin Kun looked sadly at me. 'I was like a son to Ba Da Shan Ren. If the sons of a man as blameless as Lu Liu Liang can be executed, then the disciple of Zhu Da, who opposed Manchu rule, can expect no less. My only hope is that the emperor never looks closely at the paintings of my late teacher.'

In the new year, the emperor issued a huge book he had been writing for some time, the title of which we translated as *Notes for Making Principles and Waking Up*. In it, he emphasised that the Manchus entered China to bring peace. His dynasty re-established the glory of China. He believed that he, on behalf of the great Qing dynasty, fulfilled the prime tenets of the three great religions of his nation, Confucianism, Taoism, and Buddhism, and deserved immortality. An emperor was heaven's agent, and must therefore be a man of virtue (*de*) and benevolence (*ren*). It was of no significance where the man was born or of what background he came from.

The emperor quoted ancient examples of other respected emperors who were foreign to Chinese soil. *Although I received my orders from heaven,* he wrote, *and I am the master of my people, I take care of them and give them my love, so why judge me as being Chinese or foreign?*

More and more books by him emerged: volumes of his collected quotes, the *Yu Xuan Yu Lu,* and books on the lives of obscure ancient monks.

In February, several royal painters informed me that the emperor had demanded to view paintings by Ba Da Shan Ren. I immediately went to find Jin Kun, but his house was empty. No one knew where he was living. A young boy espied me and gave me a note.

'Royal Painter Jin told me a tall foreigner would come today. How did he know?'

I smiled and gave the boy a coin.

My loyal friend Lang, the note read, *if you feel you wish to see me, I will be at the teahouse called Old Sycamore Autumn tonight after sunset. I will understand if you do not come.*

The teahouse was a beautiful one overlooking the Houhai lake. It was a bitterly cold evening and the lake was frozen. I arrived early and waited, shivering. When Jin Kun appeared, the harried look of anxiety lifted when he saw me.

'I am a fortunate man to have such a friend as you,' he said. Despite the cold, he appeared to be perspiring.

A waiter interrupted us. 'The gentlemen Jin and Lang prefer water that is not too boiled?'

'Yes,' we answered together. Native Beijing customers only ordered heavily boiled water, but he knew that Jin Kun, as a southerner, insisted on water that had only just reached boiling point.

Jin Kun and I sipped tea. Slowly my limbs warmed up.

'Delicious tea. Too high a temperature,' he reminded me, 'diminishes the flavour of the leaves.'

I watched him, relieved to see the lines in his forehead soften.

'Royal Painter Lang,' he went on. 'The matter we discussed several months ago has come about as I predicted.'

'Yes, I have heard.'

'I have several of my teacher's paintings. They must survive. They are part of China's heritage. Whatever happens to me, will you protect them until better times return? If the officials find these paintings, they will be destroyed.'

'Do they know that you have paintings in your possession?'

'It has never been a secret. Many people have seen them.'

'Then what good will it do to give me the paintings?' I wanted to say that if under torture he revealed where they were the paintings would still be destroyed, but I did not want to add to the panic I could see growing in his eyes.

'I have been working on this problem for many years. Long ago, I made copies and gave the originals to a monk. Unfortunately, he died last year so I retrieved them. May I pass the paintings to you? The emperor trusts you. I don't think he would ever search your house. I have distanced myself from all the royal painters for some time now. There is no one he could point to as a close friend.'

'Of course I will help you.' I didn't hesitate. I didn't even pause to think what would happen if I were questioned and my house searched. A friend in danger, great paintings in danger; there was no other option.

'When it is safe again, I will return them whole and undamaged to you.'

I added the words *wan bi gui zhao,* which literally meant to 'return the jade intact to the state of Zhao.' These were words I had read but never used, yet they were the first to come into my mind. They were the most formal words I knew for such a situation.

During the wars of ancient Spring and Autumn dynasty, five centuries before the birth of our Lord, a famous prime minister, Lin Xiang Ru, at great danger to himself, preserved his king's official stamp by hiding it on his person. When the danger passed and the king and kingdom were safe once more, the loyal minister returned the stamp. As he handed the symbol of authority to his ruler, he used those solemn words, *wan bi gui zhao.*

'I will bring them to you tomorrow night. Meet me here.'

The following evening, I sat alone in the teahouse waiting for Jin Kun. Night had fallen. Outside the wind howled and the streets were deserted. After a long wait, I left the teahouse, wondering how I would find him. I turned when I heard the sound of a man rushing, panting. It was Jin Kun.

'What happened?'

'Spies sent by the security office found out where I was living. I evaded them and took a very complicated route to get here. They will be very angry.'

'Did you bring the paintings?' I whispered.

'They are here.' He reached under his cloak and pulled out a rectangular wooden box, which he passed it to me. I hid it beneath several layers of cloaks. 'I must leave you now. I cannot anger them any further. Ten thousand thank you's. One hundred thousand. One hundred thousand thousand. One million.' He backed away, bowing and clasping his hands in front of him.

I reached forward and put my hand on his shoulder. 'When the dark clouds have blown away, I will find you. Whatever it takes.'

In the half-light of the snow and moon, an anguished look crossed his handsome face. It was a familiar look of a man in torment, unable to control his destiny and wondering why awful things were happening to him.

Jin Kun was put on trial as an accomplice of the treasonous Ba Da Shan Ren, though the artist had been dead for almost thirty years. The first canvas held up as proof of treason was a stark painting of a single fish, in bold, black ink, a small, powerful creature. Only I knew that the painting held up in court was a copy. The fish was painted from above with all of one eye visible and a portion of the second one. Black ink circled the eyes so that the whites of the eyeballs were accentuated. Left of the fish, he had painted large, beautiful characters in a modern running style, like a shorthand. The characters were *she shi*—be involved with life. They were prominently painted and the second character was double the size of the first. He had used the characters of his signature to send another message to the viewer. He combined the first two characters of his name, Ba Da, in such a way that they seemed to form another character, either *xiao,* to laugh, or *ku,* to cry and did the same with the last two characters of his name, Shan Ren, to form *zhi,* meaning 'to be in the midst of.'

The prosecutors claimed that the fish out of water was the artist himself, The Man of the Eight Great Mountains, a relative of the previous imperial family. The eyes expressed the disdain the artist felt for the Qing dynasty. To look at someone askance through the whites of the eyes—*bai yan xiang ren*—was to view them with scorn. The signature, the arrogant depiction of the words for crying or laughing, showed the artist's mourning for what was lost and his ridicule for what had replaced it.

Three other paintings were shown to prove the charges. The first one had, among other symbols, a peacock with three protruding tail feathers and a poem:

Peacocks, flowers, bamboo, screen
Top half of bamboo like an ink brush
As if it is listening with three ears,
As if in the middle of the night in spring.

The 'three ears' referred to in the poem was a common Chinese term for a slave. A good slave was one who seemed to grow a third ear to catch secrets of others that could be of benefit to his master. The peacock feathers represented officials in the Qing court. The emperor had the right to bestow these on his servants. They would then be worn proudly on the back of their caps; the maximum number that could be lavished on any one man was three.

Wherever he was, the emperor opened his court for official business at the fifth bell of the day. Eager officials, wanting to display their loyalty, might queue as early as the second bell of the day to await the emperor. Zhu Da, it was argued, was ridiculing the officials who, in their desire to ingratiate themselves with the emperor, queued in the middle of the night, eager to be first in line to see him.

The second painting was of a disabled eagle. He had a broken wing, a damaged beak, frail claws, and unhealthy feathers. The last painting showed a flock of swallows startled into flight. There was no indication as to what had frightened them. In each case, the paintings were interpreted as clever insults of the Qing dynasty and all who served it. There were no opposing voices.

When I was next called to an audience with the emperor, I asked if I could make a request of him.

'You have made many paintings that bring pleasure to me and have asked for nothing in return. What is your request?'

I remained bowed with my head down. 'Royal Painter Jin is a close friend, Bixia, and a great artist. I understand that he has displeased you, but I beg you to show mercy to him. I swear to you that he is a loyal subject.' I said the words and winced, expecting the worst.

'Zhen will consider your request.'

Jin Kun was pronounced guilty of treason by association. He was not imprisoned or physically punished, but he was stripped of his royal post and exiled to the harsh north-western border. The copies of the paintings were burnt. I never had a chance to bid him farewell.

To say that the Forbidden City was a sombre place hardly describes the mood. When I painted there I, at least, had the company of Chinese artist friends. The only other person I saw regularly was the charismatic prince Hong Li, who still arrived unannounced to watch me work. He was a confident, highly intelligent man with an unmistakable aura of authority. He had a classic Manchu face, oval in shape. His eyelids were invisible, hidden by the folds of his brow. He had broad cheekbones and a pointed chin. His ears were long and large, a very lucky feature according to Chinese superstition. His eyebrows were fine, like the thread of a silkworm. His firm mouth was made more so but a natural darker outline around the lips.

'Music and literature are important, but art is what I treasure most,' he told me. 'If I am fortunate enough to be chosen emperor, I expect you to serve me as you served my father emperor and my grandfather emperor. You are a great artist and have influenced many other artists. Your paintings are alive, not merely because of the colours you use, but because the animals and people convey their emotions and character.'

Fifteen days after that conversation, on the eighth of October 1735, the emperor's death was announced. It came as a great shock. He had been robust when I had last seen him. Paolo was even more baffled. The emperor had left the capital a few days earlier for a brief stay at Yuan Ming Yuan. Paolo's presence had not been required. When news of the emperor's death reached him, he rushed to Yuan Ming Yuan but was not permitted to see the emperor's body.

The security around Yuan Ming Yuan was vigilant and thorough. No one entered without permission. After the emperor's death, soldiers filled the streets. Homes were searched and many people were arrested.

Some whispered that Yin Zhen had been fatally sickened by the longevity pills, known as *Chang Sheng Xian Wan,* that he consumed in great quantity. But the majority believed rumours that he had been murdered by a female member of Lu Liu Liang's family, the man whose sons had been unjustly executed by the emperor on his fiftieth birthday. Like the other women of her family, this female had been taken into service in the palace.

According to the story that circulated, she matured into a beautiful woman and a talented musician. Yin Zhen was not a man who toyed with women. He lived life more like a monk than an emperor. He adored Han music and one instrument in particular, the ancient kong hou, a small instrument with anything from five to twenty-five strings. Only one elderly servant had known how to play the kong hou to the emperor's liking. He became ill in the fourth year of Yin Zhen's reign and never recovered. There was no one else who played well enough to satisfy Yin Zhen. Many musicians shied away from it, put off by its formidable reputation. For many years the kong hou lay idle until the soft hands of Lu Si Niang picked it up. She found a quiet corner of the palace and struggled with the instrument until she conquered it. In time, her fingers fluttered over the strings producing a rich, haunting tone. Revenge, everyone surmised, had provided the will; she needed no other teacher.

One night, as the emperor wandered around his palace he heard sweet strands of the kong hou. Guided by the sound, he found the young musician. She was only sixteen years old. Her beauty, dignity, and ability to play his treasured instrument won him over instantly. He refused to heed warnings about her origins.

She was brought to his bed chambers. She played melodies he had long missed. Then Lu Si Niang allowed her family's enemy to claim her body as his. She flattered and pleased him. When he left for his brief rest at Yuan Ming Yuan, she accompanied him. Though security was excellent, far fewer courtiers were present with their suspicions and prying eyes. Summoned to his chambers, she was not searched. It was said that she concealed a knife in her robes. In the night, amidst silence and stillness, she stabbed him and watched him die. She calmly severed his head from his body and wrapped it in a box and silk cloths. Lu Si Niang fled Yuan Ming Yuan with her prize and was never found.

The headless corpse, it was whispered, was buried with a wooden carving on its shoulders.

The Christian orders in China once more stood on a precipice. We prayed for a peaceful transition and for a kind ruler who would allow us to complete our work on Christ's behalf.

The new emperor was proclaimed. He was the fourth-born son Hong Li. Yin Zhen fathered only ten sons, six of whom died young. His favourite son, Hong Shi, had committed suicide several years earlier. Another had been adopted by another royal relative and lost his right to the succession. The official wife, Hu La Na La, produced no sons. Hong Zhou, the fifth-born son, and Hong Li were born of different mothers. Hong Zhou was a lazy, romantic dreamer. Hong Li' s mother, the Xi Concubine, was the daughter of a favoured official, a fourth-ranking member of the Board of Rites and from a noble family with many distinguished ancestors, including the second official consort of the Kang Xi emperor, but Hong Li outshone anyone else.

Despite his obvious talents, the choice of succession had a curious birth. Upon the death of Yin Zhen, an elderly, trusted confidant instructed confused officials to search behind the huge gilt banner above the Zheng Da Guang Ming palace. The banner hailed the name of the palace, four characters meaning 'fair and bright.' As the confidante had promised, the secret will of Yin Zhen was discovered—well protected in a lacquer box and wrapped in cloth—lodged snugly behind those golden words.

The will contained two documents. The first was addressed to ministers and officials. Its message was simple: *The crown passes to my fourth-born son, Ai Xin Jue Luo Hong Li.* The second document was addressed to Hong Li himself.

Hong Li was formally crowned emperor at the age of twenty-four in 1736. He inherited a united country and a robust treasury. He named his era Qian Long. His veins carried more Manchu blood than his father's. He was only one-eighth Han. He was a boy of four when I first arrived in China, and he had sat by my side over many years watching me work. Now he was the most powerful man in the country.

皇后

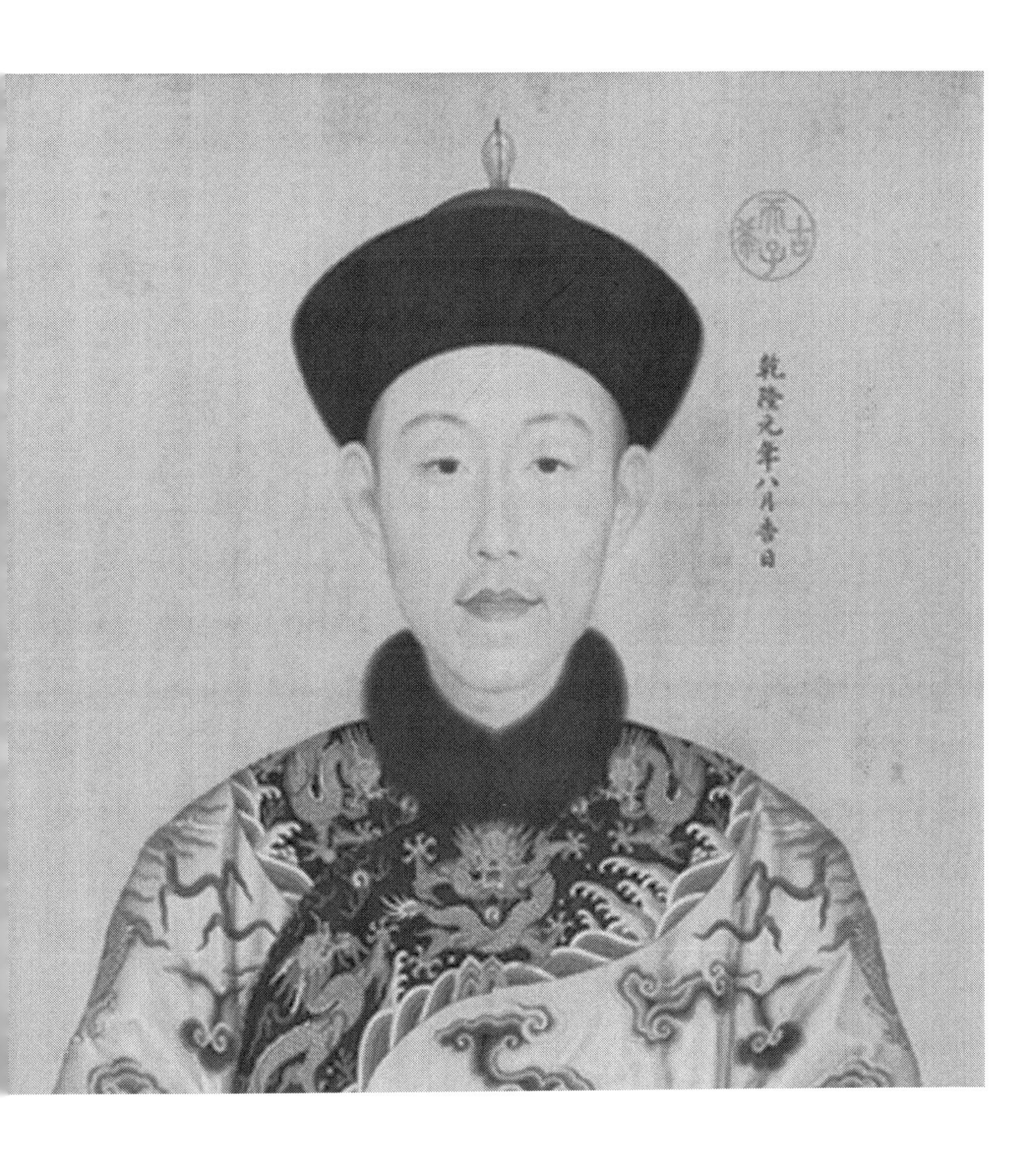
乾隆元年八月吉日

Part III

And All These Things I Saw

Heaven does not give up the winter because people dislike cold. Earth does not give up its expanse because people dislike distance. The superior man does not give up good conduct because the inferior man rails against him. Heaven has a constant way of action, earth has a constant size, and the superior man has a constant personal demonstration of virtue.

Xun Zi circa 290BC

1

Wang Rong is studying the various objects that decorate my study. He holds the bamboo brush holder that once belonged to Wu Yu. I watch though half-open eyes as, thinking I am dozing, he quizzically rubs the holder on his cheek then holds it at arm's length to see if the colour has changed. I cannot help but smile. We have known each other for fifty years. He is one of my truest friends, my confidant, and the guardian of my memories. Wang Rong holds my will somewhere in his house and has promised that my wishes will be fulfilled. I am content that Cocco will receive my enormous collection of Chinese art and craftwork; objects that have been together for decades will receive the love and care they deserve.

Wang Rong's most difficult task will be convincing the emperor to bury me with other Jesuits. It is fitting that my bones should lie with others of my kind. Life is after all a circle, a wheel, that rolls forward while remaining in place. I came to China as a Jesuit and have remained one in my heart, despite what some will say.

'Ah, you are awake.' Wang Rong says. 'Shall we go on?'

'Why not?' I say. 'Though time waits for no man, I feel it is being patient with me at the present.'

Wang Rong is familiar with these years of my life. Some of this time was not pretty and I am loathe to relive those years of anguish, but if this is to be a true account of my life I can spare no details. Without the intelligent, kind eunuch who sits elegantly in front me, I may never have emerged from the dark cave in which I had sought to bury myself.

One month after the Yong Zheng emperor's funeral, we were assembled together in the Southern Church after a communal meal. Praying with us were two legates of Pope Clement XII who had just delivered a message from him reminding us of the previous edicts regarding Chinese converts: that a Chinese Christian was not permitted to maintain any vestige of Confucian rituals of worship. We had been wryly musing over the importance they had attached to their message, since we were not only bereft of converts, but banned from creating new Christians and our numbers were too depleted to carry out evangelical work. There were no more than two score Jesuits remaining in all China.

Suddenly a troop of soldiers stormed inside. They wore the uniform of men of the Plain White Banner. My heart pounded as memories of the early days of Yin Zhen's rule and Antonio's arrest came back to me. My throat was so dry that I could hardly swallow.

'All copies of the *Da Yi Jue Mi Lu,* Notes for Making Principles and Waking Up, written by the late emperor are to be handed over to us immediately upon the orders of our ten-thousand-years-living emperor.'

Rector Ignatius walked forward and spoke quietly to the man whose shout still seemed to echo inside the tall church. 'We will honour the order of the emperor, but first we must continue with our prayers. The books will be gathered and brought to wherever you tell us.'

'Immediately! There will be no delay!' The commander's mouth hardened and he scowled. He leant forward until he was but a few inches from Rector Ignatius's face. 'Go now and find those books.'

The rector turned and gave a small movement with his head. We rushed off in several directions to gather all the volumes we possessed of books written by the late emperor. The soldiers piled them in the road in front of the church and threw a torch on to the pyre. The night sky was bright and tinged with orange and smoke billowed above many rooftops, indicating that many such bonfires were burning.

The destruction of the books was followed by many proclamations indicating a forceful change of attitude in the imperial court. Through various means, the new emperor made it clear that he was proud to be a Manchu and would make no apologies for the invasion that established the Qing dynasty. He proclaimed the Manchus to be as worthy a race as the Han. He detested his father's attempts to justify Manchu rule on the basis of historical precedents rather than on merit and strength. Foreign though Manchus might once have been to China, barbarians they were not.

The term *yi,* used to describe a foreigner, was henceforth banned, as were many other words. Study of the Han language by Manchu soldiers under the Eight Banners was forbidden. By repeating the term '*zong shu zhi bian,*' referring to what happens when there is a dispute between a conqueror and his colony, he reminded everyone who now ruled China and who were the masters.

Punishments for those viewed as critical of Manchu rule were swift and harsh. The two men released by Yin Zhen who had caused the death of the sons of Lu Liu Liang by their ridiculous anti-Manchu plots, Ceng Jing and Zhang Xi, were executed by 'a thousand cuts.' A young scholar was beheaded for a poem he wrote while taking exams for the imperial bureaucracy when he accidentally used the words foreigner *(yi)*, border *(sai)*, and barbarous *(man)*. Even Manchus were not safe from Hong Li's campaign to prove that China was part of an elite Manchu empire. A member of one of the most eminent Manchu families was ordered to commit suicide for something he had written about China's borders, in which he had unwisely used the term 'Northern Foreigners' to describe the Manchu tribes.

None of us could understand what had motivated such dramatic measures. There had been no indication of Han discontent and no discernible threats to Hong Li's rule. It was Wang Rong who suggested the reason lay in a document the late emperor had written to Hong Li about the succession.

'I have read it,' he told us. 'It said: *"I was chosen to be Emperor only because of my Father's love for you. Because of you, I fell out with my brothers and earned the name of murderer. The son I most loved, Hong Shi, was lost to me. My father's spirit has always protected you. His immense will has triumphed. Upon my death, the crown and all my power will pass to you as was my Father's command".'*

I wondered how Hong Li felt when he read that letter. His grandfather doted on him until his death when Hong Li was eleven. Yin Zhen was an efficient ruler, but he was an erratic man, prone to extreme changes in character. Though Hong Li was confident, capable, and talented and his path to the throne was effortless, was he hurt by his father's antipathy towards him and accusation hurled from beyond the grave? Whatever his thinking, his response was to attack his father's ideas. As a loyal son that was the most he could do.

The missions in China held their breath. Where would we fit into his scheme of the world? Would he use us to demonstrate his strength by expelling us and closing China to the outside world? In the end, he decreed that Christian missionaries could remain but were still forbidden to convert any of his subjects. Christianity, he said, reiterating the words of his father, has no place in China.

A few weeks after Hong Li's coronation, I was summoned to the Forbidden City. I made my first kow-tows before the new emperor.

'Rise,' he said, sitting before me on his throne with a smile brightening his long, thin face. 'Lang Shi Ning, Zhen is promoting you to a higher rank of royal painter. You are to be my personal artist.' He leant forward. 'Zhen is the third emperor you have painted for. It makes you a special man in my eyes. Zhen looks forward to reaping the benefits of your talent for many years to come.'

Wang Rong glided forward and handed me a document. 'Congratulations!' he whispered quickly. 'We are very pleased for you.'

I unrolled it and saw my name and the elegant characters that described my new rank beautifully written in vermilion ink. I was now to be referred to as *Yu Qian Hua Shi*, the 'Emperor's Painter.'

'This position gives you permission to enter freely not only the Forbidden City but also the three palaces, mine and those of my consorts.'

'Oh my,' I mumbled.

'What was that?'

'I am very honoured, Your Majesty. Your humble servant is speechless,' I said as I backed away.

Outside, I paused, weighing up the challenges that this new appointment threatened. Up to now, I had avoided contact with women, wives, and concubines. The rumours of what went on in the women's quarters made the hairs on my neck stand up—endless scheming, spying, and gossiping. The Chinese say: *Huang en hao dang*, an emperor's benevolence has boundaries. Of an emperor's lovers, they say their malevolence has no boundaries. What if I should be asked to paint them? What did I know of women and how to humour or placate them?

'Wang Rong,' I asked when I had the chance, 'will Jerome, I mean, Painter Lin, be promoted as well?'

'No. Painter Lin's art has never pleased the emperor or his father. I am sorry for him and for you. He is your great friend and now your paths must part.'

Jerome no longer even tried to use Chinese ideas or techniques. He spent most of his time managing the daily affairs of the mission. I was aware of his overall dissatisfaction at being in China. He deeply regretted leaving Europe.

When I returned home, Jerome was holding a letter in each hand. He was pale. 'This letter is from my mother. It was written two years ago and I have only just received it. I should be grateful. Some mail takes longer or never arrives. She tells me she is ill and pleads with me to return home to France. She wants to see my face and hold me in her arms before she dies. This letter is from my aunt. It was written a few months later.' He waved it in my face as emotion robbed him of speech until he finally spit out the words, 'My mother is dead. She died almost two years ago! She has been dead all this time and I never knew. I had no idea. I've gone on with my life here without praying for her soul or mourning her. What sort of a son am I?'

While he suffered the torments of grief, I stayed by his side for several days. As devout a Jesuit as he was, I believed that his mother had remained the most important person of his life. Even his love of our Lord did not surpass his love for his mother.

One evening we sat on small stools in the street in the early evening, eating soup and steamed bread we had bought from a stall. We were constantly jostled by passers-by and others pushing past us to buy food. The road was lit with hundreds of lanterns of merchants squeezed together along both sides. Food sellers and customers never spoke quietly, choosing instead to shout at each other. We put our heads close together to talk.

'We Parisians are a proud people, convinced of our superiority. You Milanese are much more tolerant. And you, especially, have been blessed by God with a silver tongue. The emperors are charmed by you. I respect you, Giuseppe. You're not false. You're accepting and see the meaning hidden in every situation. You instinctively understand which way the current is flowing and jump in without hesitation. You do not overtly seek advantage, but have the innate ability to obtain it. I, on the other hand, have accomplished so little in my years here. You have come to China and flourished as a painter while I have languished.'

'Jerome, you're still deeply hurt and see everything darkly. You are a far better artist than I am. Why do you no longer paint?'

'I do not wish to paint dogs, monkeys, horses, or birds as you do. How does that serve our Lord?'

'Then paint what you love.'

'For what purpose? No one will ever see them. The churches here have more than enough paintings.'

'You paint for your soul or to show your love of God.'

'I no longer want to paint.'

'What do you want to do?'

'I'll learn a new skill. Something more practical, but I'll never paint again.'

I handed my bowl to the stall holder. He threw it into one large bucket of hot water and the chopsticks into another. 'I'm sure that whatever you decide to do, you will succeed, Jerome.'

Jerome finished his soup. We stood up and walked along the bustling road. 'I had a dream last night,' Jerome said. 'I was in Paris, in our house. I called out to my mother to tell her I had returned, but she couldn't see me and was crying. I should never have come here. I can see that so clearly now, but there is nothing I can do about it. For the sake of our Lord, Jesus Christ, I must find a way to serve him so that my mother's sacrifice will not be in vain.'

'You're wrong, Jerome. The Lord knows you have served him with your heart and soul. You are one of the most devout men I know.'

Standing still was not possible. People moved along the road in both directions like strong currents, bumping and jolting us along as if we were flotsam in a river.

'Giuseppe, I may be devout, but I don't love God's children enough. I am moved by Christ, his words and his message, but I am not a happy man in the company of the living. I watch you. You rush through your prayers, you bow at the crucifix perfunctorily, you never lock yourself away in meditation, yet you are happy. I think about how different we are and I envy you. Jiang Shan Min is as devoted to you as if he were your son. Chinese artists flock to talk to you as an equal. And the emperor has made no secret of his affection for you for many years. You have brightened people's lives. I ask myself: which of us has better served God?'

'You, of course! There is no question.'

'I disagree.'

Before we reached the door to our house, I heard a familiar voice and ran towards it. Chen Yuan was waiting by the door and rushed forward to throw his arms around me.

'You look a bit older,' he said. 'The hair is not so bright anymore.'

'At least I still have a full head of hair,' I said, pointing to his shining scalp.

'Seppe! Look who's here!' Cocco impatiently pointed to a young girl who stood shyly beside him holding her mother's hand. I looked at her in disbelief.

'It's You Min. She's fifteen. Can you believe it?'

You Min blushed as I stared at her, a soft pink glow covering her neck and face like the blossoms on a magnolia tree. She had a small round face, with bright eyes and smooth, olive skin. She bore little resemblance to either her mother or father. The pink glow deepened to red as I watched her. As an embarrassed giggle erupted, a charming dimple appeared on her left cheek.

'Your house is like a treasure trove,' Chen Yuan said with a teasing tone in his voice as he walked around our reception room picking up stamps, porcelain figurines, and carved bamboo. 'I would never have expected you to be surrounded by so many possessions. Chinese monks would only have a single set of clothing and a bowl.'

'I am a saviour of souls and their former possessions. They would have been homeless without my intervention.'

Chen Yuan entered my studio and commented on many of the ink stones, brush holders, and brushes. His wife and daughter waited in the reception room.

'This is ancient,' he said, admiring a bronze cauldron. 'This could only have come from someone very important. An emperor, perhaps.'

'Yes, it was a present from the late emperor. He gave it to me in gratitude for *The One Hundred Horses* painting. It's very old, perhaps more than two thousand years old.'

'Your other father is an important man,' Chen Yuan told You Min when we rejoined the others. 'The emperors give him national treasures.' He waited for her response. 'Well, speak,' he ordered her in a sharp voice.

The red glow again covered her forehead and ears.

'Speak. Just say *baba* or father. Ai, how can you behave like this in your father's house?' Chen Yuan began to pace up and down, a scowl darkening his face.

You Min lowered her eyes and shook her head. The dimple disappeared.

'You Min, what is wrong?' her mother asked softly.

She lifted her eyes, stared at me, and shook her head again.

'Why don't you call me Uncle.' I suggested.

'Not acceptable. She must call you Father,' Chen Yuan said from a corner of the room.

'I think I should be called *Yang Da Shu,* the Overseas Older Uncle. Remember, it is not the *yang* that means mountain goat but the *yang* that means foreign, from across the ocean. I would not want you to think me a farm animal.'

She began to laugh. '*Da Yang Shu.*' Mischievously, You Min changed the order of the words, turning me into Big Overseas Uncle.

'I like it,' I retorted.

She brightened and Chen Yuan and his wife relaxed. We sat and drank tea and words tumbled out of all us at once. I laughed at something Chen Yuan said and glanced at the floor. It was then that I noticed You Min's feet. They were normal and healthy and big. When I looked up, the family began laughing at me.

'Ai, we were wondering when you would notice.' Chen Yuan was shaking his head. 'Her temperament is a strange one. Not like most girls. Maybe because I started to teach her to read and write from an early age. We bound her feet for less than a few months. One day, she refused to keep the bindings on. Her mother tried to convince her, but she argued that she had been given to you and that you would not want a daughter with little feet.'

I glanced with amazement at Cocco who stood looking very pleased with himself. His simple discussion with You Min nine years ago had wrought the result he had hoped for.

'This brings me to the reason for my visit.' Chen Yuan leant close to me. 'The countryside is no place for an educated woman. Her mother and I thought it best to bring her to you.'

My jaw dropped open once more. Chen Yuan ignored my reaction. Cocco covered his mouth, but I could hear his choked laughter.

'Old friend, you are getting close to the age of fifty. You Min is young and capable. She can be of help to you. We felt confident that you would want to help her.'

When I said nothing he continued, 'Would you not agree with me that a treasure like You Min should receive the best education possible?'

'I think it is a wonderful idea for You Min to continue her education in Beijing,' Cocco commented as he slapped his hands on his knees.

'And is not Brother Lang the best man to supervise her education?' Chen Yuan asked with wide eyes.

Cocco's shoulders began to shake. 'Unfortunately, Brother Lang has very little experience with women.'

Chen Yuan nodded. 'We have thought about that.'

Everyone was staring at me, but I was still speechless.

'You Min is my flesh and blood.' Chen Yuan's eyes shimmered. 'But you adopted her fifteen years ago. The child's mother and I have raised her to be favourable in your eyes. Now it is time for her education to go beyond what we can teach her in a poor, remote farming town. She is intelligent and curious and can learn much in the capital. We have heard how much the emperor respects you. Could You Min not spend two or three years in the palace to learn good manners and proper behaviour? That way she will not be a burden to you.'

Cocco came and stood by my side. 'The emperor will be very interested to hear that you have a daughter.' I ignored him.

Jerome spoke up. 'I think it an unlikely option. The Bureau for Managing the Emperor's Affairs is very strict. Palace females are either Manchurian or daughters of Chinese banner men who have adopted Manchu ways. Ordinary Han girls are rarely accepted.'

'What shall we do then?'

Again Jerome intervened and I could have hugged him. 'If you are so decided then I have a suggestion. She would not be bored and would be in the hands of intelligent people.'

'What do have in mind?'

'I suggest that she work in a church that is used by the Society of Jesus. The Southern Church.'

'A church?' Chen Yuan looked incredulous. His wife gasped.

'It's a good idea.' Cocco nodded thoughtfully. 'Uncle Chen, all the priests are men as good as Seppe and his friends. Many of them helped raise and educate me. I would not be who I am but for their attention. If you trust him, you can trust his friends. She will be safe there.'

'But is it not forbidden for Chinese to work with Christians?'

'It is only forbidden for You Min to convert to Christianity. Many Chinese help with our charities, schools, and orphanages,' Jerome answered. 'I promise you that we will do nothing that would endanger her in any way.'

'Painter Lin's suggestion is a wise one.' Chen Yuan tapped his skull. 'My years are advancing. This brain is not agile any more. If You Min is fortunate to have even a drop of influence from these special men, she will prosper. Let us be clear,' he said, turning to his wife, 'You Min is his daughter. If he believes she must go there, she goes.'

Thus I took on a new role as father-guardian of a girl child. When I turned to smile at You Min, she beamed at me, an angel with two deep dimples flashing in her rosy cheeks. From time to time, I caught her staring at Cocco. He smiled at her with great affection.

The six of us talked until it became dark. You Min and her mother quickly went out to buy meat, fish, and vegetables. When they returned, they prepared a large meal. Jerome, still grieving, said little, but Cocco was charming and full of amusing tales. He seemed to glow every time You Min laughed and pleaded with him to tell another story. Chen Yuan appeared preoccupied.

After dinner, I asked Chen Yuan to take a stroll with me. We walked in silence for a short while, carrying lanterns and stepping carefully to avoid rubbish and other things.

'Chen, old friend, I know you well enough to see that something is weighing heavily on your mind. Tell me now what the problem is.'

He looked at me with a startled expression. The light from his lantern cast long shadows across his face, like a tiger's stripes. He sighed deeply.

'Is it that obvious? For sixteen years, I have been planting fan shu. Oh, dear. The emperor now forbids us to use the term *fan*. It is one of the banned words. I must remember to call them bai shu. A lifetime's work with no result.' His lantern drooped low. 'If I cannot find a cheap and reliable way to ensure roots for each year's crops, how can the peasants grow bai shu? A food that cannot be propagated cannot ease starvation.

'Whatever we try, we cannot produce a resilient strain of bai shu. For example, the roots are delicate and suffer in cold weather. Two years ago, when we planted them, a frost destroyed the crop. Last winter, I stored thousands of sweet potatoes in a cave to protect them from changes in weather. A few days ago, the cave was opened up so that the roots could be inspected. The cave was too warm and, to my horror, shoots and leaves had already sprouted, so this year's crop will be small once more. I have come to the conclusion that I have abused His Majesty's benevolence.'

'What are you planning to do?'

He paused before answering. 'I have come to the capital to seek punishment at the hands of our ten-thousand-years-living emperor. I accepted the challenge of Sheng Zu to ease starvation. *I have failed.* I have no choice but to go to the emperor and beg to be executed. Everything is arranged for my burial.'

I thought for a second. 'You've told your family what you plan to do?'

He nodded.

I stopped and faced him, putting my lantern on the ground. I placed both hands on his shoulders. Tears trickled from the corners his eyes. 'Friend, I cannot believe I am hearing this. If you die, who will continue to plant sweet potatoes? Who will seek to ease the starvation and suffering of the masses? You say the only thing left for you is death. This new emperor seeks to rule well, to have peace, to ensure good harvests for his people. If you explain all that you have done these sixteen years for his father and grandfather, I know he will urge you to keep trying. You are the best hope he has.'

A huge sigh erupted from Chen Yuan. He turned around, his countenance completely changed. The cloud had left Chen Yuan's face as quickly as it had appeared. The old shine returned to his eyes. His nature was as changeable as spring weather. 'Thank you, Brother Lang. What you say encourages me. Though others have said the same, it is different coming from you, for you know this emperor, it is rumoured, better than anyone. My life is of no importance, but you are correct. If I die there is no one to continue my work.'

We returned to the house and Chen Yuan filled his bowl with the remains of dinner, eating with vigour. His wife looked at me with tears brimming in her eyes and mouthed the words 'Thank you' when no one else could see.

When, at the same time as You Min's arrival, Wang Rong dropped the news that as the emperor's painter I was expected to live within the Forbidden City, I was shocked.

'A house has been selected for you, near the Eastern Palace.'

'Is this absolutely necessary?'

He raised his eyebrows and nodded. 'You may keep a residence outside, but you must spend at least half of the week within the palace grounds. The emperor wishes to know that his favourite painter is close at hand.'

Jerome, Paolo, and I discussed this dramatic turn of events. Since I was now responsible for You Min, we had to decide what to do for her.

'She could not have lived with so many men anyhow, even if we are Jesuits,' Paolo said. 'You must find a house for the two of you. You realise that Cocco, of all people, cannot remain with her. He is a grown man and unmarried. You do not want to do anything that might damage her reputation. You must live within a traditional Chinese quarter where the neighbours will look after her when you are away in the palace. They will view it as a great honour to care for the ward of such an important servant of the emperor.'

I had lived with Jerome, Paolo, and Cocco for so many years that it was with great sadness that I searched for a new house.

I found a wonderful small house near a canal not too far from the Forbidden City. As Paolo had predicted, the neighbourhood was atwitter that the famous foreign personal painter to the emperor had moved in. Sharing a house with a woman was a surprise to me. So many details we men overlooked were important to her. Her capable hands transformed the house into a home and I finally understood the difference in those two simple words. She rose before sunrise and walked to the well two streets away, chatting to other women and children.

As the lady of the house and the 'daughter' of the most important man in the area, she was treated with great respect. It increased daily. Because of her, neighbours who once trembled when speaking to the emperor's painter took to calling me Da Yang Shu, Big Overseas Uncle as well. The fact that we shared a house aroused no suspicions or curiosity; all the families shared what they had and were eager to learn from us as well. You Min was particularly admired. She had humour, warmth, and understanding beyond her years. She sensed if someone was in difficulty and would rush to their assistance.

For several days, You Min and I walked to the Southern Church together. She began working as a simple cook, cleaner, and water carrier, but quickly advanced to charity work. She became particularly adept at finding shelter and clothing to help the poor during the winter months. She raised silver to obtain coarse, simple, hemp clothing and buy at a pittance cast-offs from homes of the wealthy, and she organised scores of woman to patch holes and strengthen worn spots. Despite her youth, she had recognised the need for this work and found the means to achieve the ends she desired.

I could no longer put off my move to the Forbidden City. The possessions I wanted with me were packed and carted away by imperial servants.

I was directed to the Jing Shi Fang, the Headquarters of the Eunuchs. Duan Shi Lian, now a fifth-rank official, greeted me. It was almost twenty years since that fateful life-drawing class when he had been forced by Xuan Ye to pose for my students. Our paths had rarely crossed, though each time they did, I felt he eyed me with distaste. I knew, through others, how much he hated the presence of foreigners around the emperor and his family. Though his words were polite and a large smile stayed permanently on his chubby face, age had only made him uglier and more unctuous. No matter how elegantly he dressed or how well-mannered he behaved, Duan Shi Lian reminded me of a fat, slimy toad with a poisonous tongue.

'Emperor's Painter Lang, I must explain that this is the internal household. Its rules are very different from those that exist on the outside. In here, you must study and think hard about what you do.'

'I will do my best.'

'In reality, it is not very difficult. You are an educated, reasonable man. If you follow your training and logic, everything will be all right.' Duan Shi Lian's voice was shrill, his every word spoken in a measured manner. His half-closed, bulging eyes hardly blinked. 'Your new home is an auspicious one. You are truly fortunate to be placed in the eastern portion of the internal household. Your house is behind one of the six mansions, the Ning Shou Gong, Palace of a Peaceful, Long Life. Many of the other houses around you, of course, are occupied by women, hundreds of them, but that should pose no problem for you. This young eunuch will tend to your needs. He will show you to your illustrious home.'

I took a deep breath when I walked outside with the young eunuch hovering by my elbow. He was small and thin and bursting with energy like a puppy.

'I am Wang Yi. I am a cousin of your great friend, Wang Rong. I believe he was instrumental in obtaining my assignment. It is such an honour, Emperor's Painter Lang. I am only sixteen and have much to learn, but I will serve you with all the knowledge I have. And I can always ask advice from my important cousin.,

'Then I am a lucky man. Wang Yi, my knowledge of the Forbidden City is limited. Could you tell me about some of the important buildings?'

'It would be my pleasure.' We walked quickly and he took me to a high terrace, which proved to be an excellent vantage point. 'Imagine a line drawn from the northern gate, the Shen Wu, or Martial Spirit Gate, to the southern one, the Wu or Noon Gate. The six most important palaces lie along this line. From north to south, they are: Kun Ning palace, Jiao Tai palace, Qian Qing palace, Bao He palace, Zhong He palace, and Tai He palace. The first three make up the internal household. They are divided from the remaining ones by the Qian Qing Gate. The latter three are called the external household.

'The emperor sleeps in the Qian Qing palace. The character *Qian,* as you probably know, is an alternative word for heaven. The Kun Ning palace represents earth, *Kun,* so the empress sleeps there. The Jiao Tai palace separates the emperor and his empress, heaven and earth. *Jiao Tai* means harmony, harmony between heaven and earth, between Yin and Yang. This is where the emperor and empress, um, engage in the, um—' he looked embarrassed '—the dragon and phoenix activities; their bed is the only bed allowed on the line dividing north from south. On either side of the palaces of the internal household are two more groupings of palaces, six in each section. Those in the east are of a higher rank than those of the west. In total, there are fifteen buildings that make up what we call the Three Palaces.'

He continued to point out buildings and their importance until we entered a maze of small lanes. I wondered how I would ever learn my way around. Every new turn gave way to a street that was the identical to the previous one. High walls and gates only confused me more.

Wang Yi stopped before a house. He smiled and extended his arm. 'Well, will you not go in?'

I glanced around. Curious female faces appeared in doorways and windows that shared the same courtyard.

Wang Yi leant close and whispered. 'Their curiosity is an indication of how much you are trusted around women. And you are not even a eunuch.'

I pushed the front door open. The central room was spacious and had a tall ceiling. It had been filled with furniture made from the finest mahogany. Everything had been arranged to perfection.

'The emperor gave orders to choose the best furniture. Does the furniture please you? I chose these, the tables, the chairs, cupboards, bed, and desk, with advice from my cousin, of course. Wang Rong suggested we select the simplest designs. He knows of your love of wood. Observe here, the grain—is it not beautiful, like fluttering wings? Emperor's Painter Lang, have I carried out my task properly? If you are displeased, please tell Wang Yi.'

My own things were beautifully displayed on shelves and tabletops or hung on the walls, old friends in the most unlikely of surroundings. I stared at Wu Yu's painting brushes hanging on the wall. He would never have lived here. I sat down and gazed around with mixed feelings. This could never become a home for me, yet I had no choice but to make do.

'Emperor's Painter Lang? Is everything to your satisfaction?' Wang Yi was visibly nervous. He rubbed his hands together and leant forward.

I smiled and patted him on the shoulder. 'You have done all this with a good and willing heart, and I am very grateful.'

'Oh, thank you.' He clasped his hands and brought them up to his forehead. It was then that I noticed a box on a table by the door. I walked over and picked it up, opening it slowly. Inside lay a large carved piece of jade, pale green.

'The emperor sends you a personal gift of welcome.'

A young woman knocked at the door, a tiny creature with fine, almost miniature features. She bowed over and over again. 'I am Little Qin. I have been sent to be your servant.'

'I have no need of a servant. I tend to my own needs and always have. You may go.' I turned to walk away from the door.

'If you send me away, it will be assumed that I have displeased you,' she said, clutching her hands and shifting from foot to foot in her nervousness. 'I will be punished.'

'Emperor's Painter Lang, no one of your stature is without a servant here,' Wang Yi added. 'Little Qin was very carefully selected. She is a Manchu banner woman of a good family. She is only seventeen years old but an excellent worker.'

Thus I became a European resident of the Forbidden City, but only for a few evenings each week. My neighbours were all imperial servants, more women than men. When I returned to the house I shared with You Min on the other days, I realised how much I missed the sounds and smells of the real city.

In the Forbidden City, everything was artificial and tense. I wondered how a child raised within its walls could ever understand the life of an ordinary Chinese man or woman.

I had more freedom with my new rank than I ever had before. Neither the emperor nor Rector Ignatius made demands of me. I painted from morning until night.

One evening, when I came to the Southern Church to escort You Min back home, my eyes glanced around the walls and ceiling. I had not previously noticed how much they had deteriorated.

'They must have been beautiful at one time,' Rector Ignatius said. It always amazed me how silently and unobtrusively he arrived at one's side.

'Would you like me to paint new frescoes?' I asked.

'I have prayed that someday you would ask me that question,' he answered with a smile. 'When would you like to begin?

I stayed for a few hours and studied the images. It had been many years since I had painted Christian themes, and the prospect filled me with pleasure. *You have been so good to me, Lord. I would like to express my gratitude in the best way that I know how to.*

Over the next week, I redesigned the original frescoes recalling favourite frescoes on churches in Italy. I understood what Jerome meant when he said he could not paint dogs, birds, and horses as I did. Nothing surpasses stories of the Bible as material to test the talent and heart of an artist.

The contrast between my two lives was enormous. Outside the Forbidden City, I belonged to two communities: my society and my neighbourhood. Within the Forbidden City, I lived a life like an actor in a play waiting for the curtain to fall so that I could rush home and relax.

One day, Wang Yi burst through my door. He looked from side to side like a man running from something. He paced about my room while I painted. I could hear him twitching and mumbling. I could not concentrate.

'If you do not speak to me soon and tell what your problem is, I will leave and you can pace here all day.'

'Oh, Venerable Painter Lang, I am in great difficulty. I have been ordered to the Jing Shi Fang, the Headquarters of the Eunuchs. If I am unable to serve you in the future, please do not blame my cousin.'

'Do try to stand in one place or sit down. Why have you been ordered to the Jing Shi Fang? Have you done something wrong?'

Wang Yi opened his mouth to speak then closed it again.

'Are you going to tell me why you are going to the Jing Shi Fang?'

'I cannot.'

'Have they called you alone and no one else?'

'Not exactly.'

'Are you being moved to another post?'

'Ai. You are from outside the Forbidden City. How can I convey our regulations to your red head?'

I elected a stance of disinterested silence and turned my back to finish some work. Wang Yi moaned and paced even more noisily. He stepped closer to my chair and I could feel his rapid breath on my back. He cleared his throat.

'You know that most eunuchs serve the mistresses of the household.' I kept my back turned. 'Every year, we are checked.'

'What do they check?' I was using dark pink to highlight the petals of a peony. 'Are they worried you have stolen something?'

'Ai,' Wang Yi snorted. 'I serve the women of the emperor. What do you think they check?'

I suddenly understood and turned around with my mouth open. 'It's your body they want to see. Do you have reason to be nervous? The operation was done properly, was it not?'

'Could you gaze upon it for me? What does this silly child know about the correct shape of this thing? I do not know anyone with a natural male organ. Something has altered over the past year. I fear my honourable but miserly father did not give the surgeon enough money. This is the surgeon's revenge. He did not cut enough tissue off. Venerable Lang, I worry too much. You remind me constantly that I am young. This is my only life. If they check me and are angry, I will be denied my life here. I will be forced to return home.'

I dropped my brush. 'I cannot inspect you! Why don't you ask Wang Rong? He is your cousin and is better informed of the regulations.'

'Ah, Wang Rong. Cousin Wang Rong has been promoted. He fulfils a task given only to the most important servants of our emperor. It is hard to see him these days. I should not add to his concerns. He worries that I am a eunuch of limited potential. When he sees me, he prefers to test my abilities than to listen to my concerns.'

'When are you to be inspected?'

'Two days from this day. There is a special bureau for examining our bodies. It's near the Huang Hua Gate.'

'And are you certain that you cannot stay here if it has grown?'

'If the official is kind, the court surgeon will cut off my stubble cleanly and be done with it. If he is cruel, I will depart immediately with humiliation on my shoulders.'

'Wang Yi, go to the inspection. We will face the next hurdle together if it appears. Is that satisfactory?'

'You are good of heart. I did not believe there was anything the Honourable Painter Lang could do to help, but it has relieved me somewhat to tell you my woes.' His face was so childishly forlorn that I had to suppress a smile.

Three days later, my door banged open once more and Wang Yi bounded into the house. Paolo had arrived a short time earlier. I had just finished telling him about Wang Yi's predicament. Seeing the boy's face, it was clear that all concerns were in the past.

'You showered me with luck. The stubble was nothing. No difficulties darken my path. I can serve you as before.'

'If you have problems in the future, my friend will examine you if you wish.'

Wang Yi fell to the floor and prostrated himself, greatly agitated.

'Venerable Painter Lang, do not let such sentences escape from your mouth again. Your Venerable Friend Physician Luo from Italy is the doctor of our ten-thousand-years-living emperor. He cannot tend miserable scum like me. Fortunately this outrageous thought did not occur to you earlier. If you had told anyone of such a proposal, my head and my body would be in different places. My two revered uncles,' he continued, 'in this palace, you cannot ever afford to be careless. You must be on your guard at all times. This is a place that can be very cruel and arbitrary.'

'All right. I'll be careful. At the moment, all is well. Relax, sit down, and have tea with us.'

'You are too polite. I am but your miserable slave and would not be justified to share your tea. My cousin Wang Rong is a much more worthy eunuch. He has an important position. I will try to find him and bring him to sit with you.'

Qin prepared a meal and left Paolo and me alone once more. This was the sole pleasure of living within the Forbidden City: being able to spend time with Paolo. We chatted in our mother tongue about anything that came into our minds, as if we were still the young men who had first journeyed to China. He was normally so preoccupied and busy that it was wonderful to see him relax.

'Paolo, I don't think I've ever told you how much I have treasured your friendship.'

'You don't need to. I see it often in your eyes.'

'Am I that transparent?'

'You are that genuine. Seppe, you, in turn, have given me endless hours of worry and delight.'

'Then let us hope that the latter is all that you face in the future.'

Wang Yi returned later, leading a smiling and bowing Wang Rong.

'Emperor's Painter Lang and Imperial Doctor Luo, I, Wang Rong, offer my greetings.' He dropped to the ground in an elegant posture, resting on his right knee and supported by his right fist pressed into the ground, his arm rigid. Paolo and I stood up, bowing, our hands clasped before our foreheads in a classic greeting.

'Your proud cousin keeps us informed of your success. I am pleased to welcome you into my house. May this be the first of many visits.'

Wang Rong, a seventh-rank official, wore the square hat that denoted his rank. 'It is I who am honoured to be a guest of such important men.'

What a transformation from the skinny, raw youth I had met twenty years earlier. Confidence, wisdom, and authority emanated from him, without a sign of the vanity or falseness that I saw in eunuchs such as Duan Shi Lian. His was still a gentle and sincere soul.

At one point in our conversation, I enquired about the duties of the 'important position' to which Wang Yi had referred. Wang Rong began to laugh—an elegant laugh, genuine but contained.

'You do not want to know.'

'Of course he does.' Seeing the mischievous glint in Paolo's eyes, I immediately regretted my question.

'Well, then, I shall enlighten you. I am in charge of "The Book".'

'Which book?' I had embarked on this misadventure and there was no stopping now. I looked over at Paolo who had covered most of his face with a hand. His shoulders were shaking.

'The Receive Love Book.'

I blushed deeply.

'Serves you right, you nosy old fool,' Paolo said in Italian.

'We use a beautiful word to describe my duties. I am responsible for the "dragon-phoenix" business. Every evening, as the emperor prepares for bed, I bring him The Book. He peruses the names and points to one with his golden fingers. I have the pleasure of rushing to the female palaces with a lantern calling the lucky woman. My work is the most cherished of all. Every wife and concubine, as soon as it nears darkness, desires to see my dog face.'

Even I could not fail to laugh at such a description.

'Wang Rong, I've forgotten when you actually entered the palace. Wang Yi has implied that your story is one worth hearing. Will you share it with us?'

His mood changed immediately. 'My story is like any other,' he said dismissively. He cast a sharp glance at Wang Yi who immediately cowed. 'I entered the palace during the reign of Sheng Zu. Like you two I have served three emperors.' Wang Rong began flicking his fingers as he silently counted the years. 'Ai. It is too many years to count. In order to have food to put into the mouths of my family,' Wang Rong continued, 'I was the son chosen for this dubious honour. But as you know, there is nothing good to say about this work. It comes with sacrifice. To become a person who is neither Yin nor Yang is meant to curse the next eight generations of my family.' He would say nothing more.

3

'It is good to see you, Brother Giuseppe,' Rector Ignatius said, greeting me with a large hug. 'Now quickly, I cannot wait. Show me your latest paintings.' He rubbed his hands excitedly.

'These are excellent,' he commented as he carefully examined ten new paintings I had brought along. 'Your talent grows stronger every week. So many paintings in such a short space of time. In these large scenes, you have given every person a character and an expression, no matter how small a figure they are on the canvas. And the animals are remarkable. I can feel their emotions.'

'Here are a few others that I will not give to the emperor.'

'Interesting, Brother Giuseppe. Would you like me to keep them here?'

'I believe they are safe in my studio in the Forbidden City.'

'You have quite a collection of these paintings, the ones you call your visual diary. Would you not like us to send them to the society in Italy?'

'No, I prefer to keep them close to me.'

'These are important paintings, as they depict the life of ordinary men and women. You are giving posterity a great gift. We will always know how the wealthy lived in the past, but who, before you, has taken the time to paint the servant, the worker, or the peasant? Our Lord Jesus would approve of such devotion to the poor and the forgotten. I only fear that someone will be offended by some of the scenes and destroy these paintings.'

'If I sense danger, I will arrange to get them to safety. I like to have them around me.'

'How is Cocco?' the rector asked. 'I have not seen him for several months. He used to come to walk You Min home in the evening.'

'He has received many commissions in other cities. He has been in Nanjing since January but will be home shortly, which is fortunate as I will need his help shortly.'

'With what?'

'I'm concerned that the frescoes are taking too long. I have been working for several weeks and have hardly done anything. I would like Cocco's help.'

'The work you've done is beautiful. When you finish, we will have the finest church in China.' The rector suddenly looked over my shoulder with an expression of disbelief. He raised his eyebrows quizzically. 'May I help you?'

I turned and saw a timid, perspiring Wang Yi approaching. His hands were clasped in front of his forehead while he bowed several times. He pulled a handkerchief from the purse that hung around his waist and dabbed at his flushed face.

'Honourable Emperor's Painter Lang, the gods have been kind to me and at last I have found you. The emperor sent for you, and though he has recently given you permission to work in this church, I was afraid to reveal that you were not in the Forbidden City. Oh, Emperor's Painter Lang, this is my first time in the Imperial City. It is very large and many people have not heard of the Southern Church. Perhaps I have taken too long with my quest and our ten-thousand-years-living emperor will be angry. Please, I beg you, hurry, hurry and return with me.'

'Brother Lang, I fear this means the work on the frescoes will be postponed.' Rector Ignatius looked crestfallen.

I nodded. 'It was always a possibility.'

As we rushed back to the Forbidden City, I asked Wang Yi if he knew what the emperor wanted me for. He gave me a shy look before answering.

'Emperor's Painter Lang, on the suggestion of Cousin Wang Rong, I will inform you. Did you know he has been promoted? He is now called the Tie Shen Tai Jian, the eunuch who stays closest to the body of the emperor. He felt it wisest if you knew the commission beforehand for fear that you would blanche with trepidation when you heard it from our ten-thousand-years-living emperor's precious mouth. Emperor's Painter Lang, when we return to the Forbidden City you will be asked to paint the empress, the Da Xiao Zhu Zi, honourable concubines, and the ge-ge-men, ordinary concubines.'

'Oh, dear Lord, protect me.'

'He thought you would say something worse than that.' Wang Yi giggled.

Wang Yi led me to the Kun Ming palace where the empress lived. As soon as I entered the throne room, I threw myself down on to the ground and kow-towed. A sharp smell tickled my nose, as foul as the smell of live animals and their faeces. I could not imagine why a throne room should smell like a barn.

'Missionary Lang, please rise.'

I continued to look towards that floor as was expected.

'Please, do not avert your eyes.' The emperor's voice was friendly and bemused.

'Bixia, your miserable slave is truly fortunate to be in the presence of your heavenly face. How can I dare to behold it?' I looked down again.

'Zhen grants you the right to gaze upon the emperor and his empress.'

'Thank you, Bixia.' From the corners of my eyes, I was aware of movement and heard snorts and shuffles. There were animals present!

'Missionary Lang, you have been a servant to three courts. You came to China more than twenty years ago, and your heart has always been honest and loyal. Since Zhen became emperor, you have completed many fine paintings. The fact that Zhen should reward you cannot be disputed, but Zhen is still deciding on the appropriate reward.'

Hong Li's voice had a melodic quality. He sat formally with his consort, wearing a classic fur hat of the Manchus, which resembled a miniature circus tent. The wide base swirled into a peak that was gathered to a point by a red bauble and a short white feather.

The Xiao Xian Huang Hou, the Loyal Virtuous Empress, had a face that reminded me of sunflower seed, wider at the top and tapering to a point at her chin. She was made up like a puppet in a travelling road show. Her eyebrows were extended with dark colour to her ears. Her lips were long and thin but bright red colour had been applied to create a cherry beneath her nose, the colour only covering a portion of her actual mouth. I instinctively looked for a joint, as if she were some ventriloquist's dummy. She had a long and narrow nose, similar to a beak. Diamonds sparkled on her ears. Her hat was identical to her husband's apart from a large, creamy pearl on the peak. They were married when they were fourteen and their son Yong Lian had already been named crown prince.

I quickly turned my head, hoping the emperor would not notice, but the sight of goats, sheep, pigs, and chickens made my eyes open wide and my mouth drop open. Hong Li chuckled at my reaction. I looked back at him. He motioned with his arm and eyebrows indicating that I should survey the entire room.

Apart from the platform on which their thrones rested, the large hall was a mess. Kitchen furniture and implements—tables, chairs, stoves, firewood, stone-cutting boards, gourds, plates, bamboo steamers, sauces, spices, vinegars, cooking utensils, butcher's knives—were scattered everywhere.

'The empress, as mistress of the nation, must please Zao Jun, the Kitchen God, if all the households of the nation are to be protected. Zao Jun is a most fickle, vengeful god and must be amused and flattered at all times. The implements that signify a woman's role are in this room at all times. Do queens in Europe not have the same role of protecting the hearth of every wife and mother in the nation?'

'No, Bixia. We believe in one God whom we serve in other ways. We have no Zao Jun.'

'Then your wives and mothers are free to do whatever they please without fear of retribution.'

'It is not fear of punishment that motivates our women, but the pleasure of reward in heaven.'

'Hmm. That is an interesting idea to explore: reward instead of punishment.' After a pause, he spoke. 'Zhen has a new commission to discuss with you.'

'Bixia, your miserable slave is pleased to serve you in any way you require.'

'Zhen wishes you to paint a large scroll of myself, my empress, and my wives and concubines. How does this appeal to you?'

'I am pleased to heed any and all of your wishes. When may I begin? When would Your Majesty wish it to be finished?'

'Begin tomorrow. Can you finish by the early part of the seventh month?'

'I hope to serve your wishes,' I said, bowing my head. The lump of anxiety that had arisen in my stomach when Wang Yi first mentioned the commission congealed.

'You have already been given a pass that allows you access to the three palaces and six gardens. You are free to go to the personal apartments of my wives and concubines to paint.'

'Who would Your Majesty wish me to paint first?'

'Zhen first. Then the empress. Let me introduce you to my wives and concubines.' Hong Li nodded towards a side door and I noticed that Wang Rong, expressionless, was standing in front of it.

He opened the door and called out, in a high pitched voice, the name of each female. 'Dignity Wife, enter the palace!' 'Pure Wife, enter the palace!'

He continued calling out until eleven women were gathered around the emperor and empress. After Dignity Wife and Pure Wife came Nice Wife, Obedient Concubine, Comfort Concubine, Celebratory Concubine, Smart Concubine, Happy Concubine, Honourable Concubine, Agreeable Concubine, and Old-Fashioned Concubine. As they were introduced, my eyes picked up character traits that, had I been doing an oil painting, I would have hinted at in the portrait: confidence, shyness, sensuality, playfulness, frailty, cunning, vivacity, youthfulness, dreaminess, robustness, and furtiveness.

I stared at the emperor and his twelve women as the full import of the commission hit me. I had been a celibate monk for over thirty years and had no wish to enter the lion's den, but I was being hurled into it. Sexuality waved its tentacles lasciviously, mocking me.

As this was my first commission to paint an official portrait of the emperor, I made a humble request of him. 'Bixia, may I accompany you for several days, to study you, so that I may capture your spirit properly?'

'Is this what painters do in your country?' the emperor asked.

'It is our custom to spend a great deal of time familiarising ourselves with the subjects of our paintings. We make many drawings and small preliminary paintings before the final effort.'

'Zhen begins to understand. You wish to see how Zhen spends the day. Painter Lang, when the time comes to paint the empress and my imperial women, will you also observe them in their leisure?' He leaned back and half closed his eyes, putting the tips of his fingers together.

'Oh, Bixia, your miserable slave deserves to die ten thousand deaths.' I hurled myself on to the ground.

'Ha, ha. Painter Lang, Zhen was merely playing with you. Do not worry. Stand up. Zhen knows you are a dedicated Jesuit. Human food does not interest you,' the emperor said, smiling. 'Pity. You would find much to satisfy you.'

Wang Rong explained the emperor's routine to me. 'As you know, our Manchu rulers have maintained the Chinese way of telling the time by breaking the day into twelve hours instead of twenty-four as you do. Our ten-thousand-years-living emperor eats one meal at eight bells and an afternoon one at two bells. In the evening, he consumes only dian xin, a very frugal snack. He wakes in the morning at six bells and performs some exercise. After his first meal, he reads reports, then he meets his internal cabinet and the grand secretaries of the six ministries. At noon, the entire palace rests. These two hours of your clock, between eleven and one, are viewed as a dangerous period, a time when heaven and earth, Yin and Yang, clash.

'When the emperor awakes, he uses the afternoon for personal enrichment. The palace goes to bed between the ninth and tenth bells. Between the eleventh bell of the evening and the first bell of the morning, heaven and earth mingle in harmony, so sleep during these peaceful hours nurtures the body and preserves the life of the emperor.'

During the few days that I spent in the emperor's company, I discovered that he was a man of many passions, each indulged in with energy and commitment. One of his strongest desires was to make a lasting mark on the future, to grace posterity with the art, craft, and literature of his kingdom.

'Zhen has spoken to many merchants from England, Holland, and Portugal and believes that Europe is interested in Chinese craftwork,' he said to me as we inspected furniture that had been made in a palace-funded workshop. 'We still have much to learn about Europe, but I am told that lacquer ware, furniture, porcelain, and silk will be a great success. Foreigners came here to teach us many things. Now it is our turn to teach your countries about China. Zhen would never send my citizens abroad as your kings do to find new territories and establish colonies. But I will sell the great work that my people produce. There will be Chinese crafts in every home in Europe.'

During afternoon strolls around the gardens, while he made plans for his country's economic and diplomatic future, the urge to compose a poem sometimes suddenly came upon him. Eunuchs, always in readiness, marched behind him carrying ink, paper, and boards. His favourite style of poem contained four lines with either five or seven words per line. He would stop, compose then wave a hand for a eunuch to approach him and kneel with a roll of rice paper tied to his back. The emperor placed the ink stone, pen holder, and lacquer on a platform held on the servant's head and carefully penned his newest epistle while the entourage obediently waited and murmured approval at its conclusion.

Painting, to his great regret, was not his strongest skill. He teased me sometimes about the dubious merits of Western art and I timidly argued back.

'There are artists in China who are interested in Western art. It is important that we increase our knowledge of your heritage. Painter Lang, I order you to write a book on Western art principles, particularly about this concept you call 'perspective.' And Zhen will personally draw the title for you.'

'I am very touched to be given such a task,' I told him.

I began the book instantly, working with a Chinese scholar. The ideas were those of Andrea Pozzo, the Jesuit painter who had first mentioned China to me and whose words inspired me. *Use your art for the greater glory of God,* he had told me when I was a noviciate.

After one week of work from early morning until long after dark, the emperor's portrait on the long scroll was complete. The face was the easiest part, as I knew it so well. By painting him in a three-quarter view gazing afar like a wise prophet of the Old Testament with the weight of responsibility tempered with a subtle smile, I felt I had given Hong Li all the dignity and compassion he deserved. His gown with bold dragons, swirling waves, and clouds required more attention. I laboured to capture the richness of the contrasting colours—bright yellow silk with greens, black, navy, red, and vermilion embroidery. A soft black fur collar and black fur hat highlighted the pale colouring and penetrating gaze of the youthful emperor.

I asked Wang Yi to deliver the rolled painting to the Jing Shi Fang, the Headquarters of the Eunuchs, a formality I had observed since arriving in the

Forbidden City. The office merely passed all my paintings on to the emperor. After a short time, Wang Yi brought the scroll back.

He entered my house and shook his head.

'What? Has it been shown to the emperor?' I asked him.

He shook his head again and shrugged his shoulders.

'What's going on?'

'Emperor's Painter Lang, please do not be angry with me. The Jing Shi Fang refused to give the painting to our ten-thousand-years-living emperor.'

'They have no right to do that! I will take it to the emperor myself.'

'Oh, Venerable Uncle, do not be foolish. They tell me it is the household law. If you intend to present something to our ten-thousand-years-living emperor, it must pass through the Jing Shi Fang.'

I was perplexed. 'Did they give you a reason?'

Wang Yi shook his head. 'No. I am young. What would my foolish head know? I am useless to serve you.'

'It can only be Eunuch Duan who refuses. I will go and see him.'

'I will try to find my cousin and ask his advice.'

The fat eunuch Duan Shi Lian served the empress dowager more than the emperor but, as the highest-ranking eunuch in the palace, held sway over all the others. A watery grin was permanently etched across his puffy face whenever he saw me and he rarely took his eyes off me. I felt uneasy in his presence, partly, I had to admit, because I realised that our dislike was mutual.

I took the scroll and opened it up along my high bed. I saw nothing in the portrait that indicated why the Jing Shi Fang rejected it. My servant girl, Qin, arrived with some tea. I called her over and asked her to look at my painting. When she saw the portrait, she backed away, terrified.

'Venerable Painter Lang, this will not do. I am a simple girl. How can I dare to gaze upon a portrait of our ten-thousand-years-living emperor?' Qin put her hands over her eyes and backed out of the room.

I was at a complete loss and very angry. As I strode along to the emperor's palace, my ire only grew hotter. *How dare he treat me in such a manner,* I thought. *He is trying to lower my reputation in the emperor's eyes by delaying this portrait. I will show him. I have other ways of reaching the emperor.*

In the courtyard in front of the palace, I found one of the senior ministers, whose family I had recently painted, and politely asked him to deliver the scroll to the emperor. 'He is most anxious to see this,' I explained. 'It is a portrait I have made of him.'

'It is an honour to serve as a messenger between our emperor and his favourite painter,' he answered graciously. 'I know how much he looks forward to seeing your newest creations.'

The next morning, Wang Yi stood breathless at my door, his face pale and his body trembling.

'What is going on? You look so frightened.'

'Emperor's Painter Lang, our imperial father orders you to the palace now. I think there may be trouble about the portrait, but I am too stupid to understand the problem. My cousin is very distraught and has been taken ill.'

'All I did was to avoid the Jing Shi Fang and hand the portrait to Minister Guo.'

'That is not the problem. It is much more serious. Cousin Wang Rong says the error is great and he must uncover what really happened. Unfortunately, he cannot even rise from his bed. I have never seen him like this, and I am frightened for everyone.'

I bowed before the emperor, waiting for his usual kind command for me to stand up. It did not come and I stayed prostrate, looking at my knees.

'Eunuch Duan tells us that he returned the portrait you made of me. You ignored his instructions yet presented it to me in a most unusual manner.'

'Bixia, your miserable servant was never told why the Jing Shi Fang returned the painting. Please, Bixia, allow me to bathe in your kindness. Explain how your servant has been in error.' My words echoed off the floor.

From the corner of my eye, I saw Duan Shi Lian smirking.

'Zhen allows you to raise your head. Is this the painting you made of me?' He was pointing to a scroll lying atop a desk.

'Yes, Bixia. It is what your miserable slave painted.'

'Is this a fair likeness of me?' The emperor's voice rose. His eyes were wide. He strode to the painting and picked it up to show me.

'This is a noble stance, common to portraits of kings in my country.'

He snorted. 'Impossible. Do not insult Zhen's intelligence. How could you paint such a likeness of me!' He threw the scroll down and stomped away. 'Someone come!' the emperor bellowed. Eunuchs surrounded me. 'Take him to the garden and beat him with a cane. Thirty strokes.'

Without another word, I was hauled from the room, thrown onto a high platform in the garden, and held face down by several powerful hands. Many whispered insults in my ear. My robes were pulled off, my trousers pulled down, my inner garments stripped away as well. My bare bottom lay exposed to heaven.

I was deeply humiliated but my mouth cried out, 'What is my transgression? Someone tell me!'

I was ignored. It is strange what one remembers at times of danger and panic. Many of the palace women gasped and rushed away in embarrassment. Their silk gowns crackled as they hurried out of sight. Children giggled in a distant garden. A large hound barked. I could pick out the patterns on the shoes of the eunuchs who held me. I could smell dumplings frying in the kitchens.

'Beat.' It was Duan Shi Lian's high-pitched voice. The cane smacked across my bottom. He counted each stroke. I could hear delight in his voice. The pain intensified with each stroke. I gritted my teeth and recited the most beautiful prayers I knew to take me away from this nightmare while my back arched with each blow. Nausea welled up in my throat. I chanted my prayers in Latin through clenched teeth and short, sharp breaths. Our Lord suffered far worse than this. I knew I did not deserve this punishment.

When the beating stopped, I was determined to reclaim some dignity. I got to my feet, wobbly and dizzy with pain, and somehow dressed myself. No one spoke to me. When my clothes were in order, Eunuch Duan led me back to the emperor. Walking was almost impossible. My nose ran, sweat dripped into my eyes, and blood trickled down my legs. I left a trail of red spots on the marble floor.

'Ten-Thousand-Years Sovereign, the beating is accomplished,' he proudly announced.

'Do you understand now?' The emperor's eyes were both angry and hurt.

'Bixia, your slave is too stupid and stubborn. Despite being beaten, I still do not understand.'

'Painter Lang, how dare you paint me with only one ear? Is that how little you respect us?'

I do not remember how, but I willed myself to walk the interminable distance from the palace to the gates of the Forbidden City and then home, telling myself that I would never enter the huge gates again. My back, hips, and legs swelled and the welts burned, oozed, and bled. Each step was agony, as if my skin were ripping asunder.

You Min put her hands on her cheeks when she saw me limping into the house. 'Uncle, what has happened to you? There is blood on your shoes.'

'I was beaten. With canes. On the orders of the emperor.'

'Why? What could you possibly have done?'

'I don't know. Something about painting him with only one ear.'

'Come closer. Let me help you. Lie down. We must look at the wounds and begin to clean them.'

'Let me be! I will do it myself. Just heat me some water.'

I was humiliated and shocked, feeling more like a wounded animal than a grown man. Suddenly the door swung open and Paolo rushed inside, panting.

'This is unbelievable. That it should happen to you of all people! The emperor was told that you deliberately mocked him. And he believed it. When I was told of your beating, I went to see him. I did not hesitate to tell him that I thought it was a plot to discredit you. I pointed to Duan Shi Lian, not caring who was present, and accused him on the spot. I cannot ever remember being so angry and ready to do violence to someone. The emperor has never seen me, or anyone, I should think, react so vehemently in his presence. I lunged at Duan and had to be pulled from the room. The vile, scheming serpent. Many of the cowards who allowed you to be beaten had the audacity to praise my courage afterwards. Any one of them could have stopped the farce before it began. They all know of Duan's hatred of us and his dreams of ridding China of foreigners.'

In my bedroom, Paolo removed my clothes and bathed the wounds gently before rubbing ointment on them. 'Some of the wounds are quite deep, but they are clean. We must keep them that way.'

Exhausted, I could do no more than lie upon my stomach or side. You Min came into the room and fed me broth then sat by my side stroking my hand. The pain increased by the minute and I could not restrain a moan. Paolo gave me a warm drink with ground powders. In a short time, my limbs grew numb and I became very drowsy.

I heard Wang Rong arrive and talk to Paolo. His voice was anxious and tremulous.

'When I saw the painting I almost fainted. I tried to explain to our ten-thousand-years-living emperor that it was a simple mistake, but Eunuch Duan had already fed him lies. When I tried to protest, the emperor struck me, and I was ordered to leave his presence. I expected to be stripped of my status and evicted from the palace. Then Eunuch Duan would have accomplished everything he set out to do, to destroy me and the emperor's famous painter, the Missionary Lang Shi Ning. But your outburst, Physician Luo, was so passionate and forceful that the emperor realised he had been manipulated. He was furious with Eunuch Duan, but as he is the main eunuch who serves his mother, he will not touch him.'

In my drugged state between reality and sleep, I heard the rustle of satin as Wang Rong approached me and caressed my head. 'Can he hear me?'

'I have given him a very strong sedative. I doubt he is awake.'

'Forgive me. I have failed to protect you, my dear foreign friend. I am so sorry that I did not foresee the evil schemes of Eunuch Duan. I had no idea how dangerous and evil a eunuch he really was. It seems he felt deeply humiliated at having to pose in the nude for you and your students all those years ago and waited for the most suitable moment to harm you. He laid a trap and we all fell into it. I promise you this, Emperor's Painter Lang, I will do everything I can to protect you in future.'

'Please explain to me what was wrong with the portrait,' Paolo asked.

'Let me read from a book I brought with me by a great historian called Si Ma Guang. It is called *Historical Record. Second Year of Zhen Guan Period of the Tang Emperor Tai Zong*. In this section, the Tang Tai Zong emperor sought advice from his illustrious prime minister, Wei Zheng.

'The emperor asks: *How can the ruler of a people be intelligent? How can he be stupid?*

And Wei Zheng replies: *Listening to all sides makes one intelligent*

Refusing to listen makes one stupid.

'In other words, a good ruler is a fair ruler, one who listens to all arguments from all sides, but a ruler who listens only with one ear is prejudiced and cannot be wise, fair, or enlightened.'

When I awoke, I thought about what had happened. Eunuch Duan had waited eighteen years to exact revenge. His portrait was painted in 1720. He was the first man in my life to seek my destruction. Though Paolo and Wang Rong had risked everything to protect me, I could not help feeling vulnerable and exposed. Would Eunuch Duan be satisfied to see me beaten or did he yearn for more?

Trying to rise to relieve myself, I realised that I could not move a muscle. Hearing me move, Wang Rong and Paolo rushed into my room and helped me.

'You must keep moving,' Paolo advised, 'or the pain will be worse and the joints could stiffen forever. Wang Rong, help me massage his legs.'

While they massaged me and moved my limbs, I caught a glimpse of Wang Yi standing in the doorway shaking and tearful.

'Wang Yi is permitted to remain at your side until you are well. The emperor wants you to relax at home until you are sufficiently healed. Paolo and I will come every day. Our ten-thousand-years-living emperor also said that to beat shows tenderness, to scold demonstrates love. He encourages you to read this book to learn what the wise scholars have to say about duty, responsibility, benevolence, and virtue, so that you can avoid any blunders and punishments in the future.' Wang Rong presented me with a gift, a copy of the *Four Books.*

I opened the book with tears stinging my eyes. *My Lord giveth, My Lord taketh away, and My Lord restoreth.* One man's evil is easily assuaged by another's courage or generosity. I tried to express my gratitude to Wang Rong and Paolo, but they stopped me.

'I did no more for you than you would have done for me,' Paolo said.

'The ways of evil must not be permitted to triumph,' Wang Rong added. 'Look inside the book.' He pointed eagerly.

Paolo and Wang Rong opened the book and turned the pages. The Qian Long emperor's handwriting filled the margins. It was a personal volume, which he had used for his own study and contemplation. It was his way of expressing a heartfelt apology.

You Min refused to let Wang Yi stay to care for me. 'This is our house. I have no need of you. I am perfectly capable of caring for my uncle.'

Paolo laughed. 'I do not think we have a choice. She is very forceful,' he said to Wang Yi. 'Now give us some space. I need to examine him. And please ask the neighbours to disperse. Painter Lang needs rest and quiet.'

Wang Yi and Wang Rong left the house. I could hear them talking to our curious neighbours who were asking many questions.

'The wounds are clean and beginning to close, but there will be scars, I'm afraid.'

'Paolo, no one is going to see my backside.'

He sat next to me and read one of my favourite portions of Dante's *Inferno*, the story of Francesca da Rimini, a story of star-crossed love and treachery. I was still very weak and fell into a light sleep.

I awoke briefly and heard him in quiet conversation with You Min. 'We cannot allow infection. These salves are most important. The dressings must be clean. Put fresh ones on later today and tomorrow morning. Please continue to massage his legs and help him to move his limbs. I will return tomorrow.'

'I am to be your nurse,' she announced when I was awake. 'Physician Luo has instructed me in my duties. He even agreed that a woman's hands are the best.' Her voice was defiant. Long-buried memories rose from their hiding places—mothers hugging and soothing their children, kissing a scraped knee or a bruised elbow—and I remembered the painful longing. The hunger for that tenderness and love never receded; it merely slumbered.

You Min washed my face with warm water, combed my hair, and shaved my beard. Her touch fascinated me. It was competent and gentle. I felt pampered and safe. But when she asked me to remove my clothes so that she might apply cream to my back and bottom, I refused.

'Physician Luo told me to take no nonsense from you. I have orders to summon him if you try to oppose me.'

'This is not easy for me,' I pleaded. 'Allow me to preserve my modesty.'

'And risk infection? You are being a silly, stubborn fool. Do you not wish to get well quickly? How can you apply salve when you can hardly move? I am not a young girl anymore. I am your nurse.'

My modesty was thus torn asunder by female obduracy. Her silken fingers touched my stiff, nervous body. My muscles relaxed but my heart trembled. Her hand upon skin that even I rarely touched set off internal tremors. I understood why we took vows of celibacy. The urges of the flesh have no place in a life of service to God. This small flutter revealed the bottomless hunger and thirst that the proximity of a female arouses. You Min became a wine, an intoxicating bouquet to savour and devour.

I found myself fighting both my mind and body, and I doubled and tripled my nightly meditations and confessions of sinful thoughts to exorcise the new demon I had discovered. My discipline kept the urges at bay but nothing could stop the tingling of my body.

You Min brought her work home and sat with me darning clothes for the poor, quietly sitting at a chair near my head. I grew used to the fragrance of her body and the soothing way her needle flowed through the fabric.

From morning to night, I made no move without her support. Pain and itching fought with each other to provide the greatest irritation as scabs knitted the skin together. Any small movement, a twist, a sneeze, caused them to crack. You Min checked them frequently, dabbing them with a cooling balm and wrapping soft cloth around me as if I were a baby.

My conscience and my long-neglected male nature fought viciously. My Jesuit soul insisted that You Min cease her ministrations while my body yearned for her to continue. The wounds were either taking an eternity to heal or a blessedly short amount of time depending upon my mood. Spiritually exhausted, I noticed that You Min, too, had changed. Her fingers caressed more boldly, more confidently.

'You Min,' I asked one day. 'Why did you stop binding your feet?'

'It was too painful. Everyone said that after two or three years, one gets used to the pain, but my feet were stubborn. The more we bound them, the greater the pain. Finally, I could not walk at all. My father summoned the doctor. He said that the bones had split. He advised us to take the bindings off. My mother feared that I would be taunted by people when I was ready to marry, but I really did not mind since I had decided that I would never marry. When the time is right, I will become a big-footed nun for a temple.'

I watched her as she spoke. There was contentment and pride in her voice and face.

'It would not work for you to be a nun. You would have to shave your head. If foot binding was not in your nature, neither is a bald head.' I teased her.

'Perhaps you're right.' She laughed back. 'We are gifts to our parents. Why should we bind this and change that? I do not approve.'

'What would you like to do? Would you not want to marry?'

'I would like to be useful. No well-born Chinese will want me with large feet, and I could not face a life with someone coarse or uneducated. The Manchus do not approve of foot binding, but a marriage between a Han and a Manchu is forbidden.' She giggled and gave me a quick glance. 'Perhaps a big-nosed foreigner will marry me. He would not care if I had big feet.'

'I haven't met one here in China who would be a worthy husband for you. I am afraid we will have to find a Chinese one.'

She looked startled at my comment.

Though we had shared a house for over a year, the past weeks had changed our relationship. She had flourished into a young woman and was clearly the mistress of this house while I meekly obeyed her instructions. On another level, I was aware of words unspoken, of feelings and desires smothered. There was danger lurking beneath the surface, and I prayed that the passage of time and the restoration of my former life would dissipate it.

By the time Cocco returned to the capital, I was beginning to walk without pain, and fresh, pink skin covered the lines made by the beating.

'What a shocking story,' he said when You Min told him what had happened. 'Seppe, your god is very hard on you. He grants you a great talent yet throws troubles in your path that would destroy a lesser man. I will not leave you again, not until I am certain you are safe from people like Eunuch Duan.'

'Thank you,' You Min said, 'for helping to protect my beloved uncle-father.'

It was weeks before I was able to return to the Forbidden City. When I was ready, Cocco and You Min walked me towards its great gates. With the fresh vision of their loving faces, I entered and passed by faces that knew of or had witnessed my humiliation. From somewhere I could feel eyes bore into my back and knew they belonged to Eunuch Duan. Though I looked hard, I could not find him. He kept well out of view.

I painted a new portrait of the emperor that highlighted his long, fresh, noble face. I not only painted his two ears, I exaggerated their size and brought them forward.

Next I turned my attention to the empress. When I called on her at the Kun Ning palace, Dignity Wife was with her. They were both dressed in silk robes that were virtually identical to the one the emperor had worn for his portrait. I swallowed hard and began my work. I imbued their portraits with as much dignity, style, and beauty as possible—for peace of mind and the well-being of my body.

Pure Wife, who was third in the hierarchy, resided in the Eastern Palace. Although Pure Wife was not allowed to enter the main palaces at will or to look freely upon portraits of the emperor and his consort, she too was dressed in an identical robe to that of the empress. Even her hairstyle and hat were identical.

My mind raced as I sketched her. How many spies were at work? I doubted that Duan Shi Lian would attempt another attack on me so soon after the last one, but I was wary of the emperor's women. I had heard enough stories of the scheming of palace women over the centuries to fear their displeasure. To be caned once was enough for any lifetime. I questioned every official I knew, every friendly eunuch and other painters to ascertain the potential danger of my predicament. To a person, they insisted that whatever a concubine wore, I should paint.

When I arrived at Western Palace, the fourth wife, Nice Wife, was dressed identically to the others, and so it continued. A sour taste entered my mouth. I realised that all eleven concubines and the empress would wear the same dragon-phoenix robes, the same brown fur hats, and sit in the same pose as the empress. The task before me seemed to stretch to a monotonous eternity. These women did not want to look like individuals. They all wanted to be the same person. I felt like a monkey on a leash, robbed of my creativity.

I received permission for Cocco to serve as my assistant, and he was granted limited access to the Forbidden City.

'I am happy to be a non-royal painter,' he whispered as he gazed around. 'My life is peaceful and comfortable. I have never been threatened or tormented by any eunuch, minister, or concubine. Or caned. Though I should be deferential, to my eyes the Forbidden City is no place for an ordinary man.'

'I would have to agree with you. Unfortunately, I have no choice.'

'You are also no ordinary man, Emperor's Painter Seppe!'

I brought Cocco to meet all the concubines and other wives apart from the empress. He observed them carefully and noted individual features and characteristics.

One quality was shared by all—jealousy. Each concubine insisted on viewing every preliminary painting. Oh, how the claws came out! One complained that her eyes were too small, another that her face was too long. Pure Wife felt that her expression was too bitter. Nice Wife did not want such narrow eyebrows. Comfortable Concubine objected to what she described as a fierce look in her eyes. Happy Concubine insisted she was not as fat as Comfortable Concubine. Agreeable Concubine whined that we had not captured her soft, kind features, particularly when we had made the foul-tempered Smart Concubine appear so gentle.

Cocco was quickly as addled as I had been before his arrival. My deadline approached and my head ached.

'This is an impossible piece of work,' he moaned.

'I must find a solution.'

'They have an ideal sense of themselves that is unrealistic.'

'That's it!'

'What's *it*?'

'Wait and you shall see,' I said with a smile.

In great haste, I painted portraits of eight women that were based on two types of faces, long, with either a pointed or a rounded chin, with only modest differences in lips, noses, and eyes. Cocco watched my progress with disbelief.

'Seppe, are you certain this is a wise decision?'

I spread my arms wide. 'May I introduce you to a new painting style? I call it 'idealised reality.'

He shrugged his shoulders. 'I don't know what to say. It's a bold strategy, and possibly foolhardy, but I'll help you without question. Otherwise you'll never finish in time.'

The faces were completed quickly. The robes took far longer as the embroidered designs were so elaborate. Shortly before the deadline approached, Wang Rong came to see us.

'I intend to see it first,' Wang Rong said.

'Isn't it against household law?'

'I do not intend to tell anyone about this. Do you?'

We carefully unrolled it. It was incredibly long, sixty-six Chinese feet. Wang Rong took his time looking at all the women before he began to chuckle.

'Very clever.'

Two days later Wang Yi told me that the emperor wished to see me at the palace of the empress. I made my nine kow-tows amid the odour and the mess wondering what my fate would be. The peevishness that had made me act with such determination had dissolved into anxiety, though I shared my fears with no one.

'Please rise, Emperor's Painter Lang.' Those words, spoken kindly, fell upon my ears like the sweetest music.

The emperor and his empress sat upon thrones and Dignity Wife perched on a low chair. Behind the three of them, all the other concubines were arrayed in a long line. The emperor was smiling while the women were solemn. When I saw the scroll lying at the foot of the platform, my heart raced and my throat felt parched.

'Missionary Lang,' the emperor began, and I tried to read clues from his voice, 'we are lucky. Today the empress and my concubines want to thank you personally.'

'Your Majesty is too kind. Your servant is not talented. I try with all my heart. I hope, Bixia, that you and the honourable ladies can accept my humble offering.'

'Approach for your reward.'

I moved forward and dropped to my knees. A eunuch held a lacquer plate covered with a yellow cloth. He pulled the silk away to reveal the most exquisite piece of yellow jade resting in an open, silk-lined box.

'We call this dragon's liver jade. It is a treasure from the north-west. This single piece of jade is more valuable than an entire chest of silver. Zhen thinks this is a worthy gift for you. Take it as a token of my affection for you.'

'Your worthless servant is most appreciative and humbled by such a beautiful gift. Bixia, a thousand thank yous can only begin to express my gratitude.'

'Painter Lang, with each passing day you become more Chinese.'

Cocco was waiting anxiously with You Min when I returned home.

'At least you are alive and in one piece,' You Min commented.

'Everything is fine,' I said and described the scene in the Kun Ning palace. I handed the box to Cocco. 'Here is what he gave me.'

'What a beautiful piece of jade. Look, Little Sister, have you ever seen anything so remarkable.'

'Cocco, it's yours. I want you to have it. Without your help, I would never have finished in time. It is a perfect present to give to the woman you ask to be your wife.'

'You are too generous, Seppe. Wait, there's a piece of paper in the bottom.' He handed it to me. It was written by the emperor.

I read it aloud. *'It is easy for a man with power and wealth to please many women, but it is a rare monk who can accomplish the same.'*

'I believe the emperor understood what you did,' Cocco said.

'He did appear to be rather amused.'

5

Basking in the emperor's favour, I decided the time had come to make a request, one that had been preying on my conscience since his coronation. It was a delicate matter that required the right moment in order to guarantee approval. Bowing low, I pleaded for a pardon for Jin Kun.

The emperor stroked his chin. 'Zhen remembers him. He is a great artist and can serve us well. His punishment has lasted long enough to atone for his errors. Zhen will send word that he may return to the capital.'

Jin Kun returned to the capital in October 1738. He had been gone for seven years. I was working on the frescoes in the Southern Church when he appeared, guided to me by a beaming Cocco. As I hastened down from the scaffolding, he fell to his knees.

'I won't allow this,' I said, pulling him to his feet and hugging him in a European fashion. Only when I released him did I see how much he had aged and changed. The handsome, confident artist was gone. In his place stood a timid, thin, sallow shadow of a man. Tears welled in his eyes and freely tumbled down his cheeks in long streaks while he shook his head, too overcome to speak.

'Do not be sad,' Cocco said. 'You are where you belong, and the emperor wishes you to paint for him again. My brother will help you.'

'I do not deserve the friendship and generosity you have shown me,' he said, still unable to raise his head and look at me.

'You deserve much more than I am capable of giving. I want no mention of any of this again. My only wish is to see you teaching young artists and painting according to your desires.' My innocent words opened his wounds further. I had hoped to comfort him, but I unleashed his pent-up pain and relief. His shoulders shook as he sobbed. We led him to a pew and sat down on either side of him. Of all the places for him to find emotional release and peace, there was none more appropriate in the capital. Our church, celebrating sacrifice, dedication, and resurrection, emanated with hope. I believe he felt it, though he said little.

Once he recovered his composure, the three of us walked home. Once inside, I told him to wait while I retrieved the glorious paintings I had hidden among my possessions these many years. With a degree of relief, I handed them into his trembling hands. *Wan bi gui Zhao,* I uttered, as I had promised I would when I accepted the controversial paintings. *I have returned the jade of the state of Zhao.*

Shortly after the emperor ended Jin Kun's exile, he granted another long overdue pardon, correcting another injustice of his father's reign. Wang Rong informed me that, attended only by a handful of close officials, quietly, without any ceremony or prior notice, the Qian Long emperor released his uncles from prison. Yin Ti and his two brothers had spent sixteen years imprisoned in the tomb of their father. I never saw them but was told they were all extremely frail, almost blind, and weak of mind.

Anyone could see how much the country prospered with the change in the Qian Long emperor's attitude towards foreign trade. The capital was alive with foreign specialists advising on new industries for export; Chinese-style furniture and ceramics had become highly fashionable in Europe and Chinese timbers were in demand in the colonies of North America. The emperor pursued his dream of protecting and promoting Chinese crafts by generously using Treasury funds to establish countless workshops and factories. He added to the imperial art collections and began tentatively to collect Western art. The older the relics, the greater his admiration. After the bleakness of life under his father, his reign brought light, energy, and growth.

On a fresh autumn evening You Min and I walked back home from the Southern Church.

'I am a lucky Jesuit,' I said. 'I could not wish for a more fulfilling life. Perhaps my Lord will be angry at me for expressing such satisfaction, but my happiness cannot be contained.'

'Why are you so happy?'

'What is it that makes men content? I am no different from most. Work, friends, family, and home. Never in my life have each been so rich.'

'Family?'

'Well, though I am a Jesuit, I feel—'

I did not get to finish that sentence as a heavy object struck the back of my head. I felt it fall down my back and drop to the ground. I stumbled and You Min screamed. She would not stop. 'Go away! Villains! Leave us alone!'

Doors opened and people rushed outside. Holding my head and feeling blood drip down my fingers, I was aware of the sound of several men running away. Dizzy, I collapsed and leaned against a wall. Many concerned faces surrounded me. Hands reached out to pull me to my feet and guide me home.

'White Lotus scum,' someone said.

'How could they attack him? The emperor's painter?'

'If you had not been with him they might have killed him.'

'It does not look so bad. Even though it's bleeding heavily, his skull is all right.'

'They hate all missionaries. These attacks are more frequent.'

'And more violent.'

'Help me get him inside,' You Min said. 'No more talk of violence for now. I will clean his wound and put him to bed.'

Again, I was the lucky recipient of her attentive care; again, I felt her soft hands.

'You Min, someone mentioned White Lotus. What is it? And have you known about these attacks on missionaries? I was unaware of them.'

'Father-Uncle, you live inside your paintings, not in the real world. The White Lotus group is led by a man who claims he talks to the gods. They tell him that white foreigners are evil and will destroy China. He urges all of his followers to help him rid the country of Westerners. You must be the last man in Beijing to hear about White Lotus. Now rest.'

The following evening, You Min sat quietly stitching while I sketched an idea for a large landscape painting. Though I had a large bump and a cut, I had not suffered too terribly from the rock the miscreants had thrown. You Min was silent but I sensed she was pre-occupied. Her brow was furrowed and she started to say something several times but stopped abruptly. When she finished sewing, she bit the end of the thread with her teeth and put the garment down on her lap.

'Father-Uncle, do you think of me as your daughter?'

I put my sketchbook down and looked at her. Her eyes were unusually defiant. 'Not by blood. You know that. But you are a daughter in my heart.'

She closed her eyes and spoke. 'Are Jesuits really not able to marry?'

'We are not. We swear an oath to be celibate after our training.'

'Do none of you ever take a partner?'

'I cannot speak for every Jesuit, but none of my brethren here has broken their vows. Why are you suddenly so curious about us?'

You Min's chin jutted out. 'In China we have *Hua He Shang* or "Flower Monks." Monks who are celibate but not chaste.'

'You Min, why are you talking in this strange manner? Have you heard something about one of my fellow Jesuits?'

Her eyes flashed with annoyance. 'Uncle, do you really not desire a home? Do you really want to die without ever having had a wife and children of your own blood?'

Her question took me aback. 'It is not a thought I allow to enter my mind. If we who serve God decided to marry, our greatest concerns would be for our families. Who would be left to serve the needs of the people?'

'Are you truly content to spend the whole of your life without something that is so natural? Do you never want to share your life with a woman? Are you certain your god really wants this?'

'I became a Jesuit at the age of nineteen. I swore my vows and have lived as a Jesuit for almost forty years. I understood the sacrifice I was making. I know no other life. I have no reason to question my vows now.'

She gasped. 'What do you feel for me?'

'I love you dearly. As a father should care for his daughter.'

'I am at the age that most girls marry. Why have you done nothing about finding a husband for me? Have you thought about that? I have shown you my father's letters. He grows anxious.'

Those words stung deeply. I had been selfish, ignoring his concerns as I did not wish to change the life we had created. It was indeed true that I knew of her father's concerns. In addition to seeing his letters to her, last year, when we accompanied the emperor to Cheng De, her father had brought up the subject of marriage. 'I am sorry that I have been negligent. We must begin the search for a husband immediately.'

'I have no plans at the moment.'

I looked at her. 'Surely—'

She stood up. 'Do you know why I have no plans to marry?'

'No. I do not know.'

'It is…'

'Is there a problem?'

You Min stared at me with wide eyes, then shook her head hard and turned her face away from me. In a quiet voice she said, 'It is because I cannot bear the thought of leaving you.'

'You…' I could say nothing more. The dangerous undercurrents of the past months that I had tried to ignore swirled within my chest. More than thirty years separated us. I had not granted scandalous thoughts any soil in which to grow, but her words gave them life nonetheless. Both our futures hung upon a thread; the possible repercussions of this intense yearning were frightening. If I gave in now I would not be able to control the desires ever again. I could feel them grasping at the edge of my consciousness, panting and howling to be set free. If the emperor suspected that I had repudiated my vows and way of life, he would never trust me again. How could I betray the trust of Chen Yuan who had given me his daughter to educate? How would Cocco, Paolo, or Rector Ignatius react?

A buried memory stirred, Antonio's story of his illicit love. Antonio had succumbed to his desires and taken his Tibetan princess to his bed. He had suffered terribly for that transgression.

'Why are you so blind?' You Min's voice brought me back to the present. Her shoulders began to shake. Her hands crept up to her face, covering and shielding.

'You Min, I am your father-uncle and fifty-three years old. Though I am healthy, who knows how much more life remains in me. And, dear child, how I am now is how I have always been. You cannot deny yourself marriage on my behalf. My life will go on as it has always done.' I spoke in a soft, coaxing tone, but could not control the shaking in my voice.

'Why do you Jesuits insist on punishing yourselves? The Chinese eat you, spit you out, use you, trod on you. You take pride in your denials and humiliations.'

'Our work is to spread the word of God. We do not believe that man is only capable of selfishness; if that were so, the end of the world would be at hand. We seek to bring out goodness, to create His kingdom on earth so that all men and women may feel His grace. Imagine what a wonderful world it would be then.'

You Min snatched my hand and squeezed it. My sketchbook tumbled to the floor, landing beneath her chair. 'Do you want me to go? Do you want to see me in the house of another man? To bear his sons and daughters?'

I thought of this house without You Min. I also thought of Antonio's life after Dan Zhu's death. You Min symbolised sunshine and music, order and stability. But what she suggested was impossible. And yet it was enticing. *This is sin,* I thought. This is how sin creeps into a soul, claims it and changes it.

'No. I do not wish you to leave. But...'

'You must not say "but." You have said enough. I will model my life on yours and never marry.' You Min grasped my hand firmly. Her eyes bored holes into my mine. 'Anyway, since I am a big-footed woman, no one would want me.'

I felt the pressure of her hand on mine. Such a beautiful face stared at me; only a hand's width separated us. Hot emotions welled inside me. Slowly, You Min brought her body and her face closer. Blood surged in every part of my body, pumping, pulsing. Every muscle tensed and I felt as if I were about to explode into a million pieces. She was so tender. She leant closer and parted her lips. I could see her white teeth and her tongue: a doorway to a virgin's forbidden territory. I could feel myself tumbling towards a lover's lake, crystal blue, shimmering, pure and clear and irresistible. When I parted my lips, she closed her eyes and waited. I grasped her shoulders, tingling at the curve of warm flesh under my fingers. I allowed myself to enter the current. Time stopped. A bright light seared my eyes and I put my hands up to protect my vision. Something gently pushed against my chest and I moved backwards. I shook my head and put my hands on You Min's shoulders. She was waiting for my lips. I pressed my lips on her silken hair and planted a fatherly kiss on her forehead.

'May God protect you, my child.'

You Min looked at me as if I had struck her. Without a word, she turned and left the room.

'Zhen has received excellent news, Painter Lang. Your friend Chen Yuan has produced the largest crop of bai shu, sweet potatoes, to date. He had found a reliable way to propagate the plants and to ensure high yields. It has taken twenty-three years, but at last, he has succeeded. The lao bai xing have a new food. I will go to the Tian Tan palace and thank our ancestors for this gift and I will pray that famine no longer plagues the people of the north of China.'

As he spoke, I thought about the day in 1718 when I had first met Chen Yuan. The Kang Xi emperor was busy tilling his small field in a corner of the summer palace when Chen Yuan arrived bearing the first sweet potatoes the Kang Xi emperor had ever seen. Chen Yuan was immediately dispatched to Cheng De to begin sweet potato trials. At the time, none of us would have expected it to take twenty-three years to overcome all the problems associated with successfully growing sweet potatoes.

'Merchant Chen has farmed with his heart and soul to succeed in his trials with bai shu. The words I have just heard fill me with such pride for him and hope for this great nation,' I said.

'Zhen has dispatched soldiers from the eight armies to guard the fields day and night. I have sent word that Zhen will travel to Cheng De to observe the harvest myself. Would it please you to accompany me?'

'It would be an honour to accompany you and witness this great harvest.'

'Painter Lang, you speak well. Your love for this man and Zhen's people fills me with pleasure, for Zhen knows your words to be genuine.'

You Min was understandably overjoyed with the news and squealed so loudly that neighbours came to see what the matter was. No one could understand her muffled words so I explained.

'We are truly fortunate,' someone uttered, to a chorus of agreement. 'We have the emperor's personal painter in our midst and now the daughter of the man who has ended starvation.'

Many of them crowded into our house, reaching out their hands to touch You Min as if she were a blessed being. She was far too excited to take much notice of their actions.

I could not imagine celebrating Chen Yuan's momentous achievement without Cocco and Jin Kun and left the house to find them. Though they often travelled for inspiration for their marvellous landscapes, by good fortune, both were in the capital now. Since Jin Kun's return from exile, the two artists had become collaborators and close friends. Cocco, a man who instinctively sympathised with a soul in pain, was singularly responsible for Jin Kun's spiritual rebirth. It was not an easy task as Jin Kun had suffered a great deal in the north-western border region, where he was poorly equipped, both physically and mentally, to cope with harsh living conditions. Succoured by Cocco's optimistic and enthusiastic nature, Jin Kun slowly but surely found his footing and new strength.

'I have been the recipient of so much good fortune from the moment I met Wu Yu that I am honoured to offer guidance and friendship to another deserving person,' Cocco told me when I praised his commitment to Jin Kun.

The four of us set out together, and after several long days of travel, we were in sight of Chen Yuan's fields.

'He will be near his sweet potatoes. I'm certain of it. Let us go to the fields first,' You Min insisted.

Chen Yuan's hut, full of farming materials, still occupied the same position. Though it had expanded somewhat over the years, it retained its original banner: *Sweet fountains make green melons.*

Pointing, You Min shouted, 'Look! There he is. Baba! BABA!'

Chen Yuan turned, dropped a hoe, and ran towards us with open arms and tears falling down his face. 'Daughter! I could hardly recognise you. So grown up. And Lang, old friend! And Painter Jin and Painter Jiang! Your arrival fills my heart with joy. At this momentous event, your presence is more important to me than that of our beloved emperor. What a lucky man I am.'

We all turned as You Min's mother and brothers called out and ran towards us from another field. You Min leapt like a rabbit and hurried off to meet them. Cocco followed, running as if he were a youth.

'He loves your family,' Jin Kun told Chen Yuan. 'I believe he feels he too is a part of it.'

'That would not surprise me. And it pleases me.'

Chen Yuan's appearance worried me. His colour was yellowish and he was painfully thin. 'Are you well, old friend?' I asked.

'Just a small stomach complaint. Worries about the crop. I am fine. Come, let me show you how we are preparing for our ten-thousand-years-living emperor's arrival. There have been countless officials here for days getting everything ready: fireworks, musicians, priests. Unbelievable.'

Two days later, I finished my prayers as dawn was breaking and admired a breathtaking sunrise. *God is smiling on these people who have laboured so hard for so many years,* I thought. I was certain that His divine pleasure beat in my own breast.

'How do I look?' Chen Yuan asked. He wore a new blue silk jacket and gown with a matching blue cap.

'Like a prince,' I told him, and he smiled.

His wife, with her cheeks aglow, wore a gown of expensive silk that I had brought from Beijing.

'Thank you for this gift,' she said as she patted my arm. 'I have never worn anything so fine.' She glanced past my shoulder. 'You Cheng, let me adjust that. You must look perfect for your emperor.' She fussed with her sons, even though they towered above her. When she had finished with them, she made Chen Yuan wait patiently while she adjusted his clothes and brushed off imaginary bits of fluff.

We all turned as You Min came into the room. She was wearing a dress I had had made to celebrate her eighteenth birthday. The palace seamstresses had used the finest Vietnamese silk, from a city called Xigong or Saigon. It was a soft red brocade, with delicate patterns of flowers sewn into the cloth. On the day I gave it to her, she refused to wear it.

'No,' she had said, 'I am still a girl. I am not yet grown up. I will keep this qi pao. It fits me well, don't you think? I will know when it is the right day to wear it.'

'You will be the most beautiful woman in the fields today,' Chen Yuan said, beaming with pride. 'I am told there will be many concubines with the emperor as well, but you will outshine them all.'

'Today, Father, I am wearing a dress Uncle had made for my eighteenth birthday. I refused to put it on then, but I am proud to wear it today, for I wish to honour you.'

Chen Yuan put his hands on You Min's shoulders. 'Thank you, daughter. Today we all celebrate a birth. With this harvest, we pray to heaven that the north of China never suffers famine again. Now let us all go outside and wait for our ten-thousand-years-living emperor.'

The borders of the fields had already filled with hundreds of people. Many of them had the blackest faces that only the poorest peasants possessed.

'How appropriate that they should be here to see this,' I said to Cocco and Jin Kun.

'Chen Yuan felt it was important. He sent messengers to all the nearby villages so that they could taste this new food and see their emperor. After all, he spent years experimenting on their behalf,' Cocco informed us. 'He will cook some bai shu for all the people to taste.

Huge pots were hanging on stakes that had been placed around the fields amidst the people. Tending one pot was a woman with a smiling face that I could not fail to recognise. I hurried over to make sure it was not merely my imagination.

'Mrs Zhang?'

'Missionary Lang, we meet again as I always hoped.' She tried to bow at my feet but I stopped her.

'Where...how...?' I had so many questions that I didn't know where to begin.

'I gave birth to a son, eventually. Master Chen Yuan took care of my boys soon after you left. He gave my sons work in the fields and taught them many things. Master Chen was like their uncle. My husband died while I was away, you see. My sons are here somewhere. They're men, with wives and children. They don't remember the time I was away. They'll help others plant bai shu. We haven't forgotten you. Chen Yuan tells us all about you and your great success. We're all proud. Some things work out all right.' The crooked smile hadn't changed, though her hair was grey and her skin hardened by years in the fields. Chen Yuan had never told me he had helped them.

'I'm so pleased for you.'

Drums and pipes sounded from afar and all talking ceased. Hundreds of heads turned in the direction of the music, necks stretching and twisting.

'I can't believe the emperor is coming here,' Mrs Zhang said. 'I never thought I would ever see him. Not in ten thousand years. Go, go—shouldn't you be with Master Chen? I'm pleased to have seen you again.' She waved me off as she had done on that dark mountainside fourteen years ago.

The mounted battalions of the Armies Under the Eight Banners, their colourful flags soaring high above their heads, came into view and a murmur flowed among the crowd. Behind them came Daoist priests, officials of the Board of Rites, and hordes of marching banner men. People fell to the ground as they recognised their emperor. Surrounded by princes, nobles, and senior officials, Hong Li rode on a horse known as Juan Mao Shi Zi Cong or the Curled Hair Lion Horse. He was resplendent in a gown that I recognised as one reserved for harvest ceremonies at the Tian Tan palace.

Chen Yuan and his family waited on their knees near the platform. I looked around and saw his hut in the distance, the one that held the golden hoe given to him by the emperor's grandfather. The words carved on it were never more apt: *zhuo xin chun yi*, Farm with your heart. How pleased Xuan Ye would have been to participate in this event.

The last to arrive in the procession was the phoenix carriage of the empress and eleven other carriages, each containing a concubine protected by a troop of imperial bodyguards.

The emperor dismounted and walked towards the prone family. Chen Yuan crawled to meet him. The emperor waved his hand, and two eunuchs rushed forward carrying something on a tray. The emperor lifted the cover off it, revealing a silver object.

'Take this gift, Merchant Chen. It is a small token of my appreciation for your years of sacrifice and trial. It is a silver plaque with four characters engraved on it: *yu shu ding bang*, Cultivation of Sweet Potatoes Stabilises the Whole Country. Your emperor and all the people of China thank you. Arise, please, and take this from my hand.'

Chen Yuan stood up and gingerly reached out with quaking hands for the plaque that sparkled in the early morning sun. He and his family bowed several times.

He shouted, 'Wan Sui, wan wan sui. Live ten thousand years. One million years.' The peasants shouted with him while the emperor smiled.

The emperor turned and approached an altar that had been set up earlier, and silence descended once more. He bowed to heaven and to earth. He spread drops of red wine around the base. He nodded to the head of the Board of Rites, who signalled to someone else. Musicians began to play and singing filled the air.

Firecrackers, lit to expel evil spirits, spread charred bits of paper over the ground. Two actors with large masks of baby faces ran around gathering up the rubbish, a familiar symbolic act to show that money and resources must not be wasted.

At another signal, the ceremonies came to an end. The moment to begin the harvest had arrived. Chen Yuan's eldest son stood at the near end of a long, straight line of healthy plants. Chen Yuan stood at the far end.

From his chair on the platform, the emperor stood up and shouted, 'Wait!'

With his usual confident, long strides, he descended and walked to the edge of the field. The crowd fell to its feet once more. Chen Yuan's son instantly understood the emperor's intention and moved aside. The peasants whispered excitedly to each other. The Qian Long emperor turned and gave a benevolent smile to his subjects. Eunuchs helped him take off his outer robe and slowly, meticulously, roll up his sleeves. Apart from snorting animals and flapping banners, all was still.

'Shall we pull the roots together?' he shouted to Chen Yuan.

'Your Majesty is the leader of the people. Your insignificant servant does not dare to give the order.'

'No. Today is an exception. You are the commander of these bai shu. You give the order and I will obey.'

'I humbly accept.' Chen Yuan made nine kow-tows then raised himself to his feet. 'Begin.'

The emperor and Chen Yuan bent as one and, walking along the row from either end, pulled the thick plants from the ground until they met at the middle. Tears stung my eyes and blurred my vision to see ruler and visionary working together with equal heart and strength, seeking the best for the most vulnerable. We Jesuits believe that every good action is a reflection of God's grace. I felt in my heart that I was witnessing as divine an act as any I could have imagined. They extracted from the earth more than just plants—they coaxed out hope and brotherly love.

Chen Yuan and the emperor severed the tops of the plant with knives and cleaned the earth from the root to reveal plump, red sweet potatoes. The crowd murmured their approval and delight. Pulled from the earth tenderly as if it were an infant coming into being, each potato was large, whole, and fresh. The assorted drums and pipes blasted forth again. Other workers surged forward and began to harvest rows upon rows of fat sweet potatoes.

Chen Yuan came over to where I was standing. His face was flushed. I helped him and his sons pull a huge set of Chinese scales closer to the growing pile of sweet potatoes. Official accountants took up their positions on small desks and made notes. Several called out numbers while others tallied them using large abacuses.

'Eight thousand eight hundred thirty-five jin and four ounces...Nine thousand seven hundred sixty-four jin...Ten thousand nine jin and three ounces...Eighteen thousand six hundred jin and seven...Eighteen thousand and eight hundred eighty-seven jin point seven ounces.'

'Halt!' the emperor shouted, and all activity instantly stopped.

He was chuckling quietly to himself. He held the last sweet potato to be weighed. He pulled a dagger from the sheath of one of his guards and strode over to Chen Yuan. 'Zhen is the emperor of this country and claims the right to taste a bai shu from this harvest.'

He used the dagger to remove a portion of it and weighed the remaining section. He cut off another small portion and weighed the sweet potato once more before nodding and handing it to official. 'Now you may weigh this last bai shu,' he said as he slipped the two small portions into a pouch that hung from his waist.

'Exactly nine ounces,' the official announced.

The accountant added it up on the abacus and stood up bellowing at the top of his voice, 'The total weight of this first harvest of bai shu is eighteen thousand eight hundred and eighty-eight jin.'

Chen Yuan clapped his hands, along with everyone else present. The Chinese are infinitely superstitious and numbers affect every aspect of one's life in China. By cutting off a chunk of the last sweet potato to be weighed, the emperor ensured that history would record a lucky number for this harvest, a succession of 'eights.' Peasants, officials, and soldiers roared as drums beats rose to a crescendo.

I watched Chen Yuan's face and could have sworn that the sun shone brighter in competition with the glow that radiated from him.

Jin Kun, Cocco, You Min, and I did not leave Cheng De immediately, and it was fortunate that we delayed, for as soon as the festivities ended and the imperial party disappeared, Chen Yuan fell gravely ill.

He lay in bed, his body shrinking each day. In a short time, he deteriorated like a flower that wilts and shrivels once it is plucked.

'I have been ill for some time,' he admitted to me. 'A large tumour of some sort in my stomach. Only my doctor and my wife knew the truth. For many months, I have refused to allow death near, being unwilling to bid farewell to this world when my life's work was so close to fruition. But my life's energy sits upon the fields of Cheng De and now there is nothing left to keep death away. Dearest Friend Lang, you must be father to You Min more than ever and choose a good husband for her. I entrust the honour and care of my sons and wife to you. I know you will help them if ever they need you. Though we have spent little time together, I consider you to have been my greatest friend. We were destined to meet. The gods decided that long ago. Because of you my life gained meaning and value.'

'You say too much. You made your own fate.'

'No, old friend. You made my dream possible. I never knew how to repay you. I hope that You Min has learned to love you as a father. May she bring you happiness through her marriage and children. I must rest now. Goodbye, my dear foreign friend, and live well.'

Chen Yuan spoke to each member of his family alone. When he had said all that he needed to say, he fell into unconsciousness and died shortly afterwards. He had planned his death as efficiently as he had tended his fields, leaving everything in order and well tended.

At his funeral, his sons asked if there was anything I wished to do according to my Christian customs. Though it was difficult to control my emotions, I made a short speech and ended it with the Twenty-fourth Psalm, which had long ago been eloquently translated into Chinese. I modified it slightly to make its meaning clear to my audience. *The earth and all that grows upon it is the Lord's, as well as the entire world and all of us who dwell on it. For He created it upon the seas and established it upon the floods. Who shall ascend into the presence of the Lord? Who shall stand in His holy place? Only the man that has clean hands and a pure heart, who has not sullied his soul with vanity or deceit. That man shall receive the blessing from the Lord and righteousness from the God of his salvation.*

I did not need to say more, for from the nodding of heads I saw that they believed Chen Yuan had earned a place in my heaven as well as theirs.

Hong Li issued a memoriam of his own, which was inscribed on Chen Yuan's tomb.

Chen Yuan gave up his work
When he accepted the challenge of Sheng Zu.
He spent all his wealth in order to save the country,
Guiding generations on the planting of sweet potatoes.
Contributing his whole life and energy to the task.
Zhen respected Chen Yuan.
Zhen wished to grant him a title and a post,
To publicly display his worth and great contribution to his country.
Unfortunately, he was taken from us too young and too quickly,
Zhen greatly regrets his loss.

Chen Yuan is hereby rewarded posthumously with the title of a member of the Scholarly Institute.

This title is commensurate with his efforts and will honour the next generation.

The emperor summoned leaders from all over Rehe province to the capital and urged them to employ Chen Yuan's methods to cultivate sweet potatoes and to save his people from famine.

'Chen Yuan trained many young men to help with this task. Listen to them well and follow their instructions. Their salaries will be paid from the Treasury. If these sweet potatoes are planted far and wide,' he announced, 'we will have served not just this generation of Chinese but our descendants as well. Our ancestors will thank us.'

Honours do little to ease the grief of the mourners. You Min stayed in Cheng De to be with her mother and brothers. I returned to an empty house for the first time in five years.

'Shall I move in with you until You Min returns?' Cocco asked, sensing my sadness.

'No, but thank you for your kind offer. Cocco. The older one gets the harder it is to accept change, particularly the loss of one's friends. Though I rarely saw Chen Yuan, I grieve as if he were a member of my family. Now You Min will soon marry and I will experience another change: the emptiness of a house when a child departs forever. And I say this when I am only a mock parent. What is it like for a real one?'

'You Min must have a husband who recognises the importance of her relationship with you. Most men will expect her to turn her back on her family.'

I threw myself into painting the remaining frescoes of the Southern Church, a labour of love that had already taken four years. Since frescoes are temperamental mistresses, it required all my attention, and the days passed rapidly.

The ceiling was all that remained to be done and it proved to be the greatest challenge of all, not just because of the height but because of the distortions required to create a coherent scene to be viewed from below.

All alone in my aerie, labouring with my face a few inches from the ceiling, I prepared the surface of the ceiling carefully. I ground the pure pigments and applied them to fresh lime-plaster so that they could dry together. I applied four coats of plaster: a *trullisatio*, an *arricciato*, an *arenato*, and a *intonaco*—a first coat, a second, a sand coat, and the final coat. I applied the *intonaco* only a small portion at a time, amounts I could reasonably accomplish within a session. I put the cartoon on the *arricciato* with *sinopia*, a red earth pigment, and coloured it with the final layer. I planned each painting session carefully, like stages of a journey. Nearing completion, I worked feverishly.

As I worked in 1742, a new papal bull arrived: *Ex quo singulari*. Issued by Pope Benedict XIV the bull referred to another one, the *Ex illa die* of Pope Clement XI written in 1715. By solemn decree, we were forever forbidden to graft the religion of Rome onto those of China. Christian converts, if there were any, could only serve Christ and turn their back entirely on Confucianism and rituals of ancestor worship. It was an absurd edict, one made by imbeciles in Rome who had no idea of the depth and strength of Chinese beliefs.

On the altar of our Southern Church, we had carved Chinese and Jesuit symbols together. At the very centre were the signs of our society, the cross and the entwined letters IHS, which represented the first three letters of

Jesus' name in Greek capitals. Beneath it were three nails of the cross splayed out like a fan. Surrounding the stone on three sides was a wooden frieze of dragons and the elements in which these creatures lived: earth, water, heaven, and fire.

I had always found the mixture of symbols reassuring. We Jesuits worshipped God no less well for our religious tolerance and acceptance of Chinese beliefs alongside our own. With this latest edict, I saw the end of any hope of Catholicism in China. Not only would the Chinese refuse to convert with the conditions we were forced to impose, but the emperor would view this attempt as interference in the affairs of his country, as an assault on China's sovereignty. The rift between the Vatican and China would never be healed, not in my lifetime, not in a score of lifetimes.

I finally finished the frescoes and dismantled the scaffolding. My peers and superiors were finally able to gaze upon the results of years of quiet labour. They praised the frescoes warmly, but I was disappointed. I realised that I was a better painter of Chinese images than of Christian ones. I stood alone after everyone had left, wondering why that should be.

'We have a surprise for you.' Cocco had silently crept beside me. He startled me. He and Jin Kun visited me often—without their presence I may have gone days without speaking to anyone. I thought they had taken a short journey to Hangzhou. Jin Kun stood by the entrance with a hint of a smile playing on his face. When I followed them outside, You Min appeared. She had been hiding behind a tree.

'She's come back. We went to fetch her, but only after she wrote to us saying she was ready to return.'

'I don't know what to say. You kept this from me? You had news of You Min and didn't tell me? I've been worried and no one has put me out of my misery.'

'Father-Uncle, do not be cross. It was my idea. I wanted you to finish these glorious frescoes without any interruption. They are the most beautiful things I have ever seen. We slipped inside when all the other Jesuits were there and you weren't looking.'

'Come, let us eat and celebrate her return,' Jin Kun said. 'There is much to be grateful for.'

'I want to ask you something,' You Min announced after we returned home and began to eat dinner. Her eyes were strange, defiant and challenging. 'What is your true opinion of your Cocco?' she asked. She pronounced the name as if it were Chinese: *Kou-Kou.*

'What do you mean?'

'Did you know that he came to visit me in Cheng De in order to speak to my mother about marriage?' She was carefully folding a scarf. 'My mother assumed you knew already and approved of the arrangement. Did you know anything about it?'

'No. This is the first I've heard of it.' I was dumbfounded. He had given me so many clues over the years that hinted at his intentions, but I had been too blind to notice. Did he love her, though, or was he trying to please me somehow, to keep us as one family? I tried not to show You Min my confusion. 'It's a wonderful idea. Cocco has cared for you since he first saw you. He will make an ideal husband for you. Surely you are pleased?'

'You stupid clown.' You Min scowled and hit her thighs with her clenched fists.

'Stupid?'

'You cannot admit how you really feel.' She spat the words at me. 'Do you want me to marry Cocco?'

It was all beginning to sink in. A great sense of unease filled my heart.

'Are you going to answer?' You Min glared at me.

'Ah…I…' I pushed my soup bowl away, unable to eat another mouthful.

'Are you happy to give me to someone else?'

'Cocco is not just someone else. He is like my son.'

'Oh, you idiot. Speak from your heart. Look at me. I am not a little girl any longer. I am already twenty years old.'

A fine sweat dampened my forehead. Before I could speak, You Min put her hand over my mouth. 'Say nothing if you cannot speak sincerely, from your heart. I do not want to hear your empty sermons, your Jesuit cow droppings.' She waved her hand, sending an ivory statue flying. I did not hear it shatter and assumed it landed safely.

I paced around. My body seemed to be on fire and my breath collapsed into short, sharp bursts. A violent rush of emotion threatened to sweep away all that I held sacred.

'You must speak,' You Min demanded standing her ground.

I forced the words from my dry mouth. 'Do you wish to marry Cocco?'

Those lovely dimples appeared as she scowled and slowly shook her head. 'I do not.' It came out in a soft whisper. 'I do not want to marry him, although he is a wonderful man and will make a loving, kind husband. Do you want to know why I feel this way?'

I shook my head, slowly and unconvincingly for both of us. She ignored me anyway.

'If you only reveal a corner of your heart to me, I will never leave you. I will accompany you for your whole life. Whatever you want, I will be to you: your daughter, maid, lover.' Tears streamed down her face.

'You Min, You Min, do not say these things.' I took her in my arms. Emotions robbed me of words for an eternal moment. Yes, I loved her and feared her departure, but I knew I would not forsake my bonds and the duty I owed to Chen Yuan. Nevertheless, whispers taunted me, saying that love was unlike any other emotion, luring me towards uncertainty. Images hinted at pleasures that could be mine.

Her arms encircled me with bear-like strength. I felt suffocated. She sobbed, and I rubbed her back.

'Just say it. Just say "stay with me".' You Min pushed out the words between sobs.

My words surprised me. They were pleading and desperate.

'What you propose would send me to hell. If you really love me, you must help me, my dear child. I need your strength. Only you can save me. Love me only as your surrogate father. Do not even think of any other love. The love of a daughter is the most I can hope for in this life.'

I kissed her forehead. I became aware of the fragrance of her body, the heat from her anguish. Her small breasts pushed harder against my chest with each quaking breath. I kissed her forehead again closer to her eyebrows, then I kissed the bridge of her nose and her cheeks. Her lips were parted and lush. I felt drawn to them like a fish sucked into a whirlpool.

In a flash, the image of Christ appeared across her face, distorted and unreal. He stared at me in agony, the crown of thorns on his head. His look pierced my heart until another image took its place: that of Antonio as the fire of his execution was lit. It was a look of triumph, as if he were finally free of the demons that tormented him. It broke the spell that her touch and fragrance had released. I could feel my body relax and my embrace change from one that was dangerous to one of compassion and resignation.

I separated from You Min as gently as possible. Her jaw dropped open. In her eyes, I saw recrimination and resolve.

A few days later, Cocco brought a formal contract of engagement for me to sign. I will never forget the look on his face as he handed it to me. He glowed with happiness and exuberance. How long had he nurtured this dream of marriage to You Min? I hugged him.

'Congratulations. May your dreams become reality and your joint happiness become your greatest asset. Do you remember Chen Yuan talking to you about waiting to find the right woman? You are wise, Cocco. There is no finer woman than You Min. And I have no doubt of your love for her.'

'If love means that you cannot bear to be parted and that you dream of someone constantly, I love her. Her ties to you make her more precious to me, but I marry for love only. Seppe, I will be a good husband to her.'

'I don't doubt that.'

'I could never have imagined a more perfect marriage than this one.'

The contract was quickly signed and witnessed. You Min could no longer live with me once she was engaged. From that moment, she belonged to Cocco's family, which, ironically, consisted solely of me. Not unexpectedly, You Min and I were no longer comfortable in each other's presence, and she left to live with her mother. I don't know how much Cocco was aware of what had passed between us, but if he suspected he never breathed a word.

The loneliness I feared descended like a thick fog. Though I tried to fight it, bitterness filled my heart. When You Min left, she took her smell, her sight, and her sounds with her and left a great hole; a permanent hole. The walls, ceilings, and floors swelled with memories of the happiness that had once been in my house and began to press upon me. My spirit, already fragile, shattered under the weight.

The papal bull fed ammunition to our enemies in Europe and China—Franciscans, Dominicans, Benedictines, and Jansenists as well as local officials and followers of the White Lotus movement. They smelled our vulnerability and moved closer, sensing weaker prey. Many claimed we hid behind religion to disguise our underhanded commercial activities. Some missionaries working in other provinces died at the hands of angry gentry. The number of Jesuits in China dwindled even further. Rector Ignatius, our marvellous leader, died from a heart condition.

I spent time looking at the frescoes I had painted in the Southern Church. My Lord sat on his throne in judgement above my head. I thought I had painted a peaceful expression on his face. When I looked at the completed ceilings, he appeared to be in mourning.

Low in spirit, I locked up the house that I had shared with You Min and moved all but a handful of my belongings into my house in the Forbidden City.

'Have I upset you in any way?' Cocco asked.

'Never,' I answered, putting my hand on his shoulder. 'The source of my unhappiness lies abroad. Our society is in great danger. As much as you and You Min are my family, my fellow Jesuits are as well. If they are suffering, I am too.'

'But hiding away from your friends cannot be the answer.'

'For the moment, it is.'

'I don't entirely believe you, but I will not try to convince you to take another path. Seppe,' he added, 'I have known you for twenty-five years. I know your character better than you think.'

'Perhaps better than I know myself.'

When I unpacked, I left my religious books wrapped up and my crucifix shrouded in cloth. Questions and emotions I had suppressed for so many years festered and gnawed at my gut. It hurt to look at artefacts that taunted me for the choices I had made. To numb the inner voices, I turned to wine as a willing companion. Sometimes, when I woke up from a drunken stupor gasping for breath, I shouted for help but no one responded.

The Forbidden City was no place for a depressed Jesuit. Women were everywhere. Treachery threatened in every corner. Words from Li Bai's famous poem came back to me: '*Life is to be enjoyed; do not waste wine on the moon.*'

The wine I wallowed in was the best, a gift from the emperor, called Yu Xian Weng Jiu, Wine for Meeting the Immortals. I was still sober enough to paint for him. I covered silk canvases with his playthings: horses, dogs, monkeys, and children. I painted battles and conferences with his great armies. When the emperor found me hopelessly drunk, he never criticised me. He left me with my wine, although many eunuchs would scold, slap, and kick me after his departure, unless Wang Rong was present.

'Wine has its own spirit,' he told me one day. 'Zhen, too, drinks when Zhen composes poetry. Of all the great poets, could any of them have done so much without wine?'

When I became too inebriated to hold a brush, he gently asked Wang Rong to guide me home and keep me there until my darkness had passed.

'I do not know what causes you to dislike yourself so, Emperor's Painter Lang. Can you not pray to your god for *salvation*, as you call it,' Wang Rong said.

'What God?' I spluttered. 'He abandoned me long ago. He confused me and left me to make my own choices and most of them were wrong.'

'It seems to me that you have made excellent choices.'

'What do you know of life, a eunuch who lives within these walls?' I regretted the harsh words as soon as they came out.

'This eunuch, who knows nothing, knows who is a friend and who is not.'

Paolo, dear Paolo, came to my rescue. One day he drove me outside Beijing to a large farm he had purchased. It was prosperous and well tended. From the proceeds of sales and rent, he explained, he had established a free dispensary for the poor. As the emperor's personal physician, he was forbidden to examine anyone else, but he made medicine available to all who approached him and could not afford to pay. Paolo worked like a man driven to complete a life's work in the shortest possible time.

'Seppe, what can we do to help you?' he said as we walked in the fields near the farm.

'Do you have any medicine to make me stop hating myself?'

'What is there to hate? What has precipitated this sudden depression?'

'If I understood that, I could do something about it. You cannot help me. No one can. Paolo, I don't want to discuss my feelings with anyone. Take me back to the city and leave me alone. I do not wish to see anyone.'

'Wine has only made you angry and bitter. It is distorting your sense and reason. The first thing that must be done is to sober you up. No more wine.'

'If you do anything of that sort, I will never speak to you again.'

'We shall see.'

Paolo wasted no time. The next day, the emperor ordered me to abstain from wine. When I tried to leave the Forbidden City, guards escorted me back to my house. I cursed Paolo though he was nowhere to be seen.

Duan Shi Lian, the clever serpent, appeared at my door, his bulk filling the doorway.

'Bring me wine,' I shouted at him.

He looked at me with his false, sneering grin. 'I once believed that only we eunuchs led a cruel existence. I now realise that you missionaries have a much more bitter life.'

'Why do you say that?' I snarled.

'Excuse me for being so frank. I was a man, although I am one no longer. Before the surgeon cut my organ, I at least knew about the affairs of men. My only reason for castration was poverty. But you, such a handsome, vibrant man, you are forbidden by regulations to have sexual desire. We have no capability for sex and no desire, but that devil trapped between your legs still wants his erection and ejaculation. It must be very difficult. So you cannot be compared with us. Do you think I am right?'

I was spitting with indignation, and foul words formed in my mouth, but I swallowed them, recognising a vein of truth that no one else had spotted or dared to mention. It was a terrifying moment.

'Royal Painter Lang, this slave does not know all your business, but I have heard some things. Has Painter Jiang not just become engaged to your daughter? Ai, yai, yai. In China we say that when a daughter leaves home, the father must feel disappointed.'

Duan Shi Lian came close to me. He bent down. His breath smelled of garlic and onions. I was certain I smelled an odour of decay and rottenness.

He whispered in my ear. 'You must feel lonely. I can find you a place with a clean woman. It is one hundred per cent safe. I will never reveal your secret. You can...' His hand brushed against my crotch. He began to laugh lasciviously.

My hand tightened into a fist. Duan Shi Lian saw it and quickly moved back.

'If this speech dirties your ear, just assume I said nothing. But do you really have no senses and no urges? I have heard many people say that your daughter was very pretty. She may have had big feet, but–'

He did not finish. He was too busy ducking the ink stone I hurled at him. It hit the doorframe, fell, and broke apart.

Eunuch Duan hesitated and thought for a moment. When he spoke, there was no hint of anger. He began to laugh.

'Emperor's Painter Lang, we say that if there are those with problems there are always those who are happy to solve them. You should listen well to my words. They will be of use to you some day.'

8

On the morning of my fifty-fourth birthday, I woke up yelling, 'Don't do it!' This was my twenty-first day without wine. It took a few minutes for me to calm down. Sweat soaked my bed clothes and sheets. In my dream, I was naked, nailed to a cross upside down. A hand held a knife close to my lower body while a harsh male voice cackled maliciously. When I felt the metal touch my male organ, I began to shout, which woke me.

Carnal desire was a dangerous adversary. An intense desire for sexual fulfilment and physical bodily contact, repressed for so many years, had risen up and tortured me as effectively as any inquisitor. Until You Min, I had never felt the limitations of the choice I had made. Comforted by male friendships and largely ignorant of women, I passed the years. How unfortunate that this great trial should come in my thirty-third year as a celibate Jesuit.

The face that stared back at me in the mirror was hollow and lined. I felt limp and deeply ashamed. I went to find Paolo and explain the torment I had put myself through.

'Will you hear my confession?' I asked.

'Of course,' he answered.

After I had finished, he said, 'You have behaved as a decent man and an honest Christian. We have all questioned our choice of celibacy at some point. Some have succumbed. Few have dropped to the dark depths you have experienced, but we are not all artists. As an artist, you feel things far deeper than the rest of us do; that capacity to feel is the key to your creativity. How much more you will understand for having been confronted by the blackest parts of your soul. Welcome back. We have missed your humour and energy.'

I left Paolo and went to find Wang Rong.

'Please accept my deepest apologies for anything I said that may have hurt you. I was unforgivably cruel when I was drunk.'

'Thank you for those words, but they are not necessary. I have seen into your heart, Painter Lang, and know what lies there. You were more harsh on yourself than to anyone else.'

Not long after my re-awakening, my adopted daughter and her mother returned to the capital, prior to her wedding. They stayed in my house while I moved in with Jerome.

During the preparations for the wedding, Cocco, Paolo, Jerome, Jin Kun, and I spent a few hopeless hours discussing the wedding until Cocco dismissed us all.

'Dearest Big Brothers and Honourable Jin, what do you know of weddings?' he teased.

'Nothing,' we all answered.

'Exactly. There are many things you are useful for, but this is not one of them.'

He was thirty-seven but still had the appearance and manner of a twenty-five-year-old, exuberant, enthusiastic, warm, and high-spirited. In his presence, You Min sparkled like a freshly lit fire. She had blossomed from a quiet, solemn girl into a giggling, charming, flirtatious woman. Their laughter echoed off the walls. They teased each other and played, even chasing each other around the courtyard like young children. These were sides of her I had never seen, but Cocco was not surprised.

'You have spent so little time among women, Big Brother. Clever as you are, you have no idea how complicated and intriguing they are. Whatever they say to you, they are thinking on several levels at once. We men are much more direct.'

'How do you know so much?'

He gave me a look that told me he had no intention of telling me. 'Let us just say that I am not a monk and have not lived in a monastery all these years.'

It was, of course, unusual to begin this Chinese wedding ceremony in Jerome's overtly Christian house. You Min left her 'childhood' home in the wedding palanquin, dressed in red satin. Her mother followed behind in another sumptuous palanquin. My role was even more unusual since I served as father to both bride and groom. Paolo said a few words to bless the marriage—enough to satisfy us but few enough to not taint them as Christians.

'Thank you,' her mother said to me. 'What a fine man you have chosen. My husband would be very proud. Now we are doubly joined to you and I will not lose her as a daughter as most mothers do. Jiang Shan Min assures me of that. We will be grandparents together. Is that not a delightful idea?'

The couple moved into a house near the Back Gate Bridge. I returned to my house in the Forbidden City. The look on You Min's face when I parted from them at the door to their marital home remained with me forever. In her eyes, I saw contentment without a trace of regret. Though I was happy that she was loved and was giving love in return, for an instant I felt like a discarded implement. So this is what it is like, I thought, this inexplicable adaptable spirit of womankind. I also felt a stab of jealousy for Cocco. We had shared the same parentless start in life but how different were the fruits of our life. In the end, he won the dearest and only woman in my life.

In the early summer of 1744, Wang Rong came to my studio in high spirits.

'I have been given permission by Hong Li to return home on a ying sheng visit.'

'Congratulations. But what is ying sheng?'

'Ah. It is not something you can explain. You must see it. Go to our ten-thousand-years-living emperor and request leave to join me. I think he may agree. The country air will put colour back into your cheeks.'

At my next opportunity, I asked the emperor for leave to travel with Wang Rong.

'Painter Lang, you have many paintings yet to accomplish for me. For almost one year, you lived in a dark cloud and Zhen waited patiently. Now that you are painting well again, Zhen is reluctant to lose you even for a short time.'

'Your miserable servant is happy to comply with your wishes.'

'Of course, such a visit could provide inspiration and many new pieces of work, so Zhen is of two minds.'

'Bixia, which mind shall decide?'

'Painter Lang, are you teasing me?'

'Never, Bixia. I am your humble servant.'

'You may go. But for no longer than two weeks.'

As I backed away, I caught the emperor sharing a conspiratorial glance with Wang Rong.

We left the capital before dawn in a grand carriage pulled by four horses. Wang Rong's village was called Shadow River. It lay in Zhili province only eighty miles from Beijing.

'If we travel all day, we can reach my home by nightfall.'

As we rattled and lurched on the dusty road, Wang Rong changed. For the first time I saw dark emotions: anger, bitterness, and regret.

'Are you still interested in hearing my story?' he asked.

'Of course I am. You have been a loyal friend, helping me through those dreadful months, yet I know so little about you.'

While holding the reins, he pulled out a small jug, and I poured cups of tea for us. We ate dumplings and other small treats prepared by palace cooks for our journey.

Wang Rong paused and sighed deeply. Although he had passed the age of fifty, he still had unlined, smooth, soft skin and black hair. He reminded me of a porcelain figure with a finely formed, delicate nose, forehead, and chin. He brought his brows together and pursed his lips.

'Some places are famous for tea or melons. My area in Zhili is famous for the production of eunuchs.' He laughed wryly as he said this. 'My old parents are simple peasants, the sort who rely on heaven for sustenance. When I was eight, we suffered a terrible drought. It continued year after year. I turned nine, ten, eleven under the shadow of death. I have an older brother, a younger brother, and a younger sister. My mother and father struggled to feed the four of us. In the fourth year, they decided it best to purify the body of one of their sons so that he could become a eunuch. They believed that the remuneration would be enough to support the family. This is not always the case.

'We brothers drew straws. I pulled the short one. So I became the chosen one. The gods who had not smiled on my family were even crueller to me. You can imagine how terrified I was. To purify the body requires an adept hand, a special surgeon. The skill is passed from father to son. The surgeon in our village is extremely good. Perhaps that is why my village sends so many eunuchs to the emperor. The fact that everyone tried to reassure me that the surgeon knew his work well and had skilful hands only added to my misery. The surgery would change my life not theirs.

'A contract was signed. In it, I pledged that I accepted this purification willingly and was not coerced.' Wang Rong snorted and shook his head. 'We also signed a waiver so that if something went wrong the surgeon would bear no responsibility. My father led me to the house of Surgeon Liu. We called him Liu Dao, Mercy Knife. Both my father and Liu Dao added their names to the contract. Then I knelt down, prostrating before my new master.'

Wang Rong turned his face toward mine and gazed upon me with mournful eyes.

'No matter how high I rise, this man is my master and I am his slave. My father paid Liu Dao with several bags of millet, large containers of ashes from sesame plants, and fifty sheaths of window paper. This was spring, the time when most castrations are done before flies or mosquitoes are too thick. I no longer remember if either of us cried. Liu Dao took me to a cave in a nearby mountain. The stale air and acrid smell inside stung my nose and eyes. We sealed the opening with window paper.

'A kang, or bed, stood in the far corner. It was made of bricks with an opening at its side for a wood fire. At the head and foot double rows of bricks supported a wooden platform above the brick bed. A hole was cut in the wood where my bottom would rest so that I could relieve myself without leaving the bed.

'My master explained that for three days I would eat no dry foods, only liquids. We spread sesame plant ash all over the board to provide a soft cushion for my back so that I would be comfortable during my recovery. We prepared scores of soft heads of barley plants, extracting the liquid. The empty reeds are used to drain urine from the severed penis. We boiled da ma plants to make a strong drug that takes pain away. He began to give me liquid to drink and I relaxed under the drug's influence. We added chicken eggs to the bubbling da ma water and cooked them until they were rock hard.

'On the third day, Liu Dao laid me down upon the wooden platform and strapped my arms and legs into manacles. He tied a thick rope around my waist to secure my torso to the platform.

'He washed my body well. By this point, I had drunk so much da ma water that I was hallucinating. Only when he covered my eyes did I react, but the drugs were powerful and kept me calm.

'He cut quickly. At first, my groin felt cool. Then a searing pain rose up. I opened my mouth to scream. He immediately stuck one of the rock-hard eggs into my mouth. It blocked my throat, and my body immediately tensed. At that moment, he removed my testicles. It only took two minutes to remove my penis and testicles.'

Wang Rong paused to sip more tea. I turned away and stared at the flat expanse of fields filled with rows of barley. My heart ached for him.

'Surgeon Liu kept me very drugged for the next three days,' Wang Rong continued. 'He told me later that he used portions of a pig gall bladder to stop the bleeding and help drain fluid. He placed a board between my legs to keep them apart. Another block of wood and the remaining egg separated and lifted the wounded area off the wooden base of the bed.'

Wang Rong snorted ironically. 'At least I can thank him for being an excellent surgeon. If too little is cut off the organ can re-grow. If the cut is too deep, a depression forms and passing urine becomes a problem. It sprays out like a fan, forcing the eunuch to relieve himself like a woman.

'Now I can explain the term ying sheng.' Wang Rong's voice was thick. 'Broadly speaking, the bits removed from me are worthless. But as part of the concept of purification of the body, they are precious. Liu Dao preserved them for the time I would return and claim them. He half-filled a rice barrel, called a mi sheng, with a special dry lime and placed my lost bits inside.

'When the lime had done its work, he also put the contract in it. He wrapped the barrel in an oilskin and a red cloth and, using a rope tied around the barrel, raised it so that it was hanging from a beam. As he pulled the barrel up, Liu Dao called out "hong bu gao sheng." Each word has a double meaning. *Hong*, the character for red, also refers to my life as an official. *Bu* means to pace, but carries the same sound as the word for cloth. *Gao* is both to be tall or to rise. And as *sheng* refers to the act of lifting or promotion, the act of lifting the rice barrel, *ying sheng*, also symbolises the hope for a prosperous future and many promotions.'

Wang Rong sighed, shaking his head. 'We eunuchs fear dying without having the chance to retrieve our lost parts. If we are buried without them, we remain neither male nor female for eternity. It is said that the king of the netherworld will not accept us. At some point in our lives, we visit our master and buy back the missing pieces. That is what I am going to do.' Wang Rong spat tea onto the road.

He was silent for a time before he spoke again. 'There is another reason for this visit. No eunuch wishes to die without leaving a descendant behind, so each one who is able to adopts a son. I am about to adopt the youngest child of my little brother.

'My family has prospered by their decision to purify me. It took several years, but eventually I began to send them annual gifts of silver and other objects. Can you believe that other families are jealous of mine because of my success?'

As evening approached, we entered the village. Several young excited lookouts began shouting. In a short time, firecrackers spluttered to life and soared away, while gongs and drums pounded. The entire village came to greet us.

Wang Rong's father and mother rushed towards their son and bowed to him. His parents were small, round, and healthy-looking, with heads covered in identical silver hair. They spoke together in a local dialect. After a few minutes, Wang Rong interrupted them and introduced me. I have no idea what he said, but they both came forward, giggling and clucking their admiration. They each grabbed an arm and dragged me forward.

Everyone surged around to examine me closer. Children stretched their arms to touch my hair, even though its former rich reddish-blond was faded now by many streaks of grey. They were fascinated by my fair colouring. The younger ones grabbed my hands and rubbed my skin. They looked up at me with wonderment and curiosity. Some of the little ones giggled at my nose and nostrils.

Wang Rong said something and the children backed away in fright. 'I told them to let the emperor's painter alone. Our ten-thousand-years-living emperor will not be pleased if he is harmed,' Wang Rong said.

A palanquin arrived and a young boy stepped out.

'Uncle,' he called.

'This is the boy I am adopting,' he explained.

Wang Rong mounted one of the handsome horses that had pulled our carriage. He had brought a richly decorated saddle as well.

Wang Rong's parents walked on either side of me as we walked towards the house of Surgeon Liu behind Wang Rong and the palanquin. Two mournful Chinese wind instruments wailed alongside, a la ba and a suo na. The daor jiang stood in the entrance of his house. He was a minute, shrivelled stick of a man. Wang Rong dismounted and performed his kow-tows to his master. Surgeon Liu turned and walked inside. Only Wang Rong's immediate family and I followed him. He mounted a stool and still barely reached my chin. Very carefully, Surgeon Liu brought down one of many red bundles hanging from the beam of the room.

His old hands had trouble undoing the rope and unwrapping the cloth and oilskin, and I felt anxious for Wang Rong. I tried to catch his eye but his mind was elsewhere. Surgeon Liu opened the rice barrel and pulled out the contract. Wang Rong lifted the contract and carried it outside. In front of the waiting crowd, he set it alight. A cacophony of firecrackers erupted around the house. Wang Rong and I re-entered the surgeon's house once his parents and the villagers had moved off to partake of a grand feast. I stood by his side as he peered into the barrel.

He sighed. 'I am a man again.'

I put my arm around his shoulders. He seemed so small and frail. When he was ready, we left to join the celebration.

9

Though Wang Rong had been granted a month's leave from the palace, I could not anger the emperor by staying longer than two weeks. Before I left, Wang Rong issued a prophetic warning.

'My innocent friend, you are returning to the Forbidden City alone and this worries me. I am very torn. I wish to be with my family for a bit longer, but I fear that Eunuch Duan Shi Lian may take advantage of my absence and cause you trouble. He knows how vigilant I am as far as he is concerned. We Chinese say: "Ning dei zui jun zi, bu dei zui xiao ren": You are safe to insult a gentleman, but never insult a little man. Eunuch Duan is small-minded and bitter. Dear friend, stay on your guard.'

I hurried back to Beijing and continued my work on a series of portraits of humble people. I had noticed a beautiful servant girl in the western palaces and asked her to sit for a portrait. The servants in the Forbidden City were quite accustomed to my interest in them and were generally delighted to be asked. This young girl's name was Liang Cui and she had been in the palace for four years. She was the daughter of a middle-ranking officer in one of the Armies of the Eight Banners. She was a charming, fresh-faced creature with elegant slanted eyes, pencil-thin, curved eyebrows, and skin that glowed with life. Liang Cui was as enthusiastic as she was radiant. While I painted her, she chatted about her life. She told me that female servants were forbidden to make up their faces. Only twice a year were maids allowed to apply lip colouring, during the Spring Festival and on the emperor's birthday. Any girl caught using colouring at other times was beaten.

As I finished the painting, Liang Cui asked, 'Emperor's Painter Lang, people gossip here that our ten-thousand-years-living emperor loves to look at your work. This portrait that you do of me, will you pass it up to our beloved emperor?'

'I show him many of my works. He appreciates painting and I learn from his observations.'

'May I peek at the portrait of me now even though it is not finished?'

I nodded and she tiptoed behind my back and stared at her likeness for some time. 'Emperor's Painter Lang, a person without colouring on their face is not pretty.'

'What are you saying? I believe you're very attractive. Have I not fairly captured your likeness?'

'Oh, it is wonderful and flatters me. It is only that my face is so plain. Emperor's Painter Lang, would you be so kind as to put a bit of colouring here.' She pointed to the cheeks.

'It shall be done.'

Liang Cui giggled with pleasure. 'Oh, thank you. However, if anyone asks you, you can never say that I requested you to add colour.' Her eyes showed fear.

The emperor was delighted that I was back in the Forbidden City and asked to see my most recent paintings. 'Painter Lang, this one painting of a female servant is most enchanting. Is she really so beautiful? Who is she?'

'Bixia, she is a servant in the western palaces.'

'Why has Zhen never seen her?'

'In her own words, she has never had the luck to see her emperor.'

A week later, while I was painting in my studio in the evening by candle-light, a foul, acrid odour wafted into the room. I turned around to find Duan Shi Lian watching me. We eyed each other briefly before I spoke.

'I did not hear you enter. Have you been here long?'

'Not at all. I am relieved to find you at home. It has been a long time since we met face to face. The emperor has ordered some servant to be brought to him. I believe you know her—Liang Cui, a servant in the western palaces? The emperor's interest has made the ladies of the western palaces angry and jealous. Since Wang Rong is absent, it is my job to bei gong. There are those who think it would be better if you went to fetch her. The wives and concubines of the western palaces will not waste their anger on such a beloved foreigner.'

I did not understand the term bei gong. I didn't trust him and had no intention of falling into a trap again.

'I am an artist. This is not my affair. Please leave.'

'Missionary Lang, the wives and concubines of the emperor are not to be ignored. I believe you should think about this. You may not trust me, but if you ignore me both of us may suffer.' He rubbed his hands together anxiously. I thought he was genuinely nervous but I remained wary.

'Has the emperor ordered my assistance?'

'The emperor has said that he wishes her to be led to him by the man who has brought her beauty to his attention.'

'Fine. If the emperor has so ordered, I will obey.'

'You will need this.' Duan Shi Lian pulled a long yellow silk scarf from inside his sleeve. 'I will ask Wang Yi to accompany you. He understands the ceremony.'

'What is this for?'

'When you get there, Wang Yi will explain.'

I went outside to find Wang Yi waiting with two other eunuchs who stood holding lanterns. We walked towards the western palaces. Duan Shi Lian disappeared into the darkness in another direction.

Wang Yi whispered to me, 'I don't know what's going on. I don't think Eunuch Duan is lying, but I do not trust him. Ai ya. If only Wang Rong were here.'

When I showed him the yellow cloth, he nodded.

'This ceremony is called bei gong. It means to carry a female on your back to the emperor's palace. You are getting towards your silver-haired years. It is a long way from the western palaces to the Qian Qing palace. We will carry this special present together, like father and son.'

I patted him on the shoulder. 'Like father and son,' I agreed.

In the dim lantern light, I could see how he beamed and stood more erect. 'The silk is used like ribbon to wrap the selected one,' he continued. 'Now do not be upset by what I am about to reveal. The selected one will be naked. You must wrap her up snugly. She must not catch a chill or become ill after her liaison with the emperor.'

As we walked, I kept wondering where the sting might lie, but I trusted the emperor. Apart from our one unfortunate misunderstanding, he had always treated me with affection and respect.

When Wang Yi and I arrived at the western palaces, the wives and concubines were gathered together. Nice Wife spoke for all of them and made clear how displeased they were that a servant of theirs had drawn the attention of the emperor, all because of a painting. I wondered how they knew that it was my painting that had brought Liang Cui to the emperor's attention. We waited for many uncomfortable minutes until a servant came to tell us that Liang Cui was ready

Wang Yi and I followed the tiptoeing, petrified servant until we reached Liang Cui's humble quarters. Wang Yi remained outside her tiny room. As he had warned, she lay stark naked on her bed with her body twisted and arms folded over her chest. When my tall frame filled the doorway, she gasped.

'Oh, Emperor's Painter Lang, I am so ashamed. What will happen to me?'

She curled up her body and tried to cover herself with her hands. She had been crying; her eyes were red and swollen.

'I apologise. I had no idea when I made the painting that this would be the result.'

'My mistress is so angry.'

'How did they find out? So few people know about the painting.'

'You of all people must know that every corner is filled with prying eyes and loose tongues. There are those who want to do nothing more than make trouble for others,' she sobbed. 'Now they have turned their vengeance on me.'

'The emperor is waiting for you,' I said. 'I cannot promise you anything but I would hope that he will protect you from harm.'

'Oh, thank you, Emperor's Painter Lang. Your words give me comfort.'

'Now would you kindly stand up and I will wrap you as quickly as I can.' As I began putting the silk all around her young, slender body, I became angry. Why did the emperor insist that I get involved? He did not seem to care about my reputation among his wives and concubines. What did he think I would garner from this embarrassing situation? I seemed to possess thumbs instead of fingers and the silk slipped constantly from my grip. In the end, I succeeded, after a fashion, but the result was far from elegant. I lifted her over my shoulder but almost sent her flying beyond my back, expecting more weight than was actually there.

My anger rose with each step. I was aware that Wang Yi kept pleading to help carry her, but I ignored him. Wang Yi trotted by my side. We reached the emperor's palace, and eunuchs guided me to his bedroom. They opened the door and stood in rows on both sides with downcast eyes. As I strode into the emperor's bedroom, I did not wait for instructions. I placed her upon his dragon bed. Only then did I turn and kneel before Hong Li.

'Painter Lang, have the eunuchs not explained the rules to you?'

'Bixia, this bei gong business is a matter for eunuchs not painters or Jesuits. It is beyond my knowledge and abilities.'

'Please remove the silk cloth and place this beauty at the foot of my bed. She must enter underneath the cover and crawl her way to the top,' he said.

'Certainly, Bixia.'

I did as he asked and turned around. When I looked up, I saw amusement in his eyes. To him, this was nothing more than a prank, at my expense. I could not hide my anger.

'Even though you are my servant, you dare to show your temper. Do you find this task so insulting?'

'How can your slave dare to admit such a thing?' I bowed my head but did not kneel.

'You take this too seriously. Zhen is only testing you. Zhen has observed so many of you Christians. Zhen is curious about these celibate vows you missionaries take. Do you never feel hungry for a female? This evening, Zhen wanted you to see the other side of life. Zhen is satisfied to discover that you are faithful to your ethics. Your honour can never be in doubt.'

I snorted and held my tongue though there were many words that fought to come out. The emperor's face suddenly changed expression. The humour left and a hint of guilt entered his eyes, if only for a split second.

'Fine, fine. Go now. Zhen asks no more of you.'

I remained in my studio for several days, seeing no one. I looked through my collection of paintings and sketches of ordinary Chinese. I *wonder if I will ever dare paint another servant or worker,* I thought. *Perhaps it is time to take them to the Southern Church. They can be shipped to Italy and can cause no more trouble.*

Wang Yi knocked on my door and entered. 'The women of the western palaces wish to see you.'

'I do not wish to see them.'

'Venerable Uncle Lang, it is the empress dowager who orders your presence. You cannot refuse.'

One woman ruled above all formal hierarchy, the emperor's mother. She claimed ultimate control over the six palaces. The empress dowager waited for me at the Chu Xiu palace with all the wives and concubines I had painted. This woman had all the charm of a rusty blade and a face to match. She was called Niu-Gu-Lu. The first character meant a female cow. I thought about that each time I beheld her stony face at a banquet, festival, or ceremony. It was a shame that the emperor was such a respectful son. Perhaps without his indulgence she would have been a different woman. Power without responsibility and the tempering hand of the word of God is a breeding ground for evil.

I prostrated myself.

'Arise.'

This was my first formal meeting with her. Born in 1693, she was five years younger than I. I hoped that I too did not look like an overripe peach. Though her skin was lined, her hair remained raven black. She was haughty and stern. She was richly dressed in layers of silk and brocade and wore a large hat decorated with an assortment of precious stones.

'Missionary Lang, is this painting one of yours?' She motioned to a palace female to bring forward my portrait of Liang Cui. My heart sank realising that the episode with Liang Cui was not yet forgotten or forgiven.

'Yes. Respectfully, Empress Dowager, it is the work of this small servant.'

'You foreigners paint from life, do you not?'

'Yes,' I replied.

'Was this lowly servant not made up when she posed for you?' The empress dowager pointed to Liang Cui's lips.

'I beg your pardon?'

'You heard me. *ANSWER!*' She bellowed at me, her eyes narrowing into slits that made her even uglier.

'No. When I painted her she was not made up.'

'Then how did she obtain this appearance of a sorceress?'

'This humble servant, in a burst of inspiration, added some colour.'

'Fine. Now I will see which one of you is telling the truth. Come. Bring that sorceress here,' the empress dowager hissed.

When Liang Cui arrived, she fell prostrate upon the ground. The brief glimpse I had of her revealed how much she had cried. She was pale and quaking. My mind was racing. Why did the emperor not anticipate this risk and protect Liang Cui? Or had his mother overruled him? Was this not an overreaction on the part of the palace women? The emperor was free to bed any woman he chose.

'Servant Liang, when did you come to this palace?' Niu-Gu-Lu asked.

'Four years ago. When I was fourteen.'

'Four years. That makes you an experienced servant. How is it that you do not know the rules of this palace?'

'Precious Empress, I have said over and over again, when Emperor's Painter Lang painted my portrait, your cheap servant did not wear colour,' she sobbed.

'You dare to maintain this stone mouth. Institute house punishment,' the empress dowager ordered.

Two large, fleshy eunuchs came forward. They dragged Liang Cui towards an outside stone platform.

'Please—' I started to say.

'*SILENCE!* Not another word or she will be beaten double.'

The eunuchs stripped Liang Cui's trousers and undergarments from her. All the palace females and eunuchs watched. Liang Cui was moaning and shouting out her innocence. My heart tightened. I was again a helpless witness to arbitrary, wilful use of power. My mind raced, searching for some way to stop this beating. Liang Cui was forced to lie on the platform. The eunuch holding the cane waited for his orders.

Nice Wife walked over to her and shouted in a shrill voice, 'Are you ready to talk? Is it not so that you have lied? On that day did you not apply lipstick?'

'I did not. You can beat me to death. The answer is the same. Why do you not believe the emperor's painter? Is he not a trusted servant of the emperor?'

'Beat.' The empress dowager lowered her hand.

The cane whistled through the air and struck soft flesh. Down and down it came. Tong. Tong. Thirty blows. Forty blows. At some point, Liang Cui screamed, whimpered, then fell silent. I felt sick with guilt and prayed as hard as I had for many months. *Oh Lord, I have caused the suffering of an innocent creature. Why is this happening? What lesson am I to learn from this? Was I wrong to paint ordinary people?*

'Stop beating,' the dmpress dowager ordered.

Liang Cui was motionless. Several young female servants rushed forward to wrap her in cloths and carried her gently away.

'She is to return to her home. This sort of prostitute may not remain in our palace. Send orders for her family to come for her tomorrow. Give her ten strands of silver from the Treasury.' The empress dowager glanced around at the audience of servants, ladies, and eunuchs. 'When it comes to ancestral household law there can be no hesitation. Do you all see that?'

Suddenly I caught a glimpse of Eunuch Duan skulking in the shadows and realised that he had played his evil hand in this sad cycle of events. Who knows what he had told these she-devils.

The empress dowager turned toward me. 'Missionary Lang, I see you staring at Eunuch Duan. I am fortunate to have such a wise and loyal servant in my employ.'

I did not hide my disgust for either of them, moving my eyes from one to the other; a pair of serpents whose greatest joy came from harming others.

'I am aware that my son spoils you,' I heard the empress dowager say, and I turned to look at her with undisguised hatred in my eyes. 'However, you must understand that you cannot flaunt the rules of the household. Eunuch Duan tells me that you have painted many portraits of servants of the palace. Today, I will see these works. I will judge which are moral pictures and which are not. Any which adhere to the ancient law I will allow to remain. Those that harm the honour of the emperor will be destroyed.'

'I will show them to you, Empress.' Eunuch Duan came forward. He sneered at me openly. His delight was palpable.

As she walked past me, the empress dowager stopped. 'Missionary Lang, you people from the West come to China only by the grace of emperors who want your skills. Do not forget your place. I have heard that you encourage the emperor and the princes to wear Han clothes when you paint their portraits. And then you break our rules by painting a portrait of a lowly servant girl to present her portrait to the emperor. This is outrageous. Because you have been a servant to three emperors, I have no choice but to excuse you. Do not test my patience again, however.'

She left the palace and entered a palanquin. Eunuch Duan waddled behind on tiny feet, with mincing steps.

The women of the western palace surrounded me, cackling and teasing. 'Go home to see what they are doing. Unless you still wish to see Liang Cui and paint another portrait of her.'

I left with their harsh laughter taunting me and dragged myself home. Lost in thoughts about good and evil, it took far longer than was necessary. When I arrived, the empress dowager and her entourage were leaving although a small number of imperial guards remained. A large pile of paintings, drawings, and etchings filled the centre of the courtyard. Years of work stared back at me, paintings of images I had meant to preserve for posterity: simple labourers, peasants, views of daily life, humble villages, scenes of poverty and struggle. My heart sank to see what had been selected. At a glance, it was over one-third of my work from the past two decades, all irreplaceable. The majority of my collection of stamps, porcelain figurines, jade, bronzes, and bamboo carvings were ancient and had survived for decades if not centuries. My paintings were not so fortunate. At the very top of the pile, quivering in the breeze, was the nude drawing I had made of Duan Shi Lian so many years ago when the Kang Xi emperor had forced him to pose for the life-drawing classes.

Expressionless imperial guards lit the pile with burning torches. The fire caught quickly and roared, releasing familiar odours of paint and fabric. My neighbours, who had been watching, stood around me, offering words of sympathy. I neither prayed nor mourned; there was a strange emptiness in my soul. I had once described myself as a ship cast adrift searching for a new port, with fate as the mistress of my vessel. Now I was merely a passenger aboard that ship, heading for an uncharted destination without baggage.

10

For several days after my works were burnt, I sat in my house, numbed and grieving. The ground outside was charred and the smell of smoke clung to everything. Many distinguished visitors came to offer sympathy. The respect for art in general was high amongst the Chinese and any wanton destruction upset scholars, artists, and patrons. They did not disguise their dislike of the empress dowager. A number of servants also came to say a few quick, kind words to me before rushing off.

A few days later, Wang Yi told me that Wang Rong had returned to the Forbidden City and that he had been told of my misfortune. In a short time, he appeared at my door. He held up his hand, not letting me speak.

'His Majesty is shocked and sorrowed at the loss of what he calls your "heart and blood." He asks for your indulgence and patience. The emperor is unable to punish anyone involved in the desecration and destruction of your paintings, since the action was condoned and carried out by the empress dowager. He reminds you that he is a devoted, loyal son. Perhaps you understand this as a Christian, since you are loyal to your god at all times, even if you do not understand some of his actions. However, the emperor makes this promise to you, Lang Shi Ning: *Since Zhen is unable to punish my honourable mother or those who led her to make her dreadful decision, Zhen will attempt to soften this enormous loss with a special reward, one that will leave a worthy legacy of your devotion to China.*'

'What happened to Liang Cui?'

'The emperor has sent her to Cheng De. She will have a good life there, but she will never come again to the Forbidden City as long as the empress dowager is here.'

Formalities over, Wang Rong sat down heavily. 'I blame myself. I should have returned to Beijing with you. Though I warned you of the danger, Eunuch Duan was exceedingly clever this time.'

I clasped his hand in mine. 'Wang Rong, we Christians believe that God works in mysterious ways. Please do not feel guilty. For a moment, I feared that God was punishing me for my lack of devotion, but I don't think so anymore. In the past, whenever I have feared that misfortune was an indication of His wrath, He has sent a sign to me to show that I must find my own path to Him. There is a divine purpose to Liang Cui's suffering and my loss and I feel, in my heart, that something good will come out of this.'

In the early autumn of 1744, at a cabinet meeting the emperor made three announcements: Firstly, in the New Year, Yuan Ming Yuan would become his principal residence, the Forbidden City would be used only in the autumn and winter. Secondly, the artists Tang Dai and Shen Yuan were to create a volume of paintings and poems of the forty new gardens he had added to Yuan Ming Yuan. Thirdly, I, Lang Shi Ning, was to be the chief architect for an endeavour at Yuan Ming Yuan, the construction of palaces, fountains, and gardens, to be called the Western Gardens.

The emperor had been true to his word. I was overwhelmed by his gesture. It was much more than an act of generosity to balance the treachery of Duan Shi Lian; it was a hand of friendship stretched out from one continent to another from which would be created something for posterity to enjoy. I saw it as an opportunity to recreate an image of my homeland.

In Italian I called the gardens of Yuan Ming Yuan *il giardino del perfetto splendore.* I had first visited it in 1735, a few days before Yin Zhen's death. My second visit was several years later when Jerome and I accompanied this emperor on an inspection of the vast estate. It was broken into scores of smaller sections, each of which had a theme, created with plants, water features, sculpture, and architecture: unique, self-contained havens that I called 'sceneries.'

Jerome had surprised me with his wholehearted embrace of the theories of Chinese landscape design. Though his art remained wedded to Western concepts, he was a devotee of Chinese gardens. He wrote long treatises on their designs that were included in the *Lettres Edifiantes* Jesuits regularly sent back to Europe. He hoped that the West would adopt Chinese principles and use them in Europe.

One month after his announcement of my appointment, the emperor brought several ministers and relatives to view and officially name forty new additions—twelve new pavilions and twenty-eight 'sceneries.'

Yuan Ming Yuan was aligned on a north-south axis. The entire estate was basically rectangular in shape, somewhat larger east to west than north to south. A large proportion of the estate was water, artificial lakes, ponds, rivers, and waterfalls. It was made up of three pieces put together like a puzzle. Yuan Ming was the largest and contained the emperor's main palaces. Next to it was Chang Chun—not the same as Chang Chun estate beloved by the emperor's grandfather, which was many miles away and far smaller than Yuan Ming Yuan. Overlapping both Yuan Ming and Chang Chun was Wan Chun. Throughout the estate were hundreds of cottages, halls, mansions, palaces, pagodas, covered walkways, and pavilions. Almost every hill and mountain, river, waterfall, forest, and valley was manmade.

To my eye, however, the architecture was monotonous. Building materials were wood, never stone or marble. There were no domes, cupolas, spires, or bell towers. There were only two types of roofs: an elaborate style with roofs on all four sides of the building, some with inlaid triangles on the smaller sides and others without, as well as a simpler style that left the sides of the building bare. All the tiles were grey. Serenity and beauty were achieved through the combination of buildings and landscape design.

The naming ceremony was largely confined to Yuan Ming, which had the most buildings. As the emperor's private domain, it was a celebration of the glory of his kingdom. He had filled its mansions with national treasures: precious stones of all sorts, ancient relics of bone carving and ivory carving, embroidery, porcelain, calligraphy, lacquer ware, and bronzeware. Palaces were built with wood of ancient pine trees from forests over five hundred miles away. Special preserves nurtured rare animals, fish, insects, and butterflies. Three of the lakes held nothing but goldfish, some as valuable as one thousand double strands of silver. Stones, soil, and plants from afar recreated beloved parts of China in the emperor's private domain.

We set off at dawn for the naming ceremony, following a grey brick path that led to a small mansion. Sitting upon a thin stone platform with slender red pillars and red patterned window frames beneath curved roofs, it carried the name Zheng Da Guang Ming, Fair and Bright. We proceeded to the northeast, to the next collection of palaces. The emperor had selected several names: Labour for Government and Love Good Officials, Flying Clouds, Cabinet of Peaceful Judgements, Fragrant Green Bushes, Protect the Great Harmony, Hold Pure Fragrance Palace, and the Shadow of Delicate Wood Palace.

We boarded dragon boats at the front lake and rowed around the western side of an oval island. On the far side of this island was the back lake, several times larger than its sister. Willows swayed in the breeze and birds trilled from every direction. We crossed the back lake and moored the boats then followed covered walkways into a fairy paradise overflowing with flowers and miniature mountain villages set upon small hillocks.

We stood between two square parallel courtyards overflowing with peonies. He lingered amongst the flowers until a minister whispered loudly in his ear, 'Ten-Thousand-Years-Living Emperor, one hundred more flowers await your naming them.' The term *hua*, flower, carries a hidden reference to a woman. For the emperor to dian ming or to give a name referred to the act of selecting a lover each evening from his Receive Love Book.

Hong Li chuckled and picked up his brush to write a name: *lou yue kai yun*.

Everyone began to laugh loudly, obviously enjoying a vulgar double meaning that was lost on me. I later asked Jin Kun what the four characters meant.

'*Yue*, *yun*, and *yu*, moon, clouds, and rain, all have sexual meanings,' he explained. '*Luo yue kai yun* is quite specific. It means the engraved moon parts the clouds.'

Hong Li bestowed more names on pavilions and gardens; names like Apricot Spring House, Preserve Ancient Values and Accept Modern Ideas, and Natural Painting. By noon, when we reached another artificial mountain village, the emperor decided to eat. To protect him, a eunuch who had served three emperors stood at his back while he ate. This eunuch ensured that the ancient rules concerning imperial meals were preserved. The emperor was forbidden to eat more than three helpings from any one dish. Hong Li, busy discussing plans for the afternoon, reached for a fourth helping from one dish. He was immediately stopped by the eunuch's loud bark: '*House rules!*' This occurred several more times. I lost my appetite.

After lunch we continued on our way. Apricot trees and their rotting fruit lined the route. No one was permitted to touch the fruit of Yuan Ming Yuan other than the emperor. We reached an open pavilion capped with a straw-peaked roof. The inside was decorated by a poem by Tang dynasty poet Du Mu. I recognised the calligraphy of Yin Zhen. A river flowed briskly past the pavilion.

The emperor motioned for me to stand beside him. 'Missionary Lang, tomorrow Zhen will show you the Chang Chun garden. In the north-east is the large piece of land Zhen has reserved for you. Five months from the day after tomorrow, Zhen wishes to see a plan of your idea. Next year, as soon as spring comes, the first shovels of earth will be removed.'

'As you order, Bixia. My only concern is that I do not know if we can find enough skilled labourers and craftsmen. Are such people easy to find in China?'

'If they cannot be found, you may write to Europe to recruit the labour you require. Do not worry about the cost. If there are those within your Society of Jesus in Europe with talent, ask them to come here.'

'Bixia, your insignificant servant was unaware how much importance you attached to these Western Gardens.'

'Zhen is very curious about your ways. It is good for my country to understand more. You are a great painter. Are you also capable of helping me to appreciate your architecture and styles of gardens? It must be equal to what a king would have in your country.'

'Bixia, we will not disappoint you. Upon my return to my house, I will write to the See in Macao for assistance. Within five months, I assure you that the first plans will be ready to respectfully submit.'

The next day, the Qian Long emperor continued naming buildings and landscapes. At one point we came across a strangely shaped building. The Chinese said it was built like two sets of double handled levers placed on top of one another. I knew the shape as an ancient Sanskrit symbol called a *svastika,* basically a cross with short limbs protruding from the four ends at right angles in a clockwise direction. This design was one that was meant to keep the interior cool and bright.

To my surprise, we passed through a peach grove with a simple cottage dedicated to Tao Yuan Ming, a scholar who lived over a thousand years earlier. His poems were some of the earliest Wu Yu had taught me. He had disdained society and moved to a peach orchard in Wu Ling village in Hunan province, living in a simple hut. His companions, he wrote, were lakes and mountains and farming his occupation. For many, he represented the ideal aesthetic life long admired in China.

By the end of the morning we had visited sixteen more sceneries. In the afternoon, we finally reached the eastern portion of the Yuan Ming portion of the estate that was dominated by the Fu Hai, the Sea of Good Fortune, one of the largest man-made lakes in Yuan Ming Yuan. We boarded dragon boats and visited three tiny islands in the centre, joined together by thin filaments of land. Eleven more islands bordered the lake. Temples rested upon hillocks and water tumbled down hillsides, spilling into the lake.

'Over there is the land reserved for your Western Gardens,' the emperor told me, pointing east.

As soon as he said that I was desperate to see the tract, but Wang You Dun, a scholar-calligrapher, suddenly stopped and struck a comical dramatic pose.

'Tell us your poem, Poet Wang, or Zhen shall not be able to move from this spot.'

'Our ten-thousand-years-lving emperor is the king of poetry. Your small servant can only produce the simplest of poems to give some lowly person a bit of pleasure.'

'Please, Zhen wishes to hear your poem.'

Wang You Dun gave a shake of his long silver hair and began to speak. The emperor signalled for a scribe to write it down.

Oo, Hoo

The best of ten thousand gardens,

If one has land, one must build mountains,
If one has mountains, one must dig valleys,
If one has valleys, one must open waterways,
If one has waterways, one must build bridges,
If one has bridges, one must lay down paths,
If one has paths, one must construct houses,
If one has houses, one must link them with walkways.
If mountains are not tall, then one must create obstacles,
If valleys are not deep, then one must fill them with green,
If waterways do not spout forth, then one must emphasise their cleanliness,
If bridges are not huge, then build them with style,
If paths are not long, then one must connect them,
If houses are not large, then capture their spirit,
If walkways are not luxurious, then make them blend with the surroundings,
Yuan Ming Yuan is a miraculous landscape that harmonises heaven, man, and earth!

'Good. Excellent.'

The emperor called me to his side once more. 'Zhen has seen engravings of your European castles. They are very large, hundreds of rooms. And they seem so tall. We would be so tired at the end of the day. And how do people find each other? My grandfather saw such engravings and declared that this Europe must be a very poor land, starved of territory. Our land is vast. We do not need to build our houses towards heaven. Style is the most important element, not size. *Tian ran cheng qu, ren gong miao cheng.* Create harmony between nature and man-made things.

'Our architecture reflects philosophy. For example, we always seek the middle way. Take the term "straight." We say that straight can be found within "crooked." We like the term "open," but we can see open better from within "closed." And "high" can be found within "low." Imbalance holds balance. These concepts are part of every art and craft in China. I wish for you to create architecture for Zhen that reflects European philosophy. This is my desire.'

He had finally given me a goal. I had never thought of architecture in terms of philosophy, but I understood his point. Was he really interested in logic, dialetics, and metaphysics? Only his reaction to my plans would tell me how much of Western architecture and ideas he could tolerate.

In the fading light of day, my eyes finally beheld the raw land that would become the Western Gardens.

The emperor stood and gazed at it for a time. The, he turned to me and gestured with his arm, his long sleeve shaking in a soft breeze.

'Missionary Lang, Zhen hereby grants you this land. On this land Zhen orders you to build palaces and gardens that rival any found in your country. You are free to design these buildings based on the principles of your country.' He smiled at me with unmistakable affection.

A new career beckoned me, a field of endeavour as unknown to me as China had been twenty-nine years ago.

Two days after my return from Yuan Ming Yuan, Paolo collapsed. I was with him at the time. We assumed it was his heart, but what did we know. There was not a single physician as talented as the man who lay sallow and motionless. For four days, I stayed at his side, hardly eating and barely sleeping. He hovered between life and death, unable to say much. I poured out my heart knowing I did not have long. *Paolo,* I whispered, *I have taken you for granted. You have been the truest, most constant friend in my life. You are too young to die. Do not leave me.* I held my crucifix close to my heart.

Paolo heard me at one point and smiled. 'Seppe, let me go. I am content to die now. I will wait for you in heaven, for I know you will be there with me. Even if you believe that you have been a less than perfect Jesuit, you have been a true Christian. God will not forget you.'

I wept at his words. Even gravely ill, he could see into the deepest corners of my soul and offer solace.

'You are the best man I have ever known,' I told him. 'You have given so much to everyone else. If you ask now to rest forever, I can't deny you that wish, no matter how sad it makes me.'

'Seppe, you are a great artist. I fear there will be trouble ahead because of this important commission. Follow your conscience. Always follow your conscience and God will walk with you.'

A terrible seizure gripped his body and suddenly he was gone. Paolo was only three years old than I, not yet sixty. We had spent almost thirty years together. He was a safe harbour no matter how fierce the storms. While his voice and thoughts lived on in my head, I longed for his calm face, his dignity, and his solidity. I missed all his habits—the way he tilted his head when he spoke to a patient or stroked his beard and rocked back and forth while he pondered a problem or lifted one eyebrow askance when I uttered something ridiculous.

For me, this was the hardest part of being a celibate monk. We had no children and no grandchildren of our bloodline to brighten our later years. We had to learn to bid farewell to brothers of the heart.

The Qian Long emperor heaped praise upon the memory of Paolo. He respected the written wishes of our friend and bestowed no title or honour. Quietly we buried his body on a high promontory of the West Mountains. He had said many times that he hoped to be buried where he could look towards Italy. A small headstone marked his grave. In Chinese and Latin we carved a simple epitaph: *Here lies a physician who gave his whole heart to serving the Chinese people. May he rest in peace.*

In a short time, his farm fell into ruin and his free dispensary disappeared. There were no other Jesuit physicians of his calibre or anyone capable of providing this form of charity to the needy.

11

By the spring, April 1745, several Jesuit fathers, Jerome, and I had been labouring for months over plans for the Xi Yang Lou, the Western Gardens. Our library continued to grow and we were fortunate to have prints and plans of Versailles, Vaux-le-Vicomte, Fontainebleau, and Italian villas such as the one built for the Medicis in Pratolino. We were well aware of the designs of current European architects: Neumann, Hildebrandt, Héré de Corny, Boffrand, and many others. Our problem was finding a style that was current and relevant to our stated aim yet pleasing to Chinese eyes.

The land at our disposal was T-shaped. One entered at the top of the T and walked through the centre of its head down its elongated stem.

We broke the area into sections, creating cohesive themes in each while still luring the viewer onwards. To enhance the major architectural elements, we added walls, gates, rocks, bridges, canals, brooks, and greenery.

The final design contained two palaces, three ornate fountains, a maze, and an aviary. It was an ambitious, enormous undertaking. We estimated that the Western Gardens would take fifteen years to complete.

As soon as we had begun designing the Western Gardens, letters were sent abroad asking for additional Jesuits to come to China to aid our endeavour in fields such as engineering, hydraulics, botany, clock-making, masonry, carpentry, ironmongery, decorative arts, and stonecarving. By the time the emperor saw our plans and approved them, Jesuits had already begun to arrive. Our depleted mission grew with fresh minds, eager to assist in this splendid project. An eminent Chinese architect asked to be included in our effort, a request that we readily accepted. As soon as the ground softened in the middle of spring, we were ready to begin.

The emperor insisted we complete the first palace, the Xie Qi Qu, Palace of Delights and Harmonies, within two years, no matter how much labour was needed. We employed and trained an army of Chinese as stone carvers, masons, ironmongers, and builders. Jerome was a patient and effective instructor. The Chinese labourers were cheerful, hard-working, and obedient. No matter how inherently foreign the skills we honed in them were, they applied themselves competently.

The most difficult aspect of our task was the prohibition on our free movement within Yuan Ming Yuan. We all resided in a small village called Hai Dan wasting valuable time travelling to and from the estate. Our living quarters were tiny, poorly constructed one-roomed huts. The stove was attached to a brick bed, keeping it both warm and noxious. A wooden board on top of the bed served as my table and workspace. Each of us grew more exhausted with the passing months. We arrived home late, slept little, and left our beds in the dark. A donkey cart took us to the entrance of the estate, and while it lurched from side to side, we ate our breakfast, nibbling on the food of peasants: deep fried fresh noodle cakes and sweetened soybean milk, placed inside a hollowed gourd with its top serving as a lid.

Guards kept an eye on us to ensure that no individual wandered unaccompanied beyond the boundaries of the Western Gardens.

In 1746, a most anticipated Jesuit finally arrived. His name was Father Michel Benoist, and he had a reputation for hydraulic engineering second to none. He had been given the Chinese name of Jiang You Ren, meaning friendship and benevolence. Father Michel was an unusual man, a new generation of Jesuit, trained and sent abroad under the cloud of suspicion that dogged the Society of Jesus. Physically he was far from attractive, being short with prominent features like a weasel or a ferret with a long nose setting off a sharp profile. His eyes were deep set beneath a firm forehead. His lips were long and thin. He had a square-shaped skull, sparsely covered with hair that was prematurely grey. Those features failed to do justice to the mind that lay beneath, for not only was he talented but he was highly introspective and fair in all he said and did.

By the time he arrived in China, Jesuits hardly existed any longer outside the capital. They had been arrested In Fujian, Sichuan, Jiangxi, Zhejiang, Henan, Guizhou, and Zhili. Many had had been imprisoned and tortured. In Fujian, the saintly Petrus Sanz had been hanged.

When I went and called on him at his house, he spoke bluntly. 'I have been expecting your visit, Brother Giuseppe,' he said. 'Please be aware that I do not share your passion for Chinese culture. I am a Jesuit above all, loyal to the wishes of the pope to spread the gospel in the way he sees fit. I am an engineer second.'

I knew that I would be working closely with this man and wanted to find some common ground on which we could agree. It would not be good for morale if this man, whose skills I badly needed, and I were hostile to each other. 'You can be both and still learn from a culture so ancient and rich in art, philosophy, and history.'

'No. My two disciplines are sufficient to keep me occupied for every waking moment. When I am not designing engineering works I am praying and trying to become a better servant of our Lord.'

I sighed and pondered what lesson God was trying to teach me here. 'I see. You have obviously heard about the plans for the Western Gardens or you would not be here.'

Colour surged into his cheeks and fire lit up his eyes. I braced myself, certain he was about to chastise me for working so hard to please a heathen emperor, but I was wrong.

'Yes. It is an exciting undertaking. Fountains. I adore designing fountains. They are frivolous but beautiful and I do not believe I upset our God by creating beauty with my skills. I am ready to begin tomorrow. If you wish.'

'I do wish.'

As I left him, confused by his conflicting passions, I thought about how much our society had changed in the past thirty years, and I wondered how the future would view the two schools of Jesuit beliefs: the tolerant and the obedient.

My new young colleague became totally absorbed in his work and designed the fountains of the Palace of Delights and Harmony in a blink of an eye. Father Michel was permitted to establish a workshop within Chang Chun, where he trained many assistants, and together they built simple hydraulic equipment to supply the fountains. He worked incessantly, hardly stopping to eat or sleep. I called him the water magician. Within six months, in the closing shades of autumn, he finished the fountain and immediately fell ill with fever.

When the emperor heard that the fountain was ready, he was eager to see it at work. Father Michel was the only man among us who knew how to coax every temperamental piece of equipment to perform its task properly, but he was delirious with fever. As one might have predicted, on the day that the emperor was to inspect his new delight, a vital pump refused to work. I prayed, pleaded, and, finally, cursed the hydraulics. In a mild case of panic, I organised labourers as water carriers. We raced like madmen, filling and refilling the reservoir above the castle.

The emperor arrived just as his fountain began to function. He walked all around it, unable to take his eyes off the miracle of playful water. Animals and fish, carved in stone, spat out water, which cascaded from three levels, tripping and playing into the basin. The sun shone and rainbows shimmered among the sprays. I looked up towards heaven raising my eyebrows wondering if the Creator was gazing down on this scene.

The emperor was bewitched. 'It is a treat for the spirits themselves,' he murmured. 'There is nothing so charming in all the three gardens of Yuan Ming. Bring me Father Jiang so that Zhen may personally thank him.'

'Bixia, Father Jiang is very ill. He worked too hard and has collapsed,' I said.

'Send my physician to him. Send him food from my kitchens,' the emperor said. He issued orders to a servant, and continued, 'This is very pleasing. Zhen wants more water works. Is there anything you need to finish the palaces and gardens faster?'

'Yes, Bixia. Our work could proceed faster if we could be given a place to stay in Yuan Ming Yuan and if we were not guarded quite so closely. My labourers are honest men.'

The emperor thought for a moment. 'After today, you and Father Jiang and anyone else you deem necessary may move freely within Yuan Ming Yuan at all hours. There are many empty buildings close to these gardens. We will find suitable housing and servants for you.'

He started to walk away, then stopped and turned. 'Zhen is very pleased, Painter Lang. Perhaps kings from your country will come to visit us and see what you have built here.'

As our work in the Western Gardens progressed and months became years, letters from Europe brought terrible news. The Society of Jesus was facing banishment from France and Portugal. More and more of its property and wealth was confiscated. The Jansenists, our greatest enemies, had turned opinion sharply against us. In South America our support of native Indians put us at odds with Spanish and Portuguese interests. Jesuits, it was rumoured, were being murdered by European colonists. Some feared it would not be long before the pope ordered the complete disbanding of our order. Where once I would have scoffed at the idea, I no longer could. The twilight of the Society of Jesus neared; the last Catholic brotherhood to be established and the first, possibly, to disappear.

Jerome and I were the most well-known and longest-serving Jesuits still alive in China. Wherever we went we heard people whispering to each other: *'Those are the two Christians who have served three emperors.'*

In 1748, two Franciscan fathers were executed in Beijing along with four members of a secret society whose goal was to overthrow the emperor. Though I knew little of the facts, I was aware that the mood towards foreigners and Christianity had hardened. Outside Beijing rumours germinated and spread rapidly. Many Chinese believed lies that claimed men were supposedly required to tear up a painting of Confucius while facing an image of Christ as part of the ritual of baptism. The holy water was rumoured to be endowed with powers to confuse and muddle the senses. After imbibing this liquid, young men were reportedly unable to recognise their relatives.

Rumours surrounding the conversion ritual for women were worse. One lie claimed that young women were forced to stand naked before Christ. They were then asked to lie face down upon a cushion. The priests also stripped and pressed their bodies upon those of the virgins, cutting their buttocks so that male sweat and female blood mingled in some sort of barbaric religious marriage. While the females were in a state of hallucination under the influence of the holy water, the priests turned their bodies and copulated with them. Ritual washing or baptism completed the consummation of the marriage between Christ and his female worshippers.

I was dismayed at how easily these vile rumours took root throughout the countryside. Over the course of a handful of years, I saw the eyes of country dwellers change. They began to gaze upon us with hostility and suspicion.

When I tried to explain how different things had been when I first arrived in China to Father Michel, he commented, 'Truth plods a ponderous, difficult path but lies find no obstacles in their path. Sanity is crushed by the onslaught of innuendo and falsehood. It is the same anywhere in the world. Why should your beloved China be any different?'

On a cold wintry day in 1752, I was summoned to the emperor's presence at Yuan Ming Yuan. The emperor's face, dark and angry, caused a knot to form in my stomach.

'Missionary Lang, look at this.' He handed me a report.

I tried to read the report quickly, but my unease made me stumble over the complicated language. It was about Jerome. A few words had leapt off the pages in the report: Jesuit missionary Lin Zhi Xing, females, sorcery, and evil sexual acts.

'All of you who came to China used your skills as smoke,' the emperor said when I had finished reading. 'You gained our trust by cheating. Privately, your motives were to practice dirty sexual acts upon my people. Zhen will punish all who are guilty of this.'

I threw myself to the ground and bowed. 'Bixia, do not be angry. From what your insignificant servant knows, this is all falsehood. Your slave may not be intelligent, but can assert that his friend is not evil. Missionary Lin is not guilty of the crimes mentioned here. Missionary Lin and I have spent almost forty years together here. He is as honest and sincere a priest as any I have known. Over the past ten years we have worked side by side, day after day, on the Western Gardens. He could not be guilty of the crimes reported here.

I guarantee his integrity to you with my own life. I humbly ask, Bixia, if I may investigate the matter and prove his innocence.'

'*Zhen* called you here because of the importance of the work on the Western Gardens,' the emperor replied. 'Missionary Lin is important to you. If Zhen punishes him now, the building will be delayed. Zhen allows you to investigate. Report to me as soon as you have information.'

Deeply concerned, I hurried to the Chang Chun garden. Jerome was busy in the foundry, helping a group of Chinese workers make wrought-iron gates and locks for our castles. It was wonderful to see them—small clusters of men huddled together, forming an item that would shortly adorn a door or a wall.

As I approached him, my heart pounded so loudly that I was surprised he could not hear me coming. I explained what I had seen in the official report. At first, he could not believe his ears. Then the severity of the charge hit him and colour drained from his face.

'I am innocent.'

'Of course you are. I did not doubt it for an instant. But we must ascertain where the rumours arose. Have you any enemies?'

'I hardly speak to anyone.'

'Have you been into Beijing recently?'

'I went into the city about one month ago.'

'Where did you go?'

'I went to the Southern Church, to see some of the fathers. I had letters I wanted delivered to Europe when the next ship left. Then I spent several hours in prayer and meditation.'

'And afterwards—did you go anywhere else?'

'I didn't go anywhere. By the time I finished my prayers, it was already mid-afternoon and I returned here. Oh, yes, I remember. As I approached the Western Gate, a woman grabbed the reins of my donkey. She insisted that I give her money. She claimed her sister-in-law was ill and that her brother was far away. She needed money for a doctor, I believe. I gave her some coins and she hurried off. Do you believe this simple incident can be the root of this malicious rumour?'

As I gazed into my companion's troubled eyes, I realised that I would have torn stars from the sky to protect him. But for the moment I had a greater problem: how could I trace the source of the evil rumours? The emperor had given me very little time.

The next few days passed uneasily while we questioned many people in the villages surrounding Yuan Ming Yuan. A wall of silence met us wherever we went. No matter how much I tried to discourage him, Jerome insisted on accompanying me.

On the fourth day, we were ambushed by a large group of men. They appeared from nowhere and grabbed the reins of our slow-footed donkeys.

'We are servants of the emperor,' I shouted. 'The emperor will punish you!'

I was dragged from my donkey, held by many arms, kicked and pummelled, and eventually tied up and covered with a sack filled with a powder that stung, blinded, and choked me. One more blow knocked me unconscious. When I came to, I felt the ropes being untied. Someone gently removed the sack from head.

I had trouble focusing for a few minutes. Several arms pulled me to a sitting position. Someone gave me water and another cleaned my face with a damp cloth.

'He's cut.'

'He's bleeding.'

'Can you stand up?'

My vision cleared and I saw several concerned peasants and a troop of soldiers from Yuan Ming Yuan.

'Where is my companion?' I tried to stand up. '*JEROME!*'

'What is he shouting?'

'There's no one else here.'

'There are tracks. Someone was dragged away.'

'Search for Jerome!' I shouted over and over. 'Do not let them get away. They will kill him.' Several soldiers headed off in the direction of the tracks. I could hardly breathe and realised that a rib or two had been damaged. I had no choice but to return to Yuan Ming Yuan.

The emperor insisted I describe the events. Aching and bandaged, I told him what had happened.

'This is unacceptable. Zhen will not allow farmers to judge and punish as they wish. It is the path to anarchy.' He turned to his prime minister. 'Find these villains and we will teach them to respect the law.'

One week passed, and I feared the worst for Jerome. I was beside myself, unable to eat, sleep, or work, almost hysterical with worry. Once more, I had failed to protect a beloved friend. In every spare moment, I knelt in prayer to the Blessed Mother.

On the tenth day, a vegetable farmer went to a corner of his field to inspect a cold store. Inside, he found an unconscious man. The foreigner, he told the officials, the one you are looking for. Soldiers rushed to the farm and brought Jerome back to the capital, to our mission.

When I arrived there, a physician was examining him. Jerome looked pitiful, unconscious, covered in blood, and naked. I watched as his chest rose and fell, and I thanked the Blessed Virgin for saving his life.

'Why are his thighs covered in dried blood?' I asked.

The French physician tending him said, 'I am not yet certain where the wound is.'

He gently washed away the thickest blood. That was when we all saw the mutilation. Jerome's testicles had been crudely cut away. We bathed the gaping wound and applied poultices in silence, each missionary quietly praying that infection did not set in. Using wet cloths we dripped water and soup into his dry, cracked mouth.

The rogues responsible for the attack were hunted down and arrested two days later. Since Jerome carried an official title and rank, the imperial court took little time to declare their sentence. As Christians, we did not ask for retribution, but we were not consulted. None of the twenty men had previous crimes; they were ordinary peasants. As I listened to the men's testimony, I realised that the devil does not need evil men to do his deeds if evil words can spur honest men to cruelty. The power of language to corrupt good men and women had proved stronger than one hundred years of charitable work. Demagoguery had usurped common sense, obliterated mercy, and brooked no doubt.

By some miracle, Jerome survived. It took him some weeks to recover from exposure, massive bleeding, and lack of food and water. He hardly spoke to anyone during his convalescence. He was withdrawn and morose.

12

For twelve years, I was consumed by my work on the Western Gardens. Each year I visited Beijing during the Spring Lantern Festival to see Cocco and You Min and their growing number of children. Ostensibly I was the honoured older patriarch, the one who must be obeyed. In reality I was the one the youngest children climbed upon and the older children begged for stories of the Forbidden City. It was always sad to leave them and return to my other life, the one devoid of any hint of family. My fellow Jesuits were a solitary group with little desire for friendship. Or perhaps I no longer had the energy to make new friends. I missed the companionship of Paolo and Father Ignatius.

At long last, in 1756, the Western Gardens were complete and I was permitted to lead a tour of eminent foreign dignitaries around them. The buildings were unlike anything else in Yuan Ming Yuan. The mystery that was our creation unfolded as soon as one entered the large gates. A canal trickled along the northern perimeter and we crossed it via the Bridge of Perspective. I enjoyed watching everyone's expressions as they encountered this new man-made world. Their eyes lit up.

'There are three main sections, sealed from one another by gates and arches,' I explained to my audience as we stood at the top of the T shape. 'We tell a story within each section, using architecture, sculptures, and gardens. Only from the high hillock to our left can one see the whole garden. Outside the walls of the Western Gardens, one cannot guess what lies within, as the roofs of our castles are all Chinese, covered in blue or green tiles.'

At the end of the bridge, a sculpted lion head spouted water. Beyond, to the right, still within the head of the T, stood the Xie Qi Qu, the Palace of

Delights and Harmony, a villa of three storeys with a central gallery shaped like a horseshoe. At each end of the horseshoe, we had built two-storey pavilions that seemed to stretch out to grasp a small rectangular lake just beyond their reach.

A beautiful symmetrical curved staircase led from either side of the terrace in front of the main entrance to a basin below. All around the basin, encircled by a balustrade, animals and fish spouted water. We had carved the classic Ionic and Corinthian pillars of the palace to provide the illusion of perpetual movement and decorated the capitals with marble and majolica, a white, porous porcelain.

'This palace is meant to tell the story of joy. The emperor intends to use it for concerts, either indoors or outdoors near the lake.'

Farther away, covered in delightful designs from our imaginations and bordered by trees strictly pruned into geometrical forms, was a small building housing the hydraulic instruments of our serious French father as well as his reservoir. We had decorated its roof with carved vases.

On the other side of the head of the T was our maze. It could not be constructed of greenery, as in Italy, so we had used grey bricks, embellished with rose-coloured and ivory Chinese patterns. The walls were only shoulder height. In the centre was an octagonal pavilion entered from any one of eight staircases. My guests followed me as I walked in, assuming I knew the way to the centre. Fortunately, I did—that day. We left the maze and entered a flower garden with a small, rectangular two-storey building.

'This is where the emperor can watch his wives and children playing in the maze.' The idea seemed to delight my visitors.

At the beginning of the long body of the T was 'The Birdcage,' an aviary filled with peacocks, sparrows, and other special birds. On both sides of the gateway into the next section, Father Michel had designed small fountains made of white marble. A stream gurgled nearby, turning upon itself before moving northwards once more. To the north, on the highest hill, sat the Belvedere with its special view of the square pool at the bottom of the T. To the south, we had built a small monastery amidst bamboo groves.

The Hai Yan, Huge Melting Pot Palace, the largest palace, was our greatest creation. Its white marble staircases were enlivened by fifty small fountains that brought water cascading down balustrades into a basin below.

I continued my explanation, 'The fountain here is unlike anything the emperor had seen before. We brought him to see it on his birthday, when we turned the waters on officially for the first time. Notice the twelve carved human figures along two sides. The bronze heads represent the animals of the Chinese zodiac. These twelve animals—rat, cow, tiger, rabbit, dragon, snake, horse, sheep, monkey, chicken, dog, and pig—as you know, are of great significance. On one level they represent the twelve hours of the Chinese day. On a higher level they stand for years and cycles of years.

'The hydraulics of our grand fountain includes a timekeeping function. At the beginning of every two-hour portion of the day, one animal spits water towards the centre. Twice a day, the hour of horse and the hour of rat, all the animals hurl water towards the centre.'

I did not tell them how as long as I live I will remember Hong Li's face that day we inaugurated the fountain. To celebrate the anniversary of the birth of the Son of Heaven with a magical rush of water from the mouths of the animals of the zodiac was our way of thanking him for his gift of this land and the resources to accomplish what we did. When the animals shot water through the air, he clapped his hands and laughed loudly.

I did explain to them how the emperor was beginning to house his European art collection within the palace. The walls were to be covered with tapestries made in France, at Beauvais, specially designed for this building.

'From the terrace of this palace you can see the great waterworks,' I commented.

Who would have thought my dear friend Father Michel would have had so much play in his imagination? Further down the body of the T, he had designed two pyramids surrounded by thin spouts that pushed the water high into the air. Amidst the shower of water, statues of birds, animals, and fish stared into the distance. In a larger basin, deer chased by twelve dogs stood frozen for perpetuity. Shells and spirals adorned the fountains.

To the north of this great display, in a small addition to the body of the T, stood the Observatory of Distant Waters. From here, on his throne, the emperor could admire the water fountains that so intrigued him. He never ceased to wonder at how we broke the laws of nature for him. Above his throne we had built a canopy supported by two cranes. Behind, we had designed a brick wall and five marble panels carved with bas relief of European military weapons and symbols.

'This section tells the story of respect. Respect for nature, war, the hunter, and the hunted.'

The third section had no buildings. We had built a large mound with a spiral walkway. The emperor could ride a horse to the top and survey his estate. The land was beautifully planted up to a long rectangular reflecting pool. At the end of the pool were thirteen panels that demonstrated the principles of perspective. They were positioned in two rows to form the head of an arrow, wider at the foreground taperig towards each other at the far end, with the thirteenth panel bridging the distance between the last two panels. We painted scenes of a fictional European countryside: pastureland leading the way to soft, lush hills and a village perched on a mountaintop. It was a brilliant example of *trompe l'oeil.*

'This section tells the story of illusion and the power of imagination.'

I believe everyone was impressed, or at least they said they were. One small, sharp-eyed Frenchman came up to me after the others had wandered away.

'This is a magnificent achievement. Something for Jesuits to be proud of. I pray that it lasts for centuries, but I fear for it.'

'Why is that?'

'China is rich in culture and history, but weak in weaponry and modern warfare. It is a great prize and many countries wish for a portion of it. There will be war and soldiers like to plunder. What rich pickings there are here.'

'Do you really believe this will happen?'

'It is only a matter of time. Europe has been at war for so long it knows nothing else. China has grown soft and lazy from peace.'

I was the last to leave the Western Gardens. As I reached the gate, I turned to look back at what we had achieved while reflecting on his words. I could not bear the thought of harm coming to it. Not that buildings could not be replaced, but how could the spirit be recaptured, the reasons for its inception and the dedication we had poured into every nook and cranny?

13

With my work completed an idea was planted in my brain. In all my years in China, Confucius's influence dominated above all others. I suddenly had a burning desire to visit his birthplace in Shandong province, to bring myself closer to this visionary

I made a formal request to the bishop in Beijing. He refused my plan outright.

'I am not disillusioned with Catholicism or searching for another belief system to take its place,' I explained. 'I merely feel it is time to study Confucianism and understand why its tenets are so deeply imbedded in Chinese culture. We have ignored it for too long.'

To my astonishment, Father Michel was the only one in our mission who supported me and went to speak to the bishop on my behalf.

'Why is it that we missionaries have been in China for over two hundred years but are almost invisible?' he bluntly asked the bishop. 'Why is our religion unable to gain authority in this land? Why is it without power and legitimacy? Why are people so willing to hear evil and believe it of us?'

He waited, but the bishop did not answer. Father Michel continued, 'Let me tell you what I believe. The Chinese have a contractual relationship with their gods. They make a formal request and the gods answer in one way or another. Their trust or respect for their gods depends upon this relationship. Their gods are spirits who protect peace, grant abundant harvests, produce sons, and put rice in the cooking pot. If something is troubling the Chinaman, he prays to the appropriate god. If, by chance, his entreaty is successful, he burns incense in gratitude. If he is unsuccessful, he chooses another god.

When his pleas are ignored or unfulfilled, he blames himself as unworthy. The Chinaman cannot help but respect and fear his gods under this system. On top of this is a social system established by Confucius over fifteen hundred years ago. In his system everyone knows their place and their duties. There is a very strict hierarchy and a way in which each person can strive to become an ideal member of society. It is a highly effective social system.

'We arrive in China and try to teach the Chinaman to believe in one God, one all-powerful being who grants such intangible gifts as grace and a place by His side in heaven. And we tell them that their gods are false. This social and religious system has been in place for longer than Christianity has existed. If Christianity is ever to take root in China, it must be within a Chinese context and that means that every missionary must have a firm understanding of Confucianism.'

The bishop did not even attempt to disguise his disdain. 'My answer remains the same. We cannot afford such a visit. It would be viewed as making a pilgrimage and bowing down before Confucius's image. He plays no part in what we are trying to accomplish here. I forbid this idea even being mentioned outside these walls.'

'Are you going to Qufu?' the emperor asked when I next saw him.

'No, Bixia. My superiors are opposed to it. I should never have thought of it.'

'Hmm. You serve too many masters, Painter Lang.'

A few weeks later, Hong Li sent me on a mission to the Yellow River to purchase some of the special earth, yellow loess, from its banks for Yuan Ming Yuan.

'If you cannot visit Qufu, at least you can see the source of our civilisation, the Yellow River. But of course you have already seen it when you came north from Macao.'

'No, Bixia. When I travelled to Beijing forty years ago, the riverbed was completely dry. I walked across it.'

The emperor laughed. 'It is the most tempestuous river in my kingdom. Clearly the gods wished you to arrive safely and removed any danger from your journey. Zhen hopes the gods treat you kindly this time as well.'

I was issued with all the paperwork I required including official permission to enter several provinces on both banks of the Yellow River.

'I'm sorry you aren't able to visit Qufu,' Father Michel commented when I went to say goodbye. 'But a river journey will be a time of contemplation. Brother Giuseppe, though my approach to faith is stricter than yours, I do not question your commitment to Christ. What you have accomplished in China is admirable, all the more so because you have no model to follow. No one else has touched the emperor as you have.'

His words and a hint of warmth that accompanied them surprised me. They kept me company as we headed south, sailing down several rivers and canals until we joined the Yellow River. It was full, angry, and flowing rapidly, almost touching the tops of the steep dikes on either side.

Where the ship docked at Xuzhou, an obsequious local official was waiting anxiously for me. He led me to his residence, continuously bowing and clasping his hands, insisting that I use his house as my base. He was so eager to please that I gave him the task of purchasing, packing, and shipping my soil requirements. That done, my official reason for the trip was satisfied. Now I was free to wander as I pleased for as long as I pleased. I hired a donkey and set off. I told the impudent beast to hurry, but he was stubborn. I felt heady with a freedom I had never known before.

I paused on the steep bank of the river and spoke to the river in my native tongue. 'Yellow River, please be so kind as to share some of your secrets with me. You, who flow endlessly from west to east and have the experience of countless centuries, I come to for wisdom. Are rivers not a metaphor for life? I, who once swam against the current, have long ago given in to its force. Tell me, am I a man of conviction and principle or piece of flotsam carried along by fate?'

I followed the bank until I could go no further as the path was blocked by an impenetrable rockface. As if by magic, a raft appeared, rowed by four straining men with long poles. My donkey and I waited for them on the water's edge. When they reached us and saw me they gasped, wondering what I was. After some explanation that satisfied their curiosity, they asked me where I was going. I explained that I wished to travel downstream with my donkey for no longer than one week and back upstream to Xuzhou. I told them I would pay for as much as three weeks' work. They were delighted with my offer and helped me onboard. When we stopped for a midday meal, they invited me to share their sparse bowl of onions and yellow bean paste. I offered them provisions from my bags, dried fruits and meats they had never eaten before.

I warmed to one of the raftmen, the oldest. There was an innate wisdom to him, absent in the others who were both younger and ignorant. The river had been his whole life and he drew from it to explain every aspect of human behaviour and of life as he knew it. Though he identified with the soul of the river, it was an unequal relationship. He admired, respected, and feared it. The river largely ignored him. His companions called him Qian Lao Da, Old Mr Pull. His life was a harsh and dangerous one. He was lined and toothless, thin as bones with long, pulsing muscles. When I asked him his age, he had no idea. He told time by the flow of the river and had no idea of days, months, or years.

As they pulled the raft, they sang a mournful song:

> *A man's life cannot be predicted, for thirty years the river flows on the east, for thirty years the river flows on the west.*

'What does that mean?' I asked.

'This river has a mind of its own. It often floods and changes its course,' they explained.

'Impossible.'

They laughed at me. 'How little you know, Outsider.'

Old Mr Pull would not hear of me sleeping rough on the ground as they did. He knew many local peasants and insisted that I seek lodging with them. The villagers welcomed me with curiosity and embarrassed giggles but asked surprisingly few questions. In exchange for their hospitality I recited poems or told them stories. I also discreetly left behind some pieces of silver in the morning. By the fourth night, I insisted on sleeping outdoors with Old Mr Pull. I lay on my cloth looking up at the sky, listening to the river. The very simplicity of this existence was exhilarating.

In the middle of the night a great wind arose. I pulled my cloak closer around me, but Old Mr Pull suddenly shook me frantically and shouted in my face. '*FLOOD COMING*! We must follow them.' He pointed towards the other raftmen, who were running away.

I stood up quickly and looked around. Hundreds of people were running along both sides of the broad river.

When I tried to gather my things, Old Mr Pull shouted, 'No time. Run. Get on the donkey.'

The night was as thick as black lacquer. Old Mr Pull sniffed the air. 'We head south,' he said.

We sped away from the river. He trotted next to my donkey, hardly out of breath. He wore no shoes or shirt, just ragged trousers while I was covered in layers of robes and garments and wore thick cloth shoes.

A great thundering startled us all. *Pong. Pong.* My donkey squealed in a panic and began to run wildly. Old Mr Pull shouted above the din, 'No matter what happens to me, run for your life, Master Lang!'

The thundering grew louder and more frequent. Everyone dropped whatever they were carrying and ran desperately, screaming. My donkey's flanks were covered in white foamy sweat and I could see his eyes grow wild with fear. I grabbed the stiff hair on his neck and tried to tighten my legs around his sides as a curtain of suffocating blackness descended. The screams around me increased but I could not breathe well enough to make a sound. Water began to lap around my legs. I turned to see a large wave, many feet high, bearing down from the right. The air was hot and dense. Water, soil, and debris pelted me as the earth trembled. I closed my eyes and said a prayer, to make my peace with my Lord as death approached.

Old Mr Pull appeared from nowhere and grabbed the reins of my donkey. The air was so dense that I thought my skull would crack open. I almost lost consciousness but then a huge, foul-smelling wave brushed me off my mount. As I fell, I heard Old Mr Pull screaming, 'Hold the reins. The donkey will swim!'

The water swallowed the three of us, sucking and strangling with its violent tentacles. I clung to the reins and the paddling donkey. I was surprised to discover how powerful the will to live is. My robes, sodden and heavy, threatened to pull me under. With one hand I removed several layers as quickly as my trembling fingers would allow. I choked on filthy water. Branches, tree limbs, and rubble scratched and battered me from all sides. Sometimes we were submerged and I had to fight my way to the surface. My shoes, though tied well up my calves, were torn off. We spun and were swept down river at a terrifying speed. The water tossed us about mercilessly. Then a large log hit me in the chest and everything grew blank.

The sun breaking over the horizon seared my eyes. Old Mr Pull was lying next to me. When I began to cough, spitting out water and mud, he sat up. He told me that after I had been knocked unconscious, he grabbed on to me, tying my sleeves around his chest and carrying me on his back. The donkey, exhausted from his valiant battle, disappeared under the water. He continued to hold me as we flowed on. The water had reached a high hillock and moved on, but he had clung to a tree branch. Though we were covered from head to toe with bruises and scratches, nothing appeared to be broken or badly damaged. My clothes were little more than rags.

It took me several more minutes to come fully to my senses. I had foolishly asked the river for knowledge and it had answered me by trying to take my life. Once more a stranger had saved me. Mrs Zhang had helped me escape from ignorant peasants in a mountain village and Old Mr Pull, with his strength and determination, had kept me from drowning.

Perhaps this was my lesson. My inspiration had always flowed from the hand of friendship—one human reaching out to another. I had soaked up knowledge on many levels from Wu Yu, learned friendship via Antonio, become part of a family through Chen Yuan, Cocco, You Min, and knew true companionship through Paolo. If my paintings succeeded in capturing a small proportion of the beauty of these higher emotions, I had succeeded in using my art for the greater glory of God, as was once asked of me long ago when I was still a boy. Is not the most miraculous of God's creations man himself?

'You have saved my life,' I said, looking at Old Mr Pull with gratitude. I hugged him tightly. 'How can I ever thank you?'

He was most startled by my effusiveness and blushed deeply, saying, 'It was nothing, nothing at all.'

We stood up and searched for the river that had tried to murder us, but it was nowhere to be seen. For miles, all we could see was a vast yellow desert of mud and sand and debris.

The Yellow River's wild soul had heeded a violent, destructive urge to change its course. It had spread devastation then rolled away, unpunished, unrepentant. I insisted he return with me to Xuzhou, where I would see he was rewarded. We made our way back slowly, barefoot and penniless. I travelled like a penitent surviving on handouts and charity from wherever it came. When we found the river again, it was calm, glistening in the sunshine, but it had cut a new path. A day later, the wind picked up again and rain fell. Although the currents intensified, it merely stretched its muscle at the edges and chose not to flood the land again.

Foremost in my mind was the poem Wu Yu had forced me to learn almost forty years earlier, the one written by the Tang dynasty genius, Li Bai.

You can watch the water of the Yellow River, flowing from heaven to the sea, never to return.
You can sit in front of a mirror staring at your white hair, young and shining in the morning, turning to snow in the evening.
A human life must be spent in happiness, do not shrivel before the moon.
I sing a song for you, please listen to me.

Never before did I feel the power of Mother Nature as I did during that treacherous flood. And no better example of her unwillingness to be tamed could be found than the Yellow River, fickle and lethal as well as fertile and enriching. Our rivers in Europe are timid children in comparison with this tempermental giant.

The local official in Xuzhou almost fainted when he saw me arrive two weeks after the terrible flood.

'You are alive. Thank the gods. How could I break the news to our ten-thousand-years-living emperor that I had not protected you, his illustrious architect and painter? My head would be the price he would have demanded.' He had obviously been fretting for several days, and it took him some hours to calm down. When he had composed himself again, he informed me that at least thirty thousand people had been drowned. Over one hundred thousand people had lost their homes and farms, and the river had changed its course by over one hundred miles.

I arranged for Old Mr Pull to be given a reward. The official was loath to give much, but I was adamant. Old Mr Pull had never held so much money in his life, though it was still not a vast sum. I helped him look for his companions. He was not hopeful.

'They're not the first friends I lose. Someday the river will claim me. That's the way.'

'With your reward, perhaps you could start a different life?' I asked him.

'I have no other life. I buy a small house maybe. No boat. Easy to build a raft again. Can't buy another boat if it breaks.'

14

In July 1758, I approached my seventieth birthday. As it neared, the emperor began discussing a grand celebration for my birthday. He gave me ample warning that he would use the occasion to ennoble me: I would be granted the status of a vice-minister. When I informed the society of the imminent honour, I was surrounded by furore.

Only Father Michel quietly asked me what I thought about it.

'I arrived in China forty-three years ago. Despite the work of all the Jesuits who have spent their lives in China, we have accomplished very little. My experiences cause me to doubt whether there is any future for Christianity in China. The pope has angered three emperors and the Chinese have long memories. My paintings are my only legacy for all the years I have lived here as a Catholic missionary and many have been destroyed. I am too old to have dreams and illusions. I have faithfully served three emperors and the society. If the emperor wishes to honour me, what would be my reason to refuse him?'

'Are you telling me that you view yourself more as an artist than a missionary?' Father Michel asked. 'And that your obedience rests more with the Chinese emperor than our Lord and the pope?'

'If you phrase it as such, I must answer yes to both questions. I had a different plan when I arrived. I believed that by being a painter, I could be a worthy servant of Jesus Christ and the pope. I proved only to be a worthy servant to the emperor. It has been years since I did charity work or tried to convert anyone. In everything I have done in China I have tried to imbue my painting with my love of my God and my respect for his creations. Unfortunately, Chinese images are my tools—not the Bible and saints—and the emperor is the man I most admire, not this pope who despises our society. I am at peace with my conscience that I serve the Lord well in my own way.'

Father Michel looked into my eyes for a long time, then he spoke kindly, and my heart surged with gratitude at his compassion.

'God will never condemn you, whatever your decision about this honour. You, Brother Castiglione, have been an inspiration for all who know you. For your entire life, you have served these people. I know the story of Jiang Shan Min and his wife. I can see how much they love you when they arrive with children and grandchildren. You have helped others as well at great risk to yourself. As our Lord taught us, you have been an example of friendship and constancy. Furthermore, if the emperor has any love of our culture it is because of you. God will not forget you. And to be honest,' he added in a whisper, 'between us, I believe the others are jealous that a mere brother will receive such an honour.'

His simple words comforted me in the days that followed. And never before did I feel the absence of Paolo so strongly. I thought I heard his voice telling me to follow my conscience and that all would be well.

A few days later, the rector summoned me to his quarters. 'Brother Castiglione,' Rector Johannes said to me. 'We wish to know if you intend to accept the title the emperor has offered you.'

He was a dour man from the Lowlands, perhaps twenty years younger than I. I stood before him in a room where I had stood in countless times before, which held so many memories for me.

'Yes, Rector, I do.'

'And if I forbid you to do so?' He looked at me with drooping eyes. I felt sorry for him. Like the society of which we were members, he was a relic.

'I hope it would not come to that,' I answered.

But it did, and I refused to acquiesce. I made my choice with free will, with my conscience intact. My punishment was severe. I was excluded from the society. Though I was permitted pray in the Southern Church—which was decorated with frescoes I had painted—as a Catholic, I was forbidden to wear Jesuit cloaks or to expect any succour or assistance from the society.

After my expulsion, I wrapped up and packed away my dark Jesuit robes and wore only Chinese clothes. I took out the chain that Antonio had given me before his death and put it around my neck. The small Buddha hung alongside my cross. As I had no intention of becoming a Buddhist, I couldn't explain why I did it. I can only say that the symbols of two religions hanging on my chest gave me comfort.

With the society weakened in Europe, most Jesuits found the rector's reaction extreme and unnecessary and our friendships were unaffected. Only one man's scorn hurt deeply. Jerome, my oldest surviving friend, never forgave me. From the morning I made my decision to accept the emperor's honour, he railed at me with angry eyes and I watched as four and a half decades of friendship melted away. I told myself that he had changed a great deal after his ordeal, that he used me as a scapegoat for the bitterness he harboured at the great injustice done to him and that age had robbed him of sense. There was no room in my heart for anger towards Jerome; I only felt regret. I told him that, however he felt, I would continue to fan the flames of our friendship and hold the memories dear.

The Chinese told me over and over again that it was not an easy affair for a man to live to seventy. They used the term *xi* to describe my approaching age, a term that meant 'rare and precious.'

On the morning of my birthday, I took a long walk through many of the neighbourhoods I had once lived in. I found sweet potatoes in every market that I passed. Many people sold them, already cooked, from large woven baskets. I bought one from an old toothless woman, peeled it, and ate it slowly, gazing up at the sky. *Here is the great gift you have bequeathed your countrymen. Are you beaming with pride, Chen Yuan?*

The ceremony of ennoblement filled my old man's heart with far too much emotion. As I thanked the emperor, my feelings of gratitude drifted to the mentors and friends who had helped on the long journey from wild youth to old age—the old priest in Milan who gave me a home, the Su family, Antonio, Wu Yu, Paolo, Chen Yuan, Jin Kun, Cocco, and Wang Rong—and my lower lip trembled. An imperial document, in beautiful calligraphy, was handed to me. My Chinese name had been painted by the emperor in vermilion ink in flowing cursive brushmanship. Though I had prepared an eloquent speech for the occasion, I was unable to speak.

Two people accompanied me home: Wang Rong and Jin Kun. My friend Wang Rong held the highest rank of any eunuch, the official in charge of family law. His cousin Wang Yi had taken over his former post and was now the keeper of the Receive Love Book. Wang Rong had long since orchestrated the retirement of Duan Shi Lian. I heard rumours that my enemy died soon after his retirement—some claimed he had been poisoned. Jin Kun had become a royal painter. He was also a teacher cut of the same cloth as Wu Yu, and his students adored him.

'It is a shame that we two are the only friends who could be present to witness your ceremony of ennoblement,' Wang Rong commented. He was richly dressed, with a sealskin waistcoat, blue-grey silk trousers, and a lake-green silk robe. 'I believe that there are many people whose loss you felt deeply at that moment.'

I could hide nothing from his sharp eyes.

'I have a present for you,' Jin Kun announced. He handed me a scroll.

I unrolled it and beheld a portrait of my 'family.' With a clever use of colours and perspective he had mimicked my style to perfection. There they all were, Cocco, You Min, their children and grandchildren, sitting in the courtyard of their spacious home.

'Thank you, Painter Jin. I am astonished and very moved,' I said.

'It was a challenge. I did not find it easy, but it was instructive. I have even attempted to paint with oil colours.'

'I too have a present,' Wang Rong interrupted.

He handed me a box. Inside it, resting on satin, was a small ivory carving of a creature that I did not recognise.

'This is a carving of a national treasure. Do you recognise it?' Wang Rong raised his eyebrows. I shook my head.

'This is an animal that we Chinese refer to as one of the *si bu xiang*, four things it is not; a creature that resembles other animals but is not really any one of them. One foreign missionary told me it is called a Father David's deer in your language. It has antlers but is not a deer. It has the head of a horse but is not a horse, the body of a donkey but is not a donkey, the hooves of a cow but is not a cow.'

'It is beautiful. Thank you very much. Could it be that you are trying to mock me?'

'Tease, not mock. While this is a creature that cannot be easily categorised, it is also very precious.' He looked at me with sincere, affectionate eyes.

'I agree with you that, like the animal of this carving, I am an unusual creature: a Jesuit without a mission, a Milanese who speaks better Chinese than Italian, and a painter of a school with no past and, probably, no future.'

I hung the portrait of Cocco and his family where I could see it as soon as I entered my house. Long after my friends had left me, I stared at Wang Rong's gift. The Père David's deer brought to mind another David, the great king of the Old Testament. I remembered how, as an old man, he was devastated by the treachery of his beloved son, Absalom, who slew another of his sons and sought to overthrow him, but was eventually killed by the hand of Joab. Alone with his grief he cried, 'O my son Absalom! Would to God I had died for thee, O Absalom, my son, my son!'

Why did this part of the Bible come into my mind? I believe as a silly old man I fell to musing over how blustering confidence of youth, who feels invincible and independent, ultimately is tamed in later years by commitment, companionship, and deep wells of love.

15

In 1760, the twenty-fifth year of the Qian Long emperor's reign, a tribe called the Kalmucks from Turkestan invaded the north-western region. General Zhao Hui defeated the invasion and executed the leader. Acting on the orders of the emperor, he captured the widow of the leader, a woman whose mythical beauty had been talked about along trade routes until news of it reached the ears of Hong Li.

As the grieving widow was brought from the far north-western border to Beijing, rumours about the exotic captive multiplied. She was said to have a special odour, a particularly fragrant one. If she grew hot and perspired, the tiny red drops appeared on her skin.

The emperor ordered me to accompany him to a city south of Beijing called Liang Xiang. Not only was he eager to reward the victorious troops and their general as soon as possible, but he had another reason to insist on my presence.

'Zhen wishes you to paint this woman. Therefore it is important that you see her as soon as possible. Zhen has been told that she is weak. She has cried every day. Tears fall down her cheeks and leave red streaks. General Zhao gave her a thin white porcelain vase and told her to capture her tears in it to show me how deep her grief is. The general sent word that her tears are so red that they shine through the thin porcelain.'

The soldiers were already standing in formation when we arrived. The emperor strode up to his two kneeling generals, raised them to their feet, and embraced them—a very rare act of honour. Zhao Hui was awarded the highest level of commendation: Wu Yi Mou Yong—Martial, Determined, Intelligent, and Brave. His family was elevated to high noble status. He was given imperial pearls and a ministerial position. The second general, Fu De, was awarded the commendation Jing Yuan Cheng Yong Hou—Long Distance Fighter, Sincere, Brave. He was given imperial peacock feathers with two eyes and a ministerial rank.

An honour guard with the foreign captive could just be discerned in the distance making slow progress. The emperor had sent a royal palanquin to meet them earlier along the route. While we waited, the emperor told his aides to distribute yellow umbrellas to all the ordinary soldiers. Since this yellow was a colour reserved for the emperor and his family, the foot soldiers could not contain their pride and excitement.

A murmur rose among the crowd. The horses and palanquin approached. The emperor returned to his throne and sat very still. His brows were knitted tightly together. When the strong men carrying the palanquin stopped and placed it on the ground, the newly ennobled general, Zhao Hui, walked over to it.

A flash of terror entered my brain. What if she were not beautiful or not to his liking? What would happen to her if she did not live up to the enormous expectations that preceded her?

Sitting erect and tense, the emperor stared at the sedan chair, his face now fixed in a deep frown. Zhao Hui reached inside the curtain.

My artist's eyes were alert, looking for the essence of this woman who was never more truly to be perceived than at first sight. I saw a foot begin to emerge and then she flowed out like the opening bars of a concerto, her face announcing the major theme. When I beheld her entire body, from her slim waist to her heaving chest, I saw the first buds of spring, a gentle young sapling blowing in the wind. Music and springtime resounded in her being. In all of my seventy-two years, I have never felt melody emerge from a human form. How could any man not fall in love with her? She even caused the heart of an old Jesuit to miss a beat.

The emperor's face relaxed. A new expression filled his face, one of curiosity and possessiveness. He rose and strode towards her. To a Chinese, her features were exotic. She had very white skin with dark hair peeping out beneath a head covering. Her eyes, eyebrows, and nose were perfectly symmetrical and finely formed. Her mouth was full and sensuous. Her pale skin and doleful eyes cracked my heart. What would it feel like to be a captive, ripped from everything one knew, in the control of those who murdered your husband, to be surrounded by an alien culture, spoken to in a foreign language, and dragged thousands of miles across a land to an unknown future? Her pitiful face told me all I needed to know. She did not start the war, yet she was its saddest victim. Is this what women have suffered throughout history, the hapless survivors of their men's thwarted ambitions, left to the mercy of the victors?

The emperor stopped, waiting for her to bow before him. She did not kneel. She gazed upon him with sad yet indignant eyes.

A eunuch bellowed at her. 'Insignificant slave! Kneel down before His Majesty.' He strode toward her, about to force her submission.

'How dare you,' the emperor scolded the eunuch. He reached out and took off her head covering. A cascade of blue-black hair tumbled down her back. He looked in her face. She showed no fear and did not avert her eyes.

The emperor began to smile. He turned to a eunuch, who brought a fur hat. The emperor gently put it upon her head, pushing her hair behind her shoulders. I heard music in the shrieks of the wild birds that flew overhead. The emperor spoke to a large eunuch, who shouted out to the crowd: 'No one may harm this woman who will hereby be known as the "Fragrant Concubine." Anyone who causes her to suffer offends the emperor.'

16

Along with my title, the emperor had given me a large new house and land outside the Forbidden City. He ignored my protestations, saying that he would not hear of his vice-minister living in anything less worthy. It was a four-sided house built around a square courtyard, surrounded by gardens. There were twelve rooms beautifully decorated. The central courtyard had several ponds stocked with goldfish, and mature fruit trees. The emperor insisted on supplying a full contingent of servants. Guards patrolled the external walls of my little estate. The emperor himself gave the home its title and painted the characters. He called it *Tian Guo Men*, Kingdom of Heaven's Gate. It was a fitting title, a resting place before my final resting place.

My house was never without guests or colleagues, many of whom were very talented and gaining fame in their own right. Despite the fact that I was an old man, the emperor was still eager for more paintings so I had assistants and students to help me. On a whim I decided to paint the future emperor, Hong Li, being instructed by his father, the Yong Zheng emperor. I gave it a bold, deep blue background, a technique I had never used before, yet it worked. Ignoring how fraught their relationship had been, the emperor said it evoked wonderful memories and thanked me for this tribute to his youth and his father. He carefully penned his name in one corner.

I also asked two younger Jesuit artists to make engravings of the Western Gardens. Over the months, they produced twelve copper plates. At least those in Europe who scorned the Jesuits could see something of what we had helped to achieve here.

My largest commissions involved battle scenes. These were huge rolled scrolls depicting great triumphs. It was not my favourite genre. One was called *Ma Chang Attacking the Enemy's Camp*. Another was titled *Ayusi Assailing Rebels with a Lance*. The emperor was relieved that the wars with the Dzungars had at last ended and he wished to record the great deeds of his ancestors to honour them. Fortunately I only needed to paint a few of the figures for him to be content.

One day, the emperor asked me, 'Painter Lang, do you speak the language of the Muslim border?'

'Bixia, I do not.'

Hong Li appeared very preoccupied. 'Yes. Of course, you are Italian. Your languages are different.' He hesitated. 'The woman brought back from the Muslim border—Zhen wanted to make her a high-ranking concubine, but she is opposed. She is homesick. Zhen wishes to send you to soothe her, to end this desire to return to her people. It is seven months since she arrived and her mood is no better. Calm her down so that she is content to remain in the palace. I have no desire to mistreat her.'

'Bixia offers your humble slave an honourable position. But if your slave is unable to persuade the female to heed your wishes, perhaps it will cause even more harm to her life.'

I suddenly felt afraid for her and for me. Lao Zi once said that disaster arises from fortune and fortune arises from disaster. The emperor's victory over his enemies brought disaster for Fragrant Concubine. Now it threatened my tranquil way of life.

I often asked Wang Rong how she was faring, for the face I saw briefly all those months ago often returned to haunt my daydreams. He told me that she was being kept at Yuan Ming Yuan, far away from the other wives and concubines. She barely ate or spoke and was constantly watched in case she tried to kill herself. Those who spoke her language reported that she refused any rank as a wife of the emperor and detested the name Fragrant Concubine.

'Do not worry. Zhen is sending you to her for a reason,' the emperor continued, breaking into my thoughts. 'Zhen has a strong feeling that she will respond to your gentleness and sincerity. In this way, Zhen allows you to talk to her of your religion. When can you begin?'

I opened my mouth and closed it again.

'Zhen wishes you to use your eloquence to soothe her heart. Is that so difficult to understand?'

I shook my head.

'No, Zhen did not think so. Good, you may begin immediately. Be warned, she carries a sharp knife in her clothes. Every time my ministers implore her to be reasonable, they fail.' The emperor paused. 'Ai. If my mother knew how this woman opposes me, she would have her put to death. You must not reveal her behaviour to anyone.'

'Bixia, you need not worry that I would reveal anything to the empress dowager.'

I saw as little of his mother as possible. The years had not been kind to her. An ugly soul hardens a face as it ages. In her case, she would frighten the devil away

'Bixia, has anyone tried to take the knife away?'

'Not yet. Of course we could. But this is not a method Zhen wishes to employ. To overpower her would be a mistake. One wrong step and she will seek release from me through death. Zhen has issued strict orders. She is watched night and day. Zhen truly wishes that she will turn her heart around and adapt to life in our palace. You, of all the people Zhen knows, have the ability to cure her. Zhen is sure of it.'

Fragrant Concubine resided in a special palace within Yuan Ming Yuan with a name I translated as Sitting on a Stone Veranda. It had been built between the back lake and the enormous 'Prosperity Sea Lake.' It was bright and very well placed. In all directions the eye was soothed by lush vegetation and emerald water.

Before I entered, I reflected on a side of the emperor I had never before seen. His desire for her and her fragility made him feel utterly helpless, probably for the first time in his life. He had captured a wild creature that pined for freedom while he sought to tame it.

Not far from the Sitting on a Stone Veranda Pavilion, separated by a river, was one of the nicest features in Yuan Ming Yuan, a miniature market called the Street of Buying and Selling. It looked like an ordinary village, although a very prosperous one. I lingered awhile longer wondering how I was going to accomplish my task.

Before I could open the door, a eunuch rushed out to greet me. He was very respectful, bowing low in greeting. The eunuch explained that the poor creature said very little, even to those who spoke her language. She only found solace strolling in the gardens and by feeding the birds.

'She is a gentle creature. If only she would speak to us. One word from such a silent creature would be like the song of the rarest bird.'

Inside the palace, Fragrant Concubine, looking young and defenceless, lay with her head upon the back of a daybed. Every corner of the room held a silent servant, ever watchful.

Even in her listlessness, her beauty was unmistakable, yet it was not just beauty that made her special. She was a rare gift of nature, something gentle, tender, exquisite, and, ultimately, fragile. I knew it was unjust that she had been captured and ached all the more for her loss, but could not fail to be excited to see her again.

As she heard the door open, the pitiful creature turned her head and glanced at me for a brief second. Her eyes revealed a soul in torment. I have seen animals behind cages with the same listless, empty look, but this was worse. Here was a human, capable of thought and expression, whose deepest desires were blocked. Her eyes returned to the open door, to freedom. I knew, at that instant, that I would use whatever skills I possessed to bring laughter back to that noble face, to help her accept her fate.

I began to talk in all the languages I knew, passing from Italian, to broken Spanish, Portuguese, French, Latin, Greek. She did not move. She hardly blinked.

'I feel like a fat dumb potato standing talking to myself in a host of languages,' I said in Italian. The servants glanced at me as if I were mad.

'I am Giuseppe Castiglione. A painter and a Jesuit brother.'

She did not respond.

I pulled out some chalk and paper from my robes. I quickly drew a melon from her region, the sweet ha mi melon so beloved by the Chinese. I named it for her in Chinese. 'Ha mi gua. Tian, sweet.'

A tiny ember of light flickered in her eyes. It did not fade.

My heart began to race. I drew a stringed instrument used by her people. It had four strings and a very full body, like a gourd. More light shone in her eyes. I drew another stringed instrument like our mandolin. I pretended to strum it, humming a lively tune.

I held her attention in my hand and was afraid to breathe too hard lest she snatched it back again. Her gaze twittered like that of a frightened bird, tensed and ready to flee at the first sign of trouble.

She opened her eyes wide and looked at my face, taking in my fair skin and long beard. Perhaps I was the first European she had seen since her capture. My hair was grey and white; no flecks of blond or red remained. I was an old, old man.

The eunuch came forward, excited. He asked me if I wanted a translator. I shook my head. I requested more rice paper instead.

When it came, I sketched a cartoon dog, old and mangy. Drawing like this was one of the games I used many times with children. Was this young woman not a child again, taking her first steps in a new world, grasping a new language? She half turned away, watching me from the corner of her eye. I believe she was trying to figure out who this bearded old idiot could be.

Next to the dog, I sketched a hen. I could feel Fragrant Concubine relaxing ever so slowly. I added a grey beard on to the dog, one like mine. When I gave him round green bean eyes, she giggled. I put a small cap on the head of the hen, identical to the one she wore, red and round like a skullcap. I painted large, suspicious eyes on the hen. The hen spied the bearded dog with mistrust. Laughter suddenly erupted from her. It was clear and crisp, like a spring breeze on young leaves. Two deep dimples appeared on either side of her mouth. Relief surged through me. It was but a small reward, yet worth its weight in gold.

We ended my visit on this note of mutual understanding. I had conveyed, through further sketches, that I understood her suspicions but that I was as harmless as a toothless, ageing hound from another country. She still had not uttered a word, but I sensed that a tiny thread of trust had stretched across the room between her exquisite fingers and my gnarled ones.

I met her day after day. As the emperor's spokesman, I drew scores of pictures showing her that if she promised not to kill herself, we would try to make her as happy as possible. Then she revealed that she spoke Portuguese. In her youth, she had been educated by a Portuguese priest. We moved from cartoons to language and she poured her heart out so fast that I could hardly take it in.

Her name was Alena and she was the youngest child of many and only twenty-three years old. She had loved her husband from the moment she had met him, even though he was much older and a seasoned warrior. After their marriage, he was often away fighting for months at a time. She blamed his absences on the fact that no child had been conceived. She was, foolishly, on her way to meet him when news of his death reached her. Before she knew it, she was captured and separated from everything she had ever known. Alena told me sadly that she had dreamed of such a different life for herself on her wedding night. She had hoped to produce a tribe of children and live surrounded by her parents, siblings, and all of their offspring.

After some time she admitted that, even if the emperor allowed her to leave, she could never go home. Her people would assume that she had been unfaithful in her widowhood—it did not matter if willingly or not—and would reject her. She did not want to die but was not ready to become a mistress of the emperor.

One day I explained to her that every foreigner used a Chinese name; that I was no longer Giuseppe Castiglione but Lang Shi Ning. Since China would be her home, it was time to put the name Alena away. She thought about it for several minutes.

'I do not wish to insult the emperor who has given me the title Fragrant Concubine. I will be known as Miss Fragrant from now on.'

After that day, Miss Fragrant began her lessons in Chinese with an excellent group of elderly scholars. Her mind was agile and curious and she grew more adept daily at speaking in Mandarin although she had no desire to learn to read or write it.

One day she handed the knife to me. 'If there are more people like you and my teachers around the emperor, I am safe here. I don't need this anymore.'

The emperor was overjoyed with my progress. This only made me more nervous. I too recognised she meant a great deal to me. Only in my prayers did I acknowledge how protective I felt of her. I did not want her to change or to suffer any more harm. She was perfect as she was, the most ideal image of womanhood, the finest qualities of femininity combined in one form. Once she entered the western or eastern palaces, surrounded by jealousies and pettiness, she would change. She would have to in order to survive. If she did not, she was doomed.

'Now you must paint her,' the emperor said one day. 'And you may use those oil paints you love so much.'

I leapt at the opportunity to paint her portrait. My very own Mona Lisa, I told her, though she had no idea to what I was referring. She refused to smile, but the finished portrait had enough of a hint of contentment to add mystery to her thoughts. She had come to rely on me and look forward to my visits.

'Uncle, have you ever been so sad that you wanted to die?' she asked me.

'Miss Fragrant, as a Jesuit I have never contemplated suicide nor could I help anyone else to harm themselves,' I answered.

'There are ways other than suicide to die, if one decides to. My grandmother could not bear to live without my grandfather and followed him to her grave only a few days after his death. She seemed to will her death; she used no poison or weapon.'

I thought for a moment before I answered. 'There have been times when I have endured terrible trials and I thought I could never go on, but there was always someone dear to me who encouraged me to live. I have learned that the path of love is far stronger than any other and the greatest motivation of life. I cannot explain what happened to your grandmother who I assume to have been old. Perhaps her love for her husband was more powerful than her love for her children and grandchildren or perhaps she was tired of this life. Though I am now old, I still have many reasons to live and many loved ones. You are young, and though cruel things have happened to you, Miss Fragrant, you have won the heart of the emperor. Since I have known him since he was a boy of four, I can assure you it is a heart worth winning.'

'And you, Uncle. Do you love me? I think that would mean more to me than anything, for you are older, kinder, and wiser than anyone else I have ever met.'

'Yes,' I answered without hesitating. 'I love you and want to see you safe and happy.'

The smile she rewarded me with was engraved in my memory. I did a quick painting later of her face with that smile and I kept it for my introspection.

When I delivered the oil painting to the emperor he was delighted. 'Painter Lang, this portrait shall hang in my bedchambers. It is most pleasing.'

Four months after my first encounter with Miss Fragrant, the Lotus Lantern Festival was celebrated at her doorstep, on the Street of Buying and Selling. This midsummer festival was the time when the devil supposedly released the dead to pass among the living. It followed on the heels of a lighter celebration, the Qi Qiao Jie or Asking for Skills Festival when all the women displayed their embroidery skills, praying for help and instruction from the gifted 'Female Star.'

'The empress dowager detests the Lotus Lantern Festival,' Wang Rong told me as he helped me to find a costume. 'She is terrified at the thought of the dead walking among us; afraid she may see a ghost.'

'She has good reasons to be afraid of the dead—and the living,' I muttered.

On the morning of the festival, the emperor used me to present special gifts to Miss Fragrant. The most touching gift was a gaggle of new companions. His aides had found ten cheerful, young Turkish women to serve as her new maids. The emperor had been a clever ruler tolerating the minorities of his vast kingdom. He had encouraged many to move closer to Beijing where they were treated with tolerance and solicitude. Some of the men were awarded noble titles or served in various ministries as advisors. He granted land to artisans, built a mosque, and allowed them to construct houses according to their customs. The young women were from these families.

I arrived at the Sitting on a Stone Veranda Pavilion surrounded by these colourfully attired, noisy girls and imperial guards carrying gifts. Miss Fragrant cried red tears of joy as she met her new companions. Though I had seen her tears before, I never failed to be amazed at their reddish hue. Whenever this happened and she dabbed her cheeks and eyes with a cloth it became stained.

Another gift from the emperor was a musical clock. It played three familiar songs, two of which were Italian lullabies. When they finished, I quietly began to sing one of them.

'Louder, please, Painter Lang,' she said.

'Are you sure?'

'I too love to sing. And to dance.'

'So you can sing?' I asked quickly.

She nodded her head then shook her head, but I understood her mixed feelings.

I repeated the lullaby. I could hardly finish it, as I was suddenly overwhelmed by a great feeling of nostalgia. The best memories of my youth surfaced: the smells of breadbaking, olives heavy on the trees, the choirs in the churches, the clouds that tickled the hilltops. A soft hand broke my reverie. I turned to catch the crystal glint of tears in her eyes, catching the light and reflecting a rainbow of colours. She, more than anyone, understood the sense of belonging that a homeland holds on one forever.

Miss Fragrant covered her face with her hands and sobbed. A thin line of red tears spilled out between her fingers and ran down the backs of her palms. Before I could offer her my handkerchief, she threw herself at me, burying her head in my chest. This unleashed a flood of tears from me as well, silly old fool that I had become. Her companions joined in as well, sucked in by the heady emotions. The imperial guards stood impassively, ignoring the caterwauling in the room.

Nearby at the Street of Buying and Selling, the festival swung into life as people arrived. Temporary houses and shops made of tents and curtains had been erected. All the guests were specially chosen. Only the highest nobles of Han, Manchu, and minority backgrounds, personal relatives of the emperor, and the palace eunuchs and palace woman were permitted.

Everyone present wore a disguise. Miss Fragrant emerged from her home on my arm dressed as a female skilled in the martial arts. She wore a black mask that revealed only her eyes. Wang Rong had helped me make a costume of a fierce pirate, albeit an old one. I wore a bulky helmet that hid most of my face. I felt as if I were speaking in a tunnel. Miss Fragrant found my appearance highly comical. I carried a sword in my belt. Having never carried a weapon before, I found the sensation of a heavy object hitting my thigh every second step unnerving.

The crowd was so thick that we walked toe upon heel and shoulder touching shoulder. Her companions had long disappeared, rushing off giggling, drawn to curious sights in every direction. I spoke to her in Chinese so that I did not draw attention. Feeling very secure in her mask and disguise, she was as excited as a young swallow out for its first solo flight. She almost danced along, taking in all the sights and commenting on everything though I heard little and understood less, deafened by my ridiculous helmet.

Any object imaginable could be found on the Street of Buying and Selling. Merchandise overflowed as if the largest city markets had come together in one spot. Certain shops sold seasonal items. Every package was wrapped in red and green paper. Many colourful boxes hung in long vertical strands. Miss Fragrant stood transfixed by the desserts, her eyes wide like a young child. I picked out a selection for her to taste. I knew that many of these dishes had been sent to her by the emperor, desperate to please her palate, but most had gone uneaten. Here, under the summer sky in a festive atmosphere, the food elicited a different response.

We stopped at one shop selling lanterns. Painted on the outside of the lanterns were characters representing a word puzzle. Crowds gathered around, trying to guess the solutions. The Manchu nobles vied with each other to show their knowledge of Han culture. Several of the puzzles had been designed by the emperor himself. The winners would receive a gift from him.

I explained the contest to Miss Fragrant. 'Look, this lamp reads: "*Within a four-sided city, soldiers and horses pass in two directions. Which king will be killed by whom? Only when the battle is finished will we know the result.*" Do you know what it refers to?'

She shook her head.

'This is an easy one. It describes Chinese chess.'

Whatever purchases we made were completed with fake money. With the way everyone shouted, bullied, and bargained, one would think the entire market was genuine. To add to the authenticity, actors played the part of thieves and bandits, stealing our goods and our purses. The emperor, the empress, the concubines, and the princes and princesses walked the streets as ordinary men and women.

Every form of entertainment was available, including acrobats and wonderful musicians. One could choose from three types of fortune-teller: those who based their predictions on your name, those who needed your time of birth, and those who read your palm. Magicians, fire dancers, trapeze artists thrilled everyone with their amazing feats. There were cockfights and quail fights and the guests' favourite, cricket fights.

'What is that man doing?' Miss Fragrant asked.

'He is a storyteller who uses sounds instead of words. I will tell you the story as he reveals it,' I whispered in her ear. I was so close that I could smell her special fragrance. It was not always present, but today it was, a fragrance that reminded me of myrrh.

'Well? What is happening?' she demanded.

I came to my senses and whispered in her ear. 'A middle-aged couple is chatting amicably. They enter a market and bargain with the owner of a shop. Finally satisfied, they return home to make their meal. They clean the kitchen, start the fire, blow the bellows, boil the water, and fry the food. Two guests arrive, another man and woman. The little house is crowded and happy. Then an argument breaks out. Plates are broken. A fight erupts among the hosts and their guests. It all ends in chaos.'

She marvelled at the man's skill and applauded with the audience when he finished. As dusk approached, we watched an amazing group of women acrobats perform. One woman lay on a high platform so that the crowd could get a good view of her. On her tiny bound feet she balanced a large porcelain trough. A long ladder protruded from the middle of the trough, miraculously balanced on two legs. Another young lady with bound feet climbed up the ladder. The crowd cheered their approval.

We were startled by the sound of pounding hooves. A group of horsemen charged at the crowd and everyone scattered. One horse came perilously close to Miss Fragrant and me. She grabbed my arm and screamed. The rider, wearing a copper helmet, reached down and scooped her from the ground as if she were light as a feather. She tried to hold on to me but the strength of the rider broke her grip. He placed her in front of him on the horse while she struggled wildly. Watching her distress and seeing her begin to disappear, I shouted wildly and angrily. I pulled my fake sword from my sheath and ran on my useless, wobbly old legs, as if I knew anything about sword fighting.

Out of nowhere, a Good Samaritan appeared. He wore the clothes of a Muslim but his face was covered with a mask. He spurred his horse forward and grabbed the reins of the escaping horse. The two men fought savagely with swords. Miss Fragrant slipped off the horse and ran to my arms, sobbing. The thief fell off his horse, seemingly seriously wounded, with blood running down his chest. He ran off, followed by guards who shouted for him to stop.

I held Miss Fragrant and caressed her trembling head until she calmed down. We walked towards the Good Samaritan to thank him.

He smiled. 'It is all in a day's work. No need to waste your breath thanking me. All I ask is that the young lady look upon me as a brother. Together we can be a family, brother and sister. Will she tell me her name?'

I spoke to Miss Fragrant in Portuguese. 'Did you understand what he said in Chinese?'

She nodded, still clutching me.

'Are you willing to take this brave man as a brother?'

She shook her head resolutely and spoke in Chinese. 'Uncle, I am very confused. You assured me that everything today was pretend. Yet they used real swords. I saw blood. I wish to return home.'

'Everything is all right now, my dear. I don't know how all that happened, but you are safe now. Calm down. This fine gentleman has asked you a question and you must answer. If you do not wish to become a sister to this hero, just say so. It is not an important matter.' I turned to the Good Samaritan and spoke for her. 'Brave sir, not wishing you any dishonour, the young lady does not wish to take you as her brother. Please do not feel offended.'

'Relax. Relax. We need not be brother and sister. Please ask the pretty lady if she would give me the honour of strolling with me awhile in the gardens.'

She pushed herself away from me at that point and looked at the Samaritan. 'I would be happy to do that,' she told him. 'You come with us,' she added in Portuguese.

I suddenly recognised the voice and the posture of the Good Samaritan. It was the emperor. What a performance he had just put on!

'Wonderful,' the disguised emperor said. 'Shall I lead the way?'

As the three of us strolled away from the crowded, raucous market, a sedan chair appeared and stopped before her. Miss Fragrant shook her head and pointed to the emperor's handsome steed. He pretended to misunderstand her meaning.

'I am a very good rider,' she announced.

'Ah,' he replied and lifted her upon his treasured mount. I saw him pinch the horse's stomach. It leapt forward. The emperor's horsemanship was second to none. As the startled horse lurched, he jumped on it and steadied it. In a flash, he set off for the lake, his beloved concubine safely in front of him. I stood there like a fool, my jaw hanging loose.

They were fast disappearing.

The emperor guided his horse towards one of the most charming views near the Sea of Prosperity, a garden copied from one in Hangzhou. From a distance, I watched them dismount. He was leaning over her, talking tenderly. As they walked slowly towards a wooden bridge, cold sweat began to trickle down my back. What if Miss Fragrant had no idea who was at her side? What if she said something injudicious and offended the emperor unwittingly?

I hurried as fast as my ageing limbs would allow. When I finally reached the bridge, a young guard dressed as a Daoist appeared from the side with a huge grin on his face. He held a large horsetail broom across my path, blocking the way. I moved left. So did he. I scolded him. He laughed.

'Vice-Minister Lang, our ten-thousand-years-living emperor thanks you for your help and he asks you to enjoy yourself. Elsewhere.'

I expected Miss Fragrant to turn and look for me, but she did not. When they reached the middle of the bridge, a small boat left the far bank to meet them. She allowed herself to be helped on to the boat. I was touched. The man for whom women were usually his for the asking had put so much energy and patience into soothing the broken heart of this one. As I walked away, I prayed that his charm would serve as a balm to Miss Fragrant and that they would find happiness together. How was that possible in the dark environment of the Forbidden City?

The small boat sailed towards the centre of the Sea of Prosperity and the main island. I stood in a discreet spot, watching them. Night had now fallen. A gong sounded and the bright sparks of firecrackers filled the dark sky. Smoke drifted above our heads and fading embers slowly floated towards the cool lake. Lotus lanterns twinkled in the boats moored along the banks. One large imperial dragon boat carried a huge paper palace. On the banks of the islands the nobles released paper money with Daoist words of wisdom and spells upon the water, messages meant for the lonely ghosts who were expected to discover them. Monks and lamas controlled the proceedings.

Once the large dragon boat began to sail, all the smaller boats moved away from the banks. The surface of the Sea of Prosperity filled with dancing lights of lotus lanterns. The paper palace began to burn. More firecrackers erupted while gongs and drums pounded the night air. The cacophony swelled and rolled along the calm surface of the lake and out into the gardens.

The emperor and his 'Fragrant Concubine' watched it all, hidden in a tranquil corner of the lake and peering out from the shelter of a willow tree.

17

Two days after the Lotus Lantern Festival, an imperial carriage arrived at my door. A guard announced that the emperor wished to see me on urgent matters.

He was pacing back and forth when I entered his study. 'Painter Lang,' he announced abruptly, 'Zhen orders you to build, in the shortest time possible, a collection of Muslim buildings.'

'Build Muslim buildings? Bixia, are you sending me to the Muslim borders? They are very far away and I am an old man.'

'No. Not there. Here. In the Western Gardens. The Fragrant Gui Ren is far from her homeland. Zhen wishes you to build her home village here.'

My lame brain finally understood. Miss Fragrant had relayed to me her late night conversation with the emperor. She had realised fairly quickly that her saviour had been the emperor. As night fell, he removed his mask. While the festivities rained around them, they talked. She explained that though she had given up her wish to die, she wished to remain a chaste widow in honour of her late husband. The emperor cleverly asked her if she would consent to be his wife if he could find the right gift, a gift that would lighten her heart.

'How could I answer such a question?' she said to me with glistening eyes. 'For the first time I saw the love in his heart. He has been patient with me. But my loyalty to my people and my religion is deep as well. I was pulled in two directions. I do not wish to be forced...I said yes. In my heart, I do not believe he could ever find a present that would break my resolve to remain chaste.'

Now my clever emperor was calling upon my aged skills to win her love. Whereas the years had slowed my brain, experience had honed it well and

I knew that this was an ambition too bold to be achieved. I told him so in delicate terms, without fear of insulting him.

'Bixia, your stupid servant has too small a talent and too little strength for such an order. I know nothing of Muslim culture. It would be wiser to ask a younger man with more talent.'

'Painter Lang, how can Zhen accept this ignorance as a reason? You Christian artists paint your saints, gods, prophets, and scenes from your sacred book. Have you ever seen these people or spirits? Have you ever been to the places you depict? Does it not all flow from your imagination?'

I was no match for him when determination was his motivation.

'When Zhen was four or five years old, Zhen saw the first painting you made for Zhen's grandfather. Zhen still remembers the vision Zhen experienced then. Zhen told Zhen's grandfather: this man will be a friend of an emperor and of China. Was Zhen wrong?' He looked at me with piercing eyes. I shook my head weakly.

'Good. Zhen grants you one year. No more.' He waved his hand dismissively. 'Give Fragrant Gui Ren a vision of her homeland. Remember, you may not be late,' he added, his face darkened.

I had the glimmering of an idea, ill defined still but possible. I bowed as best I could and agreed to carry out his orders.

I asked the emperor for the assistance of Brother Jerome and any other Jesuits still remaining in Beijing who had worked on the Western Gardens. Father Michel had died before his fiftieth birthday, but a few others remained. The emperor immediately issued an order. It saddened me that Jerome and other Jesuits could not willingly help me unless the emperor intervened.

Despite the gulf that existed between us, we worked well together, and at times, Jerome temporarily forgot his animosity towards me. In the Western Gardens, at the far end of the rectangular pool, we changed the paintings on the thirteen panels. We designed new canvases depicting what we thought Miss Fragrant's native land looked like. We painted many canvases for different seasons and times of the day so that we could change the scenes on the panels daily. It would be a triumph of *trompe l'oeil* if we succeeded in convincing a homesick courtesan that Turkestan was only a short distance away. The paintings on the walls were reflected in the clear water of the pool.

We made the greatest changes to the Belvedere, the elegant summer house between the two major palaces. This jewel of a building, although small, commanded the highest vantage point in the Western Gardens. From its windows, Miss Fragrant could gaze upon the perspective hill, the reflecting pool. and the *trompe l'oeil* panels.

Although I was of an age when most men are free to pray and read and while away the time, I began work on the construction of Miss Fragrant's gift.

My eyes and ears were losing their sharpness, my body bent and aching, but I remained my emperor's servant.

Wang Rong kept me informed of the goings on in the den of she-devils. Despite the emperor's best efforts, his wives and concubines knew every detail of his love for Miss Fragrant. The concubines complained bitterly to the empress dowager. They resented the love he lavished on her. These women, who were summoned as usual to his bedchamber, were well aware that Miss Fragrant denied him her body. Persisting in her unbelievable disobedience, she was rewarded with a new palace and gardens. To the she-devils this was maddening. I had long feared she would be poisoned or assassinated and hoped the emperor's protection was thorough.

The exterior of the Belvedere was European, with a beautiful wrought-iron door and symmetrical curved staircases. We only needed to change the interior. I studied as much material as existed on the art of the Muslim empires. Like the Chinese, the Muslims avoided human representation in painted and carved decorations in buildings. We mimicked their intricate designs. The final stone and marble carving exceeded my greatest hopes.

The emperor was stricter than I had ever seen him. He personally checked every detail and tolerated nothing less than perfection. We completed the work in eleven months.

On a morning blessed by heaven with bright skies and a soft wind, the emperor approached the Sitting on a Stone Veranda Pavilion. He led his beloved towards her new home. Slowly they travelled towards the Western Gardens. The palanquin stopped before the gates and they walked inside. Her eyes beheld, for the first time, the Palace of Delights and Harmony and its playful fountains. She passed the aviary and crossed the marble bridge over the stream. The palanquin climbed the high hill and halted before the Belvedere. She ascended the grand marble staircase. Inside, she gasped at the Arabic designs we had carved in the walls and ceiling. Her delicate fingers traced the familiar patterns. Along the corridor, the emperor opened the door to the prayer room. We had created a wall with stalactite patterns we had read about. A frieze contained words from the Koran. Every inch of wall and ceiling was intricately carved. Best of all, lit by oil lamps resting on a carved mahogany stand was an exquisite illuminated manuscript of the Koran.

I waited for their arrival at the door to her bedroom. Her eyes were wide with amazement and deep emotion. The floor was covered with rich carpets from Persia. Everywhere she looked, there were objects dear to her religion and homeland. Her eyes filled with pink liquid that squeezed out between her thick eyelashes. When the emperor opened the window and motioned for her to come closer, pointing towards the reflecting pool, I watched her face as her eyes gazed into the distance.

'There is a beautiful long blue lake,' she exclaimed. 'And at the end…it cannot be.' She brought her hands to her cheeks and glanced at the emperor with startled eyes. 'I can see the fields I loved and goats. There is the most beautiful mosque and mountains from my country. What sort of magic is this?'

She clutched at her white silk scarf and covered her face, red tears leaving long streaks down the scarf. Her shoulders trembled. The emperor put his arms around her and hugged her to his chest. At that moment, he was not the most powerful man in the nation but a man deeply in love. As I left the Belvedere and walked towards the reflecting pool, I could almost feel Miss Fragrant's heart open to the man who had caused her so much pain but courted her with all the tenderness he possessed.

With my work finally at an end, I returned to my home to do nothing more strenuous than walk around my gardens. I heard from Wang Rong that Miss Fragrant and the emperor had become lovers. Most of the time she remained at Yuan Ming Yuan, but occasionally, she accompanied him to the Forbidden City. I saw her a few more times when she was brought to my house to sit for another portrait. She was happier than before but a hint of sadness appeared now and then. As my hearing was failing I missed many of the things she was telling me in confidence. Perhaps it was for the best.

The emperor arrived at my house to personally pick up the new portrait.

'Painter Lang, you have captured everything about her that Zhen treasures in this portrait. It is your finest work, as if you painted it from your heart.'

It was the last painting I made. My hands finally refused to obey my commands. I would muse while watching many a sunset on how I had floated on the river of life for an unexpectedly large amount of time, dropping the best of me into the current. If my artistic contribution disappeared in a tributary downstream, it was for a reason. It was part of God's plan.

One day, three years after painting my final portrait of Miss Fragrant, my reverie was disturbed by the distressed voice of Wang Rong.

'Oh, Vice-Minister Lang, it is a most terrible day.'

'Why? How?' My mouth was dry and my chest ached. I could tell Wang Rong had been crying and a feeling of dread came over me. Even before he spoke I had a vision of Miss Fragrant, smiling from an upper storey window in the Belvedere as she waved goodbye to me, pointing at the scenes of Turkestan in the distance.

Wang Rong had great difficulty telling me his story. 'Today is the day that the emperor performs the autumn ceremony at the Tian Tan palace to pray to the ancestors and gods for a good harvest. When he left the Forbidden City, the empress dowager ordered Fragrant Concubine to be brought to her. I sent one or two soldiers, very discreetly, to tell the emperor before I accompanied her. I hoped to protect her, or at least to delay until the emperor returned. As we entered the palace, all the doors were locked behind us. Fragrant Concubine looked at me. She had no fear, only resignation in her eyes. We both knew what a dangerous situation this was.

'The empress dowager was very cold to her and asked why she had refused to obey the emperor for so long. "I had already taken vows of marriage," Fragrant Concubine explained. "My husband may have departed this world, but I was expected to be true to my vows. It is not our custom for a widow to remarry."

'The empress dowager looked at her with her eyes narrowed to tiny slits and asked one simple question. "What do you really want?"

'Fragrant Concubine took a long time to answer. She understood what game was being played and did not fight it.

'"Death," she answered slowly.

'"If I give you permission to die now, do you still want death?"

'The Fragrant Concubine knelt before the fearsome woman. "Thank you," she uttered, "for your great kindness."

'I tried to talk to the empress but was ordered to be silent. Before Fragrant Concubine was led away she asked permission to talk to me. "Please tell His Majesty that if I had not already taken the vows of marriage, I would not have refused the true love he offered me. In this life our union was fraught with difficulties, but tell him that in the next life I will love him fully and that I will await him in the land of dreams and miracles. Please find Missionary Lang as well and tell him that I am sorry. There was not enough love around me to keep me in this world. I go to a place where I will bathe in the love of my family."

'While the emperor was carrying out the solemn ceremony, the soldiers I had sent crawled to him and interrupted to convey the words I had told them to say, that Fragrant Concubine was in danger and had been taken to his mother's palace.

'The emperor ended the ceremony and spurred his horse to the Forbidden City. He reached his mother's palace and pounded on the locked gates, but nobody answered. I could hear him shouting. His mother sat on her throne without expression. While he pounded and shouted, Miss Fragrant took the rope offered to her and tied it to a beam in a small room, attended by eunuchs of the empress dowager. It was over very quickly. The eunuchs returned and nodded to the empress dowager. When the door to the palace was opened, it was left to me to tell him that she was dead. Together we went to look at her body. His grief is terrible. The emperor tells me that he will never share his heart with another woman.'

While I had known that every day their love was allowed to flourish was a gift from heaven, I had hoped that fate would give them more time. As for me, my will to live shattered that day into millions of irretrievable tiny pieces. One more life ended before its time because of jealously and treachery.

I had never known what is like to share one's life fully with a woman, but I would like to think that if I had not become a Jesuit I would never have married a woman without the same sensitive, tender qualities of Miss Fragrant. As a celibate monk, I poured my spirit and emotions into my paintings instead of into a wife and children. Perhaps it was because I had become a silly old man that I grieved for her as much as I did. When, several months after Miss Fragrant's death, the emperor visited me, he told me that he kept the porcelain vase with her red tears by his bedside beneath the two oil portraits I had painted of her.

'Zhen will protect these portraits forever.'

18

The Chinese say that the age of seventy-three is a gateway. If one makes it beyond seventy-three one can live to the next gateway of eight-four. I have no desire to live that long.

I believe Wang Rong was here, but he has departed. The memoirs are complete, but he still comes to see me as do others. I am not blind, but I don't see clearly any more. Many people like to stroke my head as if I were a child. I have been sleeping when I should be practising calligraphy. I often do that—fall asleep when the exertion of holding the brush and forming the characters depletes the tiny well of energy that remains in my body. The brush is sitting waiting for me, though the ink is completely dried. My hands are too stiff now to accomplish anything, so I gaze out into the garden. It is a beautiful day. The sun illuminates the flowers and leaves and a warm breeze drifts in through the open door.

My seventy-eighth birthday approaches. I am a well-cared for old man—the emperor insists upon it. The walls that contain our grief are built of the same material, almost upon the same terrain. Of all the work I completed for him, that which mattered most was the work that enabled him to win the love of Miss Fragrant. He is different now. He seeks more pleasure, perhaps to mask how much he misses her.

Although my house is large, I prefer to rest in my study surrounded by my beloved objects. My servants hand me the bamboo brush holders each morning so that I may rub them on my cheeks as I have always done. Some of them, the oldest, are now deep red. My failing eyes can no longer make out the details of the intricate ivory or wood carvings, but my hands caress them and recognise them, so well do I know their patterns.

Despite all the difficulties I encountered, I am grateful to God and to this country. He guided me through my angry early years to my destiny in China. Because of Him, I had the opportunity to stand, arms outstretched, between two cultures. I believe that in some way I contributed to the enrichment of Chinese culture. Though I shall disappear, I have left something behind for future generations to savour. I observed and I recorded what I saw here.

When my body is weak, I retreat to my memories. Foremost are the three exceptional emperors I have served, but there are other great people who enrich my daydreams. The departed come closer by the minute, staying with me as I muse, standing by my shoulder and talking to me. In my mind's eye they are as fresh and clear as a spring morning. Wu Yu with his blind eyes. Paolo with his far seeing ones. Antonio, young and unscathed, tugs at the Buddha necklace I wear faithfully, winking at me. 'You promised to give this to someone, but you have kept it for yourself.' Ruth caresses my hand tenderly. Chen Yuan thanks me for looking after his daughter, proud of the many grandchildren and now great-grandchildren that bear his blood. Rector Ignatius smiles benignly, full of pride for the rebellious Jesuit he protected and encouraged. Jin Kun teases me, telling me that we have another long, boring ceremonial scroll to prepare.

A new face appeared a few days ago. It was Jerome. No one told me that he died. He is young again and full of hope. I am happy for him.

The emperor visited me again today. My servants get more nervous with each visit. They never know when he may appear. This time he brought Cocco with him. 'He paints almost as well as you do,' he teased. 'He is a royal painter, my personal painter.'

The emperor showed me a new plant that is being tested. Corn, he said. The river of life flows on and there is a new Chen Yuan struggling to help his people. I nodded and tears flowed from my eyes. Cocco leant forward to dab at my face with his handkerchief.

I asked the emperor to allow me to be buried in the Jesuit cemetery. He laughed. 'Zhen will not allow you to be buried in so-called blessed ground by the Jesuits who have spurned you,' he said. 'Zhen will bury you with Chinese nobles, in the Tang Gong Sha Lar, just outside the Fu Cheng Gate. Your funeral will be a fitting testimony to your eminence in my court. Everyone will dress in white and the procession will stretch for many li. Zhen will read a memorial that Zhen will personally compose. Music and flowers will accompany you to your final resting place.'

I shrugged. Does it really matter, I wonder, where my body lies as it returns to dust?

As I sit looking out at my tranquil courtyard, my energy fading, a poem comes to mind. It is one I memorised many years ago, written in the sixteenth century by Saint Peter Canisius. Though he had probably never spared even one thought for China, it is remarkably Chinese in its mood,

I am not eager, bold
Or strong, all that is past.
I am ready, not to do,
At last, at last

Epilogue

Giuseppe Castiglione died on 16 July 1766, three days before his seventy-eighth birthday. The Society of Jesus was suppressed and disbanded by order of Pope Clement XIV in 1773. The Qian Long emperor abdicated in 1795, not wishing to serve longer as emperor than his grandfather.

Today, the Western Gardens are, sadly, little more than rubble. On 7 October 1860, French and English troops under the command of Lord Elgin (the son of the Lord Elgin who brought the marble friezes from the Parthenon to England) ransacked Yuan Ming Yuan in revenge for alleged attacks on foreign nationals during the Taiping Rebellion and ordered that all the buildings within it be burned. The French commander, General Montaulban, objected but failed to convince Lord Elgin to abandon his plan to shock and shame the Qing dynasty.

Charles Gordon, serving in the English army as a captain, wrote: '*You can scarce imagine the beauty and magnificence of the palaces we burnt. It made one's heart sore to burn them; in fact, these palaces were so large and we were so pressed for time, that we could not plunder them carefully...It was wretchedly demoralising work for the army.*'*

The priceless art collection of the Qian Long emperor was plundered. The tapestries designed by the Jesuits to hang in the palaces of the Western Gardens were destroyed. (Their twins are in Versailles.) Although the palaces designed by Castiglione were still standing early in the twentieth century, they deteriorated rapidly through neglect. It is still possible to walk among the ruins and make out the rich carvings on marble that once graced walls, balustrades, doorways, and fountains. Today, Yuan Ming Yuan serves as a painful symbol of the humiliation the Chinese suffered at the hands of the West and it is a sad legacy of the efforts of the gentle Jesuit who did so much to bridge the cultural gap between China and Europe.

Castiglione's art was all but forgotten for many years, but much of it has resurfaced, and it is highly prized by collectors of Asian art. Many of his most famous pieces can be seen in the National Museums of China and Taiwan. The portrait of Qian Long and his concubines was found by chance early in the twentieth century and now hangs in the Cleveland Museum of Art. Only in the past few decades have all twelve animal heads of the zodiac that graced the fountain in the Western Gardens reappeared.

Castiglione was buried in the Jesuit cemetery. The emperor wrote an epitaph and contributed a generous sum for his burial. The cemetery in which Castiglione lies is one of two that hold the remains of so many famous Jesuits, including Matteo Ricci. It is located in a tranquil garden behind an official building off the Chegongzhuang Road. The tombstones were desecrated twice—during the Boxer Rebellion and the Cultural Revolution—but have been restored and are all intact. It is still possible to see the resting place of Giuseppe (Josephus, in Latin) Castiglione, also known as Lang Shi Ning.

Diana Gore
London, July 2010

*Kutcher, Norman. 'China's Palace of Memory'. The Wilson Quarterly Vol 27, No I (Winter 2003), pp 30-39.

Picture credits:
All of the paintings included in this book are by Giuseppe Castiglione (1688-1766)

Front Cover: *The Pine, Hawk and Glossy Ganoderma* , 1724. Handscroll, ink and colour on silk, 242.3 x 157.1 cm, in the collection of The Palace Museum, Beijing, China.

Back Cover: *Portrait of the Qianlong Emperor,* circa 1736. Handscroll, ink and colour on silk, 242 x 179 cm, in the collection of the Palace Museum, Beijing, China.

Part I: *The Qianlong Emperor in Ceremonial Armour on Horseback.* Handscroll, ink and colour on silk, 232 x 322.5 cm, in the collection of The Palace Museum, Beijing, China.

Part II: Selection from *One Hundred Horses,* Handscroll, ink and colour on silk, 94.5 x 776.2 cm, in the collection of the National Palace Museum, Taiwan, Republic of China.

Part III: Selection from *Portraits of Emperor Qianlong, the Empress and Eleven Imperial Consorts,* 1736. Handscroll, ink and color on silk, 53.8 x 1,154.50 cm. The Cleveland Museum of Art. John L. Severance Fund 1969.31.

Made in the USA
Charleston, SC
22 February 2011